The Vision of Desire

Margaret Pedler

THE VISION OF DESIRE

BY MARGARET PEDLER

AUTHOR OF
THE HERMIT OF FAR END,
THE MOON OUT OF REACH, ETC.

"Heaven but the Vision of fulfill'd Desire
And Hell the Shadow from a Soul on Fire. "

—THE RUBAIYAT OF OMAR KHAYYAM

TO BUNTY

(F. MABEL WARHURST)

WITH MY LOVE

CONTENTS

DREAM-FLOWERS

"Beyond the hill there's a garden,
  Fashioned of sweetest flowers,
Calling to you with its voice of gold,
Telling you all that your heart may hold.
Beyond the hill there's a garden fair—
  My garden of happy hours.

"Dream-flowers grow in that garden,
  Blossom of sun and showers,
There, withered hopes may bloom anew,
Dreams long forgotten shall come true.
Beyond the hill there's a garden fair—
  My garden of happy hours!"

MARGARET PEDLER.

NOTE: —Musical setting by Margaret Pedler. Published by Edward Schuberth & Co., 11 East 22nd Street, New York.

PROLOGUE

"... It's no use pretending any longer. I can't marry you, I don't suppose you will ever understand or forgive me. No man would. But try to believe that I haven't come to this decision hurriedly or without thinking. I seem to have done nothing but think, lately!

"I want you to forget last night, Eliot. We were both a little mad, and there was moonlight and the scent of roses.... But it's good-bye, all the same—it must be. Please don't try to see, me again. It could do no good and would only hurt us both. "

Very deliberately the man read this letter through a second time. At first reading it had seemed to him incredible, a hallucination. It gave him a queer feeling of unreality—it was all so impossible, so wildly improbable!

"I want you to forget last night. " Last night! When the woman who had written those cool words of dismissal had lain in his arms, exquisite in her passionate surrender. His mouth set itself grimly. Whatever came next, whatever the future might hold, he knew that neither of them would be able to forget. There are some things that cannot be forgotten, and the moment when a man and woman first give their love utterance in words is one of them.

He crushed the note slowly in his hand till it was nothing more than a crumpled ball of paper, and raised his arm to fling it away. Then suddenly his lips relaxed in a smile and a light of relief sprang into his eyes. It was all nonsense, of course—just some foolish, woman's whim or fancy, some ridiculous idea she had got into her head which five minutes' talk between them would dispel. He had been a fool to take it seriously. He unclenched his hand and smoothed out the crumpled sheet of paper. Tearing it into very small pieces, he tossed them into the garden below the veranda where he was sitting and watched them circle to the ground like particles of fine white snow.

As they settled his face cleared. The tension induced by the perusal of the letter had momentarily aged it, affording a fleeting glimpse of the man as he might be ten years hence if things should chance to go awry with him—hard and relentless, with more than a suggestion of cruelty. But now, the strain lessened, his face revealed that charm of boyishness which is always curiously attractive in a man who has actually left his boyhood behind him. The mouth above the strong, clean-cut chin was singularly sweet, the grey eyes, alight and ardent, meeting the world with a friendly gaiety of expression that seemed to expect and ask for friendliness in return.

As the last scrap of paper drifted to earth he stretched out his arms, drawing a great breath of relief. His tea, brought to him at the same time as the letter he had just destroyed, still stood untasted on a rustic table beside him. He poured some out and drank it thirstily; his mouth felt dry. Then, setting down the cup, he descended from the veranda and made his way quickly through the hotel garden to the dusty white road beyond its gates.

It was very hot. The afternoon sun still flamed in the vividly blue Italian sky, and against the shimmer of azure and gold the tall, dark poplars ranked beside the road struck a sombre note of relief. But the man himself seemed unconscious of the heat. He covered the ground with the lithe, long-limbed stride of youth and supple muscles, and presently swung aside into a garden where, betwixt the spread arms of chestnut and linden and almond tree, gleamed the pink-stuccoed walls of a half-hidden villa.

Skirting the villa, he went on unhesitatingly, as one to whom the way was very familiar, following a straight, formal path which led between parterres of flowers, ablaze with colour. Then, through an archway dripping jessamine, he emerged into a small, enclosed garden—an inner sanctuary of flower-encircled greensward, fragrant with the scent of mignonette and roses, while the headier perfume of heliotrope and oleander hung like incense on the sun-warmed air.

A fountain plashed in the centre of the velvet lawn, an iridescent mist of spray upflung from its marble basin, and at the farther end a stone bench stood sheltered beneath the leafy shade of a tree.

A woman was sitting on the bench. She was quite young—not more than twenty at the outside—and there was something in the dark, slender beauty of her which seemed to harmonise with the southern scents and colour of the old Italian garden. She sat very still, her round white chin cupped in her palm. Her eyes were downcast, the lowered lids, with their lashes lying like dusky fans against the ivory-tinted skin beneath, screening her thoughts.

The man's footsteps made no sound as he crossed the close-cut turf, and he paused a moment to gaze at her with ardent eyes. The loveliness of her seemed to take him by the throat, so that a half-stifled sound escaped him. Came an answering sound—a sharp-caught breath of fear as she realised an intruder's presence in her solitude. Then, her eyes meeting the eager, worshipping ones fixed on her, she uttered a cry of dismay.

"You? —You? " she stammered, rising hastily.

In a stride he was beside her.

"Yes. Didn't you expect me? You must have known I should come. "

He laughed down at her triumphantly and made as though to take her in his arms, but she shrank back, pressing him away from her with urgent hands.

"I told you not to come. I told you not to come, " she reiterated. "Oh! " turning aside with nervous desperation, "why didn't you stay away? "

He stared at her.

"Why didn't I? Do you suppose any man on earth would have stayed away after receiving such a letter? Why did you write it? "—rapidly. "What did you mean? "

She looked away from him towards the distant mountains rimming the horizon.

"I meant just what I said. I can't marry you, " she answered mechanically.

"But that's absurd! You've known I cared—you've cared, too—all these weeks. And last night you promised—you said—"

"Last night! " She swung round and faced him. "I tell you we've got to *forget* last night—count it out. It—it was just an interlude—"

She broke off, blenching at the abrupt change in his expression. Up till now his face had been full of an incredulous, boyish bewilderment, half tender, half chiding. Within himself he had refused to believe that there was any serious intent behind her letter. It was fruit of some foolish misunderstanding or shy feminine withdrawal, and he was here to straighten it all out, to reassure her. But that word "interlude"! Had she been deliberately playing with him after all? Women did such things—sometimes. His features took on a sudden sternness.

"An interlude? " he repeated quietly. "I'm afraid I don't understand. Will you explain? "

Her shoulders moved resentfully.

"Why do you want to force me into explanations? " she burst out. "Surely—*surely* you understand? We can't marry—we haven't money enough! "

There was a long pause before he spoke again.

"I've enough money to marry on, if it comes to that, " he said at last, slowly. "Though we should certainly be comparatively poor. What you mean is that I'm not rich enough to satisfy you, I suppose? "

She nodded.

"Yes. I'm sick—*sick* of being poor! I've been poor all my life—always having to skimp and save and do things on the cheap—go without this and make shift with that. I'm tired of it! This last two months with Aunt Elvira—all this luxury and beauty, " she gestured eloquently towards the villa standing like a gem in its exquisite Italian setting, "the car, the perfect service, as many frocks as I want—Oh! I've loved it all! And I can't give it up. I can't go back to being poor again! "

She paused, breathless, and her eyes, passionately upbraiding, beseeching understanding, sought his face.

"Don't you understand? " she added, twisting her hands together.

His eyes glinted.

"Yes, I'm beginning to, " he returned briefly. "But how are you going to compass what you want—as a permanency? Your visit to Lady Templeton can't extend indefinitely. "

She was silent, evading his glance. Her foot beat nervously on the flagged path where they stood.

"Is there some one else? " he asked incisively. "Another man—who can give you all these things? "

A dull, shamed red flushed her cheek. With an effort she forced herself to answer him.

"Yes, " she said very low. "There is—some one else. "

"I wonder if he realises his luck! "

The palpable sneer in his voice cut like a lash. She winced under it.

"One more question—I'd like to know the answer out of sheer curiosity. " His voice was clear and hard—like ice, "You knew you were going to do this to me—last night? "

Her lips moved but no words came. She gestured mutely—imploringly.

"Answer me, please. "

His implacable insistence whipped her into a sudden flare of defiance. She was like a cornered animal.

"Yes, then, if you must have it—I *did* know! " she flung at him in a low tone of furious anger.

Involuntarily he stepped back from her a pace, like a man suddenly smitten and stunned.

"While for me last night was sacred! " he muttered under his breath.

Before the utter scorn and repugnance in the low-breathed words her defiance crumbled to pieces.

"And for me, too! Eliot, I wasn't pretending. I *do* love you. I never meant you to know, but last night—I couldn't help it. I'd promised to marry the—the other man, and then you came, and we were alone—and—Oh! "—desperately, lifting a wrung face to his. "Why won't you understand? "

But the beautiful, imploring face failed to move him one jot. Something had died suddenly within him—the something that was young and eager and blindly trusting. When she ceased speaking he was only conscious that he wanted to take her and break her between his two hands—destroy her as he had destroyed the letter she had written. The blood was drumming in his temples. His hands clenched and unclenched spasmodically. She was so slender a thing that it would be very easy... very easy with those iron muscles of his.... And then she would be dead. She was so beautiful and so rotten at the core that she would be better dead....

It was only by a supreme effort that he mastered his overwhelming need of some physical outlet for the passion of disgust and anger which swept him bare of any gentler emotion as the incoming tide sweeps the shore bare of sign or footprint. His body grew taut and rigid with the pressure he was putting on himself. When at last he spoke his voice was almost unrecognisable.

"I do understand, " he said. "I understand thoroughly. You've made—everything—perfectly clear. "

And with that he turned swiftly, leaving her standing alone in a flickering patch of shadow, and strode away across the grass. As he went, a little breeze ran through the garden, wafting the caressing, over-sweet perfume of heliotrope to his nostrils. It sickened him. He knew that he would loathe the scent of heliotrope henceforth.

CHAPTER I

ANN'S LEGACY

The sunshine romped down the Grand' Rue at Montricheux, flickering against the panes of the shop-windows and calling forth a hundred provocative points of light from the silver and jewels, the shining silks and embroidery, with which the shrewd Swiss shopkeeper seeks to open the purse of the foreigner. It seemed to chase the gaily blue-painted trams as they sped up and down the centre of the town, bestowing upon them a fictitious gala air, and danced tremulously on the round, shiny yellow tops of the tea-tables temptingly arranged on the pavement outside the pastrycook's.

It was still early afternoon, but already small groups of twos and threes were gathered round the little tables. At one a merry knot of English girl-tourists were enjoying an al fresco tea, at another staid Swiss habitués solemnly imbibed the sweet pink or yellow *sirop* which they infinitely preferred to tea, while a vivid note of colour was added to the scene by the picturesque uniforms of a couple of officers of an Algerian regiment who were consuming unlimited cigarettes and Turkish coffee, and commenting cynically in fluent French on the paucity of pretty women to be observed in the streets of Montricheux that afternoon.

Typically aloof, a solitary young Englishman was sitting at a table apart. He was evidently waiting for some one, for every now and again he leaned forward and glanced impatiently up the street, then, apparently disappointed, settled himself discontentedly to the perusal of the Continental edition of the *Daily Mail*.

He was rather an arresting type. His lean young face looked older than his five-and-twenty years would warrant. It held a certain recklessness, together with a decided hint of temper, and he was much too good-looking to have escaped being more or less spoiled by every other woman with whom he came in contact. Like many another boy, Tony Brabazon had been rushed headlong from a public school into the four years' grinding mill of the war, thereby acquiring a man's freedom without the gradual preparation of any transition period—a fact which, with his particular temperament, had served to complicate life.

Physically, however, he had come through unscathed, and his white flannels revealed a lithe, careless grace of figure. When he lifted his head to look up the street there was a certain arrogance in the movement—a hint of impetuous self-will that was attractively characteristic. The irritable drumming of long, sensitive fingers on the table-top, while he scanned the head-lines of the paper, was characteristic, too.

Suddenly a cool little hand descended on his restless one.

"You can stop beating the devil's tattoo on that table, Tony, " said an amused voice. "Here I am at last. "

He sprang up, regarding the new-comer with a mixture of satisfaction and resentment.

"You may well say 'at last'! " he grumbled. Then the satisfaction completely swamping the resentment, he went on eagerly: "Sit down and tell me why I've been deprived of your company for the whole of this blessed day. "

Ann Lovell sat down obediently.

"You've been deprived of my society, " she replied with composure, "by some one who had a better right to it. "

"Lady Susan, I suppose? "—in resigned tones.

She assented smilingly.

"Yes. A companion-chauffeuse isn't always at liberty to play about with the scapegrace young men of her acquaintance, you know. And this morning my employer was seized with a sudden desire to visit Aigle, so we drove over and lunched at a quaint old inn there. We've only just returned. "

As she spoke Ann stripped off her gloves, revealing a pair of slender hands that hardly looked as though they would be competent to manipulate the steering-wheel of a car. Yet there was more than one keen-eyed, red-tabbed soldier whom she had driven during the war who could testify to the complete efficiency of those same slim members.

"I'm dying for some tea, Tony, " she announced, tossing her gloves on to the table. "Let's go in and choose cakes. "

Tony nodded, and they dived into the interior of the shop, and, arming themselves with a plate and fork each, proceeded to spear up such as most appealed to them of the delectable *pâtisseries* arranged in tempting rows along shining trays. Then, giving an order for their tea to be served outside, they emerged once more into the sunlit street.

One of the Algerian officers followed Ann's movements with an appreciative glance. Had she been listening she might have caught his murmured, "*V'la une jolie anglaise, hein*? " But she was extremely unselfconscious, and took it very much for granted that she had been blessed with russet hair which gave back coppery gleams to the sunlight, and with a pair of changeful hazel eyes that looked sometimes clearly golden and sometimes like the brown, gold-flecked heart of a pansy. She was almost boyishly slender in build, and there was a sense of swift vitality about all her movements that reminded one of the free, untrammelled grace of a young panther.

Tony Brabazon watched her consideringly while she poured out tea.

"Montricheux has been like a confounded desert to-day, " he remarked gloomily. He was obviously feeling very much ill-used. "Tell Lady Susan she'll drive me to take the downward path if she monopolises you like this. "

"Tony, you've not been getting into mischief? "

Ann spoke lightly, but a faint expression of anxiety flitted across her face as she paused, the teapot poised above her cup, for his answer.

He hesitated a moment, his eyes sullen, then laughed shortly.

"How could I get into mischief—my particular kind of mischief—in Montricheux, with the stakes at the tables limited to five measly francs? If we were at Monte, now—"

If Ann noticed his hesitation she made no comment on it. She finished pouring out her tea.

"I'm very glad we're not, " she said with decision. "You'd be too big a handful for me to manage there. "

"I've told you how you can manage me—if you want to, " he returned swiftly. "I'd be like wax in your hands if you'd marry me, Ann. "

"I shouldn't care for a husband who was like wax in my hands, thank you, " she retorted promptly. "Besides, I'm not in the least in love with you. "

"That's frank, anyway. "

"Quite frank. And what's more, you're not really in love with me. "

Tony stiffened.

"I should think I'm the best judge of that, " he said, haughtily.

"Not a bit. You're too young to know" —coolly.

A look of temper flashed into his face, but it was only momentary. Then he laughed outright. Like most people, he found it difficult to be angry with Ann; she was so transparently honest and sincere.

"I'm three years your senior, I'd have you remember, " he observed.

"Which is discounted by the fact that you're only a man. All women are born with at least three years' more common sense in their systems than men. "

Tony demurred, and she allowed herself to be led into a friendly wrangle, inwardly congratulating herself upon having successfully side-tracked the topic of matrimony. The subject cropped up intermittently in their intercourse with each other and, from long experience, Ann had brought the habit of steering him away from it almost to a fine art.

He had been more or less in love with her since he was nineteen, but she had always refused to take him seriously, believing it to be only the outcome of conditions which had thrown them together all their lives in a peculiarly intimate fashion rather than anything of deeper root. But now that the boy had merged into the man, she had begun to ask herself, a little apprehensively, whether she were mistaken in her assumption, and she sometimes wondered if fate had not contrived to enmesh her in a web from which it would be difficult to escape. Tony was a very persistent lover, and unfortunately she was not free to send him away from her as she might have sent away any other man.

Fond as she was of him, she didn't in the least want to marry him. She didn't want to marry any one, in fact. But circumstances had combined to give her a very definite sense of responsibility concerning Tony Brabazon.

His father had been the younger son of Sir Percy Brabazon of Lorne, and, like many other younger sons, had inherited all the charm and most of the faults, and very little of the money that composed the family dower. Philip, the heir, and much the elder of the two, pursued a correct and uneventful existence, remained a bachelor, and in due course came into the title and estates. Whereas Dick, lovable and hot-headed, and with the gambling blood of generations of dicing, horse-racing ancestors running fierily in his veins, fell in love with beautiful but penniless Virginia Dale, and married her, spent and wagered his small patrimony right royally while it lasted, and borrowed from all and sundry when it was squandered. Finally, he ended a varied but diverting existence in a ditch with a broken neck, while the horse that should have retrieved his fortunes galloped first past the winning-post—riderless.

Sir Philip Brabazon let fly a few torrid comments on the subject of his brother's career, and then did the only decent thing—took Virginia and her son, now heir to the title, to live with him.

It was then that Ann Lovell, who was a godchild of Sir Philip's, had learned to know and love Tony's mother. Motherless herself, she had soon discovered that the frailly beautiful, sad-faced woman who had come to live with her somewhat irascible godparent, filled a gap in her small life of which, hitherto, she had been only dimly conscious. With the passing of the years came a clearer understanding of how much Virginia's advent had meant to her, and ultimately no bond between actual mother and daughter could have been stronger than the bond which had subsisted between these two.

It was to Ann that Virginia confided her inmost fears lest Tony should follow in his father's footsteps. From Sir Philip, choleric and tyrannical, she concealed them completely—and many of Tony's youthful escapades as well, paying some precocious card-losses he sustained while still in his early teens out of her own slender dress allowance in preference to rousing his uncle's ire by a knowledge of them. But with Ann, she had been utterly frank.

"Tony's a born gambler, " she told her. "But he has a stronger will than his father, and if he's handled properly he may yet make the kind of man I want him to be. Only—Philip doesn't know how to handle him. "

The last two years of her life she had spent on a couch, a confirmed invalid, and oppressed by a foreboding as to Tony's ultimate future. And then, one day, shortly before the weak flame of her life flickered out into the darkness, she had sent for Ann, and solemnly, appealingly, confided the boy to her care.

"I hate leaving him, Ann, " she had said between the long bouts of coughing which shook her thin frame so that speech was at times impossible. "He's so—alone. Philip represents nothing to him but an autocrat he is bound to obey. And Tony resents it. Any one who loves him can steady him—but no one will ever drive him. When I'm gone, will you do what you can for him—for him and for me? "

And Ann, holding the sick woman's feverish hands in her own cool ones, had promised.

"I will do all that I can, " she said steadily.

"And if he *does* get into difficulties? " persisted Virginia, her eager eyes searching the girl's face.

Ann smiled down at her reassuringly.

"Don't worry, " she had answered. "If he does, why, then I'll get him out of them if it's in any way possible. "

Two days later, Ann had stood beside the bed where Virginia lay, straight and still in the utter peace and tranquillity conferred by death. Her last words had been of Tony.

"I've 'bequeathed' him to you, Ann, " she had whispered. Adding, with a faint, humorous little smile: "I'm afraid I'm leaving you rather a troublesome legacy. "

And now, nearly four years later, Ann had thoroughly realised that the task of keeping Tony out of mischief was by no means an easy one. Here, at Montricheux, however, she had felt that she could relax her vigilance somewhat. There was no temptation to back "a certainty" of which some racing friend had apprised him, and, as Tony himself discontentedly declared, the stakes permitted at the Kursaal tables were so small that if he gambled every night of the week he ran no risk of either making or losing a fortune.

The chief danger, she reflected, was that he might become bored and irritable—she could see that he was tending that way—and then trouble would be sure to arise between him and his uncle, with whom he was staying at the Hotel Gloria. She recalled his hesitation when she had asked him if he had been getting into mischief. Was trouble brewing already?

"Tony, " she demanded shrewdly. "Have you been quarrelling with Sir Philip again? There's generally some disturbing cause when you feel driven into asking me to marry you. "

"Well, why won't you? He'd be satisfied then. "

"He? Do you mean your uncle? "—with some astonishment.

Tony nodded.

"Yes. Didn't you know he wanted it more than anything? Just as I do, " he added with the quick, whimsical smile which was one of his charms.

Ann shook her head.

"You haven't answered my question, " she persisted.

"Well, " admitted Tony unwillingly, "he and I did have a bit of a dust-up this morning. I'm sick of doing nothing. I told him I wanted to be an architect. "

"Well? "

"It was anything but well! He let me have it good and strong. No Brabazon was going to take up planning houses as a profession if he knew it! I'd got my duty to the old name and estate and the tenants, et cetera, et cetera. All the usual tosh."

Ann's face clouded. She devoutly wished that Sir Philip *would* allow his nephew to take up some profession—never mind which, so long as it interested him and gave him definite occupation. To keep him idling about between Lorne and the Brabazon town house in Audley Square was the worst thing in the world for him. Privately she determined to approach her godfather on the subject at the very next opportunity, though she could make a very good, guess at the reason for his refusal. It was a purely selfish one. He liked to have the boy with him. Bully him and browbeat him as he might, Tony was in reality the apple of the old man's eye—the one thing in the whole world for which he cared.

There would be nothing gained, however, by letting Tony know her thoughts, so she answered him with trenchant disapproval.

"It's not tosh. After all, your first duty is to Lorne and to the tenants. A good landlord is quite as useful a member of society as a good architect."

"Oh, if I were doing the actual managing, it would be a different thing," acknowledged Tony. "But I don't. He decides everything and gives all the orders—without consulting me. I just have to see that what he orders is carried out, and trot about with him, and do the noble young heir stunt for the benefit of the tenants on my birthday. It's absolutely sickening!"—savagely.

"Well, don't quarrel with your bread-and-butter," advised Ann. "Or with Sir Philip. He's not a bad sort in his way."

"Oh, isn't he?"—grimly. "You try living with him! Thank the powers that be, I shall get a 'day off' to-morrow. He's going over to Evian by the midday boat. The St. Keliers—blessed be their name!—have asked him to dine with them—to meet some exiled Russian princess or other."

"Lady Susan is going, too. She's staying the night there. Is Sir Philip?"

"Yes. There's no getting back the same night. This is topping, Ann. " Tony's face had brightened considerably. "Suppose you and I go up to the Dents de Loup for the afternoon, and then have a festive little dinner at the Gloria. Will you? Don't have an attack of common sense and say 'no'! "

His eyes entreated her gaily. They were extremely charming eyes, of some subtly blended colour that was neither slate nor violet, but partook a little of both, and shaded by absurdly long lashes which gave them an almost womanish softness. A certain shrewd old duchess, who knew her world, had once been heard to observe that Tony Brabazon's eyes would get him in and out of trouble as long as he lived.

Ann smiled.

"That's quite a brain-wave, Tony, " she replied. "I won't say no. And if you're very good we'll go down to the Kursaal afterwards, and I'll let you have a little innocent flutter at the tables. " Ann had no belief in the use of too severe a curb. She felt quite sure that if Tony's gambling propensities were bottled up too tightly, they would only break out more strongly later on—when he might chance to be in a part of the world where he could come to bigger grief financially than was possible at Montricheux. She glanced down at the watch on her wrist and, seeing that the time had slipped by more quickly than she imagined, proceeded to gather up her gloves. "I think it's time I went back to Villa Mon Rêve, now, " she said tentatively, fearing a burst of opposition.

But, having got his own way over the arrangements for the morrow, Tony consented to be amenable for once. Together they took their way up the pleasant street and at the gates of the villa he made his farewells.

"I shall drop into the club for a rubber, I think, " he vouchsafed, "before going home like a good little boy. "

"Don't play high, " cautioned Ann good-humouredly.

She could detect the underlying note of resentment in his voice, and she entered the house meditating thoughtfully upon the amazing short-sightedness evinced by elderly gentlemen in regard to the upbringing of their heirs.

CHAPTER II

THE BRABAZONS OF LORNE

"Ann's the best pal Tony could possibly have, so, for goodness' sake, be content with that and don't get addling your brains by trying to marry her off to him. Match-making isn't a man's job. A female child of twelve could beat the cleverest man that's hatched at the game."

Lady Susan Hallett fired off her remarks, as was her wont, with the vigour and precision of a machine-gun. There was always a delightful definiteness both about her ideas and the expression of them.

The man she addressed was standing with his back to the open French window of the pretty salon, angrily oblivious of the blue waters of Lac Léman which lapped placidly against the stone edges of the *quai* below. He was a tall, fierce-looking old man, with choleric blue eyes and an aristocratic beak of a nose that jutted out above a bristling grey moustache. A single eyeglass dangled from a broad, black ribbon round his neck. "One of the old school" was written all over him—one of the old, autocratic school which believed that "a man should be master in his own house, b'gad!" By which—though he would never have admitted it—Sir Philip Brabazon inferred a kind of divinely appointed dictatorship over the souls and bodies of the various members of his household which even included the right to arrange and determine their lives for them, without reference to their personal desires and tastes.

It was odd, therefore, that his chief friend and confidante—and the woman he would have married thirty years ago if she would only have had him—should be Lady Susan, as tolerant and modern in her outlook as he was archaic.

She was a tall, sturdily built woman of the out-of-door, squiress type. Her fine-shaped head was crowned by a wealth of grey hair, simply coiled in a big knot on the nape of her neck and contrasting rather attractively with her very black, arched eyebrows and humorous dark eyes. Those same eyes were now regarding Sir Philip with a quizzical expression of amusement.

"Besides, " she pursued. "Ann wouldn't have half as much pull with him if she *were* his wife, let me tell you. "

"You think not? "

"I'm sure. A man will let himself be lectured and generally licked into shape by the woman he wants to marry—but after marriage he usually prefers to do all the lecturing that's required himself. "

The old man shot a swift glance at her from under a pair of shaggy brows.

"How do you know? " he demanded rudely. "You're not married. "

Lady Susan nodded.

"That's why. "

"Do you mean—do you mean—" he began stormily, then, meeting her quiet, humorous gaze, stammered off into silence. Presently he fixed his monocle in one of his fierce old eyes and surveyed her from behind it as from behind a barricade.

"Do you mean me to understand that that's the reason you declined to marry me? "

She laughed a little.

"I think it was. I didn't want to be browbeaten into submission—as you browbeat poor Virginia, and as you would Tony if he hadn't got a good dash of the Brabazon devil in him. You're a confirmed bully, you know. "

"I shouldn't have bullied you. " There was an odd note of wistfulness in the harsh voice, and for a moment the handsome, arrogant old face softened incredibly. "I shouldn't have bullied you, Susan. "

"Yes, you would. You couldn't have helped it. You'd like to bully my little Ann into marrying Tony if you dared—monster! "

The grim mouth beneath the clipped moustache relaxed into an unwilling smile.

"I believe I would, " he admitted. "Hang it all, Susan, it would settle the boy if he were married. He wants a wife to look after him. "

"To look after him? " —with a faintly ironical inflection.

"That's what I said"—irritably. "That's—that's what wife's for, dammit! Isn't it? "

"Oh, no. " She shook her head regretfully. "That idea's extinct as the dodo. Antiquated, Philip—very. "

He glared at her ferociously.

"Worth more than half your modern ideas put together, " he retorted. "Women, don't know their duty nowadays. If they'd get married and have babies and keep house in the good, old-fashioned way, instead of trying to be doctors and barristers and the Lord knows what, the world would be a lot better off. A good wife makes a good man—and that's job enough for any woman. "

"I should think it might be, " agreed Lady Susan meditatively. "But it sounds a trifle feeble, doesn't it? I mean, on the part of the good man. It's making a sort of lean-to greenhouse of him, isn't it? "

"You're outrageous, Susan! I'm not a 'lean-to' anything, but do you suppose I'd be the bad-tempered old ruffian I am—at least, you say I am—if you'd married me thirty years ago? "

"Twenty times worse, probably, " she replied promptly. "Because, like most wives, I should have spoiled you. "

Sir Philip looked out of the window.

"I've missed that spoiling, Susan, " he said. Once again that incongruous little note of wistfulness sounded in his voice. But, an instant later, Lady Susan wondered if her ears had deceived her, for he swung round and snapped out in his usual hectoring manner: "Then you won't help me in this? "

"Help you to marry off Ann to Tony? No, I won't. For one thing, I don't want to spare her. And if ever I have to, it's going to be to some one who'll look after *her*—and take jolly good care of her, too! "

"Obstinate woman! Well—well"—irritably. "What am I to do, then? "

"Can't you manage your own nephew? "

"No, I can't, confound it! Told me this morning he wanted to be an architect. An architect! " He spoke as though an architect were something that crawled. "Imagine a Brabazon of Lorne turning architect! "

"Well, why not? " placidly. "It's better than being nothing but a gambler—like poor Dick. Tony always did love making plans. Don't you remember, when he was about eight, he made a drawing of heaven, with seating accommodation for the angels—cherubim and seraphim, and so on—in tiers? The general effect was rather like a plan of the Albert Hall"—smiling reminiscently. "Seriously, though, Philip, if the boy wants *work,* in the name of common sense, let him have it. "

"There's plenty of work for him at Lorne"—stubbornly. "Let him learn to manage the property. That's what I want—and what I'll have. God bless my soul! What have I brought the boy up for? To be a comfort in my old age, of course, and a credit to the name. Architect be hanged! "

As he spoke there came the sound of footsteps in the hall outside—light, buoyant steps—and Lady Susan's face brightened.

"That will be Ann, " she said. Adding quickly, as though to conclude the subject they had been discussing: "I warn you, Philip, you're driving the boy on too tight a rein. "

Sir Philip greeted Ann good-humouredly. In spite of the fact that she showed no disposition to fall in with his wishes and marry Tony, he was extremely fond of her. She was one of the few people who had never been afraid of him. She even contradicted him flatly at times, and, like most autocrats, he found her attitude a refreshing change from that of the majority of people with whom he came in contact.

"Seen Tony in the town? " he demanded. It was evident the boy was hardly ever out of his thoughts.

"Yes. We've just been having tea together. "

Sir Philip nodded approvingly.

"Excellent, excellent. Keep him out of mischief, like a good girl."

Ann laughed, a shade scornfully, but vouchsafed no answer, and soon afterwards Sir Philip took his departure.

"The twelve-thirty steamer to-morrow, then, Susan," he said as he shook hands. "I'll call for you in the car on my way to the *débarcadère*."

When he had gone Lady Susan and Ann exchanged glances.

"I've been telling him he drives Tony on too tight a rein," said the former, answering the unspoken question in the girl's eyes.

"It's absurd of him," declared Ann indignantly. "He tries to keep him tied to his apron-strings as if he were a child. And he's not! He's a man. He's been through that beastly war. Probably he knows heaps more about life—the real things of life—than Sir Philip himself, who wants to dictate everything he may or may not do."

"Probably he does. And that's just the trouble. When you get a terribly experienced younger generation and a hide-bound older one there are liable to be fireworks."

"All I can say is that if Sir Philip won't let him have a little more freedom, he'll drive Tony just the way he doesn't want him to go."

Lady Susan's keen glance scrutinised the girl's troubled face.

"You can't help it, you know," she remarked briefly.

"That's just it," answered Ann uncertainly. "I sometimes wonder if I could—ought to—" She broke off, leaving her sentence unfinished.

Lady Susan, apparently not noticing her embarrassment, gathered up her belongings preparatory to leaving the room.

"Marrying to reform a rake never pays," she said in level tones. "It's like rolling a stone uphill."

"But Tony isn't a rake! " protested Ann, flushing quickly. "There's any amount of good in him, and he might—might steady down if he were married. "

"Let him steady down before marriage, not after"—grimly. "A woman may throw her whole life's happiness into the scales and still fail to turn the balance. Without love—the love that can forgive seventy times seven and then not be tired—she'll certainly fail. And you don't love Tony. "

It was an assertion rather than a question, yet Ann felt that Lady Susan was waiting for an answer.

"N-no, " she acknowledged at last. "But I feel as though he belongs to me in a way. You see, Virginia 'left' him to me. "

"You're not called upon to marry a legacy, " retorted Lady Susan.

Ann smiled.

"No, I suppose not. " She was silent a moment. "I wish Sir Philip didn't lead him such a life. It's more than any man could be expected to stand. "

Lady Susan paused in the doorway.

"Well, my dear, don't vex your soul too much about it all. However badly people mismanage our affairs for us, things have a wonderful way of working out all right in the long run. "

Left alone, Ann strolled out on to the balcony which overlooked the lake, and, leaning her arms on the balustrade, yielded to the current of her thoughts. Notwithstanding Lady Susan's cheery optimism, she was considerably worried about Tony. She could see so exactly what it was that fretted him—this eternal dancing attendance on Sir Philip, who insisted on the boy's accompanying him wherever he went, and she felt a sudden angry contempt for the selfishness of old age which could so obstinately bind eager, straining youth to its chariot wheels. It seemed to her that the older generation frequently fell very far short of its responsibility towards the younger.

With a flash of bitterness she reflected that her own father had failed in his duty to the next generation almost as signally as old Sir Philip, although in a totally different manner. Archibald Lovell had indeed been curiously devoid of any sense of paternal responsibility. Connoisseur and collector of old porcelain, he had lived a dreamy, dilettante existence, absorbed in his collection and paying little or no heed to the comings and goings of his two children, Ann and her brother Robin. And less heed still to their ultimate welfare. He neglected his estate from every point of view, except the one of raising mortgages upon it so that he might have the wherewithal to add to his store of ceramic treasures. He lived luxuriously, employing a high-priced *chef* and soft-footed, well-trained servants to see to his comfort, because anything short of perfection grated on his artistic sensibilities. And when an intrusive influenza germ put a sudden end to his entirely egotistical activities, his son and daughter found themselves left with only a few hundred pounds between them. Lovell Court was perforce sold at once to pay off the mortgages, and to meet the many other big outstanding debts the contents of the house had to be dispersed without reserve. The collection of old porcelain to which Archibald Lovell had sacrificed most of the human interests of life was soon scattered amongst the dealers in antiques, who, in many instances, bought back at bargain prices the very pieces they had sold to him at an extravagantly high cost. Every one went away from the Lovell sale well-pleased, except the two whose fortunes were most intimately concerned—the son and daughter of the dead man. They were left to face the problem of continued existence.

For the time being the circumstances of the war had acted as a solvent. Robin, home on sick leave, had returned to the front, while Ann, who possessed the faculty of getting the last ounce out of any car she handled, very soon found warwork as a motor-driver. But, with the return of peace, the question of pounds, shillings and pence had become more acute, and at present Robin was undertaking any odd job that turned up pending the time when he should find the ideal berth which would enable him to make a home for Ann, while the latter, thanks to the good offices of Sir Philip Brabazon, had for the last six months filled the post of companion-chauffeuse to Lady Susan Hallett.

The entire six months had been passed at Mon Rêve, Lady Susan's villa at Montricheux, and with a jerk Ann emerged from her train of retrospective thought to the realisation that her lines had really fallen in very pleasant places, after all.

It seemed as though there were some truth in Lady Susan's assertion that things had a way of working out all right in the end. But for her father's mismanagement of his affairs—and the affairs of those dependent on him—Ann recognised that she might very well have been still pursuing the rather dull, uneventful life which obtained at Lovell Court, without the prospect of any vital change or happening to relieve its tedium, whereas the catastrophe which had once seemed to threaten chaos had actually opened the door of the world to her.

CHAPTER III

ON THE TOP OF THE WORLD

The rack-and-pinion railway from Montricheux to the Dents de Loup wound upward like a single filament flung round the mountains by some giant spider. The miniature train, edging its way along the track, appeared no more than a mere speck as it crept tortuously up towards the top. At its rear puffed a small engine, built in a curious tilted fashion, so that as it laboured industriously behind the coaches of the train it reminded one ridiculously of a baby elephant on its knees.

Ann was leaning against the windowless framework of the railway carriage, watching the valleys drop away, curve by curve, as the train climbed. Far below lay the lake, a blue rift glimmering between pine-clad heights. Then a turn of the track and the lake was swept suddenly out of sight, while the mountains closed round—shoulder after green-clad shoulder, with fields of white narcissus flung across them like fairy mantles. The air was full of the fragrance of narcissus mingling with the pungent scent of fir and pine. Ann sniffed luxuriously and glanced round to where Tony was sitting.

"Doesn't it smell clean and delicious? " she said, drawing in great breaths of the pine-laden air. "When I come up to the mountains I always wonder why on earth we ever live anywhere else. "

Tony smiled.

"You'd be the first to get bored if you didn't live somewhere else—now that the winter sports are over, " he returned. "After all"—mundanely—"you can't derive more than a limited amount of enjoyment from scenery, however fine. Besides, you must know this route by heart. "

"I do. But I love it! It's different every time I come up here. I think"—knitting her brows—"that's what is so fascinating about the Swiss mountains; they change so much. Sometimes they look all misty and unreal—almost like a mirage, and then, the very next day, perhaps, they'll have turned back into hard-edged, solid rock and you can't imagine their ever looking like dream-mountains again. "

Gradually, as they mounted, they left the verdant valleys, with their sheltered farms and châlets, behind. The pine-woods thinned, and now and again a wedge of frozen snow, lodged under the projecting corner of a rock, appeared beside the track. The wind grew keener, chill from the eternal snows over which it had swept, and sheer, rocky peaks, bare of tree or herbage, thrust upward against the sky.

Presently, with a warning shriek, the train glided into a tunnel cut clean through the base of a mighty rock. The sides dripped moisture and the icy air tore through the narrow passage like a blast of winter. Ann shivered in the sudden cold and darkness and drew her furs closer round her. She had a queer dread of underground places; they gave her a feeling of captivity, and she was thankful when the train emerged once more into daylight and ran into the mountain station. Tony helped her out on to the small platform.

"Which is it to be? " he asked, glancing towards where a solitary hotel stood like a lonely outpost of civilisation. "Tea first, or a walk? "

Ann declared in favour of the walk.

"Let's go straight up to the Roche d'Or. I always feel as if I'd reached the top of the world there. It's certainly as near the top as I shall ever get! " she added laughing. "I don't feel drawn towards mountaineering, so I shall probably never ascend beyond the limits of the rack-and-pinion. "

The Roche d'Or was a steep upward slope, culminating in a rocky promontory from which was visible the vast expanse of the Bernese Oberland. A railed-in platform capped the promontory, for it was a recognised viewpoint. Opposite, across a shallow valley, the Dents de Loup cut the sky-line—two menacing, fang-shaped peaks like the teeth of a wolf, and beyond them a seemingly endless range of mountains stretched away to the far horizon, pinnacle after pinnacle towering upwards with sombre, sharp-edged shadows veiling the depths between. Along immense ridged scarps lay the plains of everlasting snow, infinitely bleak and desolate till a burst of sunlight suddenly transformed them, clothing the great flanks of the mountains in cloth of silver.

Ann stood still, absorbing the sheer beauty of it all.

"It's heavenly, isn't it? " she said at last, a little sigh of ecstasy escaping her.

Tony looked, not at the hills, but at the young, eager face just level with his shoulder.

"It's probably as near heaven as I shall ever get, " he answered. "Anyway, just for the moment, I don't feel I've anything particular to complain of. "

"I suppose I'm to take that as a compliment, " replied Ann. "Anyway"—mimicking him—"I don't really think you have very much to complain of at any time. You're one of the idle rich, you know. How would you like it if you were obliged to keep your nose to the grindstone—like Robin and me? "

"I shouldn't mind"—curtly—"if I could choose my grindstone. "

"But that's just it! Robin can't—choose his grindstone, I mean. He's just got to keep slogging away at anything that turns up. "

Her face shadowed a little. They were very devoted to each other, she and Robin. From their earliest childhood their father had counted for so little in either of their lives that they had inevitably drawn closer to each other than most brothers and sisters, and the enforced separation of the last few years had been a sore trial to both of them.

"You're very fond of Robin, " observed Tony. There was a note of envy in his voice.

"Of course I am. If we could only afford to live together, I think I should be absolutely happy. "

He glanced at her quickly.

"Aren't you happy with Lady Susan? "

"Oh, yes, yes! No one could be kinder to me than she is. But—I miss Robin"—rather wistfully. "You see, we've always been everything to each other. "

"I see. And what will happen if one day you—or Robin—should get married? "

Ann skirted the topic dexterously.

"Oh, don't let's think about possible calamities on a day like this. Look! " She touched his arm, drawing his attention to a girl who had also climbed the Roche d'Or hill to see the view and had halted near them, a sheaf of freshly-gathered wild-flowers in her hand. "Aren't those blue gentians lovely? "

Tony glanced at the few vividly blue flowers the girl was jealously clasping. She had walked far in search of them and valued them accordingly.

"Do you want some? " he asked eagerly.

Ann nodded.

"Isn't it getting rather late in the year to find them, though? " she said doubtfully.

The girl with the flowers, overhearing, turned to her with a friendly smile.

"There are very few left, " she vouchsafed. "I've been hunting everywhere for them. But you may find one or two over there. " She pointed to a distant slope.

Tony's eyes followed her gesture. Then he glanced down at Ann inquiringly.

"Are you game for so long a walk? " he asked.

"I'm game for anything up in this air, " she assured him with conviction.

But, as was not infrequently the case, Ann's spirit outstripped her physical strength. The slope indicated was much farther away than it appeared and "the going was bad, " as Tony phrased it. Blue gentians proved tantalisingly elusive, and at length, rather disheartened by their unprofitable search, Ann came to a standstill.

"I think I'm beginning to feel a keener interest in tea than gentians, Tony, " she confessed at last, ruefully. "It's very contemptible of me, I own. But when I contemplate the distance we've already got to cover before we reach the hotel again, I feel distinctly disinclined to add to it. "

"I've let you walk too far! " Tony was overwhelmed with compunction. "Look here, sit down in this little hollow and rest for a few minutes before we turn back, while I just go a bit further and see if I can find you a gentian. "

He stripped off his overcoat as he spoke and rolled it together to make a cushion for her.

"No, no, I don't want your coat, " she protested. "I don't need it—really! "

But Tony was suddenly masterful.

"You'll do as you're told, " he asserted. And somewhat to her own surprise she found herself meekly obeying him.

He strode away, disappearing quickly from sight over the brow of a hill, and with a small sigh of contentment she tucked her feet under her on the improvised cushion and lit a cigarette. She had had a busy morning, and was really more tired than she knew. First of all there had been the car to clean, then there were flowers to be arranged for the house, and after that various small shopping errands had cropped up, so that Ann had found herself very fully occupied until at length, accompanied by Sir Philip, Lady Susan had departed for Evian. She wondered fugitively how the pair were enjoying themselves.

It was very pleasant sitting there. The huge boulder against which she leant sheltered her from the wind and the spot was bathed in brilliant sunshine. She finished her cigarette and lapsed into a brown study provoked by Tony's sudden question: "What will happen if one day you—or Robin—should get married? " She had never asked herself that question. It was so much an understood thing between brother and sister that, as soon as Robin found a sufficiently remunerative post, they should live together, that any alternative had not entered her head.

But now she came to think of it, of course it was quite possible that Robin might some day meet the woman whom he would want to marry. Her mouth twisted in a little wry grimace of distaste. She was sure she should detest any woman who robbed her of her brother. And if such a thing happened, she would certainly take herself off and live somewhere else. Nothing would ever induce her to remain in a married brother's house—an unwanted third.

There would always be one avenue of escape open to her, she reflected ironically—by way of her own marriage with Tony. She wished it were possible to fall in love to order! It would simplify things so much. As Tony's wife she felt sure she could keep him straight and so fulfil the trust Virginia had imposed on her. He had always shown himself sensitively responsive to her influence—like a penitent boy if she scolded him, radiant if he had won her approval. And he had a very special niche of his own in her heart. Next to Robin, there was no one she loved more.

... A sudden cloud across the sun roused her to the fact that she had been sitting still for some time, and that, at that altitude, the air held all the mountain keenness. She felt chilled, and scrambled up hastily to her feet. She would go to the crest of the hill and signal to Tony that she was ready to return.

But, to her utter astonishment, when she had climbed to the top, he was not in sight. The hill brow apparently commanded a view of the surrounding country for a distance of at least two miles, and as far as she could see there was no sign of any living creature in the whole expanse. Hardly believing her own senses, she brushed her hand across her eyes and looked again. But she had made no mistake. Tony was nowhere to be seen. The ground stretched bleakly away on every hand, untenanted by any human soul except herself.

She stood still, staring dazedly around. Tony would never have gone back without her. He must be hidden from view by some dip or inequality of the ground. Or—her heart stood still at the thought—had he slipped and fallen headlong into some hideous crevasse?

Curving her hands on either side her mouth, she called him, sending her voice ringing through the clear, crisp air. But there came no answer. Instead, the utter loneliness and silence seemed to surge up round her almost like a concrete thing. For a moment, sheer terror of what might have happened to him overwhelmed her.

"Tony!... Tony! " Her voice rose to a scream, then cracked on a hoarse note of sudden, desperate relief.

To her left the ground fell away abruptly in a precipitous ravine, and, rising slowly above the lip of the chasm, she could discern Tony's head and shoulders. Instantly her mind leapt to what had happened. Failing to find a gentian in his search over safe ground, he must have caught sight of a late blossom growing in some cranny of the rock face below, and, recklessly regardless of the danger, he had climbed down to secure it.

The mere thought of the risk he had incurred—was still incurring—sent a shiver through her. Her first impulse was to rush towards him. Then, realising that any movement of hers might distract his attention and so add illimitably to his danger, she forced herself by an almost superhuman effort to remain where she was. Motionless, with straining eyes, she watched while he slowly edged himself up. That his foothold was precarious was evident from the careful precision of his movements, so unlike Tony's usual nimbleness.

Now his arm was above the edge... both arms... he seemed to be resting a moment, leaning on his chest an instant before making another effort. Should she go to him? Her arms hung stiffly at her sides, her hands opening and shutting in an agony of indecision.

Tony was moving once more, and this time he hoisted himself up so that he succeeded in getting one knee over the top. Another moment and he would be safe.... Then, without a cry, he suddenly toppled backwards and disappeared from view, and Ann could see only the jagged edge of the ravine, stark against the sky-line.

For a fraction of a second she stood paralysed, overwhelmed with the horror of what had happened. Then, choking back the scream which rose to her lips, she set off running in the direction of the spot where Tony had vanished from sight.

CHAPTER IV

RATS IN A TRAP

Breathless, her heart thudding painfully in her side, Ann reached the ravine and, throwing herself face downwards on the ground, crawled to the edge. For an instant she closed her eyes, shrinking with a sick dread from what they might show her—Tony's young, lithe body lying broken on the rocks below, or, perhaps, only the dark blur of some awful and unmeasured depth which would never give up its dead.

It was by a sheer effort of will that she at last forced herself to open her eyes and peer downward. Immediately beneath the brink of the chasm the ground dropped vertically for a few feet, but below that again it sloped gradually outwards, culminating in a broad, projecting ledge which formed the lip of the actual precipice itself. Tony lay on the ledge, motionless, with outflung arms and white, upturned face. He had evidently lost his footing, and, after the first drop, rolled helplessly downward. Only the presence of a jagged, upstanding piece of rock had saved him from falling clean over into the depths below.

Strain as she might to see, Ann could not tell whether he were dead or merely insensible, and the agony of uncertainty seemed to drain her of all strength. For a few moments she lay where she was, unable to control the trembling of her limbs, her aching eyes staring fixedly down at the still, prone figure on the ledge below. But the paralysing terror passed, and, at length, though still rather shakily, she dragged herself to her feet. She must go to him—somehow she must get down to where he lay.

At first she could think of no way of reaching him. Although he himself had attempted, and very nearly successfully accomplished, the upward climb to the brow of the ravine, she knew she dared not attempt to make the descent at that same spot. If there were no way round, she would have to go back to the hotel in search of help. But that would take an hour or more! And meanwhile Tony was lying there untended. She couldn't wait! She must get to him—get to him at once, and know whether he were living or dead. She flung herself down on the ground once more and cast a despairing glance at the inaccessible shelf of rock where he lay. Then it appeared to her that, although narrowing as it went, it ran upwards, forming a kind of rough track below the overhanging summit which, further along, might debouch on to the crest of the ravine.

Springing to her feet, she hurried desperately along the top in the direction which the track seemed to take, and at length, with a gasping sigh of relief, came to a wide fissure that slanted down to meet it.

She was sure-footed as a deer, her slim, supple body balancing itself almost instinctively, but even so the traversing of that narrow, rocky ledge, in parts not more than a foot wide, was a severe test of her endurance. A single false step meant death, instantaneous and inevitable, and the whole terrible ten minutes which it took her to complete the short distance was poignant with the dread of what she might discover at its end.

Moving very cautiously, her bare hands sliding across the rough face of the rock as she edged her way forward, she came at last to where the ledge widened out and the ground above sloped gently upwards. A few steps more and she could see Tony's young, supine figure. The last three yards were accomplished at a run, and an instant later she was kneeling beside him, thrusting swift, urgent hands beneath his shirt to feel whether his heart still beat. The throb of it came softly against her palms—warm, and pulsatingly *alive*!

Ann rocked a little on her knees. She felt sick and giddy with reaction from the almost intolerable strain of the last few minutes. Then she caught sight of a vivid glint of blue—a single gentian bloom still tightly clasped in the boy's hand, and quite suddenly she began to cry, the tears running unchecked down her face. And it was just then that Tony came back to consciousness—to the vague consciousness of something wet splashing down on to his face. He stirred and opened his eyes.

"Tony! " Ann's voice was hoarse with relief.

His eyes blinked at her uncertainly.

"Hello! " he said rather feebly. "What's happened? "

"I thought you were killed! " she cried unsteadily. "Oh, Tony, I thought you were killed! "

He regarded her consideringly.

"No, " he replied seriously. "I'm not at all killed. Why should I be killed? " Then, clearer consciousness returning: "Am I talking rot? What's happened? "

Ann slipped her arm beneath his shoulders and raised him a little so that his head rested on her lap.

"You fell, " she said, trying to speak calmly. "You were climbing up and you fell. Where are you hurt, Tony? "

"Oh, I remember.... Yes, I fell—just as I was getting to the top. A rotten old stump gave way under my foot. "

"But where are you hurt? " persisted Ann anxiously.

"I don't think I *am* hurt. " He stretched his limbs tentatively. "No, there's nothing broken. I feel a bit buzzy in the head, that's all. "

He tried to lift himself up, but Ann pressed him back against her knees.

"Don't move! Don't move! " she cried hastily. "Lie still for a few minutes. Are you sure—*sure* you're not hurt? "

"Bet you a tenner I'm not, " he replied, with the ghost of a grin. "My head's clearing, too. I was only knocked out of time for a minute. Don't worry. " He put up his hand and touched her cheek. "Why, you're quite pale, Ann. "

"I *felt* pale—when I saw you fall, " she answered grimly. Her spirits were returning now that she was assured he was uninjured. "I was certain you must be killed. "

"It would have been one way out of it all, wouldn't it? " he replied with a touch of bitterness.

"Oh, hush! Don't speak like that. "

"I won't—if it annoys you. But, anyway, you needn't worry. I shan't die young. The gods don't love me enough. "

Ann ignored this.

"Do you think you could stand now? " she asked practically.

Tony's eyes gleamed mirthfully.

"I'm very comfortable as I am, " he remarked, rubbing his cheek against her skirt.

She resisted the temptation to smile.

"I'm not—particularly, " she returned briefly. "I've got cramp. "

He sat up at once.

"Oh, by Jove! Why didn't you say so before? "

"Because I hadn't got it before. I was much too concerned about you to have time for it. How do you feel? Shall I help you up? "

But Tony disclaimed the necessity for any assistance. As he said, he had only been knocked out of time for a few minutes. He might have been made of indiarubber for all the actual harm his fall had done him. He rose to his feet without difficulty and proceeded to help Ann to hers.

"How do we get back? " he asked. Then, glancing upwards: "I'm hanged if I'm going to try and climb up there a second time. How on earth did you get here? You didn't drop from the skies, I suppose, like an angel? "

"There's a ledge—it's rather narrow, but one can just squeeze round, and it brings you out somewhere on the top. Are you sure you can manage it, though? You won't turn faint or anything? "—anxiously.

"No"—with impish gravity. "I shan't 'turn faint or anything. ' In fact, I could dance a hornpipe here if you liked. Still, I'll hold your hand—just in case of accidents"—audaciously. "Shall I go first? Oh, by the way"—he paused. "Here's your blue gentian. Won't you have it? "

Ann felt her throat contract as she recalled what the little blue flower had so nearly cost. Her eyes filled in spite of herself.

"Good heavens! Don't cry over it! " Tony laughed carelessly. He had recovered his usual bantering manner of speech which yet always seemed to hold an undercurrent of bitterness. "It's not worth that. See, I'll chuck it away, so that it can't remind you of the unpleasant shock I gave you this afternoon. "

He tossed the flower over the edge of the ravine. For an instant it seemed to hover in the air like a blue butterfly. Then it sank slowly out of sight.

"Here endeth the first lesson, " commented Tony.

"Lesson on what? "

"On trying to get things which an all-wise Providence has considerately placed out of your reach. " Without giving her time to reply, he continued: "Give me your hand—no, you must"—as she hung back. "I'm not going to have you risking this ledge again alone. "

He extended one hand behind him, and, recognising the uselessness of argument, Ann yielded and laid hers in it. Somehow she was not altogether sorry to feel that friendly, human grip. In single file they made the perilous return journey along the narrow track, emerging at length on to safe ground. Ann withdrew her hand with a sigh of relief. It was good to feel that they were out of danger at last.

"I think we shall have to hurry if we are to catch our train, " she said, keeping determinedly to the practical side of affairs. She felt she did not want to discuss their adventure. It was too vividly impressed upon her mind and had all too nearly ended in disaster. It seemed as though, the wings of Death had brushed her as he passed by.

Tony pulled out his watch.

"Eight, as usual, " he replied. "We shall have to sprint. And I've done you out of your tea, too, " he added remorsefully.

"Oh, that! " Ann dismissed the matter with a rather uncertain little laugh. "You don't suppose I'm worrying about my tea, do you? "

He looked at her curiously.

"No, I don't suppose you are, " he answered.

They set off at a good pace, but they had wandered much further afield than they realised, and when at last the hotel, and the station which practically adjoined it, came into sight, the train was already drawn up at the platform, waiting to start. A shrill whistle cut the air warningly, and instinctively Ann and Tony broke into a run. Tony was the first to recognise the futility of the proceeding. He pulled up.

"We may as well save our breath, " he observed laconically. And even as he spoke the train, with a final shriek, moved out of the station.

Ann stood still, her eyes following it with an expression of blank dismay.

"Tony! " Her voice sounded a trifle breathless. "Do you know—have you realised—that that's the last train? "

He nodded.

"And we've missed it. "

He appeared completely unconcerned, and she turned on him with a flash of impatience. His inconsequence annoyed her.

"Yes, we've missed it, " she repeated. "How do you suppose we're going to get back without a train to take us? "

Tony's soft, slate-coloured eyes surveyed her placidly beneath their long lashes.

"I haven't the faintest idea, " he acknowledged.

"Tony! " In spite of her indignation a quiver underlay Ann's voice. Her nerves had been wrought up to a high pitch by the afternoon's events, and she felt unequal to parrying Tony's customary banter.

Immediately his manner changed. When he spoke again it was with a quiet confidence that reassured her completely.

"It's quite true, " he said soberly. "I haven't an idea at the moment. But I'll get you safely back to Montricheux this evening somehow. I promise you, Ann. So don't worry. "

The sun was hanging low in the sky by the time they reached the hotel, and when he had established Ann in an easy chair and provided her with a cigarette, together with a six-weeks'-old copy of a London magazine which he unearthed from amongst a dusty pile of luridly illustrated handbooks on Switzerland, Tony departed to make inquiries regarding their journey back to Montricheux. He returned within a very short time, his face wearing an unusual look of gravity, and for a moment he stood staring down at her without speaking.

"I've got some bad news for you, " he said at last, with obvious reluctance. "I'm not able to keep my promise, Ann. We can't get back to Montricheux to-night. "

She glanced up incredulously.

"Can't get back? " she repeated. "Oh, but we must. "

Tony shook his head.

"Can't be done, " he answered. "It seems that infernal train is the only means of getting up and down from here. You can't motor or drive. There's no road. "

The out-of-date magazine slid suddenly off Ann's knee and fell with a plop on the floor.

"Are you serious? " she asked, still hardly able to believe him. "Do you really mean we—we've got to stay the night here? "

She could read the answer to her question in the unmistakable concern which was written on his face.

"Oh, but it's impossible! " she exclaimed in deep dismay. "We can't—we can't stay here! " She sprang up, clasping and unclasping her hands agitatedly. "Don't you *see*, Tony, that it's impossible? "

"We've no choice, " he replied bluntly. "If there were any possible way of getting you back to Villa Mon Rêve to-night, I'd move heaven and earth to do it. But there *isn't*. We've no more chance of getting away from here than rats in a trap. "

CHAPTER V

THE VISITORS' BOOK

It was quite true. They were caught like rats in a trap, and Ann's heart sank. She had lived long enough to know that there are always a certain number of censorious people sufficiently ungenerous and narrow-minded to make mischief out of any awkward happening, no matter how innocently it may have occurred.

"Can't you think of any way out, Tony? " she said at last. "I—I don't seem to know what to do. " She looked round her vaguely, feeling confused and unnerved by the awkwardness of their predicament.

"There's not a châlet within reach, or I'd go off there for the night, " answered Tony, adding with a twinkle in his eyes: "And although I might, of course, sleep outside, if you preferred—on the top of the Roche d'Or, for instance! —I'm afraid it wouldn't help matters much, as my frozen corpse would require about as much explaining away as the fact that we've stayed the night here. "

He had never felt less like joking, but he was rewarded by seeing a faint smile relax the strained expression on her face.

"Don't worry, Ann, " he pursued, tucking a friendly arm into hers. "No one need ever know. But I could kick myself for landing you into this mess. It's all my fault. If I hadn't gone fooling about at the top of that ravine and come to grief we should be buzzing comfortably homeward in the train. "

"You did it for me, " cried Ann quickly. Now that the first shock of realisation was over she was recovering her usual cheery outlook on things. "You mustn't blame yourself. It's no one's fault. It's just—"

"The cussedness of things, " vouchsafed Tony, as she paused.

"Yes, Just that. Well"—she gave her shoulders a slight shrug as though she were shaking off a burden—"we may as well make the best of things. At least we shall see the sunset up here. It's supposed to be rather wonderful, isn't it? "

"I believe the sun*rise* is the special thing to see. You'll have to get up early to-morrow, ma'am. " He paused a moment, then went on with frank admiration: "Ann, you're a real little sport! There isn't one girl in twenty would have taken this business as well as you have. They'd have been demanding my head on a charger. "

"It wouldn't be any use making a fuss about a pure accident, " she returned philosophically. "Let's just enjoy it—the sunset and the moonrise and everything else. Oh! I do hope they'll give us a decent dinner! You did us out of our tea by tumbling over the precipice—don't make a habit of it, please, Tony! —and I'm simply starving. "

He nodded.

"I'll go and order some grub—and book rooms. " He paused uncertainly. "By the way, I'll have to enter our names in the hotel register, I suppose? "

"Our names? " Ann flushed nervously. "Oh, you can't—I mean—"

"Don't worry, " he said soothingly. "I shan't enter us under our own names, of course. What do you say to Smith—nice, inoffensive sort of name, don't you think? 'G. Smith and sister'—I think that'll meet the necessities of the case. "

Ann giggled suddenly.

"It's all rather funny if it wasn't so—so—"

"Improper, " supplied Tony obligingly.

"Call it unconventional, " she supplemented. "It sounds better. And now do go and order some food for 'G. Smith and sister. ' Sister is literally starving. "

Half an hour later they were light-heartedly demolishing an excellent dinner, and the manager of the Hotel de Loup was congratulating himself upon the acquisition of two unexpected guests during the slack season. Afterwards they made another pilgrimage up to the Roche d'Or to watch the sunset.

When they had reached the top, Ann stood quietly at Tony's side, not speaking. The wonderful beauty of the scene enthralled her, and words would have seemed almost a profanation, breaking across the deep, stirless silence which wrapped them round. Away to their right the golden disc of the sun was sinking royally westward, bathing the mountains in a flood of lambent light, and piercing the darkening blue of the sky with quivering shafts of scarlet and orange and saffron. Across the snow-fields shimmered a translucent rosy glow, so that they seemed no longer bleak and desolate, but lay spread like an unfurled banner of glory betwixt the great peaks which sentinelled them round. Presently the sun dipped below the rim of the horizon, and the splendour faded swiftly. It was as if some one had suddenly closed the doors of an opened heaven, shutting away the brief vision of its radiance.

In the faint, chill light of the risen moon, Ann turned to go, still in silence. She felt awed by the beauty of it all. For the time being she had forgotten the untoward circumstances which had brought her here, forgotten even Tony, except that she was vaguely conscious he was beside her, another human being, sharing with her the deep, eternal quiet of the mountains and the flaming glory of the setting sun. Then his arm slipped through hers, as they began the steep descent, and at the boyish, friendly touch of it, she came back to earth.

"Oh, Tony, I'm almost glad we missed the last train, " she said softly, "It's been so wonderful. "

"Yes, it's been wonderful, " he assented, and there was a queer, excited note in his voice. "It's been wonderful to be up here with you—right away from the rest of the world. "

Instinctively she drew a little away from him.

"I wish you wouldn't, " she said hastily.

"Wouldn't what? " He linked his arm in hers more firmly. "Help you down this hill? You might trip if I didn't. It's a very rough track" —blandly.

Inwardly Ann admitted to a feeling of helplessness. Tony eluded reproof with a skill that was altogether baffling. Now, as usual, having said what he wanted to say, he retreated behind a fence of raillery.

"You know quite well I didn't mean that, " she said indignantly.

"What did you mean, then? That I'm not to make love to you? "

"It isn't fair of you, " she urged. "Not now—here. "

"No, I suppose it isn't, " he acknowledged equably. "But I'm going to do it, all the same. Probably I'll never get you to myself again—alone on the top of the world. But I'll promise you one thing"—his voice deepened to a sudden gravity. "This is going to be the last time I make love to you. If you say 'no' to me now, I shall accept it, and it will be 'no' for always. "

Ann's heart beat a little more quickly.

"Tony—" she began protestingly.

"No. Hear me out. I know what's the matter. You don't trust me. You're afraid, if you marry me, that I'll let you down—as my father let my mother down. But I won't! I swear it. " He stood still and, slipping his arm from under hers, took both her hands in his and held them tightly. "If you'll marry me, Ann, I promise you that I'll give up gambling—every form of it—from this day forth. "

"You couldn't! " she broke in hastily.

"I could do anything—for you, " he answered simply. "Because I love you. "

There was something very touching in the boyish declaration. Ann looked up and saw his face in the moonlight, white and rather stern. It made her think of the face of some young knight of bygone days taking a sacred vow before he set forth to seek and find the Holy Grail.

He bent down to her.

"Ann, darling, " he said gently. "I love you so much. Won't you marry me? "

She felt her heart contract. He had asked her many times before—sometimes half jestingly, sometimes with a sudden imperious passion that would fain have swept everything before it. But this was different. There was a gravity, an earnestness in his speech which she could not lightly brush aside. Alone here, under the wide sky, with only God's open spaces round them, it seemed to her as though his question and her answer to it must partake of the same solemnness as vows exchanged within the hallowed walls of a sanctuary.

She wished intensely that she could give him the answer he desired. And, beyond that, she felt the urge of Virginia's trust in her. Here was her chance. At a word from her he was willing to renounce the one thing for which he craved—the thing that had wrecked his father's life, and which might some day wreck his own. Ought she to say that word—promise to marry him, even though she had no love to give him? Her mind seemed to be going round and round in a maze of uncertainty and doubt.

And then suddenly the remembrance of what Lady Susan had said rushed over her: *"A woman may throw her whole life's happiness into the scales, and still fail to turn the balance. Without love—the love that can forgive seventy times seven, and then not be tired—she'll certainly fail."*

The words steadied her. *"Without love—"* and she had no love to give Tony. Not the love that a woman should bring to the man she will call husband. Out of the turmoil of her mind this one thought emerged clear and irrefutable. And in that moment, for good or ill, her decision was taken.

"Tony." She spoke very gently, sore at heart for the pain she knew she must inflict. "I must say no, dear. If I loved you, I'd say yes very gladly. But I don't love you—not like that."

"And you won't marry me?"

"No, I can't marry you."

"Then that's finished." He spoke brusquely. "I shan't ask you again, so you needn't worry. Come along, we'll get back to the hotel. If we're going to watch the sunrise to-morrow, we'd better turn in early. And this air makes one confoundedly sleepy. I believe I could sleep the clock round."

His abrupt return to the commonplace left her feeling confused and disconcerted. It almost seemed as though she must have dreamed the brief conversation which had just taken place. It was incredible that a man could ask you to marry him, promise to forswear a deadly vice that was born in his blood, and then—almost in the same breath, as it were—casually vouchsafe the information that he "could sleep the clock round"!

He had linked his arm in hers again, and was piloting her skilfully down the uneven pathway. She stole a glance at his face. But she could learn nothing whatever from his expression. Apparently he was solely concerned with the matter of conducting her back to the hotel in safety.

They parted in the hall at the foot of the stairs.

"I hope you'll sleep all right, " said Tony, smiling down at her. "I'm afraid you'll find it a bit of a picnic, though, without any of the 'comforts of home'! "

He had hardly finished speaking when the hotel door swung open, and a man came striding in from outside. As he paused on the threshold to pull off the heavy coat he was wearing, he shot a casual glance in the direction of the two people standing together by the staircase. Then, his gaze concentrating suddenly, he stared at Tony with an odd intentness.

"Good-night, Tony. " Ann's voice travelled softly to his ears, and at the sound of it the man transferred his gaze from Tony's face to hers. He himself remained standing unobserved in the curtained shadow of the entry, and, when Ann had gone upstairs, Tony passed him on the way to his own room on the ground floor without noticing his presence.

The man's glance followed him speculatively. Strolling across to the bureau, he opened the visitors' book, flicking over the leaves till he came to the current page. He ran his fingers down the list of names, pausing abruptly at the last inscription: *"G. Smith and sister. "* Followed the illuminating word, *"London. "*

With a brief, ironical smile he closed the book. Then he, too, took his way to bed, and presently the Hotel de Loup was wrapped in the profound stillness of night.

CHAPTER VI

THE MAN WITH THE SCAR

The sun poured down on to the balcony, and even though the gaily striped sun-blind had long since been lowered the heat was intense. But in the clear, dry atmosphere of Switzerland it could never be too hot to please Ann—she was a veritable sun-worshipper—and she lay back on a wicker *chaise-longue,* basking contentedly in the golden warmth while she awaited Lady Susan's return from Evian. From below came the drowsy crooning of the lake, as the water lapped idly against the stones that edged it—a lake of a blue so deep as to be almost sapphire.

Ann's eyes rested affectionately on the scene. She had grown to love Lac Léman and the mountains amid which it lay. Opposite her, on the far side of the water, the beautiful Savoy range sloped upwards from the shore, brooding maternally above the villages which fringed the borders of the lake, while to her left the snow-capped Dents du Midi, almost dazzling in the brilliant sunshine, guarded the gracious valley of the Rhone.

It was very calm, and peaceful, and sunshiny. Here at Montricheux one could easily imagine oneself shut away for ever from all that was hard and difficult and sordid—enclosed within a charmed circle of enchanted mountains where life slipped effortlessly on from day to day. This morning Ann felt peculiarly aware of the peaceful atmosphere prevailing. It struck her how smoothly and easily the last few months had passed. To-day seemed typical of all the days which had preceded it. A little work—quite pleasant work, for Lady Susan—a measure of play, sunshine, the keen joy of beautiful surroundings—these things had made up six months of a strangely tranquil existence.

And now, as she sat communing with herself, she was conscious of a queer foreboding that this unruffled period of her life had run its course and was drawing to an end. Almost, it seemed to her, she could hear a low rustle amongst the winds of life—the faint, muttering stir which presages a storm.

Only once before had she experienced a similar sensation of foreboding, a few weeks prior to the death of her father and the subsequent discovery that she and Robin were left practically penniless. She had felt then as though a definite epoch in her life was approaching its close, and something new and difficult impending. And, in that instance, her premonition had been only too accurately fulfilled.

She tried to shake off the odd feeling of presentiment which obsessed her. But it persisted, and it was a real relief when at last the opening of a door and the sound of voices in the hall heralded Lady Susan's return. Unpleasant premonitions and such-like ghostly visitants were prone to melt away in her cheery, optimistic presence like dew before the sun, and Ann hastened out of the room to welcome her back.

But at sight of the little group of people in the hall she paused in dismay. Sir Philip and his chauffeur were supporting Lady Susan on either side, while Marie, the excitable *femme de chambre,* was wringing her hands and pouring out a voluble torrent of commiseration.

"Be quiet, Marie! " ordered Lady Susan in her brisk voice. "The end of the world hasn't come just because I've sprained my ankle! Go and get some bandages and hot water instead of squawking like a scared fowl. "

Ann hurried forward anxiously, but Lady Susan nodded reassurance.

"Don't be alarmed, my dear. It's nothing serious. I slipped on the gangway, coming off the steamer, and turned my ankle. That's all. "

"And quite enough, too! " fumed Sir Philip, as, assisted by the chauffeur, he lifted her with infinite care on to a couch. "Now, then, you clumsy fool! " This to the unfortunate chauffeur, who had released his hold a moment too soon, jarring the injured foot.

The man fled, pursued by his master's maledictions, and a few minutes later, hot water and bandages being forthcoming, Ann busied herself in tending the rapidly swelling ankle.

"What about a doctor? Don't you think you'd better have one? " asked Sir Philip, fussing helplessly round and feeling as inadequate as most men in similar circumstances. "You may have broken a small bone or something, " he added with concern.

"Doctor? Fiddlesticks! " returned Lady Susan. "Ann's all the doctor I want. There's quite a professional touch about that bandage"—extending her foot for him to see. "Thank goodness, most of our girls know how to give first aid nowadays! Now, run along, Philip, and look after that harum-scarum nephew of yours. I know you're aching to make sure he hasn't got into mischief during your absence, " she added with a touch of malice.

Sir Philip demurred a little, but finally went away, promising to look in again in the evening. But when evening came Lady Susan had retired to bed, feeling far too ill to receive visitors.

It was not until after Sir Philip's departure that she would allow herself to admit that she was suffering acutely, and then she lay back against her cushions, looking so white and exhausted that Ann was thoroughly alarmed and despatched Marie in search of the doctor, who promptly prescribed rest and quiet. By the following morning Lady Susan found herself too stiff even to wish to move. She had tripped and fallen suddenly, without being able to save herself at all, and she was more bruised and shaken than she or any one else had suspected.

For the next few days, therefore, she was relegated to the role of invalid. She was suffering a good deal of pain, and in the circumstances Ann felt disinclined to worry her with an account of the predicament in which she and Tony had found themselves during her absence at Evian. So that when Lady Susan asked her how she had amused herself that day, she merely vouchsafed that she had gone up to the Dents de Loup and stayed the night there in order to see the sunrise. Afterwards, it seemed simpler to let it rest at that, rather than enter into fresh explanations. The whole incident had come to assume much smaller proportions in retrospect, and the fact that she and Tony had not encountered any other visitors at the hotel had served to reassure her considerably.

By the end of a week Lady Susan was sufficiently convalescent to hobble about with the aid of a stick, and when Tony called with a huge sheaf of flowers for the invalid, and the news that there was a particularly good programme of music to be given at the Kursaal that evening, she insisted that Ann should go with him to hear it. Ann protested, but Lady Susan swept her objections aside.

"My dear, you've been dancing attendance on a fidgety old cripple long enough. Go along with Tony and squander your francs at boule, and drink *café mélange* or ice-cream soda, or whatever indigestible drinks the Kursaal management provides, and listen to this 'perfectly ripping programme. '" She shot a quizzical glance at Tony. "And you can tell that crabbed old uncle of yours to come to the villa and keep me amused in the meantime. "

And, since there was never any combating Lady Susan's decisions, matters were arranged accordingly.

* * * * *

It was unusually gay at the Kursaal that evening. The announcement of a special programme had drawn a large audience, and the terrace was crowded with people sitting at small, painted iron tables and partaking of various kinds of refreshment while they listened to the orchestra. Festoons of coloured lights sparkled like jewels in the dusk, and from the twilit shadows of the gardens below came answering gleams of red and orange, where Chinese lanterns spangled the foliage of the trees. Beyond the gardens lay the sleeping lake, and faint little airs wafted coolly upward from its surface, tempering the heat of the evening.

Ann looked round her with interested eyes while Tony gave his order to a waitress. She thoroughly enjoyed an evening at the Kursaal. Until she had joined Lady Susan at Villa Mon Rêve, she had never been out of England—for, though Archibald Lovell had been fond of wandering on the Continent himself, no suggestion had ever emanated from him that his daughter might like to wander with him—and the essentially un-English atmosphere of the casino still held for her the attraction of novelty. It was all so gay, so full of light and movement, and of that peculiar charm of the open air which makes an irresistible appeal to English people, condemned as they are by the exigencies of climate to take their pleasures betwixt four walls throughout the greater portion of the year.

"It interests me frightfully, watching people, " observed Ann. "Quite a lot of the people here are really enjoying the music—and quite a lot are simply marking time till the tables are open and they can go and play boule. "

Tony nodded.

"The sheep and the goats, " he replied. "Count me among the latter. But boule's a rotten poor game, " discontentedly. "Give me roulette—every time. One has the chance to win something worth while at that. "

"And a chance to lose equally as much, " retorted Ann.

She flushed a little. This was the first occasion on which Tony had referred to the subject of gambling since the day they had gone up to the Dents de Loup together. She wondered if he had spoken deliberately, intending to remind her of the fact that, since she had refused to marry him, he was perfectly free to gamble if he chose. Yet he had spoken so casually, apparently quite without *arrière pensée* that it almost appeared as though the memory of that day upon the mountain had been wiped out of his mind. He seemed unconscious of any *gêne* in the situation. During Lady Susan's brief illness he had been in and out of the villa exactly as usual, bringing flowers, running errands, cheering them all up with his infectious good humour—spontaneously willing to do anything and everything that might help to tide over a difficult time.

Now and again there flashed into Ann's mind the recollection of those few moments on the moonlit hill-side, when Tony's gravely steadfast face and proffered vow had made her think of him as some young knight of old, and she would ask herself whether she had done right or wrong in refusing him. But, for the most part, the episode seemed to her to be invested with a curious sense of unreality, an impression which was fostered by the apparently unforced naturalness of Tony's demeanour. And now she felt rather as though he were asserting his independence, his freedom to gamble.

"Lose? " He picked up her words. "You've got to be *prepared* to lose—at everything. The whole of life's a bit of a gamble, don't you think? "

"No, " she answered steadily. "I don't. Life's what you make it. "

The soft, slate-coloured eyes regarded her oddly.

"Yours will be, I dare say. Mine will be regulated by Uncle Philip, presumably. " His mouth twitched in a brief sneer. "It rather strikes me we make each other's lives. " Then, as though trying to turn the conversation into a more impersonal channel: "Rum crowd here to-night, isn't it? See that woman sitting on your left? She looks as though she hadn't two sous to rub together, yet she's been losing at least five hundred francs each night this week. She covers the table with five-franc notes and loses consistently. "

So Tony himself must have been playing at the tables every night! Ann made no comment, but glanced in the direction of the woman indicated. She was rather a striking-looking woman, no longer young, with a clever, mobile mouth, and a pair of dark, tragic-looking eyes that appeared all the darker by contrast with her powder-white hair. She was of foreign nationality—Russian, probably, Ann reflected, with those high cheek-bones of hers and that subtle grace of movement. But she was atrociously dressed. Crammed down on to her beautiful white hair was a mannish-looking soft felt hat that had seen its best days long ago, and the coat and skirt she was wearing, though unmistakably of good cut, were old and shabby. In her hand she held an open note-case, eagerly counting over the Swiss notes it contained, while every now and again she lifted her sombre, tragic eyes and cast a hungry glance towards the room where boule was played, the doors of which were not yet open.

"She might be an exiled Russian princess, " commented Ann, observing a certain regal turn of the head which wore the battered mannish hat.

Tony nodded.

"That's just what she is. She used to play a lot at Monte before the war. Now she can't afford to go there. So she lives here and plays every night—on the proceeds of any odd jewellery she can still sell. "

Ann regarded her commiseratingly. The woman seemed to her a pathetically tragic figure—a sidelight on the many tragedies hidden among that cosmopolitan crowd on the terrace. Then her straying glance shifted to a man seated alone at the next table to the

Russian's, apparently absorbed in a newspaper. Tony followed the direction of her eyes.

"That chap plays bridge at the club sometimes, " he vouchsafed. "I don't know who he is—never spoken to him. Foreigner, too, I should imagine. He's so swarthy. "

Ann bestowed a second glance on the man in question. He was wearing evening kit, and at first sight the brown-skinned face above the white of his collar, taken in conjunction with dark hair and very strongly-marked brows, seemed to premise the correctness of Tony's surmise. Suddenly the man lifted his bent head, and over the top of the newspaper Arm found herself looking into a pair of unmistakably grey eyes—grey as steel. They were very direct eyes, with a certain brooding discontent in their depths which looked as though it might flame out into sudden scorn with very little provocation.

She dropped her glance in some confusion. She felt rather as though she had been caught looking over her neighbour's garden wall. There had been an ironical glint in the regard which the grey eyes had levelled at her that suggested their owner might have overheard Tony's frank comment. Under cover of a fortissimo finale on the part of the orchestra she leant forward and spoke in a low voice:

"He's as English as you are, Tony. No one but an Englishman ever had grey eyes like that. "

But Tony's interest had evaporated. The band's final burst of enthusiasm heralded the finish of the first part of the programme and the consequent opening of the tables for boule. With a hurried "Come along, quick, " he jumped up and, with Ann beside him, was first in the van of the throng which was hastening into the rooms to play. In a few moments the gaily-lit terrace was practically deserted, and an eager-faced crowd pressed up against the green-clothed tables, each individual eager to secure a good place.

For a little while Ann contented herself with watching.

"Faites vos jeux, messieurs. Messieurs, faites vos jeux. "

The ball spun round, and the croupier's monotone sounded warningly above the whispering of notes and the clink of coin.

"Le jeu est fait. " It reminded Ann of the vicar intoning at the little church she had attended in the old Lovell Court days. Only there were no responses! Everybody was engrossed in watching the ball as it dodged in and out amongst the numbers, hesitating maddeningly, then starting gaily off on a fresh tack as though guided by some invisible spirit of malice.

"Rien ne va plus! "

Like the crack of doom came the last gabbled utterance, and the croupier's rake descended sharply on a claw-like hand which was attempting to insinuate a coin on to the cloth "after hours, " so to speak.

"Cinq! " An announcement which, five being the equivalent of the zero in roulette, was followed by the hungry rake's sweeping everything into the coffers of the bank except the five-franc note which Tony had staked on the number *cinq*.

He gathered up his winnings, and, turning excitedly to Ann, demanded why she wasn't playing.

"Follow me, " he told her. "I'm going to win to-night. I feel it in my bones. "

His eyes were brilliant under their absurd long lashes, and the smile he gave her was the confident smile of a conqueror. Ann caught the infection and began to play, staking where he staked, as he had suggested. Now and then she ventured a little flutter of her own and tried some other number, but usually her modest franc lay side by side with Tony's lordly five-franc note.

Evidently Tony's bones had the right prophetic instinct, for after every *coup* the croupier pushed across to him a small pile of notes and silver. Ann's own eyes were sparkling now. It was not that she really cared much about her actual winnings. She was staking too lightly for that to matter. But it entertained her enormously to win—to beat the bank as embodied in the person of the croupier, who reminded her of nothing so much as of an extremely active spider waiting in a corner of his web to pounce on an adventurous fly. Each time the ball dropped into the number she had backed, a little thrill of sheer, gleeful enjoyment ran through her.

Now and again, in spite of her absorption in her own and Tony's play, she was conscious of a muscular brown hand on her right that reached out to place a fresh stake on the table—never to gather up any winnings. Its owner must be losing heavily. He was betting, not only on single numbers, but putting the maximum on certain combinations and groups of numbers. And every time the long-handled rake whisked his stakes away from him.

Ann glanced sideways to see who was the unlucky player, and once more she met the same ironical grey eyes which she had last encountered over the top of a newspaper. The man who was losing so persistently was her Englishman.

He did not seek to hold her gaze, but bent his own immediately upon the table again. She stole another glance at him. He was very brown, but she could see now that he was naturally fair-skinned, although tanned by the sun. A small scar, high up on the left cheek-bone, showed like a white line against the tan. Probably he had lived abroad in a hot climate, she reflected; that deep bronze was never the achievement of an elusive northern sun. It emphasised the penetrating quality of his eyes, giving them a curious brilliance. Ann had been conscious of a little shock each time she had encountered them. She was inclined to set his actual age at thirty-six or seven, though his face might have been that of a man of forty. But there was a suggestion of something still boyish about it, notwithstanding the rather stern-set features and bitter-looking mouth. She felt as though the bitterness revealed in his expression did not rightly belong to the man's nature. It was in essence alien—something that life had added to him.

"Faites vos jeux, messieurs; messieurs, faites vos jeux. "

The croupier's droning voice recalled her sharply from her thoughts.

"Which is it to be this time, Tony? " she asked, smiling.

"Seven and *impair,* " he replied tersely. And in due course the seven turned up.

Their run of luck was continuing without a break, and plenty of amused and interested glances were cast at the young couple of successful players. They were taking it all so easily, with a careless, light-hearted enjoyment that was rather refreshing to turn to after a glimpse of some of the furtive, vulture-like faces gathered round the tables. Meanwhile, the grey-eyed Englishman continued to lose with the same persistency as his young compatriots were winning. Apparently he was playing on a system, for, in spite of his want of success, he continued steadily backing certain definite combinations. He showed neither impatience or annoyance when he lost. His face remained perfectly impassive, and Ann had a feeling that he would play precisely as steadily, remain as grimly unmoved, if the stakes were a hundred times as high as those permitted at the Kursaal. She could imagine him staking his whole fortune, losing it, and then walking out of the rooms as coolly composed as he had entered them.

Once more the ball slithered into the number she had backed, and she opened a small silken bag, that already bulged with her evening's gains, and added the winnings of the last coup. At the same moment, some one pressing from behind jolted her arm, and the bag fell with a little thud, its contents spilling out on the floor. Tony, engrossed in the play, failed to notice the mishap and went on staking, but the Englishman, apparently quite unconcerned as to the chances he might be missing, stooped at once and collected the bag and its scattered contents.

"I think I've rescued everything, " he said, as he handed it to her. "But you'd better count it over and make certain. "

"Oh, no, I won't count it. It's sure to be all right. Thank you so much. " Ann spoke rather breathlessly. For some reason or other she felt unaccountably nervous.

The man smiled.

"You've become such a Croesus to-night that I suppose an odd franc or two doesn't matter? " he suggested.

"I *have* been lucky, haven't I? " she acknowledged frankly. "It's been such fun. " Then, with friendly sympathy: "I'm afraid you've lost, though? "

He shrugged his shoulders.

"I'm used to losing, " he replied indifferently.

Somehow, Ann felt as though he were not thinking only of his losses at the tables. That note of bitterness in his voice sprang from some deeper undercurrent.

"I'm so sorry, " she said simply.

"I never expect to win, " he returned curtly. "If you expect nothing, you're never disappointed. Pray don't waste your sympathy. "

The rudeness of the speech took her aback. Yet, sensing in its very churlishness the sting of some old hurt, she answered him quietly, though with heightened colour:

"If you expect nothing, you'll get nothing. That's one of the rules of the road. "

He checked himself in the act of turning away, and regarded her with a mixture of contempt and amusement, much as one might smile at the utterances of a child.

"Don't you think we get mostly what we're looking for? " she went on courageously. "If you expect good things, they'll come to you, and if you're expecting bad things, they'll come, too. "

He gave a short laugh.

"The doctrine of faith! I'm afraid I've outgrown it—many years ago. "

"Faites vos jeux, messieurs, " intoned the croupier.

The Englishman tossed a coin on to number nine. Ann followed the circlings of the ball with a curious tense anxiety. She wished desperately that the nine would turn up.

"Numéro un! "

With a feeling akin to revolt she watched those who had staked on number one grab up their winnings, while the croupier raked in the Englishman's solitary bid for fortune.

"You see? " The bitter grey eyes mocked her. "Quite symbolical, wasn't it? "

With a slight bow he moved away from the table and passed quickly out of the room.

Ann felt disinclined to play any further. She watched Tony win, then lose once, then win again several times in succession. He was flushed and there was a look of triumph on his face.

"Haven't you finished yet, Tony? " she asked at last "I'm ready to go home when you are. "

"Go home? When I'm winning? " he expostulated. "Rather not! " Then, catching sight of her face, "Hello! You look tired. Are you, Ann? "

She nodded.

"Yes, I think I am a little. "

Tony held a five-franc note in his hand, ready for staking. Without the least sign of disappointment he stuffed it back into his pocket.

"Then we'll go home, " he said. And somewhat to the amazement of the people nearest him, who had been watching his phenomenal run of luck, he made a way for Ann through the crowd and followed her out of the room.

"That was nice of you, Tony, " she said gratefully, as they started to walk home through the deserted streets.

He threw her a quick, enigmatic smile.

"I've an obliging disposition. Haven't you found that out yet? "

Ann laughed.

"It's becoming quite noticeable, " she retorted. "Tony, you nearly broke the bank to-night, I should think. "

"Broke the bank! At five francs a time! " He kicked a pebble viciously into the roadway. "It was confounded bad luck to get a run like that with such a rotten limit. With an equal run at Monte I'd have made a fortune. Oh, damn! "

They walked on in silence for a while. There was no moon. The lake lay dark and mysterious, pricked here and there with the swaying orange light of a fishing-boat. High up, like a ring of planets brooding above the town, the great arc of the Caux Palace lights blazed through the starlit dusk.

Tony reverted to the evening's play.

"You didn't do badly, either, " he said, challengingly. "You weren't bored to-night, were you? "

An odd little smile crossed her face.

"No, I wasn't bored, " she answered quietly.

CHAPTER VII

A QUESTION OF ILLUSIONS

An air of suppressed excitement prevailed over Montricheux. It was the day when the pretty lakeside town celebrated the Fête des Narcisses, and from the smallest street urchin, grabbing a bunch of narcissi in his grubby little hand and trying to induce the good-natured foreigner to purchase his wares, to the usually stolid *h'teliers,* vying with each other as to which of their caravanserais should blaze out into the most arresting scheme of decoration on the great occasion, the whole population was aquiver with an almost child-like sense of anticipation and delight. There was to be a procession of decorated cars and carriages, a battle of flowers, and attractions innumerable during the course of the day, followed in the evening by a Venetian fête on the waters of the bay.

Tony looked in at Villa Mon Rêve shortly after breakfast.

"Taking any part in the proceedings? " he inquired conversationally.

Ann shook her head.

"We've had the car decorated in honour of the occasion, " she replied. "But we're not competing for any prize. I expect we shall just drive about the town. "

"Same here. Tour round, chucking flowers at unsuspecting people. It's a bore that you and I can't play about together, " moodily. "But we've got a female relative of Uncle Philip's on our hands—a wealthy old cousin, name of 'Great Expectations, '" with a cheerful grin. "So I've got to trot her round and do the devoted nephew stunt all day. "

"I hope you'll do it nicely"—smiling.

"I shall hear of it from Uncle Philip if I don't! "—grimly. "But you needn't worry. I got all my best manners down from the top shelf this morning and gave 'em a brush up. "

"Good boy. " Ann nodded approval.

"And by way of reward, " insinuated Tony, "you'll come to the dance at the Gloria this evening, won't you? I could come over and fetch you about ten o'clock, after this precious Venetian fête is over. I'd have liked to go on the lake, but Uncle Philip has ordained that we are to watch the proceedings from our balcony at the Gloria. After that, I should think 'cousin' will be sufficiently exhausted to contemplate the idea of retiring to bed like a Christian woman. She's seventy-nine. "

"People fox-trot at seventy-nine nowadays, " suggested Ann mischievously. "Perhaps your duties won't end at ten. " Then, seeing his face fall: "But I'll come to the dance, if Lady Susan doesn't happen to want me this evening. "

At that moment Lady Susan herself came into the room. She still limped a little, leaning on an ebony stick with a gold knob.

"Who's taking my name in vain? " she asked, as she shook hands with Tony. "I'm sure to want you, " addressing Ann, "but I suppose I shall have to go without you if Tony wants you too. "

Ann explained about the dance, adding: "But of course I shan't think of it if you'd rather I stayed at home. "

"Of course you *will* think of it, " contradicted Lady Susan with vigour. "I'd go myself if it wasn't for this wretched ankle of mine, and then"—bubbling over—"Philip and I could tread a stately measure together. I can just see him doing it! " she added wickedly.

"That's fixed, then, " said Tony. "So long. I'll call for you about ten o'clock, Ann. "

After lunch Lady Susan and Ann drove off in the two-seater, Ann at the wheel and a great basket of flowers for ammunition purposes on the floor of the car. The streets were thronged with people, and from almost every window depended flags and coloured streamers, flapping gaily in the breeze. Cars hastened hither and thither; some, elaborately decorated, were evidently intended to compete for the prizes offered, whilst others, like that of Lady Susan, were only sufficiently embellished to permit of their taking part in the Battle of Flowers, in accordance with the official regulations issued for the occasion.

The judging of the cars took place in the wide Place du Marché, and immediately afterwards the firing-off of a small self-important cannon signalised the commencement of the battle. Carriages and cars passed and repassed, flowers were tossed from one to the other, whilst showers of confetti and coloured paper *serpentins* flew through the air.

Lady Susan apparently enjoyed the fun as much as any one, and was perfectly charmed when, as the two-seater glided past Sir Philip's Rolls-Royce, he flung an exquisite spray of crimson roses into her lap, with a sprig of rosemary nestling amongst them.

"Romantic old dear! " she commented, laughing, as she retaliated with a tiny nosegay which Sir Philip caught neatly as it went sailing over his head. But her eyes were very soft as she turned to Ann. "The beauty of not being married is that you never lose your illusions. Always remember that, Ann, when you feel like commiserating the old maids of your acquaintance. "

"And are you bound to lose them if you marry? " queried Ann, steering her way deftly through the traffic and bringing the two-seater to a standstill as the stream of cars temporarily checked.

"No. But you run an excellent chance of it. Do you suppose if I'd married Sir Philip thirty years ago he'd be pelting me with roses now? "—enjoyably. "Of course not. It'd be the tradesmen's books, most likely! "

"You wicked cynic! "

Lady Susan laid her hand impulsively on the girl's arm.

"Not really, Ann, " she said hastily. "I know that if only a man remembers the roses, marriage may mean heaven on earth. But they so often forget"—a little wistfully. "And a woman does so *hate* to be taken for granted—regarded as a kind of standing dish! "

Came a regular barrage of flowers from a car to their right, and Ann, recognising a party of friends, returned them measure for measure. Meanwhile, unnoticed by her, the third-prize car had drawn alongside, intervening between herself and the car-load of friends. She had already raised her arm to speed a final rosebud on its way, and then, with a sudden shock of surprise, she recognised in one of the occupants of the prize car the Englishman with the grey eyes. He was sitting beside an extremely pretty woman and looking somewhat haughty and ill-tempered, as though the whole business of the fête bored him excessively.

She tried to check her action, but it was too late. The rosebud flew from her fingers, and the Englishman's head being directly in her line of fire, the bud, sped with hearty goodwill, hit him straight on the nose. Ann smiled—she couldn't help it. But there came no response, his expression remaining unaltered. He regarded her unsmilingly, without a hint of recognition in his eyes.

A hot flush stained her cheeks.

"Boor! " was her mental comment, and she let in the clutch viciously as the car in front of her moved forward.

Lady Susan laughed outright.

"I wonder who that handsome, sulky-looking individual is? " she said gaily. "He fairly froze you, Ann. I imagine he thinks you did it on purpose. "

Ann's face burned more hotly. That was precisely the conclusion she had arrived at herself, and the idea filled her with helpless rage.

"He struck me as quite an unusual combination of good looks and bad temper, " pursued Lady Susan. "Evidently he doesn't appreciate being pelted with roses. "

A sudden gurgle of laughter broke from Ann.

"It was rather a hard little bud, " she said vindictively. "I hope it hurt him. "

Lady Susan threw a swift glance at her.

"Do you know him? Have you met him before? " she asked.

"He was down at the Kursaal the other night—the night Tony and I had such good luck. I dropped my bag and he picked it up for me. That's all. "

Ann spoke rather shortly, and for some time afterwards appeared to be completely absorbed in manoeuvring the two-seater through the streets. They did not encounter the Englishman's car again, and eventually, after making a final circuit of the town, they returned to Mon Rêve.

In the evening Lady Susan complained of fatigue.

"I've not quite got over that fall of mine yet, " she acknowledged ruefully, when Ann suggested that perhaps she had been out driving too long in the hot sun. "Elderly ladies should refrain from tumbling about; it shakes them up too much. I should immensely like to go to bed, if you don't mind watching the Venetian fête in solitary splendour. Do you? "

She emitted a sigh of satisfaction when Ann assured her that she did not.

"Then I shall just disappear to bed with a novel. It will entertain me far more than gazing at a lot of illuminated boats paddling about the lake. "

"I think I shall take our boat out, then, " said Ann. "I'd rather like to see it all at close quarters. It's all new to me, you know. "

Lady Susan nodded. At different times they had spent a good many enjoyable hours together, pulling about on the lake, and she had complete confidence in Ann's ability to manage a rowing-boat.

"Very well. Only don't forget Tony is coming to take you to the dance at ten and tire yourself out. "

Ann laughed and shook her head, and when Lady Susan had departed to bed she threw a knitted coat over her evening frock and made her way out into the garden. It was a long, rambling garden, sheltered from the road by a high wall and, at its farthest end, skirting the lake itself. Here a small wooden landing-stage had been erected, and moored against it lay a light rowing-boat—the *Rêve.* With practised hands Ann untied the painter, affixed a light to the bows of the boat, dropped the sculls into the rowlocks, and rowed quietly out across the placid water.

One by one illuminated boats came creeping round the arm of the bay, each adding a fresh cluster of twinkling lights to the bobbing multitude already gathered there. Like a cloud of fireflies they seemed to dart and circle and hover above the dusky surface of the lake. Motor-launches flashed here and there, in and out amongst the slower craft, while from one of the lake steamers, decks and rigging outlined in quivering points of light, came the inspiriting strains of a band. Snatches of song drifted across the water, and now and again the melancholy long-drawn hoot of a syren pierced the air.

Gradually Ann drew abreast of the assembled craft, and leisurely pulled her way in and out amongst them. The decorated boats delighted her, some agleam with Chinese lanterns—giant glow-worms floating on the water, others with phantom sails of frail asparagus fern lit by swaying lights like dancing will-o'-the-wisps—dream-boats gliding slowly over a dreaming lake.

Presently she rested on her oars, watching the scene with the eager, vivid interest which was characteristic of her. So absorbed was she that she failed to notice that her own small skiff was getting rather dangerously hemmed in. To her right lay a biggish sailing vessel, blocking the view on that side, behind her a small fry of miscellaneous craft, packed together like a flotilla of Thames boats on a summer's day awaiting the opening of the lock gates. Half unconsciously she heard the approaching chug-chug of an engine mingling with the sound of voices singing lustily—the hilarious chorus of a crew of roysterers who had been celebrating not wisely but too well.

... It all happened with appalling suddenness. One moment she was watching the fairy fleet that glittered on the lake, the next a hubbub of hoarse, warning shouts filled the air, the throb of an engine pulsed violently in her ears, and a motor-boat, overloaded by half-tipsy revellers and travelling too fast for safety, drove past the bows of the sailing vessel and veered drunkenly towards her. Instinctively she clutched at her oars. But they were useless, pinned to the sides of her boat by the press of others round it. Then, from almost immediately above her, it seemed, a terse voice—curiously familiar—rapped out a command.

"Stand up! "

Hardly knowing what she did, she obeyed, yielding blindly to the peremptory order. She felt her frail barque rock beneath her feet, then strong arms grasped her—strong as tempered steel—and lifted her clean up out of the lurching boat and over its side into another.

Almost before she had time to realise that she was safe, the motor-boat crashed, head on, into the empty *Rêve,* staving in her side so that in an instant she had filled with water, her gunwale level with the lake. Then, as though some ghoulish hand had clutched at her from the depths below, she sank suddenly out of sight.

Staring with horrified eyes at the swift and utter destruction of the *Rêve,* Ann shuddered uncontrollably. But for the unknown deliverer who had snatched her bodily from the doomed boat she herself would be struggling in that almost fathomless depth of water or, stunned by the savage drive of the motor-boat's prow, sinking helplessly down to the bottom like a stone.

"Don't be afraid. You're all right. " Again that strangely familiar note in the reassuring voice.

Ann twisted round within the circle of the arms which held her and peered up at the face of their owner. A flickering gleam of light revealed a small white scar high up on the left cheek-bone.

"You! " she exclaimed under her breath. "Is it you? "

"Yes. " She could detect a note of amusement in the voice that came to her through the dusk. "Your creed has proved false, you see. I expected nothing—and here I am with an altogether charming adventure. "

"I shouldn't describe it quite like that, " she answered ruefully.

"No? But then you've lost a boat, whereas I've gained a passenger. Our points of view are different. "

The arms which held her had not relaxed their hold, and she stirred restlessly, suddenly acutely conscious of their embrace. Instantly she felt herself released.

"Will you be all right? " came in a cool voice.

"Oh, yes—yes. " Ann stammered a little. "This is a very steady boat, isn't it? "—wonderingly.

"It's a motor-boat, that's why. "

Now that the uproar occasioned by the accident had died away, she could hear the soft purring of an engine forward.

"Still, you'd better sit down, " resumed the Englishman. "The Bacchanalian gentlemen in the boat which ran you down are still blundering about, and may quite probably cannon into us. And you don't want to take a second chance of being shot out into the lake. "

"Indeed I don't. " She sat down hastily. "I—I don't really know how to thank you, " she began haltingly, after a moment. Somehow she felt curiously shy and tongue-tied with this man.

"Then don't try, " he replied ungraciously.

This was hardly encouraging, but Ann returned to the charge with determination.

"I must, " she said. "If it hadn't been for you I should certainly have been drowned. "

"Rather improbable, " he answered—as indifferently as though it really mattered very little whether she were or not. "With so many people close at hand, some one would have been sure to fish you out. You'd have got a wetting—and so would your unfortunate rescuer. That's all. Still, I'm just as glad I saw what was going to happen. I prefer to keep a dry skin myself. "

"Oh! Then you would have jumped in after me? " asked Ann, with interest.

He sat down in the stern of the boat, his arm on the tiller, and regarded her contemplatively.

"I suppose so. A man has no choice when a woman chooses to go monkeying about in a boat and gets herself into difficulties. "

"'Monkeying about in a boat! '" repeated Ann indignantly. "I suppose you'll say next that I rammed my own boat and sank it! "

"You certainly put yourself in the way of danger, " he retorted. "Who in the name of Heaven allowed you to go out on the lake alone on a fête night like this? Isn't there any one to look after you? "

"I look after myself, " she replied shortly. "I'm not a child. "

He laughed.

"Not much more, surely. How old are you? Seventeen? Eighteen? "

"Add four, " said Ann, "and you'll be nearer it. "

"So much? " He fell silent. There had been genuine surprise in his voice. Perhaps he was recalling her as he had seen her at the Kursaal—boyishly slender, her eager, pointed face alight with gay enthusiasm and amusement.

One, two, three—nine strokes. The sound of a clock striking came wafted faintly across from the shore. Ann started up.

"I must get back! " she exclaimed. "I'd forgotten all about the time. "

A brief smile crossed the man's dark face.

"So had I, " he said. And there was something in the quality of his voice which sent the colour flying up into her face.

"Why must you go back in such a hurry? " he resumed composedly. "One can watch the fête very well here. "

"I'm going to a dance—at the Gloria, " said Ann. "Some one—they are coming to fetch me, and if I'm not there—"

"'They' will be disappointed, " he finished for her, a veiled irony in his voice. "What time do your friends expect you? "

"At ten. "

"And it is now only nine. If you care to watch the fête a little longer, I can land you wherever you wish and you would still be in good time. I will guarantee your safety, " he added with a smile.

Ann hesitated. On the one hand she was thoroughly enjoying the water-fête as viewed from the security of the Englishman's motor-boat, and the unconventionality of the circumstances added a spice of adventure to the situation. On the other, like every properly brought up young woman, she was quite aware of what would be Mrs. Grundy's pronouncement on such a matter.

"You'll stay? " said the Englishman.

It savoured more of a command than a question. Metaphorically Ann threw Mrs. Grundy overboard into the lake.

"Yes, I'll stay, " she answered.

He accepted her decision without any outward sign of satisfaction, and she experienced a slight chill of disappointment. Perhaps, after all, he had only asked her to remain a little longer, not because he really desired the pleasure of her company, but merely in order that he might not be inconvenienced by the necessity of taking her back to Montricheux before he himself was ready to go. She had all the sensitiveness of youth and, once this idea had presented itself to her, she felt self-conscious and ill at ease, only anxious for the moment to arrive when she need no longer trespass on his hospitality.

And then, just as though some secret wireless had acquainted him of her discomfort, he held out his hand with a sudden smile that softened the harsh lines of his face extraordinarily.

"Thank you, " he said quietly. "When you go to bed to-night you'll be able to feel you've done your 'kind deed' for to-day. "

Half reluctantly, yet unable to do otherwise, Ann laid her hand in the one he held out to her. His strong fingers closed round it possessively and she was aware of a queer, breathless feeling of captivity. She drew her hand sharply away.

"Is it a 'kind deed'? " she asked lightly, for the sake of saying something—anything—which should break the tension of the silence which had followed.

"Is it not? To bestow a charming half-hour of your companionship on the loneliest person in Montricheux? Oh, I think so. "

"You didn't look at all lonely this afternoon, " flashed back Ann, remembering the pretty woman with whom she had seen him driving.

"At the Battle of Flowers, you mean? No. " He turned the conversation adroitly. "But I only won third prize, so I'm still in need of sympathy. Taking the third prize is rather my *métier* in life. "

"Perhaps it's all you deserve, " she suggested unkindly. "Anyway, you've nothing to grumble at. *We* didn't win anything. We weren't elaborately enough decorated to compete. "

"Yet you looked as if you were enjoying it all, " he hazarded. "Did you? "

"Yes, of course I did. Didn't you? "

"Not particularly—till some one threw me a rose. "

Ann decided to ignore the latter part of this speech.

"You're such a confirmed cynic that I wonder you condescended to take part in anything go frivolous as the fête, " she observed.

He shrugged his shoulders.

"When in Rome—Besides, it reminded me of my young days. "

"You talk as if you were a close relation of Methuselah. You're not so very old. "

"Am I not? " He paused a moment. "Old enough, at any rate, to have lost all my illusions. "

There was an undercurrent so bitter in the curtly uttered speech that Ann's warm young sympathies responded involuntarily.

"I wish I could bring them back for you, " she said impulsively.

Through the flickering luminance of the lights rimming the boat's gunwale he looked at her with an odd intensity.

"That's just what I'm afraid of, " he said. "That you might bring them back. Fortunately, I'm leaving Montricheux to-morrow. "

Ann was silent. She was vibrantly conscious of the man's strange, forceful personality. His brusque, hard speeches fell on her like so many blows, and yet behind them she felt as though there were something that appealed—something hurt and seeking to hide its hurt behind an armour of savage irony.

His voice, coolly indifferent once more, broke across her thoughts.

"Would you like to go back now? "

He spoke as though he were suddenly anxious to be rid of her as quickly as possible, and she assented hastily. His abrupt changes of mood disconcerted her. There seemed no accounting for what he might say next. He tossed a curt order to a man whom she could discern crouching forward near the engine.

"Bien, m'sieu, " came the answer, and presently the motor-boat was dexterously edging her way through the throng till she emerged into a clear space and purred briskly towards the shore.

Once more the Englishman's hand closed firmly round Ann's as he helped her out on to the little landing-stage.

"Good-bye, " she said, a trifle nervously. "And thank you so much for coming to my rescue. "

Still retaining her hand in his, he stared down at her with those queerly compelling eyes of his. She felt her breath coming and going unevenly. For a moment he hesitated, as though deliberating some point within himself. Then:

"Good-bye, " he said. And his voice was utterly expressionless. It held not even cordiality.

CHAPTER VIII

A LETTER FROM ENGLAND

The postman, entering through the garden gate which opened on to the street, found Ann busily engaged in cutting flowers. He greeted her with a smile, pleased to be saved the remainder of the distance to the house.

"*Bonjour, mademoiselle*. Only one letter for the villa this morning. " He handed her the solitary missive which the mail had brought and departed, whistling cheerfully, on his way down the street.

Ann fingered the bulky envelope with satisfaction. It was addressed in Robin's handwriting, and she carried it off to a sunny corner of the garden to enjoy its contents at leisure.

> "Dear Little Ann"—ran the letter. *"Here, at last is the good news we have both been waiting for! I have been offered exactly the kind of billet I wanted—that of estate-agent to a big land-owner. The salary is a really generous one, and there's a jolly little cottage goes with it, so that you'll be able to chuck free-lancing and come and keep house for me as we've always planned. Needless to say, I've accepted the job!*
>
> *"And now to give you all details. My future employer is one, Eliot Coventry. We've had several interviews and I liked him very much, although he struck me as rather a queer sort of chap. I should put him down as dead straight and thoroughly dissatisfied with life! Heronsmere, the Coventry place, is a fine old house—one of those old Elizabethan houses you're so cracked on. It reminds me a bit of Lovell Court. There'll be a lot to see to on the estate, as the bailiff in charge has just let things rip, and Coventry himself has been out of England for some years. In fact, he has never lived at Heronsmere. He's a distant cousin of the late owner and only inherited owing to a succession of deaths. He was abroad at the time and never even troubled to come home and have a look at his inheritance.*
>
> *"One thing I know will please you, and that is that we shall be near the sea. Silverquay is the name of the village, which is really a part of the Heronsmere property. It's comparatively small, not*

much more than a little fishing village, but the town of Ferribridge is only about ten miles distant, so you'll be able to obtain the necessities of civilised existence, I expect.

"Coventry wants me to take up the work straight away, so I should like to move into Oldstone Cottage—our future place of abode—as soon as possible. How soon do you think Lady Susan would spare you? By the way, you won't need to exercise your mind over the servant question. Knowing you were fixed out in Switzerland, I wrote off at once to Maria Coombe to ask her if she knew of any one suitable, and she promptly suggested herself! So she goes to Oldstone Cottage to-morrow to get things in order for us.

"I think I've told you everything. I've tried to imagine all the questions you would want to ask—and to supply the answers!

"Ever your affectionate brother,
"ROBIN."

Ann laid the letter down on her knee and sat looking out across the lake with eyes which held a curious mixture of pleasure and regret. The idea of sharing life once more with Robin filled her with undiluted joy, but she was conscious that the thought of leaving Lady Susan and dear, gunny Switzerland created an actual little ache in her heart. She could quite imagine feeling rather homesick for Lady Susan's kindly presence, and for the Swiss mountains and the blue lake which lay smiling and dimpling at her now in the brilliant sunlight.

Her glance lingered on the lake. She had not been on the water since the Venetian fête, nearly three weeks ago, owing primarily to the destruction of the *Rêve,* and secondly to Lady Susan's incurable aversion to a hired boat. "They roll, my dear, " she asserted, when Ann vainly tried to tempt her into giving the hireling a chance. "And the cushions have villainous lumps in sundry places. No, I'll stay on shore till we have a new boat of our own. "

So they had stayed on shore, but in spite of herself, Ann's thoughts often travelled back to the occasion of that last journey she had made on the lake—with the purr of the motor-boat's engine in her ears and the odd, unnerving consciousness of the Englishman's close proximity. She would have liked to forget him, but there was something about the man which made this impossible. Ann admitted it to herself with an annoyed sense of the unreasonableness of it. He was nothing to her—not even an acquaintance, according to the canons of social convention—and in all human probability they would never meet again.

Yet, try as she might, she had been unable to dismiss him altogether from her thoughts, and since his departure she had several times caught herself wondering, with a fugitive emotion of odd trepidation, whether he would ever return. Once she had even thought she descried him coming towards her along the Grand' Rue, and when the figure which she had supposed was his resolved itself, upon closer inspection, into that of a total stranger, bearing only the most superficial resemblance to the man for whom she had mistaken him, she experienced a totally disproportionate sense of disappointment.

The news contained in Robin's letter promised, at any rate, to end all likelihood of any further meeting. Even if, later on, the unknown Englishman should return to Montricheux, it would only be to find her gone. She derived a certain feeling of relief from this thought. There was something disquieting about the man. He made you like and dislike him almost in the same breath. On the whole, Ann felt she would be glad to be in England, freed from the rather disturbing uncertainty as to whether they might or might not meet again. People so often came back to Montricheux.

She folded up Robin's letter, and, slinging her basket of flowers over her arm, returned to the house, somewhat troubled in mind as to how she should break the news of her impending departure to Lady Susan. The difficulty solved itself, however, more easily than she had anticipated.

"At Silverquay! " exclaimed Lady Susan, when Ann had explained matters. "Now, how charming! I do think Fate is a good-natured old thing sometimes. I shall lose you and yet still keep you, Ann. You'll be living quite near me. "

Ann looked up in surprise.

"But you don't live at Silverquay! " she said.

"Almost next door, though. My home, White Windows, is in the neighbouring parish—Heronsfoot—about five miles away, three if you cut across the fields. "

"Then of course you know this Mr. Coventry? "

"No, I've never met him. I knew Rackham Coventry, from whom your man inherited, and I've heard him speak of his cousin Eliot. They were on very bad terms with each other, so that Eliot never came near the place in poor old Rack's time, and, as your brother tells you, he was abroad when the property fell in to him. Heronsmere is a lovely old house, by the way. "

"I wonder Mr. Coventry never came back until now, " said Ann. "He must take very little interest in the place. "

"He's lived abroad for years, I believe. I remember Rack's telling me he had been crossed in love, and he cut himself adrift from England afterwards. I think the girl threw him over because in those days he wasn't rich enough. She must feel rather a fool now, if she knows how things have fallen out. The Heronsmere rent-roll is enormous. "

"It rather serves her right, doesn't it? " commented Ann, with a feeling that for once poetic justice had been meted out.

Lady Susan smiled.

"Yes. Though I always feel a bit sorry for people who get their deserts. You never realise how heavy the bill is going to be when you're running it up. " She fell silent a moment, then went on: "The pity of it is that I suppose Eliot Coventry will never marry now, and so Heronsmere will ultimately go to a very distant branch of the family. He tried to get himself killed out of the way during the war, I heard. I knew a man in the same regiment, and he told me Eliot didn't seem to know what the word fear meant—'Mad Coventry, ' they called him. He took the most amazing risks, and came through without a scratch. "

"While poor Robin got badly wounded and gassed into the bargain, " said Ann. "That's why I'm so glad he's got this post. The doctors told him that an out-door job was his one chance of getting really strong again. "

"Yes, I'm very glad—for you, " answered Lady Susan ruefully. "But I shall miss you badly, child. However, if Robin wants you he must have you, and as he wants you to go as soon as possible I should think the best plan is for you to travel back to England with Philip and Tony next week. "

It was typical of Lady Susan that she wasted no time in repining, but promptly proceeded to sketch out a definite plan of action.

"But what about you? " asked Ann with some concern.

"I'll come with you all as far as Paris, and there you can drop me to do some stopping. I shall stay two or three weeks, I expect. "

Ann's face still remained clouded. She felt that it was hardly fair to desert Lady Susan so suddenly, much as she longed to join Robin as speedily as possible.

"Are you sure you wouldn't rather I stayed with you a little longer? " she suggested earnestly. "I'm sure Robin could manage for a few weeks—especially as he will have Maria Coombe. "

Lady Susan's quick dark eyes flashed over her.

"Who is Maria Coombe? " she demanded.

Ann laughed.

"Maria Coombe is a host in herself, " she answered. "She's an old Devonshire servant who was with my mother originally. I believe she came to Lovell when she was about eighteen as kitchen-maid. Then, when Robin and I were kiddies she was our nurse, and after we grew too old to need one she stayed on in a sort of general capacity. I never remember life without Maria until she got married. Her husband was killed in the war, and now she's coming to Oldstone Cottage to look after us. I'm so delighted about it, " she added. "It will be like old times having Maria around again. "

"That's really nice for you, " agreed Lady Susan heartily. "Still, I think"—smiling—"Robin will be glad to have his sister, too. And you needn't worry about me in the least. I've heaps of friends in Paris. Besides, Brett Forrester—my scapegrace nephew—is there now, and he and I always amuse each other. "

"Tony knows him, doesn't he? He mentioned having met him in London, I remember. "

"Yes. I believe they both belong to the same gambling set in town—more's the pity! " replied Lady Susan, with grim disapproval. "The only difference between them being that Brett gambles and can afford to do it, while Tony gambles—and can't. I haven't seen Brett for a long time now, " she went on musingly. "Not since last August, when he was yachting and put in at Silverquay Bay for a few days. He's always tearing about the world, though he rarely troubles to keep me informed of his whereabouts. I wish to goodness he'd marry and settle down! "

A sudden puff of wind blew in through the open window, disarranging the grouping of a vaseful of flowers, and Ann crossed the room to rectify the damage. Lady Susan's eyes followed her meditatively. She liked the girl's supple ease of movement, the clean-cut lines of her small, pointed face. There was something very distinctive about her, she reflected, and she had to the full that odd charm of elusive, latent femininity which is so essentially the attribute of the modern girl with her boyish lines and angles.

"I shall miss you dreadfully, Ann! " she exclaimed impulsively. "I wish you belonged to me. "

She was hardly conscious of the line of thought which had prompted the spontaneous speech. Ann turned round smilingly.

"It's dear of you to say so, " she replied. "I shall insist on Robin's letting me come over to White Windows as often as I like—and as you will have me! "

Lady Susan laughed and kissed her.

"You'd better not promise too much—or I shall want to abduct you altogether! " she declared. "I think Robin's a very lucky young man. "

Once the date of her departure for England was actually fixed, it seemed to Ann as though the days positively flew by. There were a hundred and one things requiring attention. Sleeping-berths must be booked on board the train, last visits paid to various friends and acquaintances, and final arrangements made with regard to the shutting up of Mon Rêve. Last, but not least, there was the packing up of Ann's own personal belongings, which, in the course of the last six months, seemed to have strayed away into various odd corners of the villa, as is the way of things.

But it was all accomplished at last, and close on midnight the little party of four travellers stood on the deserted platform at Montricheux, watching the great Orient Express thunder up alongside. Followed a hurried gathering together of hand-baggage, a scramble up the steep steps of the railway coach, a piercing whistle, and the train pulled out of the station and went rocking on its way through the starry darkness of the night.

CHAPTER IX

OLDSTONE COTTAGE

The journey from Montricheux to London accomplished, Ann was speeding through the familiar English country-side once more and finding it doubly attractive after her six months' sojourn abroad. The train slowed down to manipulate a rather sharp curve in the line as it approached Silverquay station, and she peered eagerly out of the window to see the place which was henceforth to mean home to her. She caught a fleeting glimpse of white cliffs, crowned with the waving green of woods, of the dazzling blue of a bay far below, and of a straggling, picturesque village which climbed the side of a steep hill sloping upward from the shore. Over all lay the warm haze of early July sunshine. Then the train ran into the station and she had eyes only for Robin's tall, straight figure as he came striding along the platform to meet her.

Brother and sister resembled each other but slightly. In place of Ann's tempestuous coppery hair Robin was endowed with sober brown, and for her golden-hazel eyes, with their changeful lights, nature had substituted in him a pair of serious greenish-brown ones. But they were attractive eyes, for all that, with a steady, "trustable" expression in them that reminded one of the eyes of a nice fox terrier.

"Robin! " Ann sprang out of the railway-carriage and precipitated herself upon him with unconcealed delight. "Oh, my dear, how are you? Let me have a good look at you! "

She pushed him a little away from her and her eyes flashed over his face and figure searchingly. Then she nodded as though satisfied with her inspection. Whereas when she had last seen him he had limped a bit as a consequence of his wound, to-day he had crossed the platform with the old, easy, swinging stride of the pre-war Robin, and although his face was still rather on the thin side, it had lost the look of delicacy which, a year ago, had worried her considerably.

"Isn't this all simply splendid, Robin? " she said gaily, as, after giving her luggage in charge of a porter, they made their way out of the station. "Never tell me dreams don't come true after this—if you dream them hard enough! "

He smiled down at her. Her spontaneous enthusiasm was infectious.

"It certainly looks as if they do, " he agreed. "Here's our trap. Jump in! "

She regarded the smart ralli-cart and bright bay cob with interest. The latter, held with difficulty by a lad Robin had left in charge, was dancing gently between the shafts, impatient to be off.

"*Our* trap? " queried Ann.

"Yes. It goes with the cottage, " explained Robin. "Coventry's been awfully decent over everything. Of course, he provides me with a gee to get about on, but as soon as he heard I had a sister coming to live with me he sent down this pony and cart from his own stables. Naturally, I told him that that kind of thing wasn't included in the bond, but he shut me up with the remark that no woman could be expected to settle down at the back of beyond unless she had something to drive. "

"He must be an extremely nice young man, " commented Ann, as she settled herself in the trap.

Robin gathered up the reins and they set off, the sleek little cob at once breaking into a sharp trot which carried them swiftly along the leafy country road.

"Coventry's not very young, " observed Robin, as they sped along. "Must be six or seven and thirty, at least. And I don't think *you* would describe him as 'nice' if you'd met him. He's very brusque in his manner at times, and I don't fancy women figure much in his scheme of existence. "

"Oh, well, he's of no importance beyond being the source of a perfectly topping billet for you. " Ann brushed the owner of Heronsmere off the map with an airy wave of her hand. "He's quite at liberty to enjoy his womanless Eden as far as I'm concerned. Men—other than extremely nice brothers, of course! —are really far more bother than they're worth. They're—they're so *unexpected*"—with a swift recollection of the upsetting vagaries of mood exhibited by a certain member of the sex.

Robin threw her a brief glance, then, drawing his whip lightly across the cob's glossy flanks, he asked casually:

"And how did you leave the Brabazons? "

"They're both looking very fit after three months in Switzerland, of course, but I think Tony found it a bit boring compared with Monte Carlo. They came straight on to Montricheux from Mentone, you know. "

"Tony still gambles as much as ever, then? "

Ann's face clouded.

"I'm afraid he does, " she acknowledged. "At least, whenever he gets the chance. "

"Well, he won't get much chance down at Lorne, " remarked Robin philosophically.

"They're not going down to Lorne yet. They go back to Audley Square till the end of this month. That's quite long enough for Tony to get into trouble"—ruefully. "Lady Susan says he plays a lot in her nephew's set—that's the Brett Forrester Tony sometimes speaks of as such a fine bridge player. "

"I've heard of Forrester from other people, " observed Robin. "He's got the reputation of being one of the most dare-devil gamblers in London—in every shape and form. Cards, horses, roulette—anything you like as long as it's got the element of chance in it. "

Ann's brows drew together.

"That may be all right for Mr. Forrester. As Lady Susan says, he can afford to throw money away if he chooses. Tony can't, you know. Sir Philip's pretty strict over his allowance. "

"I'm rather anxious to meet your Lady Susan, " said Robin. "It was very decent of her to let you leave her almost at once like that. "

"Lady Susan always *would* do the decent thing, I think, " returned Ann, smiling. "The other thing doesn't seem to occur to her. You'll meet her before long, as she comes straight home from Paris. Isn't it strange that you should get this berth and that we should come to live quite close to her? "

"'M. Rather a coincidence. " Robin, occupied in restraining a sudden tendency on the part of the pony to frolic a little as they neared home, replied somewhat abstractedly. He was a good whip, and under his quiet handling the cob soon steadied down to a more reasonable gait and finally pulled up decorously at a green-painted gateway. A diminutive and hugely self-important young urchin, whom Ann learned later to know as Billy Brewster, the odd-job boy, appeared simultaneously and flew to the pony's head, grasping his bridle with as much promptitude as if there were imminent danger of his bolting at sight. Billy's ultimate ambition in life was to be a groom—he adored horses—and although, at present, the exigencies of fate ordained that boots, coals, and knives should be added to his lot, he proposed to lose no opportunity of acquiring the right touch of smartness requisite for his future profession.

Ann laughed as she passed through the gate which Robin held open for her, while Billy touched his hat rapturously for the third time.

"Who is that fascinating imp? " she asked. "Is he one of our retainers, Robin? "

He nodded, smiling.

"That's Billy. He does everything Maria doesn't choose to do, in addition to grooming the horses. You will observe he is the complete groom—minus livery! "

Ann's eager glance swept the low, two-storied cottage which faced her. It was a cosy, home-like looking little house, approached by a wide flagged path bordered with sweet, old-fashioned country flowers. One of its walls was half concealed beneath a purple mist of wistaria, while on the other side of the porch roses nodded their heads right up to the very eaves of the roof. From the green-clothed porch itself clustered trumpets of honeysuckle bloom poured forth their meltingly sweet perfume on the air. And framed in the green and gold of the honeysuckle, her face wreathed in smiles, stood the comfortable figure of Maria Coombe.

Ann was conscious of a sudden tightening about her throat. The sight of Maria, with her shrewd, kindly eyes smiling above her plump pink cheeks, and her hands thrust deep into the big, capacious pockets of her snowy apron, just as she remembered her in the long-ago nursery days at Lovell, brought back a flood of tender memories—of the old home in Devon which she had loved so intensely, of Virginia, frail and sweet, filling the place of that dead mother whom she had never known, of all that had gone to make up the happy, care-free days of childhood.

"Maria! " With a cry Ann fled up the flagged path, and the nest moment Maria's arms had enveloped her and she was coaxing and patting and hugging her just as she had done through a hundred childish tragedies in years gone by, with the soft, slurred Devon brogue making familiar music in Ann's ears.

"There now, there now, miss dear, don't 'ee take on like that. 'Tis a cup of tea you be wanting, sure's I'm here. An' I've a nice drop of water nearing the boil to make it for you. "

She drew Ann into the living-room—a pleasant sunshiny room with a huge open hearth that promised roaring fires when winter came—and whisked away into the back regions to brew the tea.

Ann smiled up at Robin rather dewily.

"Oh, Robin, we ought to be awfully happy here! " she exclaimed. As she spoke, like a shadow passing betwixt her and the sun, came the memory of the morning at Montricheux, when she had been waiting for Lady Susan's coming and some vague foreboding of the future had knocked warningly at the door of her consciousness. For a moment the walls of the little room seemed to melt away, dissolving into thick folds of fog which rolled towards her in ever darker and darker waves, threatening to engulf her. Instinctively she stretched out her hand to ward them off, but they only drew nearer, closing round her relentlessly. And then, just as she felt that there was no escape, and that they must submerge her utterly, there came the rattle of crockery, followed by Maria's heavy tread as she marched into the room carrying the tea-tray, and the illusion vanished.

"There's your tea, Miss Ann and Master Robin, an' some nice hot cakes as I've baked for you. " Maria surveyed her handiwork with obvious satisfaction. "And I'm sure I wish you both luck and may a dark woman be the first to cross your threshold. "

"You superstitious old thing, Maria! " laughed Robin. "As if it could make twopenny-worth of difference whether a blonde or brunette called upon us first! "

"I don't know nothing about blondes and brunettes, sir, " replied Maria, with truth. "But they do say 'twill bring you luck if so be a dark woman's the first to cross your threshold after the New Year's in, and it seems only reasonable that 'twould be the same when you go into a new house. "

Unfortunately Maria's hopes were not destined to be fulfilled, as the first person to cross the threshold of Oldstone Cottage after Ann's arrival was Caroline Tempest, the rector's sister. "Miss Caroline, " as she was invariably called by the villagers, was a flat-chested, colourless individual with one of those thin noses which seem to have grown permanently elongated at the point in the process of prying into other people's business. Her hair, once flaxen, was now turning the ugly yellowish grey which is the fair woman's curse, and her eyes were like pale blue china beads.

She appeared, accompanied by the rector, about half an hour after Maria had brought in tea, and seemed overwhelmed to discover that Ann herself had only just arrived.

"I really must apologise, " she declared, in the voice of a superior person making a very generous concession. "I quite thought you were expecting your sister yesterday, Mr. Lovell. I told you so, didn't I, Brian? " She appealed to her brother, who nodded rather unhappily. "And we thought we'd like to call as soon as possible and welcome you to the parish. "

Ann didn't believe a word of it.

"She knew perfectly well you were expecting me to-day, " she declared when, later on, she and Robin found themselves alone again. "Though I haven't the slightest doubt she told that nice brother of hers just what she wished him to believe. She simply wanted to have first look at me so as to be able to give the village to-morrow a full, true, and particular account of what I'm like. "

However, she replied to Miss Caroline's apologies with the necessary cordiality demanded by the occasion and, ringing for Maria, ordered fresh tea. The rector protested.

"No, no, " he said hastily. "You must be far too tired to want visitors when you've only just come off a long journey. We'll pay our call another day. "

Brian Tempest was the very antithesis of his sister—tall and somewhat ascetic-looking, with a face to which one was almost tempted to apply the word beautiful, it was so well-proportioned and cut with the sure fineness of a cameo. His dark hair was sprinkled with grey at the temples, and beneath a broad, tranquil brow looked out a pair of kindly, luminous eyes that were neither all brown nor all grey. Later, when she knew him better, Ann was wont to inform him that his eyes were a "heather mixture—like tweed. " Small, fine lines puckered humorously at their corners, and there was humour, too, in the long, thin-lipped mouth.

Robin and Ann brushed aside his protest with a hearty sincerity there was no mistaking. Whatever each of them might feel concerning Miss Caroline, they were in complete accord in the welcome they extended to her brother. He was no stranger to Robin. The latter had put up at the village inn during the time occupied by Maria Coombe in "cleaning down" the Cottage and making it habitable, and the rector had dropped in to see him in a characteristically informal, friendly fashion on more than one occasion.

The two chatted together while Miss Caroline put Ann through a searching catechism as to her past, present, and future mode of life, including the age at which her parents had died, the particular kind of work she had undertaken during the war—appearing somewhat taken aback when Ann explained that she had driven a car, the making of shirts and mufflers coming more within the scope of Caroline's own idea as to what was "suitable" work for a young girl—and the length of time she had lived with Lady Susan. The coincidence of Robin's obtaining a post in the neighbourhood of Lady Susan's home impressed her enormously, as fate's unexpected shufflings of the cards invariably do impress those whose existence is passed in a very narrow groove.

"It's really most extraordinary! " she declared, scrutinising Ann much as though she suspected her of having somehow juggled matters in order to produce such a phenomenon. "Did you hear that, Brian? Miss Lovell has been living with our dear Lady Susan. " She spoke as if she held proprietary rights in Lady Susan. "Isn't it extraordinary that now she and her brother should have come to live so near White Windows? "

"I think it's a very charming happening, " replied the rector, "since Oldstone Cottage is even nearer to the rectory! "

He smiled across at Ann—a quick, sympathetic smile that seemed to establish them on a footing of friendly intimacy at once.

"Really, " went on Miss Caroline, doggedly pursuing the line of thought to the bitter end of her commonplace mind, "it's as though it were *meant* in some way—that you should come to Silverquay. "

"Probably it was, " returned the rector simply, and Ann observed a quiet, dreaming expression come into his eyes—a look of inner vision, tranquilly content and confident.

"Fancy if it turns out like that! " exclaimed Miss Caroline. "It would be a most singular thing, wouldn't it, if it was really *intended*? "

"Not at all, " answered Brian composedly. "You're speaking as though you regarded the Almighty as a thoughtless kind of person who would let things happen, just anyhow. "

"Brian! " Miss Caroline's tones shuddered with shocked reproach. Her brother often shocked her; he seemed to think of God as simply and naturally as he might of any other friend. She herself, in the course of her parochial work in the village, habitually represented Him as a somewhat prying and easily offended individual who kept a particularly sharp eye on the inhabitants of Silverquay.

She hastily turned the conversation on to less debatable ground.

"We shall have quite a lot of fresh people in the neighbourhood, " she remarked sociably. "Mr. Coventry himself is a stranger to us all, and then there will be a new-comer at the Priory, too. "

"Mrs. Hilyard, you mean? " said Robin.

"Yes. " Miss Caroline looked full of importance. "I hear she arrives to-day. The carrier told our cook that he was ordered to meet the four-thirty train this afternoon—to fetch a quantity of luggage. "

"Is there a *Mr.* Hilyard? " asked Ann casually. She could see that Miss Caroline was bursting with gossipy news which she was aching to impart.

"No, she's a widow, I hear, and very wealthy. The furniture that's been coming down by rail is of most excellent quality—most excellent! "

"How do you know, Caroline? " inquired the rector, his eyes twinkling with amusement.

"Well, *entirely* by accident, I happened to be taking a basin of chicken broth to old Mrs. Skinner—you know, she lives in one of the Priory cottages—on the very day the pantechnicons were delivering at the house, and I saw quite a number of the chairs and tables as they were being carried in. "

The twinkle in Brian's eyes grew more pronounced.

"I'm afraid you must have stood and watched the unloading process, then. "

"Well, I suppose I did—just for a minute, " she acknowledged, adding with some asperity: "It would be quite fitting if you took a little keener interest in future parishioners, Brian. "

"My interest in my future parishioners is quite keen, I assure you—though I don't know that it extends to their furniture, " replied the rector, laughing.

"Oh, well, it's nice to know that some one has taken the Priory who is in a position to keep it up properly, " persisted his sister. "Don't you agree, Miss Lovell? "

"Of course, " said Ann. "Besides"—smiling across at the rector—"as we're as poor as church mice, it's just as well the new arrival at the Priory should he rich—to even things up. "

"I think it's all very interesting, " pursued Miss Caroline, still intent on her own train of thought. "Here's Mr. Coventry come home at last to live at Heronsmere—a very eligible bachelor—and with this Mrs. Hilyard, a wealthy widow, living so near by it wouldn't be at all surprising if something came of it. "

The rector jumped up, laughing good-humouredly.

"Caroline! Caroline! I must really take you home after that, or Miss Lovell will think Silverquay is a veritable hot-bed of gossip. Coventry hasn't been in the neighbourhood a month, poor man, and here you are trying to tie him up with a lady who doesn't even arrive until this afternoon! "

"Besides, " suggested Robin, smiling broadly, "she may be a really disconsolate widow, you know. "

Miss Caroline shook her head.

"I don't think so, " she answered obstinately. "The furniture didn't look like it. One of the packages was a little torn, and I caught sight of the curtains inside. They were rose colour. "

"That was really quite bright of Miss Caroline, " observed Ann with some amusement, when the rector and his sister had started for home. "Only she didn't know it! "

CHAPTER X

A DISCOVERY

The morning breeze darted in and out of Ann's bedroom like a child tentatively trying to inveigle a grown-up person into playing hide-and-seek. With every puff a big cluster of roses, which had climbed to the sill, swayed forward and peeped inside, sending a whiff of delicate perfume across to where Ann was kneeling, surrounded by trunks and suitcases, unpacking her belongings. Pleasant little sounds of life floated up from outdoors—the clucking of a hen, the stamping of the bay cob as Billy Brewster groomed him, whistling softly through his teeth while he brushed and curry-combed, the occasional honk of a motor-horn as a car sped by in the distance. Then came the beat of a horse's hoofs, stopping abruptly outside the cottage gate.

Ann did not pause in her occupation of emptying a hatbox of its tissue-shrouded contents. Robin had ridden away almost immediately after breakfast, so she merely supposed that, having started early, he had returned early. But a minute later Maria was standing in the doorway of the room, her broad face red with the exertion of hurrying upstairs, her eyes blinking excitedly.

"'Tis Mr. Coventry himself, miss, " she announced. "He didn't inquire if any one was at home, but just followed me in and asked me to tell Master Robin he was here. "

Ann rose reluctantly from her knees, dusting her hands together.

"All right, Maria, I'll go down and see him. Perhaps he can leave a message with me for Robin. I hope, though, " she added with a faint sense of irritation, "that he isn't going to make a habit of dropping in here in the mornings. "

Only pausing to push back a stray lock of hair, she ran quickly downstairs and into the living-room.

"I'm so sorry"—she began speaking almost as she crossed the threshold—"but my brother is out. "

With a stifled ejaculation the man standing in the shadow of the tall, old-fashioned chimneypiece wheeled round, and Ann found herself looking straight into the grey eyes of the Englishman from Montricheux. For a moment there was a silence—the silence of utter mutual astonishment, while Ann was wretchedly conscious of the flush that mounted slowly to her very temples. The man was the first to recover himself.

"So, " he said, "*you* are Miss Lovell! "

Something in his tone stung Ann into composure.

"Yes, " she replied coolly. "You don't sound altogether pleased at the discovery. "

"Pleased? " His eyes rested on her with a species of repressed annoyance. "It doesn't make much difference whether we're—either of us—pleased or not, does it? "

His meaning appeared perfectly plain to Ann. For some reason which she could not fathom he found her appearance on the scene the very reverse of pleasing.

"I don't see that it matters in any case, " she replied frostily. "The fact that I happen to be your agent's sister doesn't compel you to see any more of me than you wish to. "

"True. And if I'd known you were here I wouldn't have come blundering in this morning. "

"I arrived yesterday, " vouchsafed Ann. "Won't you sit down? " she added with perfunctory politeness. She seated herself, and in obedience to her gesture he mechanically followed suit.

"Yes, you were expected to-day, weren't you? I'd forgotten, " he said abstractedly.

No one particularly enjoys being assured that they have been forgotten, and Ann's eyes sparkled with suppressed indignation.

"Can I give my brother any message for you? " she asked stiffly.

All at once he smiled—that sudden, singularly sweet smile of his which transformed the harsh lines of his face and which seemed to have so little in common with his habitual brusqueness.

"I've been behaving like a boor, haven't I? " he admitted. "Forgive me. And can't we be friends? After all, I've some sort of claim. I pulled you out of Lac Léman—or rather, prevented your tumbling into it, you know. "

He spoke with a curious persuasive charm. There was something almost boyishly disarming about his manner. It was as though for a moment a prickly, ungracious husk had dropped away, revealing the real man within. He held out his hand, and as Ann laid hers within it she felt her spirits rising unaccountably.

"I hope you'll like it here, " he pursued. He glanced round with a discontented expression. "Does the cottage furniture satisfy you? Is it what you like? "

"It's perfectly charming, " she replied whole-heartedly. "I love old-fashioned things. "

"Well, if there's anything you'd like altered or want sending down, you must let me know. There are stacks of stuff up at Heronsmere. "

"You've already sent down the one thing to complete my happiness, " she answered, smiling. "That jolly little pony. "

"Oh, Dick Turpin. Do you like him? "

"Is that his name? Yes, I like him immensely. Thank you so much for sending him. " She paused, then added rather shyly: "I always seem to be thanking you for something, don't I? First for rescuing my bag at the Kursaal, then for rescuing me, and now for Dick Turpin! "

"You can't do without a cob"—briefly. "Do you ride? "

She nodded.

"Yes. I thought of riding him sometimes. Does he ride all right? "

"Oh, he's quiet enough. But if you want to hunt next winter, you must let me mount you. " His glance rested on her slim, boyish contours. "I've a little thoroughbred mare up at Heronsmere—Redwing, she's called—who would carry you perfectly. "

"Oh, I couldn't—you mustn't—" she began with some embarrassment.

"Nonsense! " He interrupted her brusquely. "What are you going to do down here if you don't ride and drive? Lovell will have his work. But you won't. "

"I'm proposing to keep chickens, " announced Ann. "I'm not in the least an idle person. You lose the habit if you've earned your own living for several years, " she added, with a touch of amusement.

"Have you done that? "

She assented.

"Of course I have. You can't live on air, you know, and as my father didn't leave us much else, Robin and I both had to work. "

He regarded her with brooding eyes. She was so gay and cheery about it all that, against his will, his thoughts were driven back amongst old memories, recalling another woman he had known who had chosen to escape from poverty by a different road from the clean, straight one of hard work. She had funked the sharp corners of life, that other, in a way in which this girl with the clear, brown-gold eyes that met the World so squarely would never funk them.

Before he could formulate any answer there came the sound of the house-door opening and closing. He rose hastily from his chair.

"Ah! That must be your brother! " he exclaimed, a note of what sounded almost like relief in his voice. He seemed glad of the distraction, and shook hands cordially with Robin when he came in.

"I'm sorry I was out, " began the latter. But Coventry cut short his apologies.

"Don't apologise, " he said. "It has given Miss Lovell and myself the opportunity of renewing our acquaintance. "

Robin looked from one to the other in surprise.

"Have you met before, then? " he asked.

Ann explained.

"At Montricheux, " she replied. "Mr. Coventry saved me from a watery grave on the night of the Venetian Fête there. "

"From nothing more dangerous than a wetting, actually, " interpolated Coventry in his abrupt way.

"Well, even that's something to be thankful for, " returned Robin, smiling. "Will you smoke? "

He offered his cigarette-case, and the two men lit up.

"I've just been over to see Farmer Sparkes, " he continued. "He's put in a list as long as your arm of repairs he wants doing. "

Coventry laughed good-humouredly.

"I suppose they'll all be sticking me for alterations and repairs now I've come back, " he said. "What's the use of a landlord unless you can squeeze something out of him? "

"I'm afraid there is a bit of that attitude about most tenants, " admitted Robin. "I expect the new owner of the Priory will get let in for the same thing. One or two of the Priory cottages want doing up, it's true. "

"Have you seen her yet, Robin? " inquired Ann quickly, with feminine curiosity.

"Mrs. Hilyard, do you mean? No, I didn't come across her this morning. "

"*Who* did you say? " asked Coventry.

Something in the quality of his voice brought Ann's eyes swiftly to his face. All the geniality had gone out of it. It was set and stern, and there was an odd watchfulness in the glance he levelled at Robin as he spoke.

"Mrs. Hilyard—the new owner of the Priory, " explained Robin. "She arrived yesterday. "

"Hilyard? " repeated Coventry. "Some one told me the name was Hilton. You don't know what Hilyard she is, I suppose? "

"No, I don't know anything about her. But Hilyard's a fairly common name. "

"Yes, I suppose it's fairly common, " agreed Coventry slowly.

As though to dismiss the topic, he returned to the matter of the repairs required on Sparkes' farm, and for a few minutes the two men were engrossed in details connected with the management of the estate. But Ann noticed that Coventry seemed curiously abstracted. He allowed his cigarette to smoulder between his fingers till it went out beneath their pressure, and presently, bringing the discussion with Robin to a sudden close, he got up to go. He tendered his farewell somewhat abruptly, mounted his horse, which had been standing tethered to the gateway by its bridle, and rode away at a hand-gallop.

Ann made no comment at the time, as Robin seemed rather preoccupied with estate matters, but over dinner in the evening she broached the subject upon which she had been exercising her mind at intervals throughout the day.

"Robin, did you notice Mr. Coventry's expression when you mentioned Mrs. Hilyard? "

Robin looked up doubtfully from one of Maria's beautifully grilled cutlets.

"His expression? No, I don't think I was looking at him particularly. He thought she was called Hilton, or something, didn't he? "

Ann went off into a small gale of laughter.

"Does a man ever notice anything unless it's right under his nose? " she demanded dramatically of the universe at large. "My dear, " she went on, "his face altered the instant you mentioned Mrs. Hilyard's name. "

"Well, but why should it? " demanded Robin, still at sea.

"I think, " she pronounced oracularly, "that *a* Mrs. Hilyard must have played a rather important part in Mr. Coventry's life at one time or another. "

"Well, it's no business of ours if she did, " responded Robin unsympathetically.

"No. But it would be queer if the Mrs. Hilyard who's bought the Priory happened to be the other Mrs. Hilyard—the one Mr. Coventry knew before. "

"We've no grounds for assuming that he ever knew a Mrs. Hilyard at all, and if he did—as I said before, it's no business of ours. "

There never was a real woman yet who failed to be intrigued by the suggestion of a romance lying dormant in the past life of a man of her acquaintance, and Ann was far too essentially feminine to pretend that her interest was not piqued.

"No, of course it's no business of ours, " she agreed. "But still, one may take an intelligent interest in one's fellow beings, I suppose. "

"It depends upon circumstances, " replied Robin. "I'm here as Coventry's agent, and my employer's private affairs are no concern of mine. "

There was just a suspicion of the "elder brother" in his manner—only a suspicion, but it was quite sufficient to arouse all the latent contrariety of woman which Ann possessed.

"Well, Mrs. Hilyard isn't your employer, " she retorted. "So I've a perfect right to feel interested in her. "

"But not in her relation to Mr. Coventry, " maintained Robin seriously.

The corners of Ann's mouth curled up in a mutinous smile, and her eyes danced.

"My dear Robin, you can't insulate a woman as you can an electric wire—at least, not if she has any pretensions to good looks. "

"No, I suppose you can't, " he admitted, smiling back unwillingly. "More's the pity, sometimes! "

There, for the moment, the subject dropped, but the imp of mischief still flickered defiantly in the golden-brown eyes, and when, after dinner was over, Maria brought in the coffee, Ann threw out a tentative remark which instantly achieved its nefarious purpose of loosening the springs of Maria's garrulity.

"They be telling up a tale in the village about the new lady as has taken the Priory, " began Maria conversationally.

Ann sugared her coffee with an air of detachment, and watched Robin fidgeting out of the tail of her eye.

"You shouldn't listen to gossip, Maria, " she reprimanded primly.

"Well, miss, 'tis true folks say you shouldn't believe all you hear, and 'tis early days to speak, seeing she's scarcely into her house yet, as you may say. "

"You give me an uncomfortable feeling that she spent the night on the doorstep, " observed Ann.

"Oh, no, miss, " replied Maria, matter-of-factly. "She slept in her bed all right last night. But maybe, for all that, it's true what folks are saying, " she added darkly. "I'd run out of sugar, so I just stepped round to the grocer this evening after tea, and he told me 'twas all the tale in the village that this Mrs. Hilyard isn't a widow at all, and some of them think she's no better than she should be. "

An ejaculation of annoyance broke from Robin.

"The tittle-tattle in these twopenny-halfpenny villages is almost past believing! " he exclaimed angrily. "Here's an absolute new-comer arrives in the district, and they've begun taking away the poor woman's character already. "

"Well, sir, of course I'm only speaking what I hear, " replied Maria, who, with all her good points—and they were many—had the true West Country relish for any titbit of gossip, whether with or without foundation. "Let's hope 'tisn't true. But they say her clothes do be good enough for the highest lady in the land. Mrs. Thorowgood—

her that's been helping up to the Priory all day—called in on her way home just to pass the time of day with me. It seems Mrs. Hilyard has arranged she shall wash for her, and she was taking a few of her things home with her for to wash to-morrow. And she told me her own self, did Mrs. Thorowgood, that the lace on them be so fine as spider's web. "

Ann endeavoured to conceal her mirth and reply with becoming gravity.

"Maria, dear, if a disreputable character is considered inseparable from pretty undies in Silverquay, I'm afraid I shall get as bad a reputation as Mrs. Hilyard, " she suggested meekly.

"You, miss? " Maria's loyalty rose in wrathful protest. "And who *should* have good things if 'tisn't you, I'd like to know? 'Twouldn't be fitting for any Miss Lovell of Lovell Court to have things that wasn't of the very best. And as to telling up little old tales—there'll be no tales told about you, nor Mr. Robin neither, so long as I'm in Silverquay. I'll see to that! "

Thoroughly devoted, illogical, and belligerent, Maria picked up the coffee tray and stalked out of the room, leaving Ann and Robin convulsed with laughter.

CHAPTER XI

THE LADY FROM THE PRIORY

Bang! The noise of the explosion reverberated through the clear summer air, and Ann, returning home from the village by way of a short cut through the woods, smiled to herself as she heard it. She knew that sound—the staccato percussion of a burst tyre—only too well.

The main road ran parallel with the woods, and, impelled by a friendly curiosity to know if she could be of any help, she branched off at right angles and turned her steps in its direction. As she approached she could discern between the tree-trunks a car, slewed round half across the road, and the figure of a woman standing beside it and bending over one of the wheels. Her very attitude betokened a certain helplessness and inexperience, and, seeing that she was alone, Ann quickened her pace.

"Can I help you at all? " she volunteered, as she reached the roadside.

The woman straightened herself.

"Oh, if you would! " she exclaimed, with obvious relief. "My tyre's burst, and I'm ashamed to confess I haven't the faintest idea what to do. "

Ann regarded her with interest. She was past her first girlhood, a woman of about thirty, and unusually beautiful. Even more beautiful now, perhaps, than she had been in earlier days, since, in taking the first freshness and bloom of youth, the years had given in exchange an arresting quality which is only born of suffering and experience—adding a deeper depth to her eyes, a certain strength of endurance to the exquisitely moulded mouth. Silky dark hair curved back beneath her close-fitting hat like a raven's wing, sheathing her small, fine head. There was the same silky darkness, too, of brow and lashes, and when she lifted her long-fringed lids they revealed a pair of sad and very lovely eyes, the colour of a purple pansy.

"It was foolish of me to come out alone, " she pursued, as Ann proceeded in a business-like fashion to investigate the damage. "I've learned how to drive, but I know nothing at all about repairs, or tow to put on a new tyre or stepney or anything. "

"Well, the first thing to do is to pull the car out of the middle of the road, " returned Ann practically. "Then we'll have to jack her up. "

A couple of labourers, passing at the moment, lent a hand in pulling the car to one side, and when this was accomplished Ann made a raid on the tool box.

"No, no, " the owner of the car protested quickly. "I can't think of letting you do anything more. Even if you put things right, " she added, smiling, "I shouldn't have the nerve to drive back. The car spun half round when the tyre burst, and nearly frightened me to death. "

"In any case, I'm afraid there's nothing that I can do, " replied Ann, emerging from her investigations. "You've come out without a jack on board! "

The other, detecting the amused gleam in her eyes, laughed rather ruefully.

"I dare say I've come out without *anything* I ought to have! " she admitted. "My chauffeur was sent for hurriedly to the death-bed of his wife's aunt or some one, and I just thought I'd come out for a spin this afternoon and explore the neighbourhood. I never prepared for accidents! I shall have to walk home, that's all. "

"Have you far to go? "

"I live at the Priory. I've only recently arrived there—hence my thirst for exploration"—smiling.

"Then you must be Mrs. Hilyard. " Ann felt she had known it all the time.

"Yes"—pleasantly. "I'm Mrs. Hilyard. Are you one of my new neighbours? "

"A very new one, " confessed Ann. "I believe I arrived the same day that you did. I'm Ann Lovell. "

Apparently the name Lovell conveyed nothing to Mrs. Hilyard. Probably she possessed no equivalent of Maria, who was almost as full of current news as the local daily paper.

"Well, I'm very grateful to you for coming to my help. My chauffeur gets back this evening, and I'll send him down for the car. It will be all right here till then. "

She bowed very graciously, and was turning away when Ann impulsively detained her.

"Don't walk back, " she said. "Let me drive you home in my cart. Our cottage is close by, and if you'd let us give you some tea first—"

"Now, that's what I call being really neighbourly! " declared Mrs. Hilyard. "I'd love the cup of tea. But I can't put you to the trouble of driving me back afterwards. There must be a limit to Good Samaritanism, you know! "

"It won't be the least trouble, " Ann assured her. "Rather the reverse, in fact. My cob wasn't out yesterday, and it'll do him good to go out to-day. So, you see, you're providing an excellent reason for exercising him"—laughingly.

Mrs. Hilyard threw her a mischievous smile.

"Pure casuistry! " she affirmed. "But it's convinced me. I'll love to have tea with you, and afterwards you shall drive me home, and by the time I've given you as much trouble as possible, I hope we shall be really friends! "

It was only a matter of five minutes' walk from where they were standing to the Cottage, and Mrs. Hilyard exclaimed with delight at its pretty, old-fashioned aspect.

"What a delicious place! " she commented, as Ann established her in an easy chair. "I think I like it better than my Priory. You've some lovely bits of pewter up there"—nodding towards the tall old chimney-piece, where the tender moon-grey of ancient pewter mugs and dishes gleamed fitfully against the panelled wall.

"I'm afraid it isn't ours, " acknowledged Ann regretfully. "Though I love every bit of it. My brother is agent for the Heronsmere estate, and we have this cottage furnished. Oh, here he is, " she added, as Robin entered the room.

She introduced him to Mrs. Hilyard, who smilingly accounted for her impromptu visit.

"I feel that I'm imposing on Miss Lovell's good-nature in the most barefaced fashion, " she said apologetically. "But I honestly couldn't resist the suggestion of a cup of tea. "

"I'm very glad you couldn't, " replied Robin simply. And something in the tone of his voice, taken in conjunction with the serious directness of his regard, made of the short sentence more than a mere empty expression of politeness.

"I met Brian Tempest and his sister just now, " he went on, turning to Ann, "and asked them to come in to tea, so I expect they'll be here directly. "

"Tempest? That's the rector here, isn't it? " asked Mrs. Hilyard, as Ann slipped out of the room to prepare Maria for the expected "company. "

Robin nodded.

"You've not met him yet? "

"I've met no one. So far, I've done nothing but wrestle with packing-cases and the distribution of furniture"—smiling.

"It sounds pretty ghastly, " averred Robin. "I say"—impulsively. "Couldn't I—couldn't we help you at all? "

Mrs. Hilyard laughed softly. Robin thought it was one of the most delightful sounds he had ever heard, fluent and sweet as the pipe of a blackbird.

"Apparently you and your sister go about doing kindnesses, " she said, in a quick, touched way. "The very first thing she said to me was 'Can I help? ' And now, almost your first utterance is another offer of help! Is every one in the neighbourhood like that? Because, if so, I think I must have come to an enchanted village—and"—firmly—"I shall decide to remain here for the rest of my life! "

"Well" —Robin looked embarrassed—"shifting furniture about isn't exactly a woman's job. "

"I'm not actually shifting furniture myself—except a table or chair now and again, when no one else moves quickly enough to please me! But if you and Miss Lovell would come over one day soon and help me to decide about the disposition of my *lares* and *penates*, it would be the greatest help. One does so want some one to talk things over with, you know, " she added.

To Robin's ears there was a forlorn note in that frank little acknowledgment, and he was conscious of a sudden, overpowering rush of sympathy. She was lonely—he was sure of it. In spite of all her charm and quick laughter, she was not a happy woman. Some shadow from the past lay in her eyes, and when she laughed the sparkle in them was like the momentary sunlit ripple which breaks the surface of a pool for a brief instant and then is lost again in its shadowed stillness.

Ann's return to the room, synchronising with the arrival of the rector and his sister, served to detach his thoughts from the subject of Mrs. Hilyard's eyes, and when the necessary introductions had been performed, and the new owner of the Priory was joining in the general conversation with apparent light-heartedness, Robin was tempted to wonder whether he had been correct in his surmise, after all.

But later on, during tea, the clouded expression reappeared on her face, as though something had all at once turned her thoughts inward. It was when Miss Caroline, thirsting for information as usual, suddenly pounced on her with a question.

"I suppose you haven't met Mr. Coventry yet? " she demanded.

For an instant Mrs. Hilyard looked startled. Then she shook her head.

"Mr. Coventry? No. Is he an important person in the neighbourhood? "

"He's my chief, " volunteered Robin. "Heronsmere Belongs to him. "

"I'm afraid I don't even know where Heronsmere is, " submitted Mrs. Hilyard deprecatingly. "I'm quite ignorant about my neighbours, so far. "

"Silverquay is part of the Heronsmere property, " responded Miss Caroline. "But the house itself is not far from the Priory. The Coventrys have lived there for generations, " she added proudly. "They're immensely wealthy. "

With the last words an expression of something that looked like relief flitted across Mrs. Hilyard's face.

"How interesting! " she said, infusing just the right amount of cordiality into her voice. "And are there any children? I'm fond of kiddies. "

"Children? Oh, no. Mr. Coventry isn't married. Nor was the last owner. " Miss Caroline warmed to her subject. "It's funny there should be two bachelor owners in succession, isn't it? Rackham Coventry died unmarried, and both his younger brothers were killed—one at sea and the other in a railway accident. That's how it was the property came to Eliot Coventry, who's only a cousin. "

Mrs. Hilyard suddenly went very white. Fortunately, Miss Caroline's attention happened to be concentrated at the moment upon stirring the sugar into her second cup of tea, and by the time this was satisfactorily accomplished, the pretty colour was stealing back into the cheeks that had paled so swiftly.

"I'd really no idea there were any other houses at all near mine, " murmured Mrs. Hilyard, after the briefest of pauses. "I came across an advertisement of the Priory, dashed down to see it one day, and fell in love with it on the spot—partly because it seemed so far from everywhere. "

"We value our privacy in Silverquay, " said the rector, smiling. "Almost all the large houses are tucked snugly away out of sight—hidden by trees or rising ground. "

"Did you come here to be quiet, then? " asked Miss Caroline, thrusting in her oar the instant her brother had finished speaking.

"Yes, " answered Mrs. Hilyard simply.

Miss Caroline fixed her with a gimlet eye.

"How very surprising! " she remarked. "You don't look in the least like the sort of person who would choose to live in a quiet country village like Silverquay. "

"Don't I? " Mrs. Hilyard smiled. But she did not volunteer any explanation of her choice.

Here Ann, recognising Miss Caroline's now familiar methods of cross-examination, came to the rescue and diverted the conversation into a less personal channel, and shortly afterwards the Tempests left in order to pay some parochial visits in the village, Ann shepherding them as far as the gateway.

Mrs. Hilyard exchanged a sympathetic smile with Robin. "The Miss Carolines of the world are rather trying, aren't they? " she observed mirthfully. "I think she has gone away fully convinced that there is something 'queer' about me—that I'm not quite respectable, probably! "

"Ridiculous! " growled Robin in tones of wrath. "She has only to look at you! "

"Thank you"—meekly. "I'm glad you think I look—respectable. "

"You know I didn't mean that! I think you look—I think you look—" He floundered and broke off abruptly.

"Yes? " There was the tiniest rising inflection in her voice, demanding an answer.

Across the little room Robin's eyes laughed into hers.

"Perhaps I'll tell you some other time—when I know you better, " he said.

At that moment Ann returned from speeding the Tempests on their way. Mrs. Hilyard rose.

"I must be going, too, I think, " she said. "But I don't want you to trouble about driving me back, Miss Lovell. I'll walk. "

"It's no trouble at all, " Ann assured her. "Tell Billy to bring the cart round, will you, Robin? "

He nodded, and held out his hand to Mrs. Hilyard.

"Good-bye, " he said. "I'd ask you to let me drive you back, but that I've made an appointment to see one of Mr. Coventry's tenants. "

A few minutes later Dick Turpin, somewhat annoyed at being taken out of his stall just as feeding-time approached, was bearing Ann and her new acquaintance swiftly along the road towards the Priory.

Mrs. Hilyard was very silent during the first part of the drive. She appeared absorbed in her own thoughts, and from the expression of her face one might have hazarded a guess that she was inwardly debating some moot point. All at once she seemed to come to a decision.

"I think, " she said in a quiet, clear voice, "that I must have met this Mr. Coventry who lives at Heronsmere. I knew an Eliot Coventry—once. "

She did not look at Ann as she spoke, but gazed straight ahead as though the strip of bare, lonely road which stretched in front of them were of peculiarly vital interest.

"What—is he like? " she went on. Any one observing her at the moment would have gathered the impression that she was forcing herself to speak with composure—that it was not easy for her. But Ann, preoccupied with Dick Turpin's vagaries, was not looking at her.

"Oh, he's tall, " she made answer. "And has grey eyes. There's a little white scar just under one of them. "

The woman beside her drew a quick breath.

"Ah"—the sweet, *traînante* voice was a fraction uneven. "Then it *is* the man I've met. "

The ralli-cart swung round a corner into a narrow lane, and a quick exclamation broke from Ann as she recognised in the tall, striding figure approaching from the opposite direction the man of whom they had just been speaking. A beautiful thoroughbred collie bounded along beside him, looking up at his master every now and again with adoring eyes.

"Why, here *is* Mr. Coventry! " she exclaimed. "Shall I pull up? "

Without waiting for an answer she brought the cob to a standstill exactly as Eliot, catching sight of them, halted instinctively.

"Good afternoon, " she called out gaily, as he lifted his hat. "We were just speaking of you. Here is an old acquaintance of yours. "

Eliot's glance travelled swiftly from her face to that of her companion. His expression was quite impenetrable—mask-like in its impassivity. Mrs. Hilyard bent forward, holding out her hand.

"Have you forgotten me, Mr. Coventry? "

For an instant the man and woman looked deep into each other's eyes, as though to bridge the time which had passed since last they met—questioning what the intervening years had brought to each of them. But Eliot made no attempt to take the outheld hand. He did not appear to see it, and Mrs. Hilyard let it drop slowly down again on to her lap.

"Forgotten Cara Daintree? " he said lightly. "Is it likely I should? "

"Cara Hilyard, now. " She corrected him a shade nervously.

"Oh, yes. Hilyard, isn't it? Of course. "

His glance flashed over her face, searching and cold as a hawk's. She winced under it, but faced him gallantly, though a flush crept up under her clear skin.

"I hear we are near neighbours. I hope"—she forced herself to meet those hard, unflinching eyes—"I hope you will come and see me, Mr. Coventry. "

He bowed stiffly.

"Thanks, " was all he said. Then, laying his hand on the cob's shining flank, he deliberately addressed himself to Ann: "Is Dick Turpin still behaving himself properly? "

She nodded.

"He's a perfect cherub, " she assured him warmly. "Any one could manage him—even when he has an attack of high spirits. He's got a mouth like velvet. "

"There's something to be said for the driver's hands, possibly, " suggested Coventry, with a smile. "Light hands make a light mouth. Still, I'm glad to know he suits you. "

He whistled up his dog, who came racing to heel, then, with a grave bow which briefly included Mrs. Hilyard, lifted his hat and resumed his way along the lane.

Ann drove on, and ten minutes later pulled her horse up at the Priory doors. Mrs. Hilyard stepped lightly out of the trap. She moved beautifully, with a deer-like ease and grace.

"Now when will you and your brother come over to lunch? " she asked, as she shook hands. "He promised—for you both—to come and help me with advice about arranging my rooms. You must go on as you've begun—being neighbourly, you know, " she added quaintly.

"But we shall be cut out now by an older friend, " said Ann, when they had fixed a day for the lunch appointment.

"Oh, no"—quickly. "No man can take the place of a woman friend—and I hope you're going to be that? "

Ann smiled down into the lovely upraised face with frank comradeship.

"I hope so, too, " she returned heartily. "Still, it's jolly for you finding an old friend like Mr. Coventry living next door, so to speak, isn't it? "

For a moment Mrs. Hilyard hesitated. Then:

"Very jolly, " she replied, with a brief, enigmatic smile.

CHAPTER XII

A NEW ACQUAINTANCE

August had come in on a wave of such breathless heat that each day the weather-wise foretold a thunderstorm. But, although the heavy, sultry air and lowering skies seemed pregnant with impending tempest, with every evening would come a clearer atmosphere and all signs of thunder disappear until the following day, when the stifling heat closed down once more like an invisible pall.

The pleasantest spot in the vicinity of Oldstone Cottage was undoubtedly a certain corner of the garden where stood a venerable oak whose interlacing branches spread themselves into a cool green canopy, and here, in a hammock slung from one great limb of the tree to another, Ann had taken refuge. A book lay open on her knee, but, yielding to the languor induced by the oppressive heat, she had ceased to make even a pretence at reading and leaned back in the hammock, hands clasped behind her head, idly reviewing the happenings of the last few weeks.

The realisation that actually no more than a month had elapsed since her arrival at Silverquay amazed her. It seemed almost incredible, so swiftly and surely had the new life built itself up round her, with quick, deft touches—a friend here, an adopted custom there, new interests and occupations that had already become an accepted part of the day's routine.

Ann was the last person in the world to recognise how much of this was due to her own individual personality. That eager vitality of hers went half-way to meet life. She did not wait supinely for things to happen, but instinctively looked round to see what she could herself accomplish. As she had laughingly told Eliot Coventry, she was not in the least an idle person—and the newly-wired chicken-run and hen-coops already established in a corner of a field adjoining the Cottage garden testified to the veracity of the statement. It was a small thing, perhaps, but its prompt achievement was characteristic.

Equally characteristic were the new friendships she was forming. Where some people would find only neighbours, Ann's spontaneous, warm-hearted nature discovered friends. Brian

Tempest already counted as one, and her acquaintance with Cara Hilyard, begun so unconventionally, was rapidly deepening into a pleasant intimacy.

She had discarded her original theory that some long-ago romance linked Eliot Coventry and Mrs. Hilyard together. Neither of them appeared to her to be in the least thrilled by the fact of the other's proximity in the neighbourhood, nor did either make any obvious effort to avoid or cultivate the other's society. If they chanced to meet they exchanged civilities as the merest acquaintances might do, and gradually Ann came to believe that their knowledge of each other was based on nothing more profound than a slight friendship of many years ago, which had more or less petered out with the passage of time.

Cara, for all her quick sympathy and eager friendship, was reticent as regards the past, and Ann's attitude towards her held an element of that loyal, enthusiastic devotion which an older woman not infrequently inspires in one considerably younger than herself—a devotion which accepts things as they are and has no wish to pry into the secrets of the past.

One circumstance of Cara's former life had come to Ann's knowledge unavoidably—the fact that her husband, Dene Hilyard, had ill-treated her. A most trifling accident had served to reveal it. She and Ann had been gathering roses together in the Priory garden, and, in straining up to reach a particularly lovely bloom that hung from the roof of the pergola, Cara's thin muslin sleeve had caught on a projecting nail which had ripped it apart from shoulder to elbow. As the torn sleeve fell hack it revealed a trickle of blood where the nail's sharp point had scored the skin, and above that, marring the whiteness of the upper arm, an ugly, discoloured scar. Cara made a hasty movement to conceal it, catching the gaping edges of the sleeve together with her hand. Then, realising that it was too late, she let them fall apart again and met Ann's horrified eyes with a long, inscrutable gaze.

"Yes, it's ugly, isn't it? " she said bitterly. "All my married life was—ugly. "

"What do you mean? " Ann's voice shook. She felt as though she knew what was coming—the story of how Cara came by that dreadful scar—and fought against the knowledge with incredulous horror.

"Dene... my husband... he'd been reading a book which described how they branded a woman... and he tried... " She broke off, shivering violently.

"No—*no*! " Urgently the denial sprang from Ann's stricken lips, as though she sought by the sheer imperative violence of her disclaimer to make this horrible thing untrue.

Cara nodded her head slowly.

"It's quite true... he used to drink... he was half mad at times. That was one of them. "

She had never again referred to the matter, nor to any other episode of her unhappy married life, but since that day Ann had always the consciousness of something unspeakably hideous which had lain in the background of Cara Hilyard's life, marring it utterly, and the intense sympathy it aroused within her had quickened the growth of the friendship between them.

One circumstance which had assisted greatly in the "settling down" process, as far as Ann was concerned, had been Lady Susan's unexpectedly early return from Paris. The end of the first fortnight of July had found her back at White Windows.

"The heat was intolerable, my dear! " she told Ann. "And the dust. Not even for the sake of a new rig-out could I endure it. I thought of cool little Silverquay with the nice clean sea washing its doorstep every morning—and I bolted. Madame Antoinette has probably been, wringing her hands over my half-completed garments ever since! "

She was immensely entertained when Ann acquainted her with the identity of the man who had come to her assistance on the night of the Venetian fête, and chuckled enjoyably.

"Poor man! He must be frightfully bored at finding you here—established on his very threshold, so to speak! Confirmed misogynists should never indulge in the rescuing stunt—it's so liable to involve them in unexpected consequences. How does he bear up under the discovery? "

"Not at all well, " acknowledged Ann ruefully. "Sometimes I think he almost regrets he didn't let me drown comfortably in the lake while he had the chance! "

The wish she had expressed to Maria concerning her brother's then unknown employer—that she hoped he wouldn't make a habit of dropping in at the Cottage during the mornings—had certainly been very literally fulfilled. Rarely did Eliot Coventry put in an appearance at Oldstone Cottage at all, and if the exigencies of business matters took him there on any occasion when Robin chanced to be out, he usually contrived only to leave a note or message for him with Maria. More often than not, however, he would merely send word to him, asking him to come up and see him at Heronsmere. To Ann, puzzled and secretly somewhat piqued, it seemed as though he were studiously avoiding her. Once she mentioned the subject to Robin, introducing it casually into the conversation as though it were a matter of no moment—as is the way of women in regard to anything which touches them closely. Robin had dismissed it easily.

"Oh, you mustn't think anything of that, " he assured her. "I told you—women don't enter much into Coventry's life. He's a bit of a recluse as far as your sex is concerned. "

"He was quite friendly that first morning he came here, " objected Ann.

It was that which puzzled her—the apparently causeless change in his attitude. It was true that upon, first recognising in his agent's sister the girl he had rescued from her difficulties on the night of the Fête des Narcisses he had appeared disconcerted and by no means pleased to renew the acquaintance. But afterwards he had thawed considerably, and had even suggested that they should be friends. And now he was behaving as though he had repented the suggestion and were determined to show her that he had. It was not that he was a snob. She was absolutely certain that the fact that the unknown heroine of the lake episode had proved to be merely the sister of his estate agent would not have the most fractional weight with Eliot Coventry. And as she sat swinging idly in the hammock, letting her thoughts stray back over her few brief meetings with him, she felt utterly baffled to interpret his behaviour.

Rather irritably she tried to dismiss the matter from her thoughts, but it persisted in occupying the foreground of her mind, and at last, in desperation, she picked up her discarded book and began to read. For a few moments she succeeded in concentrating her attention. Then gradually, as the sunlight, piercing through the branches overhead, flickered dazzlingly on the surface of the paper, the black and white of the printed page ran together in a blur of grey and her eyes closed drowsily. With an effort she forced them open, although lifting her eyelids seemed like raising leaden shutters.

"The rain was now coming down in torrents" was the first sentence which met her glance. She read the phrase over two or three times as though it were some abstruse statement in mathematics. Its incongruousness annoyed her. It was nonsense for any one to write like that. Why, it was so hot... so hot that... The book, falling from her hand, slipped over the side of the hammock and dropped almost soundlessly on to the thick turf below.

The next thing of which she was conscious was of waking suddenly to the sound of a crisp masculine voice remarking succinctly and on a note of intense astonishment:

"Well, I'm hanged! "

Ann stirred and rather unwillingly opened her eyes to find herself gazing straight up into other eyes so vividly blue as to be almost startling. They were looking down at her with a mixture of amusement and unmistakable admiration.

"I've been asleep, " she said unnecessarily, still hardly thoroughly awake.

"You have, " agreed the owner of the blue eyes. "And I very nearly took the usual privilege accorded to the prince who's told off to waken the sleeping beauty. "

At that Arm woke up very completely. The speech savoured of impertinence, and she resented it accordingly, yet it had been so gaily uttered, with a sort of confiding audacity which appeared to take it for granted that she would not be offended, that she found it difficult to feel as righteously indignant as the occasion merited.

"Who are you? " she demanded, sitting up hastily and eyeing the intruder with extreme disfavour. He was hatless, and the sun glinted on dark red locks of the same warm, burnished hue as the skin of a horse-chestnut. The intensely blue eyes gleamed at her from under dominant, strongly-marked brows, and the beaky, high-bridged nose, long-lipped mouth, and stubborn chin all connoted the same arrogant virility.

"I'm Forrester—Brett Forrester, and very much at your service, " he replied cheerfully.

So this was Lady Susan's "scapegrace nephew"! This gay, confident person who strode forcefully into your garden without so much as a "by-your-leave, " and who conveyed the impression that he would stride forcefully into your life, equally without permission, if it so pleased him. Ann was aware of something extraordinarily vital about the man that attracted her in spite of her first instinctive feeling of aversion.

"And what are you doing in my garden? " she asked.

His blue eyes swept the girl's slim, supple figure as she lay in the hammock with a long, raking glance that missed nothing and then came back to her face.

"If I answered that question truthfully you'd pretend to be offended, " he said.

"I shouldn't pretend—anything, " she retorted. "Please tell me why you're here. "

"Oh, that's quite a different proposition! I can answer that one. I'm here as the emissary of my respected Aunt Susan. "

"Lady Susan? "

"Yes. We've just walked over from White Windows, and when we arrived and found you were out, and that the delightful old Devonshire party who opened the door to us could supply no recent data concerning your whereabouts, Aunt Susan collapsed into a comfortable chair and sent me to spy out the land. "

Ann sprang up out of the hammock.

"How good of her to have walked over in all this heat! " she said, preparing to lead the way back to the house.

"It was my doing, " he replied with an air of complacency, as they walked on together. "I only arrived yesterday and she talked so much about you that I was consumed with a quite pardonable anxiety to meet you. "

"I hope you found it worth the three-mile walk, " commented Ann dryly.

"Oh, quite, " he returned with conviction. "I always like making new friends. "

The cool assurance of the assertion annoyed her.

"We've hardly got to that stage yet, " she observed distantly.

"No. But we shall do"—confidently. "Perhaps further than that, ultimately. "

She threw him a quick glance and encountered his eyes fixed on her with a kind of gay bravado—like that of a small boy experimenting how far he dare go. It irritated her—this sanguine assumption of his that he was going to count for something in her life. She walked on more quickly.

"Aren't you rather a conceited person? " she asked mildly.

"I'd prefer to call it having decided ideas, " he returned.

"Well, you must know you can't force your ideas on other people. "

"Can't I? " He halted in the middle of the path and faced her. "Do you really think that? "

Ann avoided meeting his glance, but she felt it playing over her like lightning over a summer sky. It was as though he had flung down a challenge and dared her to pick it up. She temporised.

"Do I think—what? I've almost forgotten what we were talking about."

"No, you haven't," he returned bluntly. "You're merely evading the question—as every woman does when she's afraid to answer."

"I'm not afraid!" exclaimed Ann indignantly. "I certainly shouldn't be afraid of you," she added, emphasising the final pronoun pointedly.

"Shouldn't you?" He looked down at her with an odd intentness. "Do you know, I think I should rather like to make you—afraid of me."

In spite of herself Ann shrank a little inwardly. She was suddenly conscious of a sense of the man's force, of the dogged tenacity of purpose of which he might be capable. He had not been dowered with that conquering nose and those dare-devil, reckless eyes for nothing! She could imagine him riding rough-shod over anything and any one in order to attain his ends.

She contrived a laugh.

"I hope you won't attempt such a thing," she said, endeavouring to speak lightly. "If you do, I shall appeal to Lady Susan for protection."

"That wouldn't help you any," he assured her. "Aunt Susan would let you down quite shamelessly. She keeps a permanently soft spot in her heart for disreputable characters—like me."

When they reached the house they discovered Lady Susan located in the easiest chair she could find, placidly smoking a cigarette, her gold-knobbed ebony stick—inseparable companion of her walks abroad—propped up beside her. From outside the front door could be heard sundry scratchings and appealing whines, punctuated by an occasional hopeful bark, which emanated from the bunch of dogs without whom she was rarely to be seen in Silverquay. They went by the generic name of the Tribes of Israel—a gentle reference to their tendency to multiply, and they ran the whole gamut of canine rank, varying in degree from a pedigree prize-winner to a mongrel Irish terrier which Lady Susan had picked up in a half-starved condition in a London side-street and had promptly adopted. The last-named was probably her favourite, since, as Forrester had remarked, she had a perennially soft spot in her heart for disreputable characters.

"My dear, " she said, as Ann stooped and kissed her, "I do hope and pray that your adorable Maria Coombe is at this moment concerning herself with the making of tea. Much as I love you, I shouldn't have toiled over here in this appalling heat but for this graceless nephew of mine, who would give me no peace till I did. So I chose the lesser evil. "

Forrester seemed supremely unrepentant, but Ann noticed that when tea appeared he waited rather charmingly on Lady Susan, anticipating her wants even down to the particular brand of cigarette she preferred to smoke when, after swallowing three cups of scaldingly hot tea *à la Russe,* she pronounced her thirst satisfactorily assuaged. There was a certain half-humorous, half-tender indulgence in his manner towards her, and Ann could imagine that he would know very well how to spoil the woman he loved. But he would master her completely first. Of that she felt sure.

It appeared that he had descended upon White Windows unexpectedly. He had been cruising round the coast and, without troubling to apprise Lady Susan of his intention, had suddenly elected to pay her a visit, and his yacht, the *Sphinx,* was now lying at anchor in Silverquay Bay.

"And even now I don't know how long he proposes staying! " smiled his aunt.

"How long? " He smiled back at her. "The question is, how long will you put up with me? I don't think—now"—with a swift, audacious glance which Ann refused to meet—"that I can do better than throw myself on the hospitality of White Windows for the remainder of the summer. "

"My dear boy"—Lady Susan beamed. "Will you really? I should love to have you; you know that. And, after all"—with a twinkle—"Silverquay has its amusements. We take tea with each other, and boat, and bathe—"

"I can do all those things, " said Forrester modestly. He turned suddenly to Ann. "Can you swim? "

"I can keep up for about two strokes, " she replied, smiling. "After that, overcome by my own prowess, I sink like a stone. "

"Then I'll teach you, " he said. "We'll begin to-morrow. What time and where do you generally bathe? "

Ann raised one or two feeble objections, but they were promptly overruled, and before she quite knew how it had happened she found herself committed to a promise that she would be at Berrier Cove the following morning, prepared to take a first lesson in the art of swimming.

"It's really a very sensible idea, " approved Lady Susan. "If you'd actually tipped over into Lac Léman that night, you'd certainly have gone to the bottom if you'd had to depend on your own unaided efforts. "

"What happened? " asked Forrester with interest, and Lady Susan embarked on a graphic account of Ann's adventure during the progress of the Venetian fête at Montricheux, and of the way in which Eliot Coventry had come to her rescue.

"Coventry? Is that the morose-looking individual who lives at Heronsmere? " inquired Brett.

Ann glanced up in some surprise.

"Oh, have you met him already? "

"We came across him with Brian Tempest on our way here, " explained Lady Susan. "The two men are rather a study in contrasts, " she added. "Brian is really a great dear. I always think it's so clever of him to have preserved his faith in human nature when he's condemned to live with that oil-and-vinegar sister of his. It may be very unchristian of me"—with a small schoolboy grin—"but I simply can't abide Caroline Tempest! "

Shortly afterwards she professed herself sufficiently rested to essay the return journey to White Windows.

"I shall certainly come down to the Cove to-morrow and watch you disporting yourselves in the briny, " she said, as she kissed Ann good-bye. "Does Robin bathe with you? "

"When he has time. But Cara Hilyard is sure to be there. She swims like a fish. "

"That's the lovely lady who lives at the Priory, isn't it? You'll have to meet her, Brett. "

"If she is a Mrs. Dene Hilyard, I know her already, " he answered. "I used to meet her with her husband in London sometimes—and a pretty brute he was! I nearly ran away with her just to get her out of his clutches, " he added lightly.

"Well, she's out of them now, poor soul, for keeps, " said Lady Susan.

Later, as they walked home together across the fields, accompanied by the now jubilant Tribes of Israel, she returned to the subject.

"If you'll promise not to discredit me by running away with her, Brett, we'll go over to see your friend at the Priory. I should have to call, in any case, before long. "

"You needn't be afraid. There's not the remotest danger of my wanting to run off with her. "

"She's rather a beautiful person, " warned Lady Susan laughingly. "You'll probably lose your heart to her within half an hour. "

"I've only done such a thing once in my life, " he replied coolly. "I'm not likely to do it again. "

"When was that, Brett? " she asked with some curiosity. She had never heard of his having any serious love-affair.

"To-day, " he replied unexpectedly.

Lady Susan paused and surveyed him with unfeigned astonishment.

"Ann? " she cried. "Do you mean you've fallen in love with my little Ann—already? "

"I mean rather more than that, " he said deliberately. "I mean that I'm going to marry your little Ann. "

His aunt regarded him with a gleam of amusement.

"Ann Lovell is a young woman with a very decided mind of her own, " she observed. "It's just conceivable she might refuse you. "

Forrester returned her glance with eyes like blue steel.

"It wouldn't make a bit of difference if she did, " he said laconically.

CHAPTER XIII

"FRIENDSHIP IMPLIES TRUST"

"Can you put me up? Tony. "

Ann was sitting in the garden one morning, industriously occupied in shelling peas, when the foregoing terse wire was handed to her by the village telegraph boy. Tony's silence throughout the last few weeks had somewhat disturbed her. She had not received a single line from him since the day he had accompanied her to Victoria station and seen her safely on board the train for Silverquay, and now her brows drew together rather anxiously as she perused this unexpected message.

The telegram had been handed in at the local post office at Lorne, so it was obvious that Tony was at home, and the only reason she could surmise for his sudden request was that he had had a rather bigger quarrel than usual with his uncle.

She scribbled an affirmative reply on the prepaid form which had accompanied the wire and dispatched it by the telegraph boy, who was waiting placidly in the sunshine—and looked as though he were prepared to wait all day if necessary. Then, when she had slit the last fat pod in her basket and shelled its contents, she picked up the bowl of shiny green peas and carried it into the kitchen where Maria was busy making bread.

"Can we do with a visitor, Maria? " she asked, flapping the flimsy pink telegram gaily in front of her. "Here's Mr. Tony Brabazon wiring to know if we can put him up. "

"Master Tony? " Maria relapsed into the familiar appellation of the days when she had been not infrequently moved to cuff the said Master Tony's ears with gusto, on occasions when he took nursery tea at Lovell Court and failed to comport himself, in Maria's eyes, "as a little gentleman should. "

"Why, yes, miss, us could do with Master Tony. " Her face broadened into a beaming smile. "'Twould be like the old days to have him back, scrawling round my kitchen again and stealing the jam pasties. Do you mind his ways when Mr. Lovell he was travelling in furrin parts an' I was cooking for you and Master Robin? And there's not many can better my jam pasties when I put my mind to it, though I do say it. "

"Well, you'll have him 'scrawling round your kitchen' before long, I expect, " replied Ann.

Maria searched her face with kindly curiosity.

"You'm well pleased, miss, bain't you? "

Ann smiled.

"Very pleased. "

Evidently the answer did not convey all that Maria had hoped for, after kneading her dough energetically for a few moments, she threw out negligently:

"I used to fancy at one time that you and Master Tony might be thinking of getting married some day. I suppose I was wrong. "

"Quite out of it, Maria. " Ann looked preternaturally serious. "And, anyway, I thought you hadn't a very high opinion of matrimony and didn't recommend it? "

"Well, I will say my 'usband wasn't one to make you think a lot of it, " acknowledged Maria, still kneading with vigour. "But there! There's a power of difference in men, same as there is in yeast. Some starts working right away, and when you puts it down afore the fire your bread plums up beautiful. But I've known yeast what you couldn't get to work as it should—stale stuff, maybe—and then the bread lies 'eavy on your stomach. It's like that with husbands. I dare say some of 'em be good enough, but there's some what isn't, and George Coombe, he was one of that sort. But I don't bear him no grudge. He was a bit plaguey to live with, but he died proper—with his face to the foe, as you may say, so I've no call to be ashamed of him. "

"I'm sure you haven't, " agreed Ann warmly, and, leaving Maria to her bread-making, she ran off to feed the poultry. Much to her delight, her first brood of fluffy youngsters had hatched out the previous day.

A few hours later Tony wired *"Arriving 3.30 train to-morrow."* And now "to-morrow" had become to-day, and Ann, alone in the ralli-cart, was sending Dick Turpin smartly along the road to the station.

The station at Silverquay, as is so often the case at a seaside town, was more or less of a common meeting ground for the inhabitants, and it was quite an unusual thing not to run across some one one knew there, exchanging a library book or purchasing a paper at the bookstall. So that it was no surprise to Ann, as she made her way on to the platform, to see Eliot Coventry coming towards her, an unfolded newspaper under his arm.

Otherwise, the platform was deserted. The train was not yet signalled, and neither stationmaster nor porter had emerged into view. Without absolute discourtesy it was impossible for Eliot to avoid speaking to her, and Ann's heart quickened its beat a little as, after one swift, almost perturbed glance, he approached her. He looked rather tired, and there was a restless, thwarted expression in his eyes. So might look the eyes of a man who habitually denied himself the freedom to act as his inclinations demanded, and Ann was conscious of a sudden impulse of compassion that overcame the feeling of hurt pride which his recent attitude towards her had inspired. She responded to his greeting with a small, friendly smile, leavened with just a spice of mischief.

"So you're not going to cut me altogether, then? "

"Cut you? Why should I? " he said quickly.

She shook her head.

"I don't know why. But you've been doing the next thing to it lately, haven't you? "

Then, as he stared moodily down, at her without answering, she continued with the quaint, courageous candour which was a part of her:

"Will you tell me quite honestly, Mr. Coventry—would you rather that Robin hadn't a sister living with him at the Cottage? Because, if so, I can easily go away again. I shouldn't have any difficulty in finding a job, and Maria Coombe is quite capable of looking after Robin! "

While she was speaking a startled look of dismay overspread his face.

"Good heavens! " he exclaimed in an aghast voice. "Have I been as rude as all that? "

"Not rude, exactly. Only when first I came you seemed quite pleased that I should be at the Cottage. But now—lately—" She broke off lamely. It was difficult to put the thing into words. There was nothing, actually, that he had done or left undone. It was a matter of atmosphere—an atmosphere of chilly indifference of which she was acutely conscious in his presence and which made her feel unwelcome.

But he refused to help her out. His eyes were bent on her face, and it seemed almost as though there were a certain eagerness behind their intent gaze.

"Yes, " he repeated. "And now—lately? "

"You've been—unfriendly, " she answered simply.

The eagerness died out of his eyes, replaced by the old brooding unhappiness which Ann had read in them the day she had first seen him at the Montricheux Kursaal.

"Friendship and I have very little to say to each other. " He spoke with a quiet bitterness that was the growth of years. "Friendship implies trust. "

A bell clanged somewhere, but the signal arm fell unheeded by the man and woman whose conversation had so suddenly become charged with a strange new kind of intimacy.

"Then you don't trust me? " There was a hurt note in Ann's voice. She was not used to being distrusted.

Coventry smiled ironically, as though at some secret jest of which the edge was turned against himself.

"Sometimes I almost do, " he said. "But on the whole—forgive me! —I haven't a blind faith in your sex. " He paused, then added rather grimly: "A burnt child fears the fire, and I had my lesson many years ago."

"So you really deserve your reputation?"

"My reputation?"

"Current gossip sets you down as a confirmed misogynist, you know."

"For once, then, current gossip is correct."

The whistle of the approaching train shrilled piercingly through the air and, startled back to a realisation of the present, Ann glanced hastily up the line.

"You're meeting some one?" asked Eliot, his eyes following the same direction. She assented, and he turned as though to leave her. All at once he swung round on his heel and said brusquely:

"You need never imagine you're not wanted at the Cottage. I like to think of you there."

Without waiting for an answer he lifted his hat and strode away, and a minute later, with a harsh grating of brakes, the train ran into the station and Ann moved quickly towards it.

Tony sprang out on to the platform and hurried forward to greet her. He was looking thinner than when she had last seen him. His face was a little haggard, and the eyes beneath their long lashes were hard and bright.

"This is awfully good of you, Ann," he said, speaking a trifle awkwardly. "Does Robin mind my suddenly billeting myself on you like this?"

"Mind? Why, of course not! We're both delighted. And there's some one else who is nearly bursting with excitement at the idea of seeing you again—Maria Coombe. You haven't forgotten her?"

"Forgotten old Maria? By Jove, no! My ears tingle yet when I think of her." And for an instant a smile of amused recollection chased away the moodiness of his expression. "Is she with you at the Cottage, then? "

"Yes. She volunteered to come to us, and you may guess we jumped at the idea. To have dear old Maria back smooths our path in life considerably, bless her! And I love to listen to her Devon accent! It sounds so homelike. "

Tony seemed rather subdued on the homeward drive, but his spirits rallied when they reached the Cottage, where Robin was waiting for them at the gateway, with Billy Brewster hovering importantly in the middle distance. Maria welcomed the new arrival with open arms, and the tea she had prepared for the occasion was a rich display of what she could accomplish in the way of cakes and pasties when she "put her mind to it. " Tony did full justice to them and chaffed her unmercifully, to her huge delight, and for the moment one might have imagined him nothing but a big gay schoolboy, home for the holidays.

It was not until later on, when Robin had gone out again, and he and Ann were sitting smoking together under the latter's favourite oak, that he unburdened his soul.

"I'm everlastingly grateful to you for answering my S. O.S. so promptly, " he said then. "Uncle Philip was simply making life unbearable at home. "

Ann was swinging gently in the hammock, while Tony had flung himself down at full length on the sun-warmed turf. Her eyes rested on him reflectively.

"How was that? " she asked.

"Oh"—impatiently—"the usual thing, of course! Money! I asked him to let me have a hundred or two extra, and he simply went straight up in the air over it. "

"A hundred or two! Oh, Tony, have you got into debt again? "

"I haven't been running up bills, if that's what you mean. But I've had bad luck at cards—and of course I had to square things up. "

Ann suppressed a sigh. It was the same old story—that ineradicable gaming spirit which had come down from sire to son through half a dozen generations, and which seemed to have concentrated in full strength in the offspring of poor Dick Brabazon.

A few questions elicited the facts. Following upon his return from Switzerland Tony had been playing cards regularly, with, as he explained, "the most infernal luck—I made an absolute corner in Yarboroughs night after night. " The set of people with whom he mixed played unusually high points—Brett Forrester's set, as a matter of fact, although he himself had cleared out of town early in order to go yachting. Then, after losing far more than he could afford to pay, Tony had tried to recoup his fortunes by backing a few horses, and another hundred had been added to his original losses. Ultimately, when he and his uncle had gone down to Lorne, he had been compelled to make a clean breast of things and ask for money with which to settle his debts. "Debts of honour, " he had termed them, and the description acted like a red rag to a bull. Sir Philip had lost his temper completely.

"'Debts of honour' you call 'em, you young jackanapes! " he had raged. "I call them debts of the dirtiest dishonour you could pick up out of the gutter! " He swept Tony's indignant remonstrances to one side. "If you call it honourable to play for money when you haven't got it to pay with if you lose, a sense of honour's a different thing from what it was in my young days. Why—why—why—" he spluttered, "it's no better than stealing! You deserve a damn good hiding, let me tell you, and it's what you'll get one of these days if you can't keep straight, you young devil! "

The old man had stormed on for a heated half-hour or so, while Tony had stood by and listened to him, white-faced and furious, his haughty young head flung up and his teeth clenched to keep back the bitter answers that fought for utterance. Finally, his hand still shaking with rage, Sir Philip had written a cheque that would cover his nephew's losses.

"That's the last time I pay your gambling debts, " he had said as he flung down the pen. "You've an allowance of six hundred a year, and if you exceed that again I'll fire you out of the house neck and crop, and be damned to you! "

"I'll go now, sir—at once, if you wish! " Tony had returned with cool insolence.

"Go? Where would you go, I'd like to know? " Sir Philip had flung at him sneeringly. And just to prove that he could and would go if he chose, and because he was filled with a wild spirit of revolt and anger, Tony had despatched a telegram to Ann and had quitted Lorne the very next day.

"He was insufferable! " he declared stormily. "Great Scott! Does the man think I'm a child to be cuffed into obedience? I warned him for his own sake he'd better never lay a finger on me! "

"He never would, Tony, " said Ann. "Of that I'm sure. He's far too fond of you, for one thing. "

"No, I don't suppose he would, really, " conceded Tony. "But when he flies into a rage, he hardly knows what he's saying or doing. He's got the Brabazon temper all right, the same as I've got the family love of gambling. "

"Oh, Tony, I wish you'd give it all up! " exclaimed Ann impulsively. And then the colour rushed hotly into her face as she recalled with sudden vividness the circumstances in which he had once offered to renounce every form of gambling.

Absorbed in the interests of the new life in which she found herself, the recollection of that moonlit night on the steep side of Roche d'Or had slipped into the background of her thoughts. Now it leaped abruptly into the forefront, and she felt helpless and constrained, unable to urge her appeal. The answer Tony could give back was so obvious.

"I haven't the least intention of giving it up, " he said in a hard voice. "It's the chief pleasure in life to me. Trailing around Lorne and harrying his tenants happen to be Uncle Philip's pet enjoyments. I don't ask him to give those up. And I reserve the right to amuse myself in my own way. "

He switched the conversation on to another subject, and, after a decent interval, excused himself on the plea that he must "unpack his traps. "

Ann watched him stalking back to the house with gravely wistful eyes. Neither by word nor look had he implied the slightest recollection of the occasion when he had asked her to be his wife nor of her answer, and she realised that with the ingrained pride of his race he chose to consider the incident as closed. "*Then that's finished,* " he had said at the time. "*I shan't ask you again.* " And he had meant every word of it. With a headstrong determination he had accepted his dismissal and henceforward regarded himself as free to make ducks and drakes of his life if it so pleased him. She shrank from the knowledge. It seemed to lay a heavy sense of responsibility upon her.

Yet she could not find it in her heart to regret her decision. She felt deeply thankful that the mothering, protective impulse which had almost led her into promising to marry Tony had been stayed by Lady Susan's wise words. This hot-headed, undisciplined boy, despite his lovableness and charm, was not the type of man who would make a woman of Ann's fine fibre happy as his wife. Perhaps, unconsciously to herself, she was mentally contrasting him with some one else—with a man who, stern, and embittered though he might be, yet gave her a curious feeling of reliance, a sense of secret reserves of strength that would never fail whatever demand life might make upon them.

It seemed to her as if she and Eliot had drawn nearer to each other during their talk together on the deserted railway platform—as though some intangible barrier between them had been broken down. She could not put into actual words the thought which flitted fugitively through her mind—it was too vague and indeterminate. Only she was subconsciously aware that some change had taken place—that their relation to each other was curiously altered.

As she lay in bed that night, her mind a confused jumble of the day's happenings, one thought rose clear above the medley—the memory of his last words to her:

"You need never imagine you're not wanted at the Cottage. I like to think of you there. "

CHAPTER XIV

THE ETERNAL TRIANGLE

Under Brett Forrester's tutelage, Ann's progress in the art of swimming proceeded apace. Since his arrival at White Windows, the weather had been perfect—still, dewy mornings, veiled in mist, melting by midday into a blaze of deep blue skies and brilliant sunshine—and every day Ann and Mrs. Hilyard, accompanied by Forrester and very often by Robin in addition, might have been seen descending to Berrier Cove, the favourite bathing beach of the neighbourhood. Quite frequently, too, Lady Susan would join them in the water—she was an excellent straight-forward swimmer, though "without any monkey tricks, " as she regretfully acknowledged. On these occasions the Tribes of Israel would sit in a mournful row along the shore, watching the proceedings with concerned brown eyes. They themselves, individually and collectively, exhibited an unfeigned distaste for every form of aquatic sport which, Brett wickedly suggested, might be due to some subconscious atavistic emotion relative to the Red Sea episode. When they had suffered their adored mistress's temerity in silence for as long as canine toleration could be expected to endure, one or other of them would lift up his voice in a long-drawn wail of protest, the others would immediately join in, and the chorus of howls continued to make day hideous until Lady Susan issued from the water and hurried into her tent to dress.

Punishment and persuasion proved equally futile as a corrective. Inexplicable though it appeared, their mistress apparently derived some obscure satisfaction out of the process of splashing about in the wet sea, and because they loved her they bore it as long as they could. But after the expiration of a certain time-limit nothing could quiet them except Lady Susan's prompt emergence from the water.

Tony's arrival had added yet another member to the bathing contingent. He seemed to have forgotten all his troubles, and entered with zest into any and every sort of amusement which Silverquay afforded. A letter Ann had received from Sir Philip was primarily responsible for this care-free attitude. "Keep Tony as long as you want, " the old man had written. "But you may tell the young fool he can come home when he likes. I shan't bite his head off. " A slow, pleased smile had dawned on Tony's face as Ann read out this particular extract from the letter. Quarrel as he and his uncle might, they were genuinely fond of each other, and although Tony would not for worlds have admitted it, the knowledge that Sir Philip was really seriously annoyed with him had weighed heavily on his mind.

Since the removal of this incubus he had reverted to his usual high spirits and, between them, he and Brett Forrester had "made things hum, " as he described it. Boating, bathing, and picnics had been the order of the day, and the latest proposal, emanating from Forrester, was that they should all dine one evening on board the *Sphinx*. The date had been fixed to coincide with a night of full moon, and the invitations included both Eliot Coventry and the two Tempests.

The former had taken but little part in the summer diversions inaugurated by Brett and Tony. Nevertheless, he had been persuaded into joining one of the picnics. On this occasion the hostess had been Lady Susan, and she had simply declined to accept his refusal.

"Man was not made to live alone, " she had assured him. "We know that by the Garden of Eden arrangements, it's not the least use going against old-established custom, my dear man. So you'll come, won't you? " And somehow with Lady Susan's kind, merry dark eyes twinkling up at him he had not been able to find the ungraciousness to refuse.

But when the occasion came he had contributed very little to the gaiety of nations. He left early, on the ground that he had an appointment to keep in Ferribridge, and Ann felt as though he had joined the party more in the capacity of a looker-on than anything else. She said as much to him a day or two later when he chanced to meet her in the village, executing household shopping errands, and they had walked home together.

"You are quite right, " he answered. "That's what I am—a looker-on at life. I've no wish to be anything else. "

He no longer avoided her now, as he had been wont to do, and an odd sort of friendship had sprung up between them. But it was often punctuated by some such speech as the foregoing, and Ann felt that although he had sheathed the sword he was still armoured with a coat of mail. It was difficult to bring these almost brutal speeches, ground out of some long-harboured bitterness, into relation with the sweetness of that sudden, rare smile of his. The man was an enigma. He asked for friendship and then, when it was tentatively proffered, withdrew himself abruptly as though he feared it.

Brett Forrester proceeded along diametrically opposite lines. No nuances or subtle shades of feeling complicated life for him. He knew exactly what he wanted and went straight for it, all out, and Ann was conscious that she was fighting a losing battle in her effort to keep him at a distance. He had never, so far, made deliberate love to her, but there was a certain imperious possessiveness in his manner, a definite innuendo in his gay, audacious speeches which she found it very hard to combat. He seemed entirely oblivious of any lack of response on her part, and there was a light-hearted, irresponsible charm and camaraderie about him that was difficult to resist.

"What's the matter with you this morning? " he demanded one day when Ann had successfully infused a little formality into her manner.

"Nothing. Why should there be? " she returned.

"No reason at all. Only you seemed to be emulating the stiffness of a ramrod, and I thought you must be getting frightened of me—rigid with fear, you know"—impudently.

What could any one do but laugh? It was useless to try and treat him with aloof dignity if he promptly interpreted it as a sign of fear.

"I don't see anything in you to inspire terror, " Ann submitted.

"You don't? Good. Then come along down to the Cove, and I'll teach you a new stroke. "

And then, as though to contradict every opinion she or any one else might have formed of him, he was as painstaking and encouraging over the swimming lesson which ensued as though his whole reputation depended on her proficiency.

A day or two later, when Ann, accompanied by Tony and Robin, descended to Berrier Cove for her morning dip, it was to find the beach, at that time usually dotted about with bathers in varicoloured bathing suits and *peignoirs*, deserted by all save the hardiest and most determined.

The weather had changed with all the abruptness with which the English climate seems able to accomplish such transitions. A strong gale of wind was blowing, and the placid blue sea which, even at high tide, had been lapping the shore very tranquilly throughout the last fortnight, was converted into a rolling, grey-green stretch of water, breaking at its rim into towering waves.

"It looks a bit too rough for you, Ann, " observed Robin, surveying the scene doubtfully, "I don't think even your new-found prowess at swimming will be of much use to you to-day. "

"It would be all right once you're through the breakers, " suggested Tony. "There's a chap swimming out there, I see. "

He pointed to where a wet, dark head bobbed up and down like a cork beyond reach of the waves that reared themselves up to an immense height before they crashed down in a flurry of whirling foam on the beaten shore.

"Tough work, though, " replied Robin. "There's the deuce of a current running over there, and Ann's not an experienced enough swimmer to tackle a drag like that. "

Ann's face had fallen. The idea of foregoing her daily plunge did not commend itself to her in the least.

"I don't see why I can't have a dip—just get wet, you know, " she remonstrated wistfully.

"You mustn't think of such a thing! " came in quick, imperative tones. Startled, she turned round to find Forrester standing at her elbow, with Cara Hilyard beside him. Amid the hurly-burly of noise created by the breakers she had not noticed the sound of their approach.

"Do you hear? " he repeated. "You mustn't think of bathing to-day. "

Ann's head went up. The imperious speech, uttered as though it were a foregone conclusion that she would meekly obey its mandate, roused her to instant opposition.

"But I *am* thinking of it, " she replied, masking her irritation beneath an outward assumption of calm.

"I really don't think you should, " said Cara persuasively.

"You're not bathing to-day, are you, Mrs. Hilyard? " put in Robin quickly, a look of swift anxiety on his face.

She shook her head, smiling.

"No. I'm afraid I'm too big a coward. "

"I should rather put it that you've got too much sense, " returned Robin. "It really isn't safe for any but a very strong swimmer to-day. "

"Safe! " exclaimed Brett, angrily, snatching at the last word and flinging it, as it were, in Ann's face. "Of course it isn't safe! "

"Then what's the meaning of that? " asked Ann pertinently, pointing to the bathing suit he carried on his arm.

"Oh, I'm going in. It would take more than this bit of sea to drown me"—carelessly.

He was making no idle boast. As Ann well know, he was almost as much at home in the water as he was on land. And presently, when it had been decided that only the three men should risk the roughness of the breakers, she stood watching him with quiet, unstinted admiration as, timing his plunge to a nicety, he met a large billow as it rose, dived sheer through its green depths, and emerged into the comparatively smooth water on the further side before its white, curving crest could thunder down on to the shore.

Robin and Tony made but a brief stay in the water—the former curtailing the proceedings because he very much preferred the idea of keeping Mrs. Hilyard company where she sat in a fold of the rocks. Meanwhile Ann's gaze was riveted enviously on Forrester's sleek red head as it appeared and disappeared with the rise and fall of the swelling sea. He looked as if he were thoroughly enjoying the buffeting he was getting.

"I should like to go in—just for a few minutes, " she said discontentedly. There are few things that draw the genuine sea-lover more strongly than the longing to plunge into the tantalising, gleaming water and feel the rush and prick of it and its buoyancy beneath one's limbs.

Cara looked up in dismay.

"You're not thinking of going, after all? " she exclaimed. "Oh, don't, Ann! "—urgently. "It's really too risky to-day. If one of those big breakers knocked you down you wouldn't have time to get up again before another came. I once saw a woman drowned just in that way. It was horrible. She was flung down by a huge breaker, and before she could pick herself up a second wave broke over her. She had no chance to get her breath. And there wasn't any one near enough to help her. I saw it all happen from the cliff. " She shuddered a little at the recollection.

"And if one of those waves *didn't* knock me down, " retorted Ann, "I should have the most glorious dip imaginable. Honestly, Cara"—coaxingly—"I wouldn't do more than just dash in and out again. "

"Well, ask Robin what he thinks first, " begged Cara.

Ann shook her head.

"I'd much rather ask him after! " she answered whimsically, "In fact, I'm going to sneak into the water before he and Tony finish their respective toilettes. "

Without more ado she vanished into the tent which she usually shared with Cara, and in a very short space of time reappeared equipped for the water, the tassel of her jaunty little bathing-cap fluttering defiantly in the wind. Slipping out of her *peignoir*, she let it fall to the ground and emerged a slender, naiad-like figure in her green bathing-suit. She ran, white-footed, to the edge of the water and danced into the creaming foam of a receding wave, while Cara watched her with inward misgivings. Even from where she sat she could see how strong was the undertow—each wave as it retreated dragging back with it both sand and pebbles, and even quite large stones, in a swirling seaward rush against the pull of which it was difficult to maintain a footing. Ann, lithe and supple though she was, staggered uncertainly in the effort to retain her balance, her feet sinking deep into the shifting sand, as she turned to wave a reassuring hand to the solitary watcher on the beach.

And then it happened—the thing which Cara had foreseen must almost inevitably ensue. She had a momentary glimpse of the slim naiad figure swaying against a background of sea and sky, then a terrific wave towered up behind it, blotting out the horizon and seeming for an instant to stand poised, smooth and perpendicular like a solid wall of green glass. She saw Ann's face change swiftly as she realised her danger, the upward fling of her arms as she tried to spring to the surface in an effort to escape the full force of the wave and be carried in on its crest. But it was too late. With a crash like gun-thunder the huge billow broke, and to Cara's straining eyes it seemed that Ann's light form was snatched up as though of no more moment than a floating straw and buried beneath a seething, tumbling avalanche of waters.

She sprang to her feet and ran towards the water, shrieking for help as she ran. But the noise of the sea drowned her cries so that neither Robin nor Tony, still dressing in one of the tents, heard anything amiss. Even as she called and shouted she realised the utter uselessness of it. No weak woman's voice could carry against that thunderous roar. In the same instant, she caught sight of Brett's head and shoulders in the distance, and she waved and beckoned to him frenziedly. With a choking gasp of relief, she caught his answering gesture before he turned and headed straight for the shore, shearing through the water with a powerful over-hand stroke that brought him momentarily nearer.

Though actually not more than a few seconds, it seemed to Cara an eternity before the huge wave which had engulfed Ann spent itself. Then, as it receded she discerned her figure struggling in the backwash, and as the girl at last dragged herself to her knees Cara rushed waist-deep into the foaming, eddying flood in a plucky effort to reach her. But, before she could get near enough, the suction of the retreating wave had swept Ann out of her reach and the next incoming breaker thundered over her again. Cara herself barely escaped its savage onslaught, and as she staggered into safety she turned a desperate, agonised face seaward. Brett was still some yards away, and Ann would die—die with succour almost at hand! Her own helplessness drove her nearly frantic. She was beating her hands together and quite unconsciously repeating Brett's name over and over in a sick agony of urgency.

"Brett! Brett! God, let him come in time!... Brett! Brett! Brett!... "

The retreating wave revealed once more the slight girl-figure, spent and effortless this time, tossing impotently in the churning backwash. Forrester would be too late! A third wave would batter the life out of that fragile body. Cara's voice died into a strangled sob of despair.

... And then came the sound of racing footsteps, something passed her like a flash, and the white spray flew up in a dense cloud as a tall figure hurled itself headlong into the sea. For an instant Cara could distinguish nothing but a dark blot and the blur of flying spume as it spattered against her face. Then, with a shaking cry of utter thankfulness, she saw Eliot Coventry come striding out from amid the maelstrom of surging waters, bearing Ann's unconscious form in his arms.

He carried her swiftly beyond reach of the hungry, devouring waves and, laying her down on the sand, tore off his coat and placed it beneath her head. At the same moment Forrester reached the shore and raced towards them, and as Eliot straightened himself it was to meet the other man's eyes blazing into his—savage, challenging eyes, like those of a tiger robbed of its prey. For an instant the two men remained staring straight into each other's faces, while on the ground between them lay Ann's slender, white-limbed body, limp and unconscious.

To Cara, hurrying towards them as fast as the wet skirts which clung about her would allow, the brief scene seemed like a picture flung vividly upon a screen. In that moment of fierce stress the innermost thoughts of the two men were nakedly revealed upon their faces—if not to each other, at least to the clear, unerring vision of the woman, who caught her breath sharply between her teeth in a sudden blinding flash of enlightenment.

The little group seemed to her symbolical—the two men standing face to face like hostile forces, with the young, girlish figure lying helplessly between them.

CHAPTER XV

ANCIENT HISTORY

Ann opened her eyes and stared incuriously up into a blank, indeterminate expanse of white. It was quite without interest—conveyed no meaning to her whatever. Moreover, her eyelids felt inexplicably heavy, as though they were weighted. So she let them fall again, and the placid, reposeful sense of nothingness which had been momentarily interrupted enveloped her once more. She was conscious of no particular sensation of any kind, neither painful nor pleasurable, but merely of an immense peace and tranquillity.

Presently a faint feeling of curiosity concerning that odd expanse of white overhead filtered into her consciousness, gradually increasing in strength until it became a definite irritation, like the prolonged light scratching of a finger-nail up a surface of silk. She opened her eyes again reluctantly. It was still there, immediately above her—a formless stretch of dull white. She wondered whether it extended indefinitely, and her eyes travelled slowly along until they were arrested by a narrow line of demarcation. Here the expanse of white ceased abruptly, at right angles to a misty blue surface in the centre of which glimmered a square of light. Ann's mind seemed to struggle up from some profound depth where it had lain quiescent and feebly and disjointedly signalled the words: "Ceiling... wall... window.... " And finally, with an immense effort, "Room. "

After that the cogs of her mental machinery began to move in a more normal manner, though still slowly and confusedly. She recaptured the memory of a blurred murmur of voices and of some fiery liquid being poured down, her throat which stung and smarted abominably as it went down. Later had followed a pleasant dreamy consciousness of warmth which had brought with it realisation of the fact that previously she had been feeling terribly cold. Then voices again—notably Maria's this time: "She'll do now, Mrs. Hilyard, mum. 'Tis only warmth she wants. "

Why did she want warmth? When it was summer. She was sure it *was* summer. She remembered seeing the sun overhead—hanging in the middle of the sky just like one of those solid-looking gold halos which the Old Masters used to paint round the head of a saint. At least... had it been in the sky... lately? To-day? And then, accompanied by a rush of blind terror, came recollection—of an overcast sky and grey, plunging sea, and of a wild, futile, suffocating struggle against some awful force that had tossed her hither and thither as a child might toss a ball, and had finally surged right over her, blotting out everything.

A little moan of horror escaped her, and immediately Robin's dear familiar voice answered reassuringly:

"You're quite safe, old thing—tucked up in bed. So don't worry."

He was bending over her, and she made an instinctive effort to sit up. The movement sent a stab of agony through her whole body, and she gasped out convulsively:

"It hurts!"

In a moment his arm was round her shoulders, and he had laid her gently back against her pillows.

"Yes. I expect you're pretty well bruised from head to foot," he said in a tone of commiseration.

Ann regarded him uncertainly.

"I feel so queer. What's happened to me? Where—where am I?" she asked.

Robin had the wisdom to answer her quite simply and naturally, telling her in a few words just what had occurred, and, her mind once set at rest, she lay back quietly and very soon dropped off into a sleep of sheer exhaustion. Afterwards followed a timeless period marked by the comings and goings of Maria with hot-water bottles and steaming cups of milk or broth, alternating with intervals of profound slumber. Through it all, waking or sleeping, ran a thread of wearisome pain—limbs so stiff and flesh so bruised that it seemed to Ann as though the wontedly comfortable mattress on which she lay had been stuffed with lumps of coal.

One break occurred in the ordered sequence of sleep and nourishment. This happened when Tony quitted Silverquay to rejoin his uncle. The day following Ann's enforced retirement to bed, a brusque letter had come from the old man, in which he concealed a genuine longing to have his nephew with him again beneath an irritable suggestion that he was probably outstaying his welcome at the Cottage. Robin laughingly reassured Tony upon the latter point, but at the same time he agreed that the young man's return to Lorne might be advisable, since it was obvious Sir Philip was feeling his loneliness considerably more than the proud old autocrat was willing to confess.

So Tony had tiptoed up to Ann's room, when she had roused herself sufficiently to wish him good-bye and bestow upon him a parting injunction "to be good. " After which she dropped back once more into the lethargy of weakness, painfully conscious of the fact that relief was only to be found in lying torpidly still and silent.

But all things come to an end in time—though the disagreeable ones seem to take much longer over it than the nice ones—and at the end of a few days Ann was able to sit up in bed without groaning and take an intelligent interest in the fact that her room was lavishly adorned with roses.

"Where did all the flowers come from? " she demanded of Maria.

"Why, 'tis Mr. Forrester what sends they, miss, " came the answer, uttered with much satisfaction. Brett had a "way" with him against which even downright Maria Coombe was not proof. "He've a-called here to inquire every day since you was took bad. Very attentive and gentlemanlike, I call't. "

"Very, " agreed Ann with becoming gravity. "And who else—hasn't any one else"—correcting herself quickly—"been to inquire? ".

"'Deed they have! 'Twas 'Can't I see Miss Lovell to-day, Maria? ' with first one and then t'other of them. But I told them all the same"—with grim triumph. "'Not till I gives the word, ' I told them. "

"Who has called, then? " asked Ann curiously.

"Her ladyship up to White Windows, she came, and Mrs. Hilyard, and the rector and that there long-faced sister of his—all of 'em have been, miss. And the squire—he've sent his groom down to ask how you were going on. "

"The squire? "

"Mr. Coventry, I'm meaning—he as pulled you out of the water. You ought to be main grateful to him, Miss Ann, for sure."

A faint colour stole up into Ann's white cheeks.

"Oh, I am. You had better send back a message by the groom to that effect," she said curtly.

Maria surveyed her with frank disapproval.

"You should take shame to yourself, speaking that way, miss," she admonished severely. "But I expect you'm hungry-like, that's what 'tis. And I've a beautiful young chicken roasting for your lunch. You'll feel different when you've got a bit of something solid inside you."

The roast chicken, combined with a glass of champagne, certainly contributed towards producing a more cheerful outlook on life, and when, later on in the afternoon, Mrs. Hilyard called, armed with some books for the invalid, and was graciously permitted by Maria to come upstairs, Ann welcomed her with unfeigned delight.

"Well, it's quite nice to see you alive," smiled Cara as they kissed each other. "I really thought you were going to drown before my very eyes the other day."

"Instead of which I've turned up again like a bad penny!"

"Thanks to Mr. Coventry. If he hadn't chanced to be taking a constitutional in the direction of Berrier Cove that morning, I don't know what would have happened."

Ann was not looking at her. Instead, her gaze was directed towards the open window as though the view which offered were of surpassing interest.

"I wondered how it was he came to be on the spot just in the nick of time," she said negligently.

"That was how," nodded Cara. "He'd been for a walk along the shore, and luckily came home by way of the Cove."

"I suppose I shall have to thank him," remarked Ann gloomily.

Cara looked a trifle mystified. Then she smiled.

"It would be—just polite, " she submitted.

Ann frowned.

"I always seem to be thanking him! " she complained, and, in response to the other's glance of inquiry, recounted the various occasions on which Coventry had rendered her a service.

"Not a bad record of knight-errantry for a confirmed woman-hater, is it? " she added with a rueful touch of humour.

"He wasn't always a woman-hater, " answered Cara slowly. Her pansy-dark eyes held a curious dreaming look.

"I'd forgotten. Of course, you'd met him before you came here. Did you know him pretty well? "

"It was so many years ago, " deprecated Cara, with a little wave of her hand which seemed to set her former friendship with Eliot away in the back ages. "But I knew a good deal about him—we knew his people when I was a girl in my teens—and I can understand why—how he became such a misanthrope. "

Ann made no answer. Somehow she felt she could not put any direct questions about this man whose changing, oddly contradictory moods had baffled her so completely and—although she would not have acknowledged it—had caught and held her imagination with equal completeness. Perhaps she was hardly actually aware how much the queer, abrupt owner of Heronsmere occupied her thoughts. Mrs. Hilyard, however, continued speaking without waiting to be questioned.

"Eliot Coventry has had just the sort of experience to make him cynical, " she went on in her pretty, dragging voice. "Particularly as regards women. His mother was a perfectly beautiful woman, with the temper of a fiend. She lived simply and solely for her own enjoyment, and never cared tuppence about either Eliot or his sister. "

"Oh, has he a sister? " The question sprang from Ann's lips without her own volition.

"Yes. She was a very pretty girl, too, I remember. "

Ann's thoughts flew back to the day of the Fête des Narcisses, recalling the pretty woman whom she had observed driving with Eliot in the prize car. Probably, since he so disliked women in general, his companion on that occasion had been merely his sister! She felt oddly pleased and contented at this solution of a matter which had nagged her curiosity more than a little at the time.

"Mrs. Coventry—the mother—was utterly selfish, and insisted upon her own way in everything. " Cara was pursuing her recollections in a quiet, retrospective fashion which gave Ann the impression that they had no very deep or poignant interest for her. "If she *didn't* get it—well, there were fireworks! "—smiling. "Once, I remember, Eliot crossed her wishes over something and she flew into a perfect frenzy of temper. There was a small Italian dagger lying on a table near, and she snatched it up and flung it straight at him. It struck him just below one of his eyes; that's how he came by that scar on his cheekbone. She might have blinded him, " she added, and for a moment there was a faint tremor in her voice.

"What a brute she must have been! " exclaimed Ann in horror.

"Yes, " agreed Cara. "He was unlucky in his mother. " After a pause she went on: "And he was unlucky in the woman he loved. He wasn't at all well-off in those days, and she threw him over—broke off the engagement and married a very wealthy man instead. "

Ann felt her heart contract.

"I suppose that's what makes him so bitter, then, " she said in a low voice. "Probably—he still cares for her. "

"No. " Cara shook her head. "Eliot Coventry isn't the sort of man to go on caring for a woman who'd proved herself unworthy. I think—I think he'd just wipe her clean out of his life. "

"It would be what she deserved, " asserted Ann rather fiercely.

"Yes, I suppose it would. But one can feel a little Sorry for her. She spoilt her own life, too. "

"Did you know her, then? "

"Yes, I knew her. I think the only excuse to be made for her is that she was very young when it all happened. "

"I'm young, " said Ann grimly, "but I hope I wouldn't be as mean as that. "

"You? " Cara's eyes rested with a wistful kind of tenderness on the flushed face against the pillows. "But, my dear, there's a world of difference between you and the girl Eliot Coventry was in love with. "

She got up and, moving across to the window, stood looking out. Below, the pleasant, happy-go-lucky garden rambled desultorily away to the corner where stood the ancient oak supporting Ann's hammock—a garden of odd, unexpected nooks and lawns, with borders of old English flowers, without definite form and looking as if it had grown of its own sweet will into its present comeliness. But the garden conjured up before Cara's mental vision was a very different one—a stately, formal garden entered through an arch of jessamine, with a fountain playing in its centre, tinkling coolly into a marble basin, and a high-backed, carved stone bench set beneath the shade of scented trees. Above all pulsated the deep, sapphire blue of an Italian sky.

The pictured garden faded and Cara turned slowly back into the room. Her eyes looked sad.

"Poor Eliot! " she said. "It's all ancient history now. But one wishes it was possible to give him back his happiness. "

When she had gone, Ann lay thinking over the story she had just heard. So it was all true, then—the tale that Eliot had been jilted years ago! It threw a vivid flash of illumination on the many complexities she had come up against in his character. The two women who should mean most in a man's life had both failed him. He bore on his body a scar which surely he must never see reflected in the mirror without recalling the travesty of motherhood that was all he had ever known. And scored into his soul, hidden beneath a bitter reticence and unforgiving cynicism, lay the still deeper scar of that hurt which the woman who was to have been his wife had dealt him.

Ann's annoyance with him because he hadn't troubled to call personally to ascertain how she was melted away in a rush of pitying comprehension. She was conscious of an intense anger against that unknown woman who had so marred his life. She hoped she was being made to pay for it, suffer for it in some way!

And then, all at once, came the realisation that if she had remained faithful, Eliot would probably have been married years ago... she herself would never have met him.... A burning flush mounted to her very temples, and she hid her face in her hands, trying to shut out the swift, unbidden thought which had wakened within her a strange tumult of emotion. When at last she uncovered her face, her eyes held the wondering, startled look of a young fawn.

She was very young and whole-hearted, utterly innocent of that great miracle which transforms the world, as yet unrecognising of the voice of love—the Voice which, once heard, can never again be muted and forgotten. And now something stirred within her—something new and disturbing and a little frightening.

It was as though she had heard some distant call which she but half understood and, only partly understanding, feared.

CHAPTER XVI

DREAM-FLOWERS

The news of Mrs. Hilyard's visit to the Cottage soon spread abroad, and the following day, when she was allowed downstairs for the first time, Ann held quite a small reception.

Lady Susan, escorted by Forrester and the ubiquitous Tribes of Israel, was the first to arrive. Afterwards came the rector and Miss Caroline, and even Mrs. Carberry, a somewhat consequential dame whose husband was Master of the Heronsfoot Foxhounds, and who had hitherto held rather aloof from anything approaching intimacy and merely paid a stately first call on the Cottage people, unbent sufficiently to take tea informally with the invalid.

She did not, however, bring her daughter, a girl of Ann's own age, with her. A shrewd, rather calculating woman, she had fully recognised the possible attraction that might lie in Robin's steady, grey-green eyes. And since her plans for her daughter's future most certainly did not include marriage with any one so unimportant—and probably hard up—as a young estate agent, she judged it wiser to run no risks. She extracted from Ann a full, true, and particular account of her bathing adventure, and the information that it had been the owner of Heronsmere who had come to the rescue did not appear to afford her much pleasure.

"He's not here this afternoon? " She glanced quickly round the party of friends who had gathered in the pretty, low-ceiled room. "But I suppose he has called already to make sure that you're safe and sound? " There was a kind of acrid sweetness in her tones.

"Oh, no, " replied Ann, sensing the woman's latent antagonism. "Why should he? "

"Why, indeed? " Mrs. Carberry laughed dryly. "After all, he can't really feel very grateful to you for procuring him a soaking, can he? A man does so hate to be made a fool of. "

"I really don't know what he felt, " retorted Ann sweetly, but with heightened colour. "You see, I was unconscious. "

"Just as well for you, perhaps. " Again that unpleasant little dry laugh. "One feels so *draggled,* doesn't one, with one's hair all lank and wet? "

Miss Caroline's maidenly mind seemed chiefly oppressed with the immodesty of being rescued from drowning by a member of the other sex.

"How unfortunate it was that Mrs. Hilyard couldn't reach you! " she said, when she got Ann to herself for a few moments. "You must have felt very uncomfortable. "

"Uncomfortable? " Ann's clear eyes met Miss Caroline's blue bead ones inquiringly.

"*Dreadfully* uncomfortable, I should think"—with sympathy. "You—you had nothing on, I suppose"—lowering her voice impressively—"but your bathing-gown? "

"Nothing at all, " answered Ann, maintaining her gravity with difficulty. "One hasn't usually, you know—to go into the water. "

"But you had to be carried *out* of the water, hadn't you? You must have found it most embarrassing! Most embarrassing! "

"I don't think I did, " said Ann.

"Not? "—chidingly. "Oh, Miss Lovell, I can't believe that! Any nice-minded girl—I'm sure, if it had been me I should have fainted out of pure shame at finding myself in a man's arms—without a *peignoir*! "

"Well, that was just it, you see. I *had* fainted. So"—the corners of her mouth trembling in spite of herself—"I wasn't able to put on my *peignoir.* "

"I see. " Miss Caroline looked slightly relieved. "Then you didn't really know any more about it than one does when having a tooth out under gas? What a good thing! Dear me! What a good thing! And I'm sure Mr. Coventry will try to forget all about it. Any gentleman would. Really, such a—a contretemps makes one feel one ought almost to be fully clothed for bathing, doesn't it? "

She hopped up like a hungry little bird that has just been fed and flitted across the room to talk to Mrs. Carberry, and Ann wondered dryly if she were confiding in the M. F.H. 's wife particulars of the kind of costume she deemed suitable to the occasion when drowning.

Brett Forrester took her vacated seat at Ann's side.

"I'm really very much obliged to Coventry, " he remarked, by way of opening the conversation.

"Are you? " she replied innocently. "What for? "

"Why, for saving you for me, of course. I couldn't possibly have got there in time myself. And I don't like losing my belongings"—placidly.

She stared at him.

"If you're referring to me, " she said aloofly, "I'm not your 'belongings. '"

His bright blue eyes flashed over her, and for a moment his face seemed to wake up as he responded swiftly:

"But you will be—some day. So"—with a resumption of his former placidity—"as I said, I'm very much obliged to Coventry for saving you for me. "

"Brett, don't be so ridiculous! It isn't even funny to make jokes like that, " she answered with some impatience.

He remained quite unperturbed.

"I didn't intend to be funny. And I'm not joking. I'm perfectly serious. "

"Then you were never more mistaken in your life. "

"Mistaken? "—with childlike inquiry.

"In what you said just now. "

Forrester's eyes danced wickedly.

"I say such a lot of things, " he complained. "If you can specify which particular thing, now? "

"You know which I mean, perfectly well, " protested Ann indignantly. "That I—that you—what you said just now about 'belonging'! " She brought it out with a rush.

"I meant it. "

They were alone in the room. The others, conducted by Robin, had all trooped out to inspect what Lady Susan gaily insisted upon referring to as the "Cottage Poultry Farm, " and distantly through the open window came the fluttered cackling of the White Leghorns and Rhode Island Reds, resentful of this unaccountable intrusion of strangers into their domain.

Brett laid his hand suddenly on Ann's arm and thrust his face near hers.

"I meant it, " he repeated, and his voice roughened oddly. "I've meant it ever since the day I found you fast asleep in the hammock. "

She drew back a little. The nearness of his arrogant, suddenly passionate face to hers filled her with a sense of panic. His eyes were like blue fire, scorching her.

"Don't! Don't be absurd, Brett, " she said hastily. "Why—why"—seeking for some good reason to set against his abruptly declared determination—"you hardly know me! Only just on the surface, that is. "

"I know all I need to, thank you. I know you're the woman I want to marry. No"—checking with a gesture the impulsive negative with which she was about to respond—"you needn't bother about refusing me. I'm not asking you to marry me—not at this moment. "

Ann took a fresh hold of herself.

"That's just as well, " she said, trying to match his coolness with her own. "As I told you—you don't really know anything about me. I may"—forcing a smile—"have a perfectly horrid character, for all you can tell. "

"You may, " he replied indifferently. "It wouldn't worry me in the least if you had. " Then, with a strange intensity, he went on: "I shouldn't let anything that had happened in the past stand between me and the woman I wanted—if I wanted her badly enough. "

Ann stiffened.

"I think you're talking very funnily, " she observed. "I don't understand you at all. "

"Don't you? " Once more that swift, searching glance of the brilliant blue eyes. "In plain English, then, it wouldn't matter in the slightest to me what the woman I loved had done in the past. She may have sown her little crop of wild oats if she likes. The past is hers. The future would be mine. And I'd take care of that"—grimly.

"This is all very interesting, of course, " said Ann repressively. "But I don't see how it affects me. "

"Do you really mean that? " He rapped out the question sharply—so sharply that she almost jumped.

"Certainly, I mean it, " she replied with a slight accession of hauteur that sat rather charmingly upon her. She rose quickly, as a sound of voices heralded the return of the rest of the party. "And I'd prefer you not to talk to me any more—like that, " she added.

Forrester's eyes followed her as she moved back into the room and began chatting pleasantly with her returning guests. There was a look of amusement in them mingled with a certain unqualified admiration.

"Game little devil! " he muttered to himself.

Soon afterwards the M. F.H. 's wife rose to go, and, graciously offering the Tempests a lift home in her car, swept them away with her. When they had taken their departure Lady Susan declared that Ann was looking tired and that it was high time she and Brett started on their homeward tramp.

"You'll be feeling quite yourself again by next week, my dear, " she said. "Just in time for Brett's party on the *Sphinx,* " she added, smiling.

A faint look of hesitation crossed Ann's face. Brett saw it instantly.

"You promised to come, " he said swiftly, almost as though he dared her to retract her acceptance.

Ann forced herself to meet his glance. She was conscious of an inward qualm of fear and wished to heaven that she had never accepted the invitation to dine on board his yacht. But she was determined not to show the white feather and faced him coolly. After all, in these enlightened days a man couldn't very well carry you off by force and *compel* you to marry him! Though she reluctantly conceded that if any man in the world were likely to attempt such a thing it would be some primitive, lawless male of the type of Brett Forrester.

"Certainly I promised, " she told him. "And I've every intention of keeping my promise. "

Lady Susan glanced quickly from one to the other of them and her dark brows puckered up humorously.

"What have you been doing to her, Brett? " she demanded, as she and her nephew trudged homeward side by side. "Have you quarrelled? "

"Quarrelled? Certainly not. I've only"—smiling reminiscently—"been giving her a peep into the future. It will be less of a shock when it comes, " he added matter-of-factly.

If he had wished to establish himself in Ann's thoughts he had certainly succeeded. Odd snatches of his conversation kept recurring to her mind—his coolly possessive: *"I don't like losing my belongings, "* followed by that equally significant: *"The future would be mine. "* It was outrageous! Apparently Brett Forrester had never got beyond the primitive idea of the cave-man who captured his chosen mate by force of his good right arm and club, and subsequently kept her in order by an elaboration of the same simple methods.

No question of other people's rights and privileges ever seemed to enter his head. Splendidly unmoral, he had gone through life driving straight ahead for whatever he wanted, without a back thought as to whether it might be right or wrong. That aspect of the matter simply did not enter into his calculations. And because there was still a great deal of the "little boy" in him—that "little boy" who never seems to grow up in some men—women had always found excuses and forgiveness for him, and probably always would.

Even Ann could not feel as offended at his audacity as she would like to have done. There was something disarming in the very fact that he never seemed to expect you to feel offended. And though, on that first afternoon she had been allowed downstairs, he had shaken her nerve somewhat, she was inclined to attribute this to the circumstance that she was still physically a little weak—not quite her usual buoyant self. The impression of sheer dynamic force which he had left with her was very vivid, and might have lingered with her longer, troubling her peace of mind, but for an unexpected happening which served to direct her thoughts into another channel.

It was one afternoon a day or two later, and Ann, was sitting in a sunny corner of the garden, idly dipping into the books which Cara had lent her. The previous day the weather had been cloudy and rather cool, and Maria, the martinet, had sternly vetoed Ann's modest suggestion that she was now sufficiently recovered to go outdoors again.

"My dear life! And take your death of cold 'pon top of bein' near drowned? " Maria had demanded witheringly. "I wish the Almighty had weighed you in a bit more common sense when He set about making you, Miss Ann—and no disrespect intended to Him! "

She flounced away indignantly. But on this balmy summer's afternoon not even the kindly old despot of the Cottage could find any objections to such a mild form of dissipation, and accordingly Ann was basking contentedly in the hot sun, thankful at last to be released from the devoted but somewhat exacting ministrations of Maria.

She felt deliciously lazy—too lazy even to concentrate on any of the novels which Cara had brought her. She had no particular craving at the moment either to be thrilled by adventures or harrowed by the partings of lovers. But a slim volume of verse held her attention intermittently. It was more suited to her idle humour, she reflected. You could read one of the brief lyrics and let the book slide down on to your knee and enjoy the quivering blue and gold, and soft, murmurous, chirruping sounds of the summer's day, while your mind played round the idea embodied in the poem.

She turned the pages idly, skimming desultorily through the verses till she came to a brief two-verse lyric which caught and held her interest. It was a very simple little song, but it appealed to the shining optimism and belief which was a fundamental part of her own nature—to that brave, sturdy confidence which had brought her, still buoyant and unspoiled and sweet, through the vicissitudes of a girlhood that might very easily have cradled an embittered woman.

"Beyond the hill there's a garden,
  Fashioned of sweetest flowers,
Calling to you with its voice of gold,
Telling you all that your heart may hold,
Beyond the hill there's a garden fair—
  My garden of happy hours.

"Dream-flowers grow in that garden,
  Blossom of sun and showers,
There, withered hopes may bloom anew,
Dreams long forgotten shall all come true,
Beyond the hill there's a garden fair—
  My garden of happy hours!"

[Footnote: This song, "Dream-Flowers, " has been set to music by Margaret Pedler. Published by Edward Schuberth & Co., 11 East 22nd Street, New York.]

Ann's thoughts turned towards Eliot Coventry, the man who had told her he was "old enough to have lost all his illusions. " Need one ever be as old as that, she wondered rather wistfully? Surely for each one of us there should be a garden where our dream-flowers grow—dream-flowers which one day we shall pluck and find they have become beautiful realities.

She was reading the verses through for the second time when a shadow seemed to move betwixt her and the sun, darkening the page. She glanced up quickly to find Coventry himself standing beside her.

"I hope I haven't startled you, " he said. "Maria told me you were in the garden and left me to find my own way here. I think"—smiling—"some cakes were in imminent danger of burning if she took her eye off them, so to speak. "

Ann shook hands and hospitably indicated a garden chair.

"Won't you sit down? " she said, though a trifle nervously. "Or are you in a hurry? " It had startled her to find the man of whom she had at that moment been thinking close beside her.

"I'm in no hurry, " he said, sitting down. "I came to inquire how you were getting on. "

A spark lit itself in her eyes.

"I wonder you didn't send your groom instead, " she flashed out quickly. "It would have saved you the trouble. "

Coventry was silent a moment, while a slow flush rose under his sun-tanned skin.

"I think perhaps I deserved that, " he admitted at last. His glance met and held hers. "Will you at any rate try to believe I had a good reason for doing what I did? "

She hesitated.

"But—then why have you come now? What's happened to the 'good reason'? "

"I've scrapped it, " he said tersely. Then, almost as though he were arguing the matter out with himself, he added: "A man can take risks if he likes—if the game's worth the candle. "

"And—is this particular game—worth the candle? "

A sudden smile broke up the gravity of those deep, unhappy eyes of his.

"I can't answer that question—yet. "

Ann was silent. The sense of constraint left her and an odd feeling of contentment took its place. He was no longer cold and distant and aloof—in the mood to dispatch a groom with a message of inquiry! The friend in him was uppermost.

"I think yon deserve a thorough good scolding, " he went on presently. "What possessed you to attempt bathing in a rough sea like that? Seriously"—speaking more earnestly. "It was a most foolhardy thing to do. "

Ann's eyes, goldenly clear in the sunlight, met his frankly.

"I think I went—partly because I was told not to, " she acknowledged, smiling.

His lips twitched in spite of himself.

"Good heavens! What a woman's reason! "

She nodded.

"I suppose it was. But I never dreamed the waves could be as strong as they were. I felt absolutely helpless to stand up against them, and the ground seemed to be slipping away under my feet all the time, dragging me with it—oh, it was horrible! "—with a shiver of recollection. "And I have to thank you—again—for coming to the rescue! " she resumed more lightly after a moment. "I think I must really be destined to end my days in Davy Jones's locker—and you keep frustrating the designs of fate! "

"Well, don't trouble to go out of your way to give me another opportunity, " he advised dryly.

Ann laughed.

"I won't, " she promised. "Especially as it must go against all your principles to have to take so much trouble over a woman. "

He made no answer, and, fearing she had unwittingly wounded him in some way, she hastened to change the conversation. She had instinctively come to know that beneath his brusque exterior he concealed a curious sensitiveness, and, remembering all that Cara had told her of the man's history she regretted her insouciant speech as soon as it was spoken.

"Are you going to the dinner-party on board the *Sphinx*? " she asked, grasping hurriedly at the first topic that presented itself.

A quick ejaculation escaped him.

"I'd clean forgotten all about it, " he replied. "No, I didn't intend going. I must send along a refusal, I suppose. "

"Why? "

"Why? " He looked at her rather blankly. The monosyllabic question, uttered so naturally, seemed to take him aback. "Why? Oh"—with a shrug—"these social gatherings don't appeal to me. I prefer my own company. "

"It's very bad for you, " observed Ann.

"What is? My own company? "

"Yes"—simply.

He was silent a moment. Then he asked abruptly:

"Will you be there—on the yacht, I mean? "

She bent her head, conscious of the sudden flush that came and went quickly in her face.

"Yes. Robin and I are going. "

"In that case"—there was an infinitesimal pause and, although she would not look up, she was sensitively aware of the intentness of his gaze—"in that case, I shall change my mind and go, too. "

"You'll meet plenty of friends there, " replied Ann. "Lady Susan, of course, and the Tempests, and Mrs. Hilyard. "

"Acquaintances only, " he returned shortly.

"Well, at least you'll admit that Mrs. Hilyard is an 'auld acquaintance', " she said, laughing. "And she's so pretty! I do love people who are nice to look at, don't you? "

"Yes. " Just the bare monosyllable, rather grudgingly uttered—nothing more.

"Don't you think she's very beautiful? " asked Ann in some astonishment at the lack of enthusiasm in his tones.

"Yes. But, after all, that's only the outside of the cup and platter. It's the soul inside the shell that matters. "

"Well, I should think Cara has a beautiful soul, too, " replied Ann loyally.

"Probably you know her better than I do, " he said indifferently. Then, as though to change the subject: "What book have you been reading? " He picked it up from her lap, where it lay face downward, open at the lyric which had been occupying her thoughts when he joined her. "Oh, verse? "

"I felt too lazy to begin a novel, " she explained.

His eyes travelled down the brief lines of the little song she had been reading, his face hardening as he read.

"Charmingly optimistic, " he observed ironically, as he closed the book. "I'm afraid, however, that the 'garden of happy hours' is a purely imaginary one for most of us. "

"Of course it's bound to be—if you don't believe in it. You've got to *have* dream-flowers first, or naturally they can't materialise. "

"I suppose all of us have had our dream-flowers at one time or another, " he replied quietly. "And then the frost has come along and scotched them. But I forgot! "—with a short laugh. "You're one of the people who believe that if you think and believe them hard enough, your dreams will come true, aren't you? I remember your flinging that bit of philosophy in my face the first time we met—at the Kursaal. "

"Yes, " she acquiesced. "But if you haven't any, they can't come true, can they? "

"I don't imagine that what we hope or think makes any perceptible difference, " he said shortly.

"That's because you're a cynic! I think it makes *all* the difference. Robin and I are a concrete example of it. We've always wanted to live together—we hung on to the thought in our minds all the time circumstances kept us apart. And now, you see, here we are—doing precisely what we wanted to do. "

"I see that you're a very good advocate, " he replied smiling. And then Robin came out of the house and joined them and the conversation drifted away on to more general lines.

It was late in the afternoon before Coventry finally proposed taking his way homeward—so late that Robin suggested he might as well make it still later and stay to dinner with them. Rather to Ann's surprise he consented, and, in spite of his assertion, earlier on, that he "preferred his own company, " he seemed thoroughly to enjoy the little home-like *dîner à trois*. There was something about the cosy room and the gay, good-humoured chaff and laughter of brother and sister which conveyed a sense of welcome—partaking of that truest kind of hospitality which creates no special atmosphere of ceremony for a guest but encompasses him with a frank, informal friendliness.

Perhaps, as Maria moved briskly in and out, changing the plates and dishes, and not forbearing to smile benignly upon her young master and mistress if she chanced to catch the eye of one or other of them, some swift perception of the pleasant, simple homeliness of it all woke Eliot to comparisons, for just as he was leaving he said with characteristic abruptness:

"Thank you both immensely. To-night's been a great contrast to my usual evenings in that great empty barrack of a dining-room at Heronsmere. "

Unconsciously he spoke out of a great loneliness, and Ann's heart ached for this supremely hurt and bitter soul which sought security from further hurt behind the iron barriers of a self-imposed reserve and solitude.

Presently the sweet summer dusk, fragrant of herb and flower, enfolded them as they stood together at the Cottage gate. A sudden silence had fallen between them. Ann tried to break it, utter some commonplace, but no words would come. At length he held out his hand, and, as hers slid within it, he spoke with a curiously tender gravity.

"Good-bye, " he said. "Don't let the cynics spoil the world for you. I hope you'll find your happy garden—whoever doesn't. "

"I hope every one will, some day, " she answered rather low. Somehow her voice didn't seem very manageable. "Even cynics. "

"I'm afraid I've missed the way there. " Still holding her hand in his, he stared down at her with an odd, tense expression in his eyes. "Ann, do you think I shall ever find it again? "

His voice vibrated to some unlooked-for emotion, and Ann, hearing and dimly sensing the demand it held, was suddenly afraid, shrinking back into the reserves of her young, unconquered womanhood. She tried to withdraw her hand from his clasp.

Then, from somewhere above her bent head, she heard a low laugh, half tender, half amused.

"You shall tell me to-morrow, little Ann, " he said.

She felt his lips against her palm, and a minute later she was standing alone by the gate with the sound of Eliot's receding steps coming faintly to her ears through the scented dusk.

CHAPTER XVII

A SPRIG OF HELIOTROPE

The light of a pale young moon filtered in through the chinks of the blind and crept towards the bed where Ann lay tremulously awake, overwhelmed by the sudden revelation—which had come to her—the revelation of her love for Eliot Coventry.

Too unselfconscious to be much given to introspection, she had never asked herself whither the last few months had been leading her. But now, an hour ago, the touch of Eliot's lips against her hand and the sudden, passionate demand in his voice had torn aside the veil and shown her her own heart.

With a shy, almost childlike sense of wonder, she realised that her love for him was not a thing of new or sudden growth. It had been slumbering deep within her, unrecognised and unacknowledged, ever since that moment when their eyes had first met across the Kursaal terrace at Montricheux. Like a little closed bud it had lain curled in her heart, to open wide when the sun kissed its petals.

And that Eliot loved her in return she had now no doubt. In that brief, poignant moment of understanding, as they stood together in the warm starlit dusk, he had revealed it. She could still feel his lips crushed suddenly against her palm, and hear his shaken voice: "Ann, do you think I shall find the way? "

The way to the garden of happy hours! They would find it together. He had known many bitter hours, and out of them had learned a dogged scepticism—a cynical mistrust of the thing which is called love. And with all the young, uplifting faith that was in her Ann vowed to herself that what one woman had pulled down, destroyed, she would build up and make live again.

She was no longer frightened of love—not even of a love that by the very nature of things might exact far more from her than from most women. She would never be afraid of the big claims which life might make on her. Hitherto, whatever had come her way she had met with a gay courage and confidence, and now that the biggest thing of all had come to her, with its shadow of incalculable demands upon her womanhood, she would go to meet that, too, with the same brave steadfastness.

With the unerring instinct of the mother-woman, she realised how Eliot had fought against his love for her, tried to withstand it, utterly distrustful of her sex, and she smiled with a tenderly amused indulgence as she recalled his sudden withdrawals and brusquenesses. His sending down a groom to inquire how she was—it had hurt her badly at the time to think he cared so little. But now she recognised that it was because he cared so much—so much that he had begun to be afraid. So he had hidden behind his groom!

And with the realisation of how much he cared—*must* care, to have striven so hard to hide and fight it down—she was shaken with a shy, quivering ecstasy, a hesitant sweetness of need and longing that pulsed through every nerve of her. The thought of the morrow almost frightened her. He would come to-morrow—come to tell her all that he had left unsaid, to claim that promise of surrender which a woman both loves and fears to give.

... It was late when at last she slept, and she woke to find the sunlight streaming in through her window, and Maria standing at her bedside, an appetising breakfast-tray in her hands and a world of shrewd suspicion in her twinkling eyes. Last night she had chanced to look out of her kitchen window—which admitted of a slanting glimpse of the Cottage gateway—and had drawn her own deductions accordingly.

"You've had a brave sleep, Miss Ann, " she observed, as she deposited the tray she was carrying on a small table beside the bed. "Mr. Coventry stayed late, I reckon? "

Ann flushed a little, smiling. She did not resent the kindly inquisitiveness which gleamed at her out of Maria's sharp old eyes, but she had no mind to gratify it at the moment.

"Not very late. I think he left by about eleven o'clock, " she answered, with quite a good assumption of indifference. "But I expect being out in the fresh air for the first time for several days made me sleep rather soundly. Why didn't you call me as usual? I'm not an invalid any longer, you know. "

"I thought if so be you'd a mind to sleep on, 'twouldn't do you no harm, " vouchsafed Maria rather grumpily. She was inwardly burning with curiosity, but felt unequal to the task of coping with her young mistress's facility for eluding tentative inquiries, so she stumped downstairs to the kitchen regions, and left her to consume her breakfast in solitude.

Ann hurried through the meal as quickly as possible. She felt tremendously alive to-day, and the breezy sunshiny morning, the blue sky with white fleecy clouds blowing across it, the wheeling swallows, all seemed curiously in accord with her mood. She rose and, dressing quickly, went about her various household duties with a subconscious desire to get them finished and out of the way as soon as possible, and thus be free for whatever the day might bring forth.

That afternoon she and Robin were due at the rectory for tea. It was what Miss Caroline called her "day, " a bi-monthly occasion when she sat in state—and a villainous shade of mauve satin—to receive visitors. During the winter this sacred rite resolved itself chiefly into an opportunity for tea and feminine gossip in a hot, ill-ventilated room, but in the summer it was rather a pleasant little function. Tea was served in the pretty old rectory garden, and the proceedings developed on the lines of an informal garden-party at which most of the neighbours, of both sexes, showed up. For although Miss Caroline was of too inquiring a mind to be very popular, the rector himself was beloved by men and women alike.

The morning hours seemed to Ann interminably long. Insensibly she was keyed up to a delicate pitch of expectancy, her ear nervously alert for the sound of a familiar footstep on the flagged path. And as the leaden moments crawled by, and the warm, sunshiny silence which enfolded the Cottage remained unbroken, a vague sense of apprehension crept into her heart. The glamour of those moments alone with Eliot at the gate, the pulsating sweetness of the thoughts which, in the night, had sent little quivering rivulets of fire racing through her veins, grew dim and uncertain. Had she misunderstood—mistaken him? The bare idea sent a swift stab of fear through her whole being. But in a few moments her faith in the man she loved returned, and with it her serenity. She was ready to laugh at herself. Probably, she reflected, he had merely been detained by some unexpected piece of business which had cropped up necessitating his attention—and, as a matter of fact, this was precisely what had occurred.

So that when at length she and Robin made their way down a shady path and emerged on to the rectory lawn, dotted about with groups of people, and she perceived Coventry's tall, lean figure in the distance, leaning rather moodily against a tree, she reproached herself for having doubted him even for an instant. While she was greeting Miss Caroline and the rector her heart seemed to be singing a little p? an of happiness all to itself.

"... so glad to see you. " Ann came suddenly down to earth, and tried to focus her attention on. Miss Caroline's hospitable gabble. "Such a lot of people here this afternoon, too.... I'm so pleased. And a *beautiful* day, isn't it? Even Mr. Coventry has been tempted out of his shell. He'll be quite a social acquisition to the neighbourhood soon, at this rate. "

She turned to envelop Robin in a similar flood of meaningless prattle, while Ann and Tempest sauntered on together.

"Yes, " said the latter, his eyes resting thoughtfully on Eliot's distant figure. "It's a real joy to me to see Coventry here. He's too much of a hermit. I'm afraid, though, " he admitted with a rueful laugh, "I rather badgered him into coming. And I expect now he is here he's not exactly blessing me for my persistency! Will you go and be very nice to him, Ann"—he had dropped into the friendly usage of her Christian name, and Ann liked it—"and get me out of hot water? "

"I don't suppose you're in it very deeply, " she returned, with some amusement at his air of apprehension.

"Well, I really *made* him come, " confessed the rector apologetically: "I simply wouldn't take 'no'. "

"And you know perfectly well that nobody ever resents what you 'make' them do, " said Ann, smiling. "'The rector have a way with him, ' as Maria remarked the other day. "

Tempest's mouth curved in a responsive smile

"Did she? Nice woman, your Maria Coombe. But I expect the real truth of the matter is that the rector has a particularly kind and long-suffering flock. "

"A good shepherd makes a good flock, I think, " said Ann softly. And for the hundredth time wondered how so human and lovable a man came to possess a sister of Miss Caroline's description.

"Ha! There you are, Coventry! " exclaimed Tempest, as they came abreast of the solitary figure. "I've just been telling Miss Lovell that I fancied you weren't altogether blessing me for having lured you out of your lair to this sort of parish pow-wow. "

"Not at all. It's very good of people like you and Lady Susan to bother about me, seeing that, even when I am dug up, I'm afraid I'm very poor company. "

Eliot smiled rather briefly as he answered, but there was a certain friendly good-humour in his eyes as they rested on the other man's face. As Ann had remarked, no one ever resented the rector's kindly strategy.

"Have either of you seen the greenhouses? " demanded Tempest presently. "No? Oh, you must. We're rather conceited over our show of flowers this year. "

Accordingly they progressed towards the hot-houses, collecting Lady Susan and Cara, and one or two other scattered guests, as they went. Ann felt hemmed in. It began to look rather as though she and Eliot would not get a moment to themselves throughout the afternoon. Then she found him at her side, and something in the quickly amused glance of his eyes, as they swept over the gradually increasing numbers of the party, and then met her own, served to comfort her.

"The world is too much with us, " he murmured.

After that it seemed as though they were companions in distress, linked by a secret, wordless understanding, and Ann walked on with a lighter heart.

Cara was a few paces ahead, flanked by Robin and the local doctor, who were each endeavouring to secure her undivided attention. She was looking very lovely, in an elusive frock of some ephemeral material veiling a delicate prismatic undertone of colour. She always dressed rather wonderfully, every detail perfect. There was a kind of frail, worldly charm about her clothes—the sort of charm you never find in the clothes of a thoroughly good and virtuous woman, as Lady Susan trenchantly observed one day.

Ann herself was acutely conscious of that faintly languorous, mysterious atmosphere of charm with which Mrs. Hilyard seemed to be invested, and she had sometimes wondered how Eliot was able to resist it and treat her with the same cool detachment which he accorded to other people. To her there was something magnetic in Cara's personality. Perhaps her very silence about herself, and the vague background of an unhappy marriage of which Ann was dimly aware, contributed towards it. She glanced up to see Eliot gazing straight ahead, apparently supremely oblivious of that slender, gracious figure in front, moving lightly betwixt Robin and the stooping, rather clever-looking doctor.

Presently they all trooped into the hot-houses—warm and fragrant with the smell of freshly-watered earth, and a rather fierce-looking gardener paused in his work to exhibit this or that particular plant in which he took a special interest. But the pride of the rectory was the orchid-house, and insensibly everybody gravitated towards it.

Ann and Eliot were strolling along a little behind the rest, and she paused a moment to rifle a pot of heliotrope of a spray of clustered blossom.

"Heavenly stuff! " she exclaimed, sniffing it rapturously. "Smell it! " And she held it out just under Eliot's nose, obviously expecting him to share her enthusiasm.

Nothing in the world brings back the past so poignantly as remembered scents—neither sight nor sound. A pictured face, the refrain of a song, may chance to stir the pulse of memory, but a remembered fragrance—intangible, unseen—seems to penetrate to the inmost soul itself, ripping asunder the veil which the years between have woven and refashioning the dead past for us as vividly as though it had never died. Even the very atmosphere of the moment rushes back, and thoughts and feelings we had begun to believe inert and negligible reassert themselves with the old irresistible force with which they swayed us years ago.

As Ann light-heartedly proffered her sprig of heliotrope, Eliot's face whitened beneath its tan, and with a swift, almost violent movement he snatched the spray from her hand and, flinging it on to the ground, set his foot upon it.

She looked up in astonishment, then shrank back with a low exclamation of dismay as she saw his face. It was altered almost out of recognition—the mouth set in a grim straight line of bitterness, the eyes so hard that they looked cruel.

"What is it? " she faltered. "What have I done? "

With an immense effort he seemed to recover himself.

"Nothing, " he returned harshly. "Only reminded me that a man is a double fool who tempts Providence a second time. "

Ann quivered as though he had struck her.

"I—I don't understand, " she said, her voice hardly; more than a mere thread of sound.

He gave a short laugh.

"Don't you? Will you understand if I tell you this—that I'm shut out from the 'happy garden' by the gates of memory, now and always. "

She made no answer. For the moment she was physically unable to reply. But she understood—oh, yes, she understood quite well. He had repented that short, poignantly sweet moment of last night, repudiated all that it implied. He did not trust her—did not believe in her! And he was telling her in just so many words.

The revulsion of feeling left her stunned and dazed. She had been so entirely happy—had already given herself in spirit in response to his unspoken demand, and now with a single roughly uttered phrase he had closed the gates—those unyielding gates of memory—and thrust her outside.

And then her pride came to her aid. He should never know—never guess—how he had hurt her. With the pluck that is born of race, she smiled at him quite naturally.

"Well, you needn't have closed your gates so hard on my wee bit of heliotrope! Look, you've crushed it completely! " She pointed to where it lay, broken and bruised, between them.

He picked it up, and tossed it aside—a poor little corpse of heliotrope.

"I'll get you another piece, " he said shortly.

"No, no! " she checked him, laughing. "We shall have that alarming-looking gardener on our track if we steal any more! Mr. Tempest says he doesn't even allow him to pick his own flowers. Let's join the others, and escape from the wrath to come. "

It was pluckily done, and when they rejoined the rest of the party few would have suspected from her insouciant manner that she and Eliot Coventry had been engaged upon anything more heart-searching than a botanical discussion.

But that night Ann lay wakeful until the pale streamers of dawn fanned out across the sky, while Eliot Coventry, pacing restlessly to and fro in his silent study, gibed at himself with a savage irony because, though he had successfully steeled himself to meet, unmoved, the woman who had violated all his trust in her, a whiff of the sweet, heady scent of heliotrope had flooded his whole being with a resurgent bitterness so deep and so indomitable that it had utterly submerged his dawning faith.

CHAPTER XVIII

A BATTLE OF WILLS

One man sows and another reaps, and sometimes the harvest is a curiously unexpected one for the reaper. Coventry had sown harshness and distrust, and Brett reaped a harvest of kindness and favour in the quarter where he least anticipated it.

Ann, exasperated by his cool impertinence at their last meeting, had merely vouchsafed him the briefest of greetings when they had met at the rectory party, and had consistently avoided him for the remainder of the afternoon. But when, with his usual debonair assurance, he presented himself at Oldstone Cottage the following day, she received him with unwonted graciousness and appeared to have entirely forgotten that he had given her any just cause for offence.

Yesterday she had felt crushed by the magnitude of the blow which had fallen on her, and in her treatment of Forrester she had almost mechanically adopted the detached and chilly attitude prompted by her annoyance with him. But to-day reaction had set in, and, like many another of her sex, she sought to exorcise the pain which one man had inflicted by flirting recklessly with another. It is a method which has its risks, more especially if the second man happens to be dangerously in love, but a woman hurt as Ann had been hurt does not stop to count risks, but only seeks blindly for something—anything—that may serve to distract her thoughts and keep at bay memories of which the smart and sting is too intolerable to be borne.

Forrester was quick to perceive her altered attitude towards him and to take advantage of it, although, with a diplomacy foreign to his usual tactics and perhaps based on Lady Susan's warning counsels, he kept himself well in hand. Vaguely recognising behind the alteration in Ann's manner some impulse of which he could not fathom the source, he merely accepted the fact of the change and set himself to amuse and entertain her—to hold her interest without frightening her.

During the next few days he was with her almost constantly. One day he rowed her over to a distant promontory, when they picnicked together on the brow of the cliffs, afterwards exploring the woods which crowned them. Another time they motored into Ferribridge, where Ann, long denied the sight of a shop window, revelled in the opportunity to spend her pennies and shopped riotously. Yet another time, on the day preceding that fixed for the dinner-party on board the *Sphinx*, they rode together on the downs—Ann mounted on Dick Turpin, Brett on a bad-tempered, unruly mare which Lady Susan had bred and which the grooms at White Windows were terrified to back.

Forrester's horsemanship was superb. He had hands of steel and velvet, and fear was an unknown quantity to him. Ann watched the ensuing tussle between man and beast with unequivocal admiration. The mare, a big raking bay, with black points and a white blaze, sulkily obeyed her rider's curbing hands upon the bridle whilst they rode through the lanes, but when they emerged upon the wide, swelling sweep of the downs, she evidently decided that the moment had come to assert her independence.

She commenced operations by going straight up in the air—so straight that for an instant Ann thought she must surely topple backwards, and wondered with a little breathless thrill of admiration how Brett contrived to keep his seat at all at such an angle. Possibly the mare wondered also, for, coming down once more on all four feet to find the hated incumbrance still astride her back, she reared again, immediately. Ann had a vision of two black hoofs pawing the air indignantly, then, swift as a flash of light, Brett had flung himself forward on the mare's neck and brought his crop down on her head between the pointed ears. She came down to earth with a bang, plunged violently, then, giving an evil twist to her whole body, started bucking with all the wicked energy that was in her.

Brett had a magnificent seat, but twice she nearly had him out of the saddle, and it is certain that if he had not been blest with almost inexhaustible staying power, combined with a pliant strength of muscle, he would have come off second best in the contest of wills, for the mare seemed tireless, and looked as though she could go on bucking—and enjoying the process, too—till the crack of doom. Finding, however, that she could not rid herself of Forrester by the same methods which had proved easily successful with the stable lads at White Windows, she uttered a squeal of rage, laid back her ears, and bolted hell-for-leather across the downs.

This proved altogether too much for Dick Turpin's composure. He was seized with a spirited desire to go and do likewise, and for a moment or two Ann had her hands full. Gradually, however, she steadied his first wild rush to a gallop, then to a canter, and finally, as he eased into a trot, she dared to direct her attention elsewhere and look round to discover what had become of Brett.

She caught her breath with a gasp of dismay. Far ahead she could see the bay mare streaking across the downs, with Brett still square in the saddle, headed straight for the edge of the cliffs. From the way she tore along Ann knew she must be practically out of hand, and, if Brett were unable to turn her, the next few minutes would see horse and rider leap into space, to fall headlong down on to the rocks two hundred feet below.

Instinctively she urged her cob in pursuit, though subconsciously aware of the utter futility of it—of her absolute helplessness to avert disaster. Sick with horror, she could see the mare rocketing wildly towards the brink of the cliff. Almost she thought she could hear the thunderous beat of the maddened hoofs racing the beat of her own heart as it thudded in her ears, feel the wind of that reckless rush towards destruction. Nearer... nearer to the cliff's edge.... Ann's whole body stiffened convulsively in anticipation of the inevitable catastrophe.

Then, just when it seemed as though the end were come, the mare gave a shrill scream of terror and swerved violently in her stride, with a suddenness that sent her staggering to her knees. She slithered along the turf, then, scrambling to her feet, stood stock still, her head thrust forward, snorting with fright.

What followed was so surprising that Ann, about to urge her pony onward, pulled up in astonishment. In some miraculous way Brett had retained his seat in the saddle, and instead of dismounting, as she expected him to do, he lifted his arm and brought his crop hard down on the mare's quarters, so that she leaped forward, and the next moment he was sending her along as fast as she could gallop, while his arm rose and fell like a flail, thrashing her unmercifully. They fled past Ann at racing speed, and she watched, dumb with amazement, while Brett steered a huge semicircular course on the downs, keeping the animal he rode at full stretch the whole time. When at last they came back and pulled up, the mare's breath was sobbing in her throat, while Brett himself, hatless and deadly pale beneath his crop of ruddy hair, was almost reeling in the saddle.

Rather stiffly he dismounted and, slipping the reins loosely over his arm, walked towards Ann, the mare following him meekly, like a beaten child. He looked fagged out, but his blue eyes still gleamed with their old indomitable fire.

"Brett! How could you? " exclaimed Ann breathlessly, as they approached.

"How could I—what? "

"Gallop the mare like that, just after she'd run away? She might have bolted with you again. "

He threw back his head and laughed.

"Not likely! She'll never try those tricks with me again. Will you, old lady? "—and he rubbed the black velvet muzzle at his side with a kindly hand. To Ann's astonishment, the mare, dripping with the sweat of sheer exhaustion, her coat striped with the hiding Brett had given her, pushed her head forward, nuzzling his sleeve.

"She bolted the first time for her own amusement, " he continued. "The second gallop was for mine"—grimly. "Don't you see, she'd have bolted again whenever the fit took her if I hadn't punished her. The only cure was to make her gallop till she was dead beat. She knows which of us is master now. And she doesn't bear me any grudge, either. Do you, old thing? " And he patted the mare's streaming neck.

"I wonder she doesn't, " said Ann. "Wasn't it—rather brutal of you? "

"Not a bit. Merely necessary. And neither people nor animals bear a grudge when once they are mastered, fair and square. " His eyes, with a gay, dare-devil challenge in them, flashed up and met hers. "You'll find that out some day, " he added.

"I hope not, " replied Ann stiffly. Then, remembering how near death he had been, she softened. "Anyway, I'm thankful you're alive. I don't know how you managed to pull the mare round as you did. "

"*I* pull her round? My dear girl, if it had rested with me, we should both be lying in smithereens at the present moment, on the rocks below. She realised the drop just in the nick of time, and wheeled before we got to it. "

"What do you mean—she realised it? How could she? "

For a moment Brett's eyes held a curious gravity.

"I can't tell you, " he said at last, simply. "Only I know horses have a kind of instinct which very often warns them of danger. I've seen a similar thing happen once before, in the hunting field. A man was riding straight for a high bank that looked just like an ordinary on and off jump. You couldn't see what lay beyond it, and on the further side there was a forty-foot drop into a quarry. His horse had its forefeet actually on the bank—and then it must have sensed the danger, for it swung right round, just as the mare did to-day. "

As he finished speaking, he gathered up the reins and remounted.

"We'd better be jogging homeward, I think, " he said. "The mare's too hot to stand about. I don't want her to catch cold. "

They rode slowly over the springy turf, the bay mare beaten but not cowed, responding docilely to every touch of Brett's hands on the bridle. She had learned her lesson, recognised the man who rode her as her master.

Ann was very quiet, her thoughts preoccupied with the happenings of the afternoon. In some sort, they shed a fresh light on the character of the man beside her. It was impossible not to admire his cool composure in the face of danger, and his unexpected kindliness to the mare, once he had asserted his supremacy over her, and her responsiveness to his caress, had astonished Ann considerably. She had thought Brett purely brutal when she had watched him force the frightened, flagging horse anew into a gallop, but no man could be all brute to whom an animal would turn with such mute confidence as the mare had shown when the struggle between them was over.

Behind Brett's careless courage, Ann recognised an insistent force and dominance that frightened her. If he could be so invincibly determined to subdue the will of a horse, how would it fare with any woman whom he had made up his mind to conquer? Would his persistency at last beat down her opposition? Or, if the woman's will were strong enough to resist him, would the fight between them go on—endlessly? Somehow she could not imagine Forrester laying down his weapons to admit defeat.

They were now approaching the big headland flanking Silverquay harbour, and, as the waters of the bay came into view, Ann's eyes went instinctively to the *Sphinx,* where she rode at anchor, specklessly clean and shining in the brilliant sunlight. She had often admired the yacht, with her long, graceful lines that promised speed, and on occasion, when she had steamed out of the bay, Ann missed her from her accustomed anchorage—feeling rather as though a bit of the landscape had vanished, leaving a gap. But now, for the first time, she was conscious of a disagreeable impression at the sight of the yacht gleaming there in the sun. It seemed as though it were there on guard, watching... waiting... motionless and silent, like a sleek cat watching at the mouth of a mousehole. Interminably patient. She glanced at Forrester, riding quietly at her side, and recalled his battle with the bay mare. He and the yacht—his yacht. Both so quiet, and both with such an infinite latent capacity for swift, directed action.

She shivered a little, and was aware of an inward sensation of relief when the horses at last pulled up at the gate of the Cottage and Billy Brewster flew out from the stables to take charge of the pony. The sight of the boy's rubicund, commonplace face gave her a feeling of reassurance, seeming to restore the normal, everyday atmosphere which the uncomfortable train of thought evoked by the *Sphinx* had momentarily dissipated.

"Well, I suppose I shan't see you to-morrow—until the evening? " Brett, standing by her side, the mare's bridle over his arm, was regarding her with an oddly mocking expression in his eyes. She almost felt as though he had been reading her thoughts. "I shall be going backwards and forwards to the yacht, to see that everything is shipshape for my party to-morrow night. "

"Don't forget to hang up a full moon in the sky, by way of decoration, " suggested Ann, trying to speak lightly.

"The matter shall receive attention, " he replied gravely. "Aunt Susan and I shall go aboard early, of course, but the dinghy will be waiting for you all at the jetty at half-past seven. " He shook hands, sprang into the saddle, and a minute later his horse's hoofs clattered away into the distance.

Ann turned and walked slowly up the path into the house. She wondered whether—now—Eliot Coventry would be at the dinner on board the yacht. She had not seen him since the day of the rectory garden-party, and she could think no other than that he had deliberately kept out of her way.

CHAPTER XIX

ACCOUNT RENDERED

Dinner was over on board the *Sphinx*, and the whole party were gathered on deck for coffee. It had been a very perfect little dinner. Forrester was a confirmed diner-out in London, and no one knew better than he how to arrange a menu. Lady Susan played hostess charmingly, and under her benign influence the various unsympathetic elements included in the party had fused together more pleasantly than might have been anticipated.

Coventry had duly arrived, and although, as luck would have it, he found himself seated next to Mrs. Halyard, the fact that no one but the two people most intimately concerned were aware of any particular reason why they should not sit together enabled them to carry off the situation without visible effort. It had been a matter of more difficulty to merge Miss Caroline's personality into the prevailing atmosphere, but every one helped. They were all used to the fact that if they wanted to enjoy the rector's company they must be prepared to put up with his sister's, since the canons of a country neighbourhood forbade inviting the one without the other, and on this particular evening Forrester had chaffed her into such good humour that she became quite skittish, and contributed some truly surprising outbursts of frivolity to the general conversation.

"Rejuvenation while you wait, " Robin had murmured to Cara, under cover of the buzz of talk.

Mrs. Hilyard had laughed that low, pretty laugh of hers which was always free from the least suspicion of "cattiness. " "I defy any one to maintain a grown-up attitude when Brett decides that they shan't, " she made answer.

Thanks to the arrangement of their respective seats at the table, Ann had been able to avoid holding any conversation with Eliot without provoking comment. She had dreaded meeting him again, feeling that it would be difficult to re-establish the merely friendly relations which had existed between them until one tense, glowing moment had swept aside convention and pretence and let each see deep into the other's heart.

But the meeting passed off more easily than she had dared to hope. They exchanged brief greetings on the quay, where Brett Forrester's guests had collected together and were waiting to board the yacht's dinghy, and during the short passage across the bay to where the *Sphinx* lay anchored she and Cara and Miss Caroline had sat chatting together in the stern of the boat, leaving the three men to talk amongst themselves. And now, as the whole party emerged on to the deck for coffee, Ann found herself safely wedged in between Brett and the rector, with Coventry, much to her relief, established at the other end of the semicircle of chairs.

It was a glorious evening. The moon—"according to, orders, " as Brett had laughingly reminded her—hung like a great lambent globe in the sky, throwing a shimmering track of silver across the waters of the bay, and dappling the ripples of the sea beyond with shifting Jack-o'-Lantern gleams of light. The deck of the *Sphinx* shone with an almost dazzling whiteness, accentuated by the black patches of sharp shadow flung across it.

Ann sat quietly enjoying the peaceful beauty of it all, oblivious to the hum of conversation around her. For the time being she lost that sense of fear and dread of the yacht which had so curiously obsessed her yesterday. Now it seemed but a component part of the beautiful scene—to shoreward, a ragged string of cottage lights climbing the hill-side, speaking of hearth and home and of rest after the day's labour, and beyond, the still, calm moon and tranquil bay, and the yacht, with its whiteness and sharp-cut shadows, lying motionless like some legendary vessel carved in alabaster.

"What's your opinion, Ann? "

The question startled her, severing the dreaming thread of her thoughts. She roused herself with a smile.

"My opinion about what? I'm afraid I didn't hear what was being said. "

"About pains and penalties, " explained Cara,

"They sound unpleasant. "

"They are—very, " agreed Lady Susan with her jolly laugh. "The question under discussion is whether we all eventually have to pay up for our misdeeds—even in this world. "

"I think we do—in some form or another, " said Tempest quietly. "Only perhaps we don't always recognise the penalty, *as* a penalty, when it comes. "

"Then it seems rather a waste, doesn't it? " suggested Brett idly.

The rector's quiet eyes rested on the speaker.

"I don't think so. If we recognised it as a punishment, we should probably resent it so much that it wouldn't do us any good—just as spanking doesn't really do a child any good but only rouses its naughty temper. Whereas when it comes unrecognised, even though it may be the outcome of our own mistaken actions, it educates and changes us—does, in fact, just what punishment is really designed to do, acts as a remedial force. I think God often works like that. "

"Only, sometimes, the sinner isn't the only one who pays, " threw in Coventry shortly.

"He's the only one who doesn't pay, generally speaking, " answered Brett, with a grin. "He flourishes like a green bay tree instead. I never dream of paying for my sins, " he added cheerfully.

Tempest smiled—that tolerant, good-humoured smile of his which always took the sting out of anything he might say.

"You're not at the end of life yet, Mr. Forrester, " he observed quietly.

Brett laughed.

"Are you threatening me with an 'account rendered' of all my evil deeds—to he paid for in a sort of lump sum? "

"Even that might be preferable to having your punishment spread out all over your life, " said Cara, with a faint note of weariness in her voice which passed unnoticed by all except Coventry, who threw her a quick, searching glance.

"Like thinly spread butter? " suggested Brett blithely.

"Cara didn't say anything about it being thinly spread, " retorted Ann, laughing. "I should think yours might be rather thick. "

Amid the general laughter and chaff which followed the original topic of conversation was lost sight of, and presently some one suggested a game of auction. Miss Caroline's blue bead eyes gleamed at the very sound of the word. She loved a game of bridge, but for parochial reasons adhered firmly to stakes of not more than a penny a hundred. Tempest had vainly argued with her that she might equally as well play for a more usual amount, such as sixpence or a shilling, and this without outraging the susceptibilities of the parish—that if she played for money at all the principle involved was precisely the same, but she either could not or would not comprehend. Bridge at a penny a hundred was apparently an innocent occupation—at anything higher, an awful example.

"Then we'll play for a penny a hundred, " declared Lady Susan good-humouredly, when Miss Caroline had explained her scruples. "Who'll play? You will, Mr. Tempest? And you, Robin? That'll make one table. What about you others? "

"I don't play bridge, " said Brett mendaciously, adding *sotto voce* to Lady Susan: "A least, I can't afford to play for a penny a hundred, beloved aunt. " Then aloud: "Besides, Ann wants to see all over the boat, so I'm going to trot her round. "

Ann laughed in spite of herself, never having expressed any such desire as was thus coolly attributed to her. But she submitted good-naturedly enough to being carried off by Brett on a tour of inspection, whilst Lady Susan and the rector, accompanied by Robin and Miss Caroline, went below to play bridge, leaving Mrs. Hilyard and Coventry alone together on deck.

A silence fell between them. Throughout the whole time which had elapsed since they had both come to live at Silverquay they had never before been actually alone. By tacit consent they had mutually avoided such a happening, and now, without any possibility of escape, it seemed to Cara that they were suddenly enfolded in a solitude which shut out the rest of the world entirely.

She twisted her fingers nervously together, vibrantly conscious of Coventry's tall, silent figure beside her, and her breath struggled a little in her throat at the memory of all that had once linked their lives together, of which there remained now only an abiding bitterness and contempt.

The silence seemed to close round her like a pall, suffocating her. She felt she could not endure it a minute longer.

"I hardly expected to see you here to-night, " she said at last, the usual sweetness of her voice roughened by reason of the effort it cost her to speak at all.

"No. Dinner-parties aren't quite in my line, " returned Eliot dryly. "But, having been fool enough to say I'd come, I keep my word. "

He glanced towards her as he spoke, and she flushed faintly beneath his scrutiny. The latter part of the speech pricked her like an arrow sped from the past, though it was difficult to estimate from the man's impassive face whether or no he had actually intended to imply a deeper significance than the surface meaning which the words conveyed. Cara felt that she must know—at any cost she must know.

"Is that meant as a—protest? " she asked, assuming an air of playful indifference which she was very far from feeling. "Am I intended to take it as a rebuke? "

Perhaps the light detachment of her manner jangled some long-silent chord, roused an echo from the past, for his face darkened.

"You can take it so, if you wish, " he said curtly.

She was silent. In that brief question and answer she had covertly appealed for mercy and had received judgment—the same judgment which had been pronounced against her years ago. She had never thought it possible that Eliot would learn to care for her again. She knew the man too well to believe that he would have any love left to give the woman who had despoiled him of all a man values—broken his faith, destroyed the ideals that had once been his. Moreover, she had seen clear down into his soul that day at Berrier Cove, when Ann had come within an ace of death, and she knew that on the ruins of the old love a new love was building.

But, deep within her, she had hoped that Eliot's savage bitterness towards her might have softened with the passage of time—that perhaps he had learned to tincture his contempt for her with a little understanding and compassion, allowing something in excuse for youth and for the long, grinding years of poverty which had ground the courage out of her and driven her into making that one ghastly mistake for which life had exacted such a heavy penalty. She knew now that she had hoped in vain. He was as merciless as he had been that day, ten years ago, when he had turned away and left her alone in an old Italian garden, with the happy sunlight and the scent of flowers mocking the half-realised despair at her heart.

"Then you haven't ever—forgiven me? " she said at last, haltingly.

He stared at her.

"Isn't that rather a curious question to ask? You killed everything in life that mattered—damned my chances of happiness once and for always.... No, I don't think I've forgiven you. I've endeavoured to forget you. " He paused, then added with a brief, ironic laugh: "It was a queer joke for fate to play—bringing us both to the same neighbourhood. "

"I didn't know, " said Cara hastily. "You know that, don't you? I had no idea you lived here when I bought the Priory. Even when I heard—afterwards—that a Mr. Coventry owned Heronsmere, I never dreamed it could be you. You see, I was told he was very wealthy—"

"And the Coventry you knew was—poor! "

It was like the thrust of a rapier, and Cara winced under the concentrated scorn of the bitter speech.

"You are very merciless, " she said, her voice shaken and uneven.

"Then leave it at that, " he rejoined indifferently. "I've no particular grounds for being anything else. The past is dead—and it won't stand resurrection. "

"Does the past ever die? " she demanded, a note of despair in her voice. "I think not. "

He looked at her curiously—at the beautiful face, a trifle worn and shadowed, with its sad eyes and that strangely patient curve of mouth.

"What do you mean? " he asked sharply.

"One pays, Eliot. "

He shrugged his shoulders.

"Oh, yes, one pays. But, in this particular instance, I thought it was I who paid and you who took delivery of the goods. "

She sprang up.

"Then you were wrong! " she exclaimed in low, passionate tones that, in spite of himself, moved him strangely. "If you paid, I paid, too—every day of my life. Oh, I had my punishment"—with a little laugh that held more anguish than any tears. "Full measure, pressed down, running over. "

He bent his sombre gaze on her.

"I don't think I understand, " he said slowly.

"Don't you? " With a swift movement she thrust back the loose tulle sleeve which veiled her arm, uncovering the ugly, rust-coloured scar which marred its whiteness.

"That—that—? " He stammered off into a shocked silence, his eyes fastened on the scar, so unmistakably that of a burn.

"That is the symbol of my married life, " she said with a curious enforced calm. She let her sleeve fall back into its place. "Did you never hear? Dene drank—it was no secret. He was quite mad at times. "

"And he—ill-treated you? "

"When it amused him. He had a passion for cruelty. I never knew it till I married him. I found out afterwards he had been the same even as a child. He loved torturing things. " She paused, then added with a simplicity that was infinitely pitiful: "So you see, I had my punishment."

"I was abroad. I never knew," said Eliot, as though in extenuation of something of which he inwardly accused himself. "I never knew," he repeated resentfully. "By God!"—with a sudden suppressed violence which was the more intense by reason of its enforced restraint—"if I'd known, I'd have freed the woman I once loved from degradation such as that!"

Used so unconsciously, without intent, the word "once" wounded her more cruelly than any of his deliberately harsh and bitter utterances had had power to do. It set her definitely outside his life, relegated her to a past that was dead and done with—made her realise more completely than anything else could have done that, as far as Eliot was concerned, she no longer counted in his scheme of existence.

"The woman I once loved"—Cara clenched her hands, and bit back the cry of pain which fought for utterance. For an instant she felt sick with pain—as though some one had turned a knife in a raw wound. Then, with an effort, she regained her self-control.

"Thank you," she said gently. "But no one could have helped me—least of all you, even had you been in England."

They fell silent for a while. Eliot stood staring out across the moon-flecked waters, and in the silver radiance which made the night almost as light as day Cara could see the harsh lines which the years had graved upon his, face, the grim closing of the lips, and the weariness that lay in his eyes. Half timidly she laid her hand on his arm.

"I wish I could give you back your happiness," she said unevenly.

He turned and looked at her, and now there was neither pity nor compassion in his gaze—only that hardness of granite with which she was all too familiar.

"Unfortunately, that's out of your power," he said coldly. "You only had power to wreck it."

He glanced down distastefully at the hand on his sleeve, and she withdrew it hastily. But, with a sudden strength of purpose, born of her infinite longing to repair the harm she had done, she persisted, daring his anger.

"There's Ann, " she said simply.

She was surprised it hurt so little to put it into words—the fact that he loved another woman. But, since the day she had first realised that he cared for Ann, she had been schooling herself to a certain stoical resignation. She recognised that she had forfeited her own claim to love when she had married Dene Hilyard because he had more of this world's goods than the man to whom she had given her heart, and she felt no actual jealousy of Ann—only a wistful envy of the girl for whom the love of Eliot Coventry might yet create the heaven on earth which she herself had thrown away.

"There's Ann, " she said.

For an instant Eliot's face seemed convulsed, twisted into a grim mask of agony.

"Yes, " he said hoarsely. "There's Ann. And because of you, I can't believe in her. "

It was like an accusation flung straight in her face. She shrank back as though he had struck her. So he cared for Ann—like that.... And because of what she had done, because of her sin of ten years ago, he would not trust her—would not trust any woman.

"You make my 'account rendered' a very heavy one, " she said unsteadily. Then, on a note of increasing urgency: "Don't judge Ann—by me, Eliot. She's different... the kind of woman God meant women to be. If you care for her, you won't make her pay—for what I did. "

His expression altered slightly. A new look came into his eyes—of uncertainty, as though he were regarding things from some fresh angle. But he made no answer, and before Cara could speak again Robin's cheerful voice broke in upon them.

"We've just finished our rubber, " he called, as he came towards them. "Will you folks come and take a hand? "

Then, as neither of them made any immediate response, he paused uncertainly and glanced in, an embarrassed way from one to the other, vaguely conscious that his appearance on the scene had been inopportune. Womanlike, Cara was the first to recover her self-possession.

"Yes, of course we'll come, " she said quickly. "But I haven't played cards for so long that I'm sure whoever is unlucky enough to draw me for a partner will be thankful Miss Caroline has limited the stakes to a penny a hundred. "

The ease with which she spoke sufficed to reassure Robin completely.

"You'll play, Coventry? " he said, as they all three turned and walked towards the companion-way.

"I'll cut in—and take my chance, " answered Eliot.

Cara glanced at him swiftly. His mouth wore a grave little smile, as though the words bore for him a second and deeper meaning than the obvious one of their reply to Robin's question.

CHAPTER XX

REFUSAL

The process of making a tour of the *Sphinx* had been a lengthy one. The yacht was beautifully appointed, and there had been much to examine and admire. Brett, who loved every inch of her, from the marvellous little gold figure of a sphinx, which he had had specially designed and carved as a mascot, down to the polished knobs and buttons in the engine-room, had expatiated with considerable length and fervour upon her various beauties and advantages, and by the time he and Ann emerged on to the deck once more it was to find it deserted by the rest of the party.

Brett moved a couple of deck-chairs into a sheltered corner.

"You must be tired, " he said remorsefully. "I've kept you standing about an unconscionable time while I yarned on about my old tub. If you'll sit down here, I'll go and fetch you a wrap. "

Ann subsided into one of the chairs not unthankfully.

"But I don't want a wrap, " she protested.

"You will, presently. You must remember it's September, even though it is a warm evening. "

He departed on his errand, returning shortly with a wrap for her shoulders, together with a light rug which he proceeded to tuck carefully round her. She was reminded of the first occasion on which they had met, when the charming way in which he had waited upon Lady Susan had moved her to the reflection that he might be rather an adept in the art of spoiling any woman. But she had not forgotten that he would want to master her first—as he had mastered the bay mare, afterwards coaxing her into friendship.

They conversed desultorily for a time. Then, tossing away the cigarette he was smoking, Brett shot an abrupt question at her.

"Well, so you like the yacht? " he demanded.

She nodded.

"I think it's just perfect, " she answered cordially.

"I'm glad. Because"—he leaned forward and looked at her intently with a curious sparkling light in his eyes—"I hope you'll spend a good deal of time on board her. "

"I? " Ann endeavoured to speak as casually as possible, warned by that sudden danger-signal.

"Yes. Wouldn't you enjoy cruising about the world a bit? "

"Are you thinking of inviting us all to go for a trip in the *Sphinx*? I'm afraid, " shaking her head, "we're most of us much too busy people to go racing off half across the world at a moment's notice. "

"I wasn't thinking of inviting you all, " he returned coolly. "Even if the yacht could accommodate you. I was limiting the proposed yachting party to you—and me. "

Ann moved restlessly.

"Don't be absurd, Brett. "

He laughed—that gay, triumphant laughter of his which always made her a little afraid. It sounded so sure, so carelessly confident.

"Then don't fence with me any longer, " he retorted. "What's the use of pretending, anyway? "

"Pretending? I'm afraid I don't understand. " She threw a quick, dismayed glance down the length of the deck, devoutly wishing that some one would come along and interrupt them. But there was nobody in sight except one of the crew—and he was keeping his eyes very studiously turned away from the corner where they were seated.

"You don't understand? " Brett's voice roughened a little. "Haven't I made it clear what I want? I want *you*—"

"No, no! " Ann jumped up from her chair precipitately. "Don't say it, Brett! Please don't. I—I don't want to hear. "

There was a note of urgent pleading in her hurried speech, but if he heard it he paid no attention. He was on his feet as quickly as she was. Perhaps if she had looked at him she would have realised that she was drawing upon, herself the very thing she was trying to avoid. But she had averted her face, afraid of the blue flame of his eyes, and his quick movement, silent and certain as the leap of a panther, filled her with a sudden irrational terror. She started to run. Then, her feet entangled in the rug which had slipped to the floor when she sprang up from her seat, she stumbled and pitched helplessly forward.

But she did not reach the ground. Brett's arms closed round her like a vice of steel, and the next moment she felt his lips on hers—on her eyes, her throat, the gleaming curve of moon-white shoulder, straining against them in fierce, possessive kisses that seemed to drain her of all strength to resist.

At last:

"Now do you understand? " he demanded hoarsely. "I love you!... God in heaven! I wonder if you know how much I love you! "

"No, no! " She struggled to free herself from his arms, but he held her in a relentless grip that no power of hers could fight against.

"Let me go! " she gasped, finding herself helpless against him.

His eyes burned down on her.

"I'll let you go when you promise to be my wife—not before. Say you love me, Ann! "

"But I don't—I don't love you at all. Let me go, Brett! " She made another futile effort to release herself, but his grasp never slackened.

"You *shall* love me! " he declared violently.

With the imperative need of the moment Ann found her courage returning. She realised now that it was to be a battle between them, and she was filled with a cold fury against this man who tried to enforce his will on hers. Suddenly she ceased to struggle, and, bending her head back so that she could see his face, confronted him with a cool, proud defiance.

"I shall hate you if you don't release me at once, " she said quietly.

Her face, so close below his own, was milk-white in the moonlight, and her hair glimmered with strange, lurking lights. Wavering gold of hair and eyes and scarlet line of lips—they roused the devil in him. His mouth crushed down on hers once more.

"You may hate me—but, all the same, you'll marry me! I swear it! " he said with grim assurance.

"I wouldn't marry you if you were the last man on earth. "

It was very quietly uttered, but the absolute conviction of her answer seemed to arrest him. He loosened his clasp of her body, but with the—same movement his fingers slid to her wrist, prisoning it.

"Who would you marry? " he demanded.

She stood perfectly still, unresisting to the grip of his hand on her wrist. There was a mute suggestion of scorn in this very surrender to physical coercion, a poise that asserted an utter freedom of spirit—a freedom of which he could not rob her.

"You don't expect an answer to that question, do you? " she returned.

"Is it young Brabazon—Tony Brabazon? " he pursued, ignoring her reply and speaking with an odd kind of eagerness.

Ann was silent. The instinct of her sex was working in her—the instinct to conceal her real hurt, to throw dust in the eyes of the man who was seeking to tear her secret from her. So she remained silent, and the sudden gleam in Brett's eyes showed that he believed he was answered.

"Then you have thought of marrying—Tony Brabazon? " he said searchingly.

"Perhaps I have, " she admitted, reflecting with a brief flash of humour that, in this particular instance, the simple truth was quite the most misleading thing imaginable.

Brett regarded her with a peculiar expression in which resentment and a certain need of indulgence were strangely mingled.

"And you've thought better of it? " he continued, rather as though he were stating a fact of which he had some intrinsic knowledge. Ann felt a trifle puzzled. He and Tony were only card-room acquaintances, and it seemed unlikely that the latter would have confided in him. Yet Brett certainly spoke as though his cognisance of how matters stood betwixt herself and Tony were based on something more substantial than mere guesswork.

"That, also, is possible, " she answered non-committally.

"And just as well, " commented Brett. "He's a harum-scarum rake of a boy. All the same, as I told you once before, the past doesn't matter to me. It's the future that counts. "

He paused, as though he expected her to volunteer some reply. But she merely eyed him with a look of steady indifference.

"You understand, Ann? " he said, with a species of urgency in his tones.

"It sounds quite simple, " she replied shortly. "I think I understand plain English—though what you say doesn't interest me. Do you mind releasing my wrist, now? "

"You won't run away if I do? "

She shrugged her shoulders.

"Where could I run to—on the yacht? Besides, I've no wish for every one to know about this ridiculous scene, " she added scornfully, with a downward glance at her prisoned wrist.

His eyes glinted as he released his hold, but he allowed the contemptuous speech to pass without remark. She lifted her arm, frictioning her wrist where his grip had scored a red mark round it. A tumult of anger against him seethed inside her. Her lips felt soiled and she put up her hand and rubbed them distastefully. He interpreted the action with lightning swiftness.

"No, " he said, a note of grim triumph in his voice. "You can't undo it. "

"I wish, " she said with quiet intensity, "I wish I'd never set foot on board your yacht. "

"It wouldn't have made a bit of difference, " he assured her unconcernedly. "If it hadn't happened here, it would have happened somewhere else. Just as it doesn't matter in the least your refusing me—by the way, I suppose I'm to understand you *have* refused me? "—mockingly.

"Certainly I've refused you. "

"Very good. But even that won't make an atom of difference. You're going to marry me, you know, in the long run. "

"I'm not—" she began, then checked herself wearily. "Oh, don't let's go over it all again! " She was very pale, and there were dark shadows of fatigue beneath her eyes.

"We won't, " he replied amicably. "We'll go down and see how those reckless penny-a-hundred gamblers are getting on, instead. "

With one of the amazingly sudden transitions of which Ann had already discovered he was capable, he dismissed the whole matter as though it were of no importance, and, gathering up her wraps, preceded her in the direction of the companion-way. Here they were met by the bridge players. Their game finished, they were all coming up on deck, laughing and talking as they came. Ann drew back, nervously unprepared for the sudden encounter, but Brett covered her momentary confusion by genial inquiries as to who had won.

"I've won two and fivepence, " announced Miss Caroline in satisfied tones. She appeared supremely contented with the evening's harvest.

"These tiresome people are talking of going, Brett, " complained Lady Susan. "Do stop them. "

"Of course I'll stop them, " he replied promptly. "They've all got to drink my health and good luck to the *Sphinx* before they go. It's her birthday, to-day, by the way, " he went on, addressing everybody collectively, "and I insist upon the occasion being properly honoured. "

He continued pouring out a stream of light-hearted nonsense, focussing every one's attention on himself, and thus giving Ann time to recover her poise. When, finally, she joined in the general conversation, she was quite composed once more, although she still looked somewhat pale and tired.

The scene with Brett had exhausted her more than she knew. The man's sheer vitality and force were overwhelming, and his efforts to impose his will on hers, to force from her some response to the flaming ardour of his passion, had left her feeling mentally and spiritually sore and bruised, just as, physically, she had ached all over after the buffeting she had received from the waves at Berrier Cove. She longed inexpressibly for the peace and quiet of her own room, and she felt thankful when at length the moment for departure actually arrived.

Lady Susan glanced keenly at her once or twice as they were rowed across the bay to the now deserted quay, but she refrained from making any comment on the girl's appearance of fatigue. It was only as they were walking up the tarred planking of the jetty together, somewhat behind the rest of the party, that she asked with a queer mixtures of tenderness and humour:

"May I guess, Ann? "

"There's—nothing—to guess, " said Ann bluntly.

Lady Susan came to a standstill and stood looking down at her with eyes that laughed.

"So you've turned him down? " she queried.

Ann nodded silently.

"Well"—incisively—"it will do him a whole heap of good. He's much too inclined to think the entire world is his for the taking. "

Involuntarily Ann laughed outright at the palpable truth of the statement, and with that spontaneous laughter was borne away much of the hurt pride and resentment which had been galling her.

It was, after all, absurd to take an irresponsible being like Brett Forrester too seriously.

"I don't altogether envy Brett's wife, " pursued Lady Susan judicially. "Still, she'd never find life monotonous, whatever else. He'd probably beat her and drag her round by the hair when he was in a rage. But he'd know how to play the lover, my dear—don't make any mistake about that! "

"I may be old-fashioned, " said Ann demurely. "But I don't think I feel particularly attracted by the prospect of being beaten and dragged around by the hair. "

Lady Susan's dark eyes twinkled.

"All the same, I don't fancy Brett will allow a little prejudice like that to stand in his way. If I know my nephew—and I think I do—he won't meekly accept his *congé* and run away and play like a good little boy. "

"Oh, I think he quite understands, " replied Ann a trifle breathlessly.

Lady Susan shook her head.

"My dear, " she said, "Brett is delightful, and I'm ridiculously fond of him. But I'm bound to admit that he hasn't any principles whatever. And he never understands anything he doesn't want to. "

CHAPTER XXI

THE RETURN

The October sunshine slanted across Berrier Cove, flinging a broad ribbon of light athwart the water and over the wet, shining sands left bare by the outgoing tide. Its furthermost point reached almost to Ann's feet, where she sat in a crook of the rocks, resting after a five-mile tramp along the shore before she tackled the steep climb up to the Cottage.

The sea was wonderfully calm to-day—placid and tranquil as some inland lake, and edged with baby wavelets which came creeping tentatively upward to curl over on the sand like a fringe of downy feathers. Ann could not help vividly recalling the day when she had so nearly lost her life at that very spot. It seemed incredible that this quiet sea, with its gentle, crooning voice no louder than a rhythmic whisper, could be one and the same with the turbulent, thunderous monster which had almost beaten the breath out of her body.

And then her thoughts turned involuntarily to Brett Forrester. He was not unlike the sea, she reflected, in his sudden, unexpected changes of mood—with the buoyant charm he could exert when he chose, and that contrasting turbulence of his which left whoever ventured to oppose him feeling altogether breathless and battered.

Latterly, Ann had been finding it very difficult to understand him. Since the night of the dinner on board the *Sphinx* he had studiously refrained from the slightest attempt to make love to her. Sometimes, indeed, she was almost tempted to ask herself if that violent scene on the yacht could really have occurred between them or whether she had only dreamt it. It seemed so entirely incompatible with the easy attitude of friendliness which he had adopted towards her ever since. She would have liked to interpret this as signifying that he had accepted her refusal as final, but some inward prompting warned her that Brett was not the man to be so easily turned aside from his purpose. Meanwhile, however, it was a relief to be free from the subtle sense of importunity, of imperious demand, of which, when he chose, he could make her so acutely conscious.

Thinking over all that had passed between them on the yacht, she wondered curiously why he had so persistently referred to Tony. It seemed almost as though he were jealous of the boy—regarded him as some one who might prove an obstacle to the accomplishment of his own desires. Yet she could not recall anything which might have given him that impression. There had been nothing in the least loverlike in Tony's attitude towards her during his visit to the Cottage.

On the contrary, she had been inwardly congratulating herself upon the fact that he had evidently determined to abide by the answer she had given him that night in Switzerland, as they came down from the Roche d'Or—although she would not have been the true woman she was if she had not secretly wondered a little at the apparent ease with which he had adapted himself to the altered relations between them! Pride had counted for a good deal. That she guessed. But, since Tony's departure, she had begun to speculate whether there might not perhaps be some other reason which would better account for his submitting without further protest to her decision. And in a brief sentence, contained in a letter she had received from him only that morning, she thought she had discovered the key to the mystery.

> *"Uncle Philip and I depart to Mentone next week, "* he had written. *"Naturally, he hates the idea of my being anywhere in the vicinity of Monte Carlo, but as he doesn't seem able to throw off the effects of a chill he caught out shooting, our local saw-bones—in whom, he has the most touching faith—has decreed Mentone. So Mentone it is. Lady Doreen Neville and her mother will also be there, at their villa, as Lady Doreen is ordered to winter in the south of France. Afterwards the doctors hope she will be quite strong. "*

It was in the name Neville that Ann thought she detected a clue to Tony's altered demeanour. She recollected having met Lady Doreen on one occasion, about a year ago, when she herself had been paying a flying visit to the Brabazons at their house in Audley Square—a frail slip of a girl with immense grey eyes and hair like an aureole of reddish gold. She had been barely seventeen at that time, slim and undeveloped, and her delicacy had added rather than otherwise to her look of extreme youth. Ann had regarded her as hardly more than a child. But she knew that a year can effect an enormous alteration in a girl in her late teens—sometimes seeming to transform her all at once from immature girlhood into gracious and charming womanhood. Lady Doreen had "come out" since Ann had met her, made her curtsy at Court and taken part in her first London season, and it was not difficult to imagine her, delicate though she might be, as extremely attractive and invested with a certain ethereal grace and charm peculiarly her own.

And that Tony had seen a good deal of her in town last July Ann was aware. He had mentioned her name more than once during his visit to the Cottage, and it seemed to Ann quite likely that, sore because of her own definite refusal of him, he had sought and found consolation in the company of Lady Doreen.

Looking back, she fancied she remembered a certain shy embarrassment in Tony's manner when he had spoken of her. She had thought nothing about it at the time, being preoccupied with her own affairs, but now, in the light of this new idea which had presented itself to her, she felt convinced that there was something behind the slight hesitation Tony had evinced when referring to the Nevilles.

A little smile, almost maternal in its tenderness, curved her lips. She had always hoped that Tony's love for her might prove to be only a red-hot boyish infatuation, grounded on propinquity and friendship, which the passage of time would cure, and if, now, man's love was being born in him and she could keep the old friendship, it would give her complete happiness. But she questioned rather anxiously whether Doreen Neville was possessed of a strong enough character to keep him straight. She was so sweet and fragile—the kind of woman to be petted and cossetted and taken care of by some big, kind-hearted man, not in the least the type to steady a headstrong young fool, bent upon blundering on to the rocks.

Tony's letter was in the pocket of her coat, and, pulling it out, she ran through it again. There was no further mention of Doreen Neville, but she found that there was a postscript scribbled in a corner, in Tony's most illegible scrawl, which she had overlooked when reading the letter at breakfast time.

> *"Much as you disapprove, little Puritan Ann, do wish me luck at the tables! Such, luck as we had that night at Montricheux. Do you remember? "*

Ann's heart contracted suddenly. Was she ever likely to forget—to forget that day when, for the first time, Eliot Coventry's grey, compelling eyes had met and held her own? Since then she had touched heights and depths of happiness and despair which had changed her whole outlook on life. Love had come to her—and gone again, and only through sheer pluck and a pride that refused to break had she been able to face the fact and hide her hurt from the world at large.

Eliot's sudden disappearance from Silverquay last month had made things a little easier for her. He had left home the day following that of the dinner-party on board the *Sphinx*, and the knowledge that there was no danger of meeting him had helped to lessen the strain, she was enduring. Previously she had been strung up to a high nervous tension by the ever-present fear of running across him unexpectedly, and it had brought her infinite relief when she learned that he had gone away. Since then a strange numbness seemed to have taken possession of her. It was as though some one had closed the door on the past, very quietly and carefully.

Dully she recalled the night after Eliot had shown her he had no intention of claiming her love as a succession of interminable hours of mental and physical agony. But now she was hardly conscious of pain—only of a stupefied sense of loss. She felt as if her life were finished, as though all the days and years that lay ahead of her were entirely empty and purposeless. Sometime or other, she supposed, she would come alive again, be able to feel and realise things once more. But she dreaded the coming of that time. Better this apathy, like the stupor of one drugged, than a repetition of the anguish she had already suffered.

It seemed as if she were endowed with a species of double consciousness—an outward, everyday self which laughed and talked quite readily with the people she knew, walked and rode, read and wrote letters just like any one else, and a strange inner self which led a dumb, dreaming existence, drearily remote from everything that made life keen and sentient.

Suddenly a tremor of wind ran between the great boulders of the cove, whining eerily. It savoured of coming autumn, and Ann watched the quiet sea bunch itself up into small, angry tufts of foam as the breeze which seemed to have sprung up from nowhere fled across it. Then, feeling suddenly chilled, she rose from where she was sitting and turned rather wearily homeward.

Her way lay through the village, and as she climbed the steep hill which rose abruptly from the bay, in first one cottage, then another, lights twinkled into being, like bright, inquisitive eyes peering through the falling dusk. Absorbed in her thoughts, she had lingered on the shore longer than she intended, and when she reached the top of the hill she instinctively quickened her pace and hastened along the somewhat lonely stretch of road which led to the Cottage.

Just as she was within a short distance of the gate, she caught the sound of footsteps coming from the opposite direction. There were few people abroad in the lanes, as a rule, at this hour of the evening, and the idea that the approaching pedestrian might prove to be a tramp leaped quickly to Ann's mind. She was seized with a sudden nervousness, born of the dusk and loneliness of the road and of her own bodily fatigue, and she broke into a run, hoping to reach the Cottage gate before the supposed tramp should turn the corner. But the steps drew nearer—striding, purposeful steps, not in the least like those of a tramp—and an instant later the figure of Eliot Coventry rounded the bend in the road and loomed into view.

Ann's heart gave a sudden leap, then started beating at racing speed. The meeting was so utterly unlooked-for that for a moment a feeling akin to terror laid hold of her. Taking the last few yards which still intervened betwixt her and the safety of the Cottage at a rush, she almost fell against the gate, seeking with blind, groping fingers for the latch. But it seemed to be wedged in some way, and she tore at it unavailingly.

"Let me open that for you. "

Eliot's voice, rather grave but with the ghost of a quiver in it which might have betokened some inward amusement, sounded above her head. Then, as she still struggled vainly to move the recalcitrant latch, he went on quietly:

"Are you trying to run away from me—or what? "

Ann straightened herself and made a snatch at her fugitive dignity.

"No—oh, no, " she said, endeavouring to steady her flurried tones. Her heart was still playing tricks, throbbing jerkily in her side, and her breath came unevenly. "Only you startled me. I thought you were a tramp. "

She fancied he concealed a smile in the darkness.

"Not very complimentary of you, " he answered composedly.

"It wasn't, was it? I'm so sorry, " she agreed in eager haste. "Have you come to see Robin? I'm afraid he's out. He said he should be back rather late to-night. "

"No, " he replied evenly, "I've not come to see Robin. " Then, with a sudden leap in his voice: "I came to see you, Ann. "

"To see me? " she murmured confusedly.

"Yes. Am I to tell you all about it out here in the cold, or may I come in? "

Without waiting for her answer, he quietly lifted the latch which had refused to move for her trembling fingers, and silently, half in a dream, she led the way into the house.

There was no light in the living-room other than that yielded by the logs which burned on the open hearth, but even by their flickering glow she could discern how much he had altered since she had last seen him. He was thinner, and his face had the worn look of a man who has recently passed through some stern mental and spiritual conflict. There were furrows of weariness deeply graven on either side the mouth, and Ann felt her heart swell within her in an overwhelming impulse of tenderness and longing to smooth away those new lines from the beloved face. Before she knew it, that imperative inner need had manifested in unconscious gesture. Her hands went out to him as naturally and instinctively as the hands of a mother go out to her hurt child.

But he did not take them in his. Instead, he seemed almost to draw away from her, his hands slowly clenching as though the man were putting some immense compulsion of restraint upon himself.

"I've come back, Ann, " he said slowly. "I've come back. "

Her outstretched hands dropped to her sides. She was trembling, but she forced herself into speech.

"Why did you go? " she asked very low.

"I went—to see if I could live without you, to try and put you out of my life.... And I can't do it. " He spoke with a curious deliberation. "If ever a man fought against love, I fought against it. I'd done with love—it's the thing I've cut out of my plan of life these ten years. " His mouth twisted wryly as if even yet the memory of the past had power to stab him. "I distrusted love. And I distrusted you. " He stopped abruptly, still conveying that impression of a man forcibly holding himself in check.

"And—and now? " Ann's voice was almost inaudible.

They had been standing very still, held motionless and apart by a strange intensity of feeling, but unconsciously she had drawn closer to him as she spoke. As though her instinctive little movement towards him snapped the last link of the iron control he had been forcing on himself, he suddenly bent forward, and, snatching her up into his arms, held her crushed against his breast, kissing her with the overwhelming passion of a man who has been denied through dreary months of longing. Heedless of past or future, Ann yielded, surrendering with her lips the whole brave young heart of her.

Presently his clasp relaxed, and she drew a little away from him.

"Ann, " he said unsteadily, "little dear Ann! "

She met his gaze with eyes like stars—clear and unafraid.

"You haven't said yon trusted me! " A note of tender amusement quivered in her voice. "Do you, Eliot? "

For a moment his eyes seemed to burn out at her from under his heavily drawn brows.

"Trust you? " he said hoarsely. "I don't know whether I trust you or not!... But I know I want you! "

And once more he swept her up into his embrace.

"My beloved! "

His kisses rained down on her face—fierce, imperious kisses that seemed to draw the very soul out of her body and seal it his, and when at last he let her go she leaned against him, tremulously spent and shaken with the rapture of answering passion which had kindled to life within her.

"Tell me you love me! " he insisted. "Let me hear you say it—to make it real! "

And turning to give herself to him again, she hid her face against his shoulder, whispering:

"Oh, you know—you know I do! "

*****

Half an hour later found them still together, sitting by the big, old-fashioned hearth which Eliot had plied with logs till the flames roared up the chimney. Robin had not yet come back; he had ridden into Ferribridge early in the afternoon, leaving word that he would probably be late in returning. Once Maria had looked into the room to ask if she should light the lamps, and the lovers had started guiltily apart, Ann replying with hastily assumed indifference that they did not require them yet. Old Maria, whose eyesight was still quite keen enough to distinguish love, even from the further side of a room lit only by the lambent firelight, retired to her own quarters, chuckling to herself. "So 'tez the squire as was courtin' the chiel, after all. An' me thinkin' all along as how 'twas young Master Tony! Aw, well, tez more suitin' like, for sure—him with his millions and my Miss Ann. " Maria's ideas as to the riches with which the owner of Heronsmere was providentially endowed might be hazy, but at least she did not err on the side of underestimating them.

Meanwhile, Eliot and Ann, placidly believing that Maria was none the wiser for her brief entrance into the room—all newly-acknowledged lovers being apparently blessed with an ostrich-like quality of self-deception—continued talking together by the firelight.

"That first day I saw you, " Eliot was saying. "It was at the Kursaal. Do you remember? "

Ann laughed and blushed a little.

"I'm not likely to forget, " she said mirthfully. "You were so frightfully rude. "

"Rude? I? " He looked honestly astonished.

"Yes. Didn't you mean to be? I was sympathising with you so nicely over losing at the tables—and you nearly bit my head off! You looked down your nose—it's rather a nice nose, by the way! "—impertinently—"and observed loftily: 'Pray don't waste your sympathy'! "

Eliot laughed outright.

"Did I, really? What a boor you must have thought me! "

"Oh, I did"—fervently. "And then there was the day of the Fêtes des Narcisses, when I hit you with a rosebud by mistake. You glared at me as if I'd committed one of the seven deadly sins. "

"So you had—if occupying the thoughts of a 'confirmed misogynist' who had forsworn women and all their ways counts as one of them! "

A silence fell between them. The lightly uttered speech suddenly recalled the past, and each was vividly conscious of the bitter root from which it sprang. The man's face darkened as though he would push aside the memory.

"But that's past, " said Ann at last, very softly.

He turned to her curiously.

"So you know, then? "

She flushed.

"Yes, I know—I heard. People talk. But I've not been gossiping, Eliot—truly. "

A brief smile crossed his face.

"You—gossiping! That's good. But I might have guessed you would hear all about it. Even one's own particular rack and thumbscrew aren't private property nowadays"—bitterly. "I wonder how much you know. What have you heard? "

"Oh, very little—" she began confusedly, her heart aching for the bitterness which still lingered in his voice.

"Tell me, " he insisted authoritatively. "I'd rather you knew the truth than some garbled version of it. "

Very reluctantly Ann repeated what she had learned from Mrs. Hilyard—the bare facts of that unhappy episode in his life which had turned him into a soured, embittered man.

"Anything more? Do you know who the woman was—her name? "

"No. Only that she was very young"—pitifully.

"I believe, " he said, cupping her face in his hand and turning it up to his, "I believe you are actually *sorry* for her? "

"Yes, I am. I'm sorry for any one who makes a dreadful mistake and loses their whole happiness through it, " she answered heartily.

"I'm afraid I don't take such a broad-minded view of things, " he returned grimly. "I haven't a forgiving disposition, and I believe in people getting what they deserve. You'd better remember that"—smiling briefly—"if ever you feel tempted to try how far you can go. "

"Do you know, I think you're going to prove rather an autocratic lover, Eliot? " she said, laughing gently.

"All good lovers are, " he answered, drawing her into his arms once more with a sudden, swift jealousy. "Don't you know that? It's the very essence of love—possession, A man asks everything of the woman he loves—past, present, and future. He will he satisfied with nothing less. "

The words, uttered with an undercurrent of deep passion, struck a familiar chord in Ann's mind. They were like, and yet unlike, something she had heard before. For a moment she puzzled over it, the connection eluding her. Then, all at once, it flashed over her, and she remembered how Brett Forrester had said: *"The past doesn't matter to me. It's the future that counts. "* These two men, Eliot and Brett, loved very differently, she thought! With Brett, love meant a passionate determination to possess the woman he desired whether she surrendered willingly or with every fibre of her spirit in revolt. But to Eliot, love signified something deeper and more enduring. He wanted all of the woman he would make his wife—soul as well as body, past as well as future, the supreme gift which only a woman who loves perfectly can give and which only a man whose love is on the same high plane should dare to ask.

"I should never be content with less, " Eliot went on. "I think if you were ever to fail me, Ann—" He broke off abruptly, as though the bare idea were torture.

"But I shan't fail you! " she replied confidently. "I love you"—simply. "And when one loves, one doesn't fail. "

His arms tightened their clasp about her till she could feel the hard beating of his heart against her own.

"Heart's dearest! " he murmured, his lips against her throat.

Presently she lifted her head from his shoulder and regarded him with questioning eyes.

"You didn't tell me what would happen to me if I *did* fail you? "

"Don't speak of it! " he said sharply.

"But it's just as well to know the worst, " she persisted laughingly. She felt so sure—so safe—with his arms round her that she could afford to joke a little about something that could never happen. "Would you cut off my head—as Bluebeard cut off the heads of his wives? "

For a moment he made no answer. Then:

"I should simply wipe you out of my life. That's all. "

He spoke very evenly, but with such a note of absolute finality in his quiet voice that Ann quivered a little as she lay in his arms—as one might wince if any one laid the keen edge of a naked blade against one's throat, no matter how lightly.

"Ah! Don't let's talk of such things! " she cried hastily. "Don't let's spoil our first day, Eliot. Do you realise"—with a radiant smile—

"that this is the first—the very first—day we have really belonged to each other? "

So they talked of other things—the foolish, sweet, and tender things which lovers have always talked and probably always will—things which are of no moment to the busy material-minded world as it bustles on its way, but which are the frail filaments out of which men and women fashion for themselves dear memories that shall sweeten all their lives.

But time will not wait, even for lovers, and Eliot had been gone over an hour when at last Robin returned from Ferribridge.

"Cast a shoe and had to wait an unconscionable time to get my horse shod, " he explained briefly.

"You must be starving, " commiserated Ann, "I'll tell Maria to bring you in some supper at once. I've had mine. " But she omitted to add she had hardly eaten anything at the little solitary meal which succeeded Eliot's departure.

Maria's indignation as she carried out the half-touched dishes had been tinctured with a certain philosophic indulgence. "Ah, well! " she commented. "They do say folks that be mazed wi' love can't never fancy their victuals. Seems like tez true. " In response to which Ann had merely laughed and kissed her weather-beaten old cheek.

In true masculine fashion, it was not until the cravings of his inner man were satisfied that Robin began to observe anything unusual in the atmosphere. But when at last he had finished supper, and was filling his beloved pipe preparatory to enjoying that best of all smokes which follows a long day's riding and a cosy meal, it dawned upon him that there was something unaccustomed in Ann's air of suppressed radiance. She was hovering about him, waiting to strike a match for him to light up by, when the idea struck him. He regarded her attentively for a minute or two with his nice grey-green eyes and finally inquired in a tone of mild amusement:

"What is it, sister mine? Has some one left us a fortune, or what? There's something odd about you to-night—an air of—*je ne sais quoi!* "—with an expansive wave of his hand.

"'I'm engaged to be married, sir, she said, '" remarked Ann demurely.

"Engaged? Great Scott! Who to? " Robin manifested all the unflattering amazement common to successive generations of brothers when confronted with the astounding fact that the apparently quite ordinary young woman whom they have hitherto regarded merely as a sisterly adjunct to life has suddenly become the pivot upon which some other man's entire happiness will henceforth turn.

But afterwards, when he had had time to assimilate the unexpected news, he was ready to enter whole-heartedly into Ann's happiness—just as throughout all their lives he had been always ready to share with her either happiness or pain, like the good comrade he was.

"I shall miss you abominably, " he declared. "In fact, I shall forbid the banns if Coventry wants to carry you off too soon. "

"You absurd person! " She laughed and kissed him. "Why, living at Heronsmere, I shall be able to look after you both. Little brother shan't be neglected, I promise you! "

They sat over the fire talking till the grandfather's clock in the corner struck twelve warning strokes. Robin knocked out the ashes of his pipe.

"We'd better be thinking of turning in, old thing, " he observed. "Even newly-engaged people require a modicum of sleep, I suppose"—smiling across at her.

"We're not telling people we're engaged, yet, " Ann. cautioned him.

Robin looked up.

"No? Why not? " he asked laconically.

"I wanted—I thought it would be nice to have a few days just to ourselves, " she replied uncertainly.

"That's not the only reason. "

Ann hesitated.

"No, " she acknowledged at last. "It isn't. Perhaps I'm 'fey' to-night. I don't feel quite material Ann yet"—with a faint smile. "And—somehow—I'd rather no one knew for a little while. "

CHAPTER XXII

WILD OATS

Lady Susan came briskly into the morning-room at White Windows, and the four privileged members of the Tribes of Israel who, being allowed the run of the house, were basking in front of a cheery fire, rose in a body and rushed towards her, jealously clamouring for attention. She patted them all round with a beautiful impartiality, cuffed the Great Dane for trampling on a minute Pekingese, settled a dispute between the truculent Irish terrier and an aristocratic Chow, and proceeded to greet her nephew.

"I've got an errand for you this morning, Brett, " she remarked, as she poured out coffee.

Forrester, who was lifting the covers of the hot dishes on the sideboard, glanced round over his shoulder.

"At your service, most revered aunt. What particular job is it? Which will you have? Bacon and eggs, or fish? "

"Bacon. I want you to go over to Heronsmere, if you will, and bring back that pedigree pup Mr. Coventry promised me. "

Brett surveyed the privileged classes on the hearth-rug with a ruminative eye.

"Are you proposing to add yet another to your collection of dogs? " he inquired with some amusement. "You must pay over quite a young fortune to the Government every year in the shape of dog-licenses. "

Lady Susan smiled deprecatingly.

"Well, I really didn't intend to add to their number just at present, " she admitted. "But I couldn't resist a pup by Mr. Coventry's pedigree fox-terrier. It's a first-class strain, and lie promised he'd pick me out a good puppy. "

"Then hadn't you better wait till he comes hack to make the selection for you? "

"He *is* back. "

Brett, who was in the middle of helping the bacon and eggs, paused abruptly, and a delicately poached egg promptly slid off the spoon he was holding and plopped back upon the dish, disseminating a generous spray of fat.

"Damn! " he ejaculated below his breath. "Who told you Coventry was back? " he went on in an expressionless voice.

Lady Susan chuckled and tried to restrain the Irish terrier's manifest intention of leaping on to her lap.

"My dear boy, haven't you learned yet that nothing takes place in a tiny village like Silverquay without everybody's knowing all about it—and a little more, too! The comings and goings of an important personage like the owner of Heronsmere certainly wouldn't be allowed to pass without comment. " Here she quieted the Irishman's misplaced exuberance with a lump of sugar. "Through the comparatively direct channel of my maid, who had it from Mrs. Thorowgood, the laundress, who had it from the unsullied fount of Maria Coombe herself, I've even received the additional information that Mr. Coventry paid a long visit to Oldstone Cottage yesterday. "

"He probably would, " returned Brett. "After being away nearly three weeks he'd naturally want to see his agent. "

"Only, " remarked Lady Susan reflectively, "it appears that he must have gone to see his agent's sister. Robin was in Ferribridge yesterday. I met him just setting off there, and he said he'd got a long afternoon's work in front of him. "

Brett preserved a brooding silence.

"I merely told you by way of giving you a friendly warning, " observed his aunt, after a moment.

His blue eyes flashed up and met the mirthful dark ones scanning his sulky face amusedly.

"Thank you, " he said grimly. "I'll see that your warning is not neglected. "

"Now what in the world did he mean by that? " Lady Susan asked herself, and the question recurred to her again when, an hour or so later, he swung down the drive in the dog-cart at a reckless pace which sent a shiver through her as she watched him turn the corner almost on one wheel.

She was under no delusions respecting her nephew, as she had once admitted to Ann. But she was indulgently attached to him, and so genuinely devoted to Ann herself that she would have welcomed a match between the two. During the time they had lived together she had grown to love Ann almost as a daughter, and she felt that if she became her niece by marriage the girl would really "belong" to her, in a way. She had even come to a mental decision that if such a desirable consummation were ever reached she would settle a fairly large sum of money upon Ann on her wedding day. "For, " as she shrewdly argued to herself, "Brett's already got more than is good for him, and every woman's better off for being independent of her husband for the price of hairpins. "

She had seen comparatively little of Coventry and Ann together. Moreover, although she guessed that the former might be attracted to a limited extent, she did not regard him as a marrying man, nor had she the remotest notion of for how much he counted in Ann's life. Had she suspected this, she would most certainly have let things take their course, and the little warning hint which she had half banteringly dropped at breakfast, and which was destined to bear such bitter fruit, would never have been uttered.

Forrester covered the few miles that separated White Windows from Heronsmere at the same reckless pace at which he had started. He seemed oblivious of the animal between the shafts of the high dog-cart, directing it with the instinctive skill of a man to whom good horsemanship is second nature. His thoughts were turned inward. His eyes, curiously concentrated in expression, gleamed with that peculiar brilliance which was generally indicative with him of some very definite intensity of purpose. The groom who took charge of the foam-flecked horse when he reached Heronsmere glanced covertly at his arrogant face and opined to one of his fellows in the stables that "Mr. Forrester had precious little care for his horseflesh. Brought his horse here in a fair lather, he did. "

Coventry, who was attending to a mass of correspondence when Brett was shown into his study, shook hands with the superficial friendliness that not infrequently masks a secret hostility between one man and another.

"Hope I'm not disturbing you? " queried Brett lightly.

Eliot shook his head.

"I've no particular love for my present task, " he replied, with a gesture towards his littered desk. "I'm trying to overtake arrears of correspondence. Sit down and have a smoke. " He tendered his case as he spoke.

"Price you've got to pay for three weeks' gallivanting, I suppose? " suggested Brett, helping himself to a cigarette and lighting up.

"I should hardly describe my recent absence from home as—gallivanting, " returned Eliot, with a brief flash of reminiscence in his eyes.

"No? Well, you don't look as if it had agreed with you too well, whatever it was, " commented the other candidly. "I should say you've dropped about half a stone in weight since I last saw you. "

"Just as well—with the hunting season commencing, " returned Eliot indifferently.

Brett nodded, and, changing the subject, proceeded to explain the object of his visit.

"The prospect of an addition to her kennels produces much the same effect on Aunt Susan as the promise of a new toy to a kiddie, " he added. "She's almost dancing with impatience over it. "

Coventry smiled.

"We won't keep her in suspense any longer, then, " he replied. "You shall take the pup back with you. Come along to the stables and I'll show you the one I thought of sending her. "

He rose as he spoke, tossing the stump of his cigarette into the fire, and Brett followed him out of the house and down to the stables where, in an empty horse-box, the litter of puppies at present resided. Cradled in clean, sweet-smelling straw, they were all bunched together round a big bowl of bread and milk—a heterogeneous mass of delicious fat roly-poly bodies and clumsy baby paws and tails that wagged unceasingly. At sight of the visitors, they deserted the now nearly empty bowl of food and galloped unsteadily towards them, squirming ecstatically over their feet and sampling the blacking on their boots with inquisitive pink tongues.

"This is the chap, " said Coventry. And stooping, he singled out one of the pups and picked it up.

All the hardness went out of Brett's eyes as he took the little beast from him and fondled it, the puppy responding by thrusting against his face an affectionate moist black muzzle, still adorned with drops of milk from the recently concluded morning feed.

"He has all the points, " remarked Eliot. "I think he's the pick of the litter. "

"Undoubtedly, " agreed Brett, casting a knowledgeable eye over the others. "Though they're a good lot, and you ought to find a winner or two amongst them. "

"Like to see the horses? " asked Coventry, and Brett assenting very willingly, they made a tour of the stables.

"That's a nice little mare, " remarked Forrester, pausing by the stall of a slim chestnut thoroughbred, who immediately thrust her head forward and nosed against his shoulder.

"Yes. And knows her job in the hunting field, too. I'm going to offer her to Miss Lovell for the season. "

The puppy Brett was carrying in the crook of his arm uttered a plaintive squeak as the breath was abruptly jerked out of his fat little body by the sudden pressure of the arm in question.

"An offer that won't be rejected, I imagine, " replied Brett. He accompanied his host out of the stables, and the two men turned towards the house. "Miss Lovell's quite a good horsewoman—and a very charming young person into the bargain. "

"Very charming, " agreed Coventry shortly. The idea of discussing Ann with any one, above all with Brett Forrester, was utterly distasteful to him.

"A somewhat flighty young monkey, though, " pursued Brett pensively. "It's that touch of red in her hair that does it, I suppose. " He laughed indulgently.

Coventry making no reply, he continued conversationally:

"You never inquired into her past history, I suppose, when you engaged her brother as your agent? "

Inwardly Coventry anathematised the promise he had given Ann to keep their engagement secret for the present. It sealed his lips against the innuendo contained in Forrester's speech.

"I certainly did not, " he responded frigidly. "I was not engaging—her. "

Brett appeared entirely unabashed.

"No. Or you might have found she couldn't show quite such a clean bill as her brother, " he returned, smiling broadly.

By this time they had re-entered Coventry's study. Decanter and syphon, together with a couple of tumblers, had been placed on the table in readiness by a thoughtful servant. Eliot glanced at these preparations with concealed annoyance, but, compelled by the laws of hospitality, inquired curtly:

"Will you have a drink? "

Brett assented amicably and established himself in a chair by the fire, the puppy sprawling beatifically across his knees while he pulled its satin-smooth ears with caressing fingers.

"You can never trust red hair, " he went on, accepting the drink Coventry had mixed for him. Then, catching the other's eye, he threw back his head and laughed with that impudent, friendly charm of his that discounted half his deviltries. "Oh, I can guess what you're thinking! And you're quite right. I ought to know—because I'm one of the red-headed tribe myself. "

"It certainly passed through my mind, " admitted Eliot.

"Well, you can't trust 'em. It's true. There's always a bit of the devil in them. And I happen to know that that demure little person down at your cottage has sown quite a sprinkling of wild oats. "

"Wild oats in a woman are a very different thing from wild oats in a man, " remarked Eliot, pouring himself out a whisky.

"Yes. But they're a deal more nearly related nowadays than they were before the war. Staying the night at a hotel with a man pal is sailing a trifle near the wind, don't you think? Anyway, it's carrying a flirtation rather far. "

The syphon, beneath Eliot's sudden pressure, squirted out a torrent of soda. Brett's eyes scintillated as he watched the slight accident.

"You're implying a good deal, Forrester, " said Eliot gravely, as he dried his coat with his handkerchief.

"Oh, I know what I'm talking about. I was there, you see, and caught the little limb of Satan red-handed, so to speak—though, of course, she doesn't know it. " Then, as Eliot remained stonily silent, he proceeded loquaciously: "It was last June or thereabouts. I was stopping a night or two at the Hotel de Loup, up in the mountains above Montricheux—know it? "

"Yes, I know it, " replied Coventry mechanically.

"There wasn't a soul in the place except me—out of the season, you know. And one beastly cold night, when I marched into the hotel after a confounded long tramp, who should I see but a man I knew saying good-night to an uncommonly pretty girl at the bottom of the stairs. I kept tactfully out of the way till the good-nights were over, as I thought at first he must have committed matrimony while I'd been abroad and that they were on their honeymoon. I never got the chance to ask him, as he bolted past me down one of the corridors before I had time to speak. So I took a squint at the hotel visitors' book and found they'd registered as 'G. Smith and sister'! That settled it. The chap's name wasn't Smith, and I happened to know he'd never had a sister—either by that name or any other! So I just chuckled quietly to myself and mentally congratulated him on his good taste—the girl was quite pretty enough to excuse a slight deviation from the strict and narrow path. " He paused to light a fresh cigarette, his eyes, between narrowed lids, raking the other man's impenetrable face. Throughout the telling of the story Coventry had sat motionless, like a figure carved in stone. Only, as the recital proceeded, his eyes hardened slightly and his closed lips straightened into a stern, inflexible line. Having lit his cigarette, Forrester airily resumed the thread of his narrative.

"What follows is really rather interesting—the long arm of coincidence with a vengeance! My revered aunt brings me to Oldstone Cottage and sends me into the garden on a voyage of discovery to find Miss Lovell. And I find her asleep in the hammock—the identical young woman I'd seen up at the Dents de Loup with Tony Brabazon. "

"*Brabazon!* " The name seemed jerked out of Coventry's lips without his own volition. A curious greyish pallor had overspread his face, and behind the hardness of his eyes smouldered a savage fire that seemed to wax and wane, struggling for release.

"Yes, Brabazon, " replied Brett carelessly. "It seems he and old Sir Philip and Aunt Susan and Miss Lovell were all stopping at Montricheux. I'd no idea my aunt was staying there, or I'd have run down and looked her up. But we hardly ever correspond. My address is always such a doubtful quantity"—with a laugh. "You see, I'm liable to dash off to the ends of the earth at a moment's notice, if the spirit moves me. " He rose, tucking the puppy under his arm. "Well, I must be getting back. Aunt Susan will be on tenterhooks till she sees this youngster. "

Coventry accompanied him to the door and signalled to the groom who was walking Brett's horse slowly up and down.

"I shouldn't repeat that story to any one, if I were you, Forrester, " he said, speaking with some effort, as they shook hands.

"Good Lord! Not I! What do you take me for? " laughed Brett easily. "I only thought it might amuse you, Lovell being your agent. "

The groom brought the horse and trap to a standstill in front of the house door, and touched his hat.

"I've kept the horse moving about, sir, as he was a bit hot, " he said, addressing Brett.

The latter nodded and tipped the man generously. Meanness, at least, was not included amongst his many faults.

"Quite right, " he replied. "Got a basket handy for the pup? "

The man lifted down from the front of the dog-cart a basket he had put there in readiness, and the puppy, wailing pathetically, was deposited inside.

"Never mind, old man, " observed Brett, bestowing a final reassuring pat on the small black and tan head. "It'll soon be over. "

A minute later he was driving swiftly down the avenue, an odd expression of mingled triumph and amusement in his eyes.

CHAPTER XXIII

THE TEETH OF THE WOLF

The gate clicked and Ann peeped rosily out of her bedroom window. She had been expecting that click all morning—waiting for it with every sense alert and with absurd, delicious little thrills of happiness chasing each other through her veins. Several disappointing clicks had preceded it—one which merely revealed a new baker's boy who hadn't troubled to discover whether the Cottage boasted a back-door or not, and another heralding the entry of Billy Brewster, armed with a stout broom and prepared to sweep the flagged path clean of the minutest particle of dust. So that Ann had at last been reluctantly compelled to fall back on the same explanation which had served her once before—that Eliot must have been detained at Heronsmere by unexpected business.

But now the afternoon had brought the desired click of the gate, and she could see his tall, well-knit figure striding up the path below. She leaned out of the window and called to him:

"Coo-ee! I'm up here! "

The charming voice, vibrant with that tender, indescribable inflection which a woman's voice holds only for the one beloved man, floated down to him, and instinctively he looked up. For an instant his glance lingered, and ever afterwards there remained stamped indelibly upon his memory the impression of her as she leaned there like the Blessed Damozel leaning "out from the gold bar of Heaven. "

The sun glinted on her hair, turning it into a nimbus of ruddy gold, and there was something delicately flower-like in the droop of her small bent head on its slender throat. It reminded him of a harebell.

His expression hardened as he fought down the tide of longing which surged up within him at the sight of her, and from some disused corner of his subconscious mind the lines of the old Persian Tentmaker seemed to leap out at him and mock him:

> "Heav'n but the Vision of fulfill'd Desire,
> And Hell the Shadow from a Soul on fire. "

The vision which had been his was shattered, utterly destroyed—destined to be forever unfulfilled.

... But Ann remained joyfully oblivious of anything amiss.

"Walk straight in, " she called through the window. "I'm coming down. " And with a gay wave of her hand she withdrew into the room. Followed a light sound of footsteps on the stairs, and a minute later the door of the living-room flew open to admit her.

Eliot, who had been standing with his back to the room, staring out of the window, wheeled round as she came towards him with hurrying feet and thrust her eager hands into his.

"You've come at last! I thought you'd be here the minute after breakfast, " she began, her face breaking into smiles. "If you were a story-book hero you would have been!... Oh, I know you'll say it was business that kept you. But that's only an old married man's excuse"—mirthfully. "I shan't allow you to offer it to me until we've been married for years and years! "

Thus far she had run on gaily with her tender nonsense, but now she checked herself suddenly as she read no answering smile on his face and felt her hands lie flaccidly ungripped in his.

"Eliot"—she drew back a little—"why don't you speak? What is it? " Her hands clutched his spasmodically, and a sudden frightened look blurred the radiance in her eyes. "Oh, my dear! What is it? Have you had bad news? "

Very slowly, but with a strange, deliberate significance, he freed his hands from her clasp and put her away from him.

"Yes, " he said quietly, "I've had—news. " At the frozen calmness of his tones she shrank back as one shrinks from the numbing cold of the still air that hangs above black ice.

"What is it? " she breathed. "Not bad news—for us? "

Her eyes were fastened on his face, searching it wildly. A quick and terrible fear clamoured at her heart. Was there something in the past, something of which she had no knowledge, that could arise—*now*—to separate them from each other? That long-ago episode which had wrecked his youth—had the woman who had figured in it some material hold upon him? Could she—was it possible she could still come between them in some way? Ann had heard of such things. It seemed to her as though, betwixt herself and Eliot, there hovered a dim, formless shadow, vague and nebulous—a shadow which had crept silently out from some memory-haunted corner of the past.

"Not bad news—for us? " she repeated quiveringly.

"That depends upon how you choose to regard it, " he replied. "Ann"—the ice broke up and he came to the point with a suddenness that was almost brutal—"why haven't you been straight with me? "

"Straight with you? " she repeated wonderingly. "But I have been straight with you. "

"What a woman would call straight, I suppose! " he flung back. "Which means concealing everything that you think won't be found out. "

The indignant colour rushed up into her face, then receded, leaving it deadly pale.

"But I have nothing to conceal, " she answered. "Eliot—I don't understand—"

"Don't you? " lie said, and the measureless contempt in his voice stung like the lash of a whip. "Think back a bit! Is there nothing you've kept from me which I ought to have known—nothing which makes the love you professed only last night no more than a sham? "

For a moment Ann gazed at him in speechless silence. Then a low, passionate denial left her lips.

"Nothing! " she said.

Eliot took two strides towards her, and, gripping her by the shoulders, dragged her closer to the window so that the remorseless sunlight poured down on to her face.

"Repeat that! " he commanded savagely. "Will you dare to repeat that—that unutterable lie? "

His eyes, blazing with a terrible anger that seemed, to scorch her like a flame, searched her face with a scrutiny so pitiless, so implacably incredulous, that it was almost unbearable. But she endured it, and her clear golden eyes met his unflinchingly.

"It was the truth! " she said. Her voice sounded to herself as though it came from a great distance away. It had an odd, tinny sound like cracked metal.

He released her suddenly, almost flinging her from him, and she staggered a little, catching at the back of a chair to steady herself. His roughness roused her spirit.

"Eliot! Are you mad? " she exclaimed.

He stared at her, that burning ferocity of almost uncontrollable anger which had possessed him dying slowly out of his face.

"Mad? " he said grimly. "No, I'm not mad—now. I was mad yesterday—when I believed in you. "

The stark agony in his voice smote her to the heart.

"Eliot"—she moved towards him, her hands held out appealingly—"what have I done? Won't you tell me? I don't understand. "

"No? " His lips drew back over his teeth in a grimace that was a dreadful travesty of a smile. "Then I'll ask you a simple question. Perhaps—after that—you'll understand. Have you ever stayed at the Hotel de Loup? "

"The Hotel de Loup? Why—" The word "yes" was on the tip of her tongue. But before she could utter it the whole, overwhelming realisation of what he suspected rushed over her, and she checked herself abruptly, stunned into silence. With the amazing speed at which the mind can work in moments of tense excitement, she grasped instantly all that must have happened. Some one—she could not imagine who it was—had found out about that night which she and Tony had been compelled to pass together at the Hotel de Loup, and had made mischief... told Eliot, putting the worst construction on it... and he believed... Oh! What did he not believe? A burning flush bathed her face, mounting to her very temples—a flush of shamed horror, and she fell suddenly silent, staring at him with wide, horrified eyes.

"So you do remember? " he said, his voice like cold steel.

"Yes. " She answered him mechanically—like a doll which says "yes" or "no" when some one touches a spring.

"And you were not there alone, I believe? "

The other spring this time. "No, " answered the doll.

"Brabazon was with you—Tony Brabazon? "

"Yes. " Again the parrot-like reply.

"Then I don't think there is any need to continue this conversation. " As he spoke, Eliot turned and walked towards the door. Ann watched him without moving. She felt almost as though she were watching something that was happening in a play—something that had nothing whatever to do with her. Then, just as his hand was on the latch of the door, the strange numbness which had held her motionless and silent seemed to melt away.

"Eliot, come back! " she cried out, and there was a note so ringingly clear and decisive in her voice that involuntarily he halted. "I have listened to you, " she went on quietly. "Now—you will listen to me. "

He retraced his steps to her side, like a man moving without his own volition, and stood waiting.

"Well? " he said tonelessly. "What is it you wish to say? I am listening. "

"It's quite true that I stayed at the Hotel de Loup, " she said. "And it's true that Tony Brabazon was with me. But I have nothing to ask your forgiveness for. " She lifted her head, meeting his gaze with eyes that were very steady and unashamed. There was something proud and at the same time infinitely appealing in the gesture. But Eliot regarded her unmoved.

"Do you expect me to believe that? " he asked contemptuously. "I'm not a blind fool!... Do you remember, I told you that a man asks all of a woman—past as well as future. Well, you can't give me the past. It belongs to some one else—to Brabazon. I suppose you meant to marry him. And then I come along—and I'm worth more. I don't flatter myself I'm more attractive! "—grimly. "Years ago a woman threw me over because I was poor. And now another woman is ready to throw over some one else and marry me because I'm rich. It's the same stale old story. You're not going to ask me to believe you accepted me from disinterested affection, are you? "

While he spoke, Ann had been standing motionless, every nerve of her taut and strained to the utmost. Outwardly unflinching, inwardly she felt as though he were raining blows upon her. It was all so sordid and horrible. It dragged love through the clinging mire of suspicion and distrust till its radiant wings were soiled and fouled beyond recognition.

"I'm not going to ask you to believe—anything. " She spoke very quietly. A bitter, tortured pride upheld her. "If you can think—that—of me, it would be useless asking you to believe anything I might say. Yesterday"—her voice trembled but she steadied it again—"yesterday you told me that the essence of love was possession. It isn't, Eliot.... It's faith... and trust. "

In the silence that followed the man and woman stood gazing dumbly at each other, and for a brief moment love and faith hung quivering in the balance. Then the balance tilted. The heavy burden of suspicion weighed it down, and without another word Eliot turned and left the room.

Ann did not move. She stood quite still, her arms hanging straight down at her sides. The Dents de Loup—wolf's teeth! Well, the jaws of the wolf had closed, crushing her happiness for ever between their merciless white fangs.

She knew now the meaning of that nebulous, distorted shape which had seemed to come betwixt her and the man she loved. It was the grey shadow of distrust which had sprung out from the hidden places of the past and now lay, dark and impenetrable, dividing them for ever.

CHAPTER XXIV

AFTERMATH

"I beg your pardon! "

Instinctively Cara apologised, although actually the collision had been no fault of hers. The man with whom she had collided had been striding along with bent head, completely absorbed in his own thoughts, and had awakened too late to the fact that some one was coming towards him along the narrow bridle-path through the woods. He lifted his hat mechanically and murmured some sort of apology, but his eyes remained blank and seemed to look through and beyond the woman into whom he had just cannoned without seeing her—certainly without recognising her.

Cara was startled by their expression of strain. They seemed to glare with a hard, unnatural brilliance, as though the man's vision were focused upon some terrible inner presentment. She laid a detaining hand on his sleeve, but he appeared quite unconscious of her touch and she gave his arm a little shake.

"Eliot! " she said quickly. "Eliot! Are you trying to cut me? "

As though by an immense effort he seemed to come back to the consciousness of his material environment.

"To cut you? " he repeated dully. He brushed his hand across his forehead. "No, of course I wasn't trying to cut you. "

He looked shockingly ill. His face was grey and lined, and his shoulders sagged as though he were physically played out. The boots and leggings he wore were caked with mud, and his coat had little torn ends of wool sticking up over it, as if he had been walking blindly ahead, careless of direction, and had forced his way through thickets of bramble rather than turn aside to seek an easier path.

"What have you been doing with yourself? " she asked rather breathlessly. In every nerve of her she felt that something terrible had happened. "You look"—trying to summon up a smile—"as if you'd been having a battle. "

"I've been walking. "

"Far? "

He gave a sudden laugh.

"To hell and back. I don't know the mileage. "

"Eliot, what do you mean? "

He looked down at her, and now that dreadful glare which had so frightened her had gone out of his eyes. They were human once more, but the naked misery in them shocked her into momentary silence. She would have liked to run away—to escape from those eyes. They were the windows of a soul enduring torture that was almost too intolerable to be borne. It was only by a strong effort of will that she at last forced her voice to do her bidding.

"What has happened, Eliot? " she said, speaking very gently. "Can't you tell me? "

He stared at her a moment. Then:

"Why, yes, " he said. "I think I could tell you—part of it. It might amuse you. I've found you were not the only woman in the world who counts the shekels. You wouldn't marry me because I was poor. Now another woman is ready to marry me just because I'm rich. There's only one drawback. "

"Drawback? "

"Yes. Quite a drawback. You see, it doesn't appeal to me to be married because I've a decent income, any more than it appealed to me ten years ago to be turned, down for the opposite reason. "

Cara shrank from this bitter reference to the past.

"You can be very cruel, Eliot, " she said unsteadily.

"Cruelty breeds cruelty, " he replied with indifference. "Still, I'm beginning to think I was too hard on you, Cara, in the past. It seems finance plays an amazingly strong hand in the game of love. But it's taken two women to teach me the lesson thoroughly"—with a short laugh.

"Two? "

"You—and Ann. "

"Ann! I don't believe it! " The words burst from her with impulsive vehemence.

His face darkened.

"While I can believe no other. In fact"—heavily—"your poor little sin shows white as driven snow beside—hers. "

"You're wrong. I'm sure you're wrong, " insisted Cara. "I don't know why you believe what you do—nor all that you believe. I don't ask to know. It wouldn't make any difference if you told me. I know Ann. And however black things looked against her, nothing would ever make me believe she was anything but dead straight. "

"Most touching faith! " jeered Eliot. "Unfortunately, I have a preference in favour of believing the evidence of my own senses. "

She drew nearer to him, her hands pressed tightly together.

"Eliot, you're deliberately going to throw away your happiness if you distrust Ann, " she urged, beseechingly, "I've told you, she's not like me. She's different. "

"She's no better and no worse than other women, I suppose, " he returned implacably. "Ready to take whatever goods the gods provide—and then go on to the next. "

Cara turned aside in despair. She could not tell—could not guess—what had happened. She only knew that the man whose happiness meant more to her than her own, and the woman she had learned to love as a friend, had somehow come to irretrievable misunderstanding and disaster. At last she turned back again to Eliot.

"Would you have believed this of her—whatever it is you do believe—if it had not been for me? "

He reflected a moment.

"Perhaps not, " he said.

She uttered a cry that was half a sob. So the price of that one terrible mistake she had made was not yet paid! Fate would go on exacting the penalty for ever—first the destruction of her own happiness, then that of Eliot and of Ann. All must be hurled into the bottomless well of expiation. There was no forgiveness of sins.

It was useless to plead with Eliot—to reason with him. It was she herself who had poisoned the very springs of life for him, and now she was powerless to cleanse them. With a gesture of utter hopelessness she turned and left him, and made her way despondently homeward through the gathering dusk.

She reached the Priory just in time to encounter Robin coming out of the gates. He sprang off his horse and greeted her delightedly.

"I came over to bring you a brace of pheasants, " he explained. "As you were out, I deposited them in the care of your parlourmaid. "

Cara thanked him cordially, and then, as he still lingered, she added:

"Won't you turn back and come in for a cup of tea? Have you time? "

"I should think I have! " The mercurial rise in Robin's spirits betrayed itself in the tones of his voice. "I was hoping for an invitation to tea—so you can imagine my disappointment when I found that you weren't home. "

She laughed, and they walked up to the house together, Robin leading his horse. A cheery fire burned on the hearth in the square, old-fashioned hall which Cara had converted into a living-room. As they entered she switched on the lights, revealing panelled walls, thick dim-hued rugs breaking an expanse of polished floor, and, by the fire, big, cushioned easy chairs which seemed to cry aloud for some one to rest weary limbs in their soft, capacious embrace.

"Ann's always envious of your electric light, " remarked Robin. "Being only cottage folk"—smiling—"we have to content ourselves with lamps, and they seem prone to do appalling things in the way of smoking and covering the whole room with greasy soot the moment you take your eye off them. "

"I know. They're a frightful nuisance, " said Cara, ringing the bell for tea. "But lamp-light is the most becoming form of illumination, you know—especially when you're getting on in years, like me! "

Robin helped her off with her coat, lingering a little over the process, and gazed down at her with adoring eyes.

"Don't—talk—rubbish! " he said, softly and emphatically.

Perhaps he might have gone on to say something more, but at that moment a trim parlourmaid came in and began to arrange the tea-table beside her mistress's chair, and for some time afterwards Cara skilfully contrived to keep the conversation on impersonal lines. It was not until tea was over that Robin suddenly struck a more intimate note again. He had been watching her face in silence for a little while, noticing that it looked very small and pale to-day in its frame of night-dark hair, and that there were faint, purplish shadows beneath her eyes.

"You look awfully tired! " he remarked with concern. "And sad, " he added. "Is anything bothering you? "

She was silent for a moment, staring into the heart of the fire where the red and blue flames played flickeringly over the logs.

"I've been taking a look into the past, " she said, at last, "It's—it's rather a dreary occupation. "

"I know, " he said quietly. "I know. " Ignorant of that earlier past of hers, in which Eliot Coventry had played a part, he was thinking only of her unhappy married life, about which he had gathered a good deal from other people and a little—a very little—from Cara herself. But even that little had let in far more light than she had imagined. Robin's insight was extraordinarily quick and keen, and a phrase dropped here or there, even her very silences at times, had enabled him to make a pretty good conjecture as to the kind of martyrdom she had suffered. It made his blood boil to think of the mental—and even physical—suffering she must have endured, tied to the brute and drunken bully which it was common knowledge Dene Hilyard had been.

"Don't you think, " he went on gently, "that you could try to forget it, Cara? Don't dwell on the past. Think of the future. "

"I'm afraid that's rather dreary, too, " she answered, with a sad little smile. "It's just... going on living... and remembering. "

He leaned over her and suddenly she felt the eager touch of his hand on hers.

"It needn't be that, Cara, " he said swiftly. "It needn't be that. " She looked up at him with startled eyes. Her thoughts had been so far away, bridging the gulf between to-day and long-dead yesterday, that she had almost to wrench them back to the present. And now here was Robin, with a new light in his eyes and a new, passionate note in his voice. "Cara—darling—"

With a sudden realisation of what was coming, she drew her hand quickly away from him.

"No—no, Robin—" she began.

But he would not listen.

"Don't say 'no' yet. Hear me out! " he exclaimed. "I love you. But I don't suppose—I'm not conceited enough to suppose that you love me—yet. Only let me try—let me try to teach you to love me! Don't judge all men by one. You've had a ghastly time. Let me try—some day—to make you happier. "

He was so eager, so humble, so entirely selfless in his devotion, thinking only of her, that she was touched inexpressibly—tempted, even. Ah! If she could only put all the past aside, out of sight, and take this love that Robin offered her and hold it round her like a garment shielding her from the icy blasts of life! But she had nothing to give in return for this splendid, brave first love he was offering her. She must play fair. She dare not take where she could not give. Very gently she put him from her.

"You don't understand, " she said. "You don't understand. Robin, I wish—I wish I could say 'yes. ' But I can't. It isn't—Dene—who stands between us. I'm not a coward—I'd take my chance again if I could love again—"

"But you never loved him? You *couldn't* have loved him! " he protested incredulously.

"My husband? No. But—I loved some one once. And I threw away my happiness—to marry Dene. Oh, it was years ago, Robin—" She broke off and lifted her eyes appealingly to his face. "Must I go on? That's—that's really all there is to tell you. Only don't you see—I—I can't marry you. "

"No, I don't see—yet, " returned Robin stoutly, though her words had dashed the quick, eager look of hope from his face. "This—this other man, the one you cared for—is he coming back to marry you? "

"Coming back? No! " For once the sweet voice was hard—bitterly hard. "He has gone out of my life for ever. "

A look of relief came into his eyes. He took her hands into his and held them very gently.

"Then in that case, " he said, "there's still a chance for me. Not now—not yet. I wouldn't try to hurry you. But you'll let me go on loving you, Cara—after all, you can't stop my doing that! "—with a crooked little smile. "And some day, perhaps, you'll come to me and let me try and make you happier again. I think I could do that, you know. "

"Ah, no, Robin! I couldn't come to you—not like that. I couldn't take all your love—and only give you second best in return. It wouldn't be fair. "

He laughed a little.

"I think 'fairness' just doesn't come into love at all, " he said, with a great tenderness. "One just loves. And I'd be very glad to take that 'second best'—if you'll give it to me, Cara. Oh, my dear, if you only knew, if you only understood! A man can do so much for a woman when he loves her—he can serve her and protect her, and take all the difficult tasks away from her and leave her only the easy ones—the little, pretty, beautiful things, you know. He can stand between her and the prickles and sharp swords of life—and there are such a lot of prickles, and sometimes a terribly sharp sword.... I want to do all these things for you, Cara. "

She shook her head silently. For a moment she could not find her voice. She was too unused to tenderness—out of practice in all the sweet ways of being cared for.

"No—no, Robin, " she said at last. "I'm grateful—I shall always be grateful, and—and happier, I think, because you've said these things to me—because you've thought of me that way. But you must keep them—keep them for some nice girl who hasn't wasted all her youth and lost her beliefs—who can give you something better than a bundle of regrets and a second-hand love. You'll—you'll meet her some day, Robin. And then you'll be glad that I didn't take you at your word. "

But Robin appeared quite unimpressed.

"No, I shan't. I don't want any 'nice girl, ' thank you, " he returned, and his head went up a little. "If I can't have you, no one else is going to take your place. But I shall never give up hope until you've actually married some other man. And meanwhile"—smiling a little—"I shall propose to you regularly and systematically, till you give me a different answer. I suppose"—tentatively—"you couldn't give it to-day? "

Cara pushed him gently away from her, but she did not withdraw her hands from the strong, kind, comfortable clasp in which he held them.

"Oh, Robin, you're ridiculous! " she said, a little break in her voice. "I'm speaking for your own good—really I am. "

"And I think I'm the best judge of that, " he answered, regarding her with a quiet humour in his eyes. "But I won't bother you any more to-night, " he went on. "Only I shall come back. " He lifted the hands he held and kissed them—kissed them with a kind of reverence that made of the slight action an act of homage. "I shall come back, " he repeated, his eyes looking straight into hers.

Then, with a sudden reversion to the commonplace and everyday, he glanced at the clock.

"I must be off! " he exclaimed. "Ann will be wondering what has become of me—and, as soon as she's quite sure I'm safe and sound, she'll give me a scolding for being late for dinner, " he added, laughing.

Ann! Cara was conscious of an overwhelming rush of self-reproach. Ann miserable—and alone. And she had been keeping Robin here with her—or, at least, had let him stay. Should she warn him? Prepare him? She hesitated. But her hesitation was only momentary. Whatever had occurred betwixt Ann and the man who loved her, it was Ann's secret, and she alone had the right to decide whether Robin should be admitted into it or not. But he must go home—now, at once!

"Why, yes, " she said urgently. "You must hurry back, Robin. Ann may be—feeling lonely. "

Half an hour later Robin strode into the living-room at the Cottage to find Ann sitting by the window, curiously still, and staring out impassively into the dusk with blank, unseeing eyes. At sight of her—white and motionless as a statue—a queer sense of foreboding woke in him, and he stepped quickly to her side.

"Ann! " he exclaimed. "Ann, what is it? "

She remained quite still, as if she did not hear him. He touched her shoulder.

"What is it, Ann? " he repeated urgently.

At the touch of his hand she glanced stupidly towards him. Then, shivering a little as though suddenly cold, she got up stiffly out of her chair. But still she did not speak. Robin slipped his arm round her.

"Ann—dear old thing, tell me. What's happened? " he entreated.

At last she answered him.

"Nothing much, " she said. "Oh, nothing at all, really. " She gave a funny little cracked laugh. "Only—I'm not—engaged any longer.... I told you I was 'fey' last night. "

Almost before she had finished speaking, he felt her slight young body suddenly become a dead weight on his arm. She crumpled up against him, and sank into the blessed oblivion of unconsciousness.

*****

The following morning two rather strained young faces confronted each other across the Cottage breakfast table. After Ann had recovered consciousness the previous evening, she had confided to Robin something of what had taken place during the interview between herself and Eliot. He had vainly tried to dissuade her, urging that she was too tired to talk and had much better go to bed and rest.

"I'd rather tell you now—to-night, " she had insisted. "Then we need never speak of it again. And there's very little to tell. Eliot has broken off his engagement with me because he thinks I've deceived him. "

Robin's anger had been deep but inarticulate. When he spoke again it was reassuringly, soothingly. All else he had kept back.

"*You* deceive him—or any one! If he thinks that, then he doesn't know you at all, little sister. And what's more, if he can think that of you, he isn't good enough for you. "

"The trouble is"—with a pale little smile—"that he thinks I'm not—good enough—for him. "

She would give no reply to Robin's impetuous demand for an explanation.

"No, dear old boy, don't ask me, " she had said painfully. "It—it doesn't bear talking about. He just doesn't think me good enough. That's all. "

But the following morning, when he asked her if she would like to leave Silverquay, a look of intense relief overspread her face.

"Would it be possible? " she asked on a low, breathless; note of eagerness. Then her face fell. "Oh, but we can't think of it! It's much too good a post for you to throw up. "

Robin made no answer. But in his own mind he resolved that, if it were possible, he would find some other post—one which, while it would not take him entirely out of reach of the Priory, would yet spare Ann the necessity of ever again meeting Eliot Coventry, or of feeling that they were dependent for their livelihood on the man who, he was instinctively aware, had hurt her in some deep, inmost sanctuary of her womanhood—hurt her so unbearably that she could not bring herself to speak of it.

He rode across to Heronsmere as soon as breakfast was over, and it did not require a second glance at Eliot's haggard face to tell him that Ann was not alone in her intensity of suffering. He was appalled at the change which two days had worked in the man before him, and for an instant sheer pity almost quenched the burning intention of his errand.

"You wanted to see me, Lovell? "

As Eliot turned the grey mask of his face towards him, Robin mentally visioned Ann's own face as he had last seen it, and his heart hardened.

"Yes, " he said, speaking rather jerkily. "I want to resign my post as your agent. "

A momentary change of expression showed itself on Eliot's face, fleeting as the passage of a shadow across a pool.

"To resign? " he repeated mechanically.

"As soon as you can find some one to take my place. "

Coventry remained silent, his fingers trifling absently with a small silver calendar that stood on his desk, pushing it backwards and forwards.

"That's rather a strange request, " he said at last.

"I don't think so, " answered Robin, quietly, looking at him very directly.

He returned the glance with grave eyes.

"I suppose I understand what you mean, " he said slowly.

"I suppose you do, " returned Robin bluntly. "But we needn't speak of that. I came merely to ask you to accept my resignation. "

Again Eliot made no immediate response. He was trying to realise it—to visualise the Cottage empty, or occupied by some one who was no more than an ordinary estate agent—just his man of business. To conceive Silverquay void of Ann's presence, know her no longer there, be ignorant of where she was in the big world... whether well or ill.... He found that the bare idea wrought an exquisite agony within him. It was like probing a raw wound.

"No! " He spoke very suddenly, his voice so harsh that it seemed to grate on the quiet of the room. "No. You can't leave, Lovell. Our arrangement was six months' notice on either side. I claim that notice. "

Robin drew a deep breath.

"I hoped you would consent to waive it, " he said.

"I don't consent. I claim it"—decisively. "You can't leave under six months. " Coventry rose from his chair as though to indicate that the interview was at an end, hesitated a moment, then added abruptly: "I'm going abroad. I must have some one in charge whom I can trust. I shall be leaving England to-morrow. "

CHAPTER XXV

THE HALF-TRUTH

There are few truer sayings than the one which cautions us that evil is wrought by want of thought as well as want of heart. When you are unlucky enough to get a combination of the two, the evil accomplished is liable to assume considerably increased proportions.

On the morning following Eliot's visit to the Cottage, want of thought, in addition to a very natural semi-maternal pride, led Maria Coombe into confiding jubilantly into the ear of Mrs. Thorowgood—laundress and purveyor of local gossip—the fact that her Miss Ann and "the Squire up to Heronsmere" were going to make a match of it. Mrs. Thorowgood, not to be outdone, responded to the effect that she had "suspicioned" all along that this was going to be the case, and that when she had heard in the village yesterday that Mr. Coventry had gone straight to the Cottage upon his return that afternoon to Silverquay—with Mr. Lovell away in Ferribridge, too, and all! —she felt sure of it. "So I'm not surprised at your news, Mrs. Coombe, " she concluded triumphantly. "Not surprised at all. "

Having thus successfully taken the wind out of Maria's sails, she proceeded on her way delivering the clean laundry at various houses in the district, and in the course of a few hours the news of Mr. Coventry's engagement to Miss Lovell was being glibly discussed in more than one servants' hall as an accomplished fact. By the afternoon, conveyed thither by the various butchers, bakers, and greengrocers who had acquired the news in the course of their morning rounds, the information had spread to the village.

Meanwhile, during the progress of Brett Forrester's visit to Heronsmere in search of the puppy his aunt so ardently desired, a prying servant had chanced to pause outside Eliot's study door, inspired by a fleeting inquisitiveness to learn with whom her master was closeted. A single sentence she overheard sufficed to convert that idle curiosity into a burning thirst for knowledge. So she remained at the key-hole listening post until it was satisfied, and later on, armed with a fine fat piece of gossip, the like of which did not often come her way, she sallied forth to spend her "afternoon out" in the village.

Thus it came about that the two streams of gossip—one emanating in all innocence from Maria Coombe, the other having its origin in the conversation overheard between Eliot and Brett—met and mingled together and were ultimately poured into the ears of Miss Caroline, busily engaged in parochial visitation. An evil fatality appointed that the first person she subsequently encountered should be Mrs. Carberry, the M. F.H. 's wife, with whom, in a flutter of shocked excitement, she promptly shared the dreadful story she had heard. This, of course, carried then gossip into another stratum of society altogether.

"I can hardly believe it's true! I'm sur*prised*! " twittered Miss Caroline. "Although, of course, Miss Lovell is certainly rather unconventional, I've always looked upon her as quite *nice*. But to spend a night—like that—at a hotel—" Words failed her, and she had to rely upon an unusual pinkness of her complexion to convey adequately to Mrs. Carberry the scandalised depth of her feelings.

"Perhaps I'm not so surprised as you are, " returned the M. F.H. 's wife. "I never cared for the girl. After all, she was merely a companion-help. "

"Companion-chauffeuse, " corrected Miss Caroline diffidently.

"Companion-help, " repeated Mrs. Carberry, unmoved. "And no one would have taken her up at all if Lady Susan hadn't made such a silly fuss of her. It's absurd, when her brother's nothing more than Mr. Coventry's estate agent. I always think it's a great mistake to take people like that out of their position. One generally regrets it afterwards. "

"Still, I believe the Lovells were quite a good family—West Country people—lost money, you know. " Miss Caroline's conscience drove her into making this admission. Also, she wanted very much to know how Mrs. Carberry would meet it. Mrs. Carberry took it in her stride.

"That's just it. They've lost money—mixed with the wrong sort of people. Losing money so often involves losing caste, too. If this story proves to be true, I shall be very glad indeed that I never allowed my daughter Muriel to make friends of these Lovells. We shall soon know, " she added, a note of hungry anticipation in her voice. "The part about the engagement is true, without doubt, since it came direct from the Oldstone Cottage cook. Besides, one could see that this Lovell girl was angling to catch Mr. Coventry. If the engagement is broken off, we may feel pretty sure, I think, that the rest of the story's true, too. "

Privately, she hoped it would prove true, since a man is very often caught at the rebound, and, judiciously managed, it seemed quite possible that Coventry, shocked and disgusted at Ann Lovell's flightiness of character, might turn with relief and admiration to so modest and well-brought-up a girl as her own daughter. To see dear Muriel installed as mistress of Heronsmere had been her ambition from the first moment of its new owner's coming to live at Silverquay, and when Miss Caroline had volunteered the news of Ann's supposed engagement to him, it had come as a rude shock to her plans. But this had been so swiftly followed by the story of Ann's scandalous behaviour in Switzerland that she had speedily reacted from the shock, and was already briskly weaving fresh schemes to bring about the desirable consummation of a marriage between her daughter and Eliot Coventry. Decidedly, Mrs. Carberry was not likely to help stem the tide of gossip setting against Ann!

The day following, the news that Eliot had left England for an indefinite stay abroad flew like wildfire through the neighbourhood, and, in consequence, substance was immediately given to the stories already circulating. There could be no longer any further doubt as to what had happened—Coventry had asked Miss Lovell to marry him, and then, discovering how she had forfeited her reputation somewhere on the Continent, had broken off the engagement between them the very next day.

Silverquay fairly buzzed with the tale. Everybody jumped to the same conclusion and told each other so with varying degrees of censure and disapprobation. Miss Caroline, eager as a ferret, even paid a special visit to Oldstone Cottage, to obtain confirmation of the dreadful truth. Having previously assured herself that Robin and Ann were both out, she darted into the Cottage on the plea of delivering the monthly parish magazine and, naturally, lingered on the doorstep to chat a little with Maria.

"Surely there's no truth in this story I hear, Maria? " she opened fire after a few minutes devoted to generalities.

"What story may you be meaning, ma'am? " inquired Maria blandly. She had heard the tale, of course, from half a dozen different sources, and was inwardly fuming with loyal wrath and indignation—the more so in that she dared not mention the matter to her young mistress whose still, pale composure had seemed to fence her round with a barrier which it was beyond Maria's powers to surmount.

"Why—why—" Miss Caroline fluttered. "The story that she stayed the night at a hotel in the mountains with young Mr. Brabazon when she was on the Continent. "

"And did you suppose 'twas true? " demanded Maria scornfully, her arms akimbo, her blue eyes gimleting Miss Caroline's face.

"I—I don't know what to think, " began Miss Caroline feebly.

Maria looked her up and down—a look beneath which Miss Caroline wilted visibly.

"Well, 'tis certain sure no one would pass the night with you, miss, on any mountain top, " she observed grimly. "And 'tis just as sure they wouldn't with Miss Ann—though there'd be a main diff'rence in the reason why! " And with a snort of defiance she had flounced back into the house, slamming the door in Miss Caroline's astonished face.

To Ann herself, the sudden cloud of obloquy in which she found herself enveloped heaped an added weight to the burden she already had to bear, and compelled her to take Robin fully into her confidence. It was a mystery to her how the story of the Dents de Loup episode had leaked out in the neighbourhood. She utterly declined to believe that Coventry himself would have shared his knowledge of the incident with any one. But that it *had* leaked out was cruelly self-evident, and the worst part of it was that the malicious gossip was founded on so much actual fact that it was difficult—almost impossible, in fact—to combat or refute it. She felt helpless in the face of the detestable scandal which had reared itself upon a foundation of such innocent truth.

"I wish Coventry had accepted my resignation, " fulminated Robin fiercely. "This is a perfectly beastly business. That vile scandal's all over the place. "

"I know, " assented Ann indifferently. It hurt her that certain people should think ill of her as they did, but after all, the ache in her heart hurt much more. A man stretched on the rack would probably take little notice if you ran a pin into him. The lesser pain would be overwhelmed by the great agony. And although the first realisation of the gossip that had fastened on her name filled Ann with bitter indignation and disgust, it became a relatively small matter in comparison with the total shipwreck of her love and happiness. It did not really matter very much that Mrs. Carberry had cut her pointedly in the middle of Silverquay, or that some of the village girls whispered and pointed at her surreptitiously as she passed. These were all external things, which could be fought down. But the wound that Eliot himself had dealt her had pierced to the very core of her being.

"Well, " Robin resumed thoughtfully after a brief silence. "I've *got* to stay here till the six months are run out. But you needn't, Ann. You had better look for a post of some kind till I'm free—"

"A post! " She laughed rather bitterly. "I've a good recommendation for any post, haven't I? A story like this would be sure to follow me up somehow, and I should probably be politely requested by my employer to leave. '

"Then go away for a bit. I'll find the money somehow. I won't have you baited by all the old tabby-cats in the neighbourhood. "

Ann stood up, her head thrown back proudly on its slim young throat.

"*No,* " she said with decision. "No, Robin. I'm not going to run away from village gossip. I'm going to face it out. "

Robin sprang up.

"Well done, little sister! " he exclaimed, a ring of wholehearted admiration in his voice. "We'll stick it out together—stay here and live it down. " He held out his hand and, Ann laying hers within it, they shook hands soberly, just as in earlier days they had so often shaken hands over some childish pact.

The loyalty of Ann's friends, of Lady Susan and of Cara and the rector, was a very real consolation. Lady Susan had descended on the Cottage the moment the story came to her ears—which happened to be on the very day following Coventry's departure from Silverquay. Brett, she vouchsafed, had run up to town unexpectedly for a few days. "And he's just as well out of the way, " she added briskly, "till we've got this tangle straight"—little dreaming that her nephew was responsible for the whole knotting of the tangled skein. By kindly probing she elicited the real, grim tragedy which lay behind all the gossip, and her anger against Eliot knew no bounds. But once she had given characteristic expression to her opinion of men in general, and of Eliot in particular, she promptly set to work to try and mend matters.

"*I* can explain to Eliot how you came to be at the Hotel de Loup that night, " she asserted. "He won't presume to doubt me! "

"No. But he *has* presumed to doubt me, " replied Ann bitterly. "So it wouldn't help in the least if you explained all day. "

"How do you mean—wouldn't help? "

"Because what matters is whether Eliot himself trusts me—not whether he has everything explained to him, " said Ann. "He must trust me because I'm trustworthy—not because you guarantee me. "

"My dear—that's the ideal attitude. But"—Lady Susan sighed and smiled in the same breath—"we've got to make allowances for poor human nature. We're all so very far from being ideal in this sinful old world. Be sensible, Ann darling, " she coaxed, "and let me assure Eliot you were up at the Hotel de Loup alone. "

Ann shook her head.

"You can't, dear Lady Susan. Because—I wasn't alone. Tony and I were there together. "

Lady Susan turned on her a face of blank astonishment.

"You weren't alone? " she exclaimed. "But—I don't understand. Philip told me that Tony ran over to Geneva that day and stayed the night there! "

"Did he? " Ann's heart grew very soft at the thought of Tony's boyishly crude effort to protect her from the possible consequence of their night's sojourn at the hotel. "I'm afraid Tony let him think that on my account—in order to shield me.... I should have told you all about it at the time, " she went on, "only—don't you remember—you had sprained your ankle, and you were in so much, pain that I just didn't want to bother you with the matter. "

Lady Susan looked distressed.

"But, my dear, what possessed you to stay the night up there—with Tony? You must have known people would talk if it ever became known. "

"Well, it was just a sheer bit of bad luck, " explained Ann, and forthwith proceeded to recount the whole adventure which had befallen her and Tony at the Dents de Loup. "We *had* to stay there, " she wound up. "We'd absolutely no choice. But we met no one. Not a soul. And I can't conceive how the story has got out. "

"And now there's all this wretched tittle-tattle about you! " chafed Lady Susan. "My poor little Ann, it really is a stroke of the most fiendish ill-luck. "

Ann nodded.

"Yes. Don't you see how impossible it is for me to clear myself? We *were* there. It's true. "

"I do see, " replied Lady Susan in a worried tone. "It's just the kind of coil that's hardest of all to straighten out. A lot of untrue gossip founded upon actual fact—and there's nothing more difficult to combat than a half-truth. "

"Oh, well"—Ann jumped up restlessly out of her chair. "It's smashed up everything for me. And when you've crashed I don't suppose a little ill-natured gossip more or less matters very much. Did you know Mrs. Carberry cut me this morning in the village high-street? " she added with a smile.

"Did she indeed? " said Lady Susan, a grim note in her usually pleasant voice. "Of course, the whole business is nuts to her—she's aching to plant that prunes-and-prisms daughter of hers on Eliot Coventry. Well, I think I carry weight enough in the neighbourhood to put a stop to that kind of insolence. " She paused reflectively. "I shall open my campaign with a big dinner-party—and you and Robin will come to it. I'll shoot off the invitations to-morrow. Don't worry, Ann. If, between us, your friends can't manage to scotch this kind of dead-set some people are making at you, my name's not Susan Hallett. " She rose and slipped her arm round Ann's shoulders in a gesture of unwonted tenderness. "And for the rest, my dear—try and believe things will come straight in the end. You're in the long lane, now—but you'll find the turning some day, I feel sure. "

The following morning Brian Tempest arrived at the Cottage. Ann greeted him with a smile, half sad, half bitter.

"Have you come to call down fulminations of wrath on my devoted head? " she asked.

The rector's kind eyes were puckered round with little creases of distress.

"Did you think that? " he asked.

She smiled—and there was less of bitterness in the smile this time.

"No, " she answered frankly. "I didn't. I thought you'd come to pay a kindly visit to the outcast. "

"I came, " he said simply, "to tell you—if you need telling—that I don't believe one word of this ridiculous story which is flying round, and that I'm going to fight it with every bit of influence I can bring to bear. "

"You dear! " replied Ann softly. A wan gleam of amusement flitted across her face. "But it's true, you know—Tony and I did stay at the Hotel de Loup together. "

No remotest glimmer of doubt, or even of astonishment, showed itself in the steady glance of Tempest's "heather mixture" eyes.

"Did you? " he returned placidly. "Well, I suppose neither of you has the sole monopoly of any hotel in Europe. "

"Then you're not shocked? "

"Not in the least. I conjecture that some accidental happening drove you both into an awkward predicament. Feel like telling me about it all? "—with a friendly smile.

Ann felt exactly like it. There was something in Brian Tempest—in his absolute sincerity and his broad, tolerant, humorous outlook on things—which attracted confidence as a magnet attracts steel, and before long he was in possession of the skeleton facts of the story, and had himself, out of his own gifts of observation and sympathetic intuition, clothed those bare bones with tissue.

"And what do you propose to do? " he asked, when Ann ceased speaking.

"Stick it out, " she returned briefly.

Tempest watched the brave fire gather and glow in the golden-brown eyes. He nodded contentedly.

"I was sure you would, " he said. "And don't worry overmuch. *Think* that it will come right. Even"—with a kindly significance—"the part that hurts you most—and I know that's not the general gossip. Don't let your thoughts waver. There's no limit to the force of thought, you know. "

"You believe that, too, then? " said Ann quickly.

"I'm sure of it, " he answered quietly. "Thought is the one great miracle-worker. Why"—with a laugh—"if you want immediate proof, it was a bad thought, some one thinking wrongly, that started all this present trouble. So that the right thought—the thought that it will all work out straight, held by you and by all of us who are your friends—is the obvious antidote. God never made a law that only works one-sidedly. If thought forces can work evil, they can assuredly work infinite good. "

"You're an excellent 'cheerer-up, '" said Ann, later on, when he was going. "You *have* cheered me, you know, " she added gratefully.

"Have I? I'm glad. And now, I want you to cheer me. "

"You? " Her voice held surprise.

"Yes, me." He hesitated a moment. "Ann, I'm going to throw myself on your mercy. I know—to my deep shame I know that my sister has been one of the people who have helped to circulate this unfounded story about you. I want you, if you can, to try and forgive her—and me."

"There's nothing to forgive you for," protested Ann.

"She's my sister. Part of her burden must be mine. Nor have I any excuse to offer for her. Some people look through a window and see God's sunshine, while others see only the spots on the window-pane. We are as we're made, they say—but some of us have got a deal of re-making to do before we're perfected."

"Don't worry." Unconsciously Ann sought to comfort him in the same familiar, everyday language which he himself had used to her. "Don't worry one bit. I've no feeling of ill-will towards Miss Caroline. It's just her way—one can't help one's way of looking at things, you know"—quaintly. "And I'm quite, quite sure she never meant any harm."

"So that's the way *you* look at things?" He smiled down at her, his eyes very luminous and tender. "Thank you, Ann, for the way you look at things—the plucky, generous, splendid way."

And when he had gone Ann was conscious of a warm glow round about her heart—that gladdening glow of comfort and thanksgiving which the spontaneous, ardent loyalty of real friends can bring even to the heaviest heart.

CHAPTER XXVI

ENLIGHTENMENT

"I've turned up again like a bad penny, you see. "

Brett, ushered into the living-room at the Cottage by a very depressed-looking Maria, made the announcement with his usual debonair assurance.

"So I see, " replied Ann, shaking hands without enthusiasm. "How are you? "

He looked at her critically—at her face, paler than its wont, her shadowed eyes, the slight lines of her figure—grown slighter even during the brief span of a week.

"*I'm* all right, " he returned pointedly. "But I can't say as much for you. What have you been doing in my absence? Pining? "—quizzically.

"Not exactly, " she answered dryly. "I've had—oh, various worries. Nothing to do with you, though. "

"I'm not so sure, " replied Brett, with a flash of sardonic humour, the significance of which was lost on Ann.

"Then I'm afraid you'll have to take my word for it, " she responded indifferently.

"Are you worrying about this slur on your fair name? " he demanded next, as airily as though he were inquiring if she was worrying about the trimming of a new hat. "My revered aunt has told me all the news, you see. "

Ann winced.

"Brett, how can you speak like that? " Her voice trembled. "It—it isn't anything to laugh at. It's horrible! "

He regarded her in silence. Then:

"No. It isn't anything to laugh at, " he said suddenly. "It's my chance. "

He took a quick step towards her and she retreated involuntarily.

"Your chance? " she replied. "What do you mean? "

"My chance to prove that I'm a better lover than Coventry. I understand he's so shocked that he's bolted out of England"—sneeringly. "Well, I'm not. I've come back to ask you to marry me. "

Ann quivered at his mention of Eliot's name, but with an effort she forced herself to answer him composedly.

"I can only give you the same answer as before—no, Brett. "

"Do explain why, " he returned irrepressibly. "I don't care tuppence what people say. In fact, if they dared to say anything after we were married I should jolly well break their heads for them. So that's that. But surely I'm as good a fellow as Coventry—who's apparently cried off at the first sign of storm. I suppose that's what's happened, isn't it? "

She turned and faced him, a spark of anger in her eyes.

"Whatever it is that has happened between Eliot and me, it has nothing to do with you, " she said haughtily.

His eyes flickered over her face.

"But I can guess! " he replied imperturbably.

"You? —Guess? How—" She broke off, shaken, as so often before, by his air of complete assurance.

He looked at her with quizzical eyes.

"Shall I tell you? " he said tantalisingly. "Yes, I think I will. " He paused, then finished quietly: "I happened to be in Switzerland last spring—when you were. "

There was no misunderstanding the intentional significance with which he spoke—no evading the impression that some definitely evil menace lay behind the brief statement of commonplace fact. To Ann it seemed as though some horror, lurking in the shadows of the fire-lit room, had suddenly stirred and were creeping stealthily towards her—impalpable but deadly, nauseous as the poisonous miasma rising from some dark and fetid pool. She shrank back, instinctively putting out her hand as though to ward off whatever threatened.

"You—you? " she stammered.

"Even I"—blandly. His gaze fastened on her face. "I spent a couple of nights—at the Hotel de Loup. " Then, as she shrank still further away from him, he added lightly: "Dickens of a lonely place, too! "

"Then—then—" Ann's throat felt dry and constricted, but she struggled for utterance. "Then it was you who told—"

"Yes, " he cut in quickly. "It was I who told Coventry about your little escapade up there with Tony Brabazon. "

"Ah—! " A choked cry broke from her lips, and she leaned helplessly against the wall behind her.

"It was all quite simple, " went on Brett coolly. "You see, I read the entry in the hotel register—and I happened to know that Brabazon had no sister. " He rattled glibly on, recounting the episode of the Hotel de Loup with much the same air of inward entertainment with which he had narrated it to Coventry himself. When he had finished he looked across at her with a kind of triumph, no whit ashamed of himself.

There was a long silence. Ann swallowed once or twice, trying to relieve the dreadful feeling of tightness in her throat.

"I suppose, " she said at last, speaking with difficulty, "I suppose you told Eliot—on purpose—to separate us? "

She was staring at him with incredulous, horror-stricken eyes. This thing which he had done seemed to her unspeakable—treacherous and contemptible beyond all description. She had the same dazed appearance as some one who has just witnessed a terrible catastrophe—so terrible and unlooked-for as to be almost beyond credence. For an instant her stricken expression and slow, painful utterance brought the faintest possible look of shame to Brett's face. But it was only momentary and passed as swiftly as it had come.

"Well, " he confessed, "I didn't want you to marry Coventry, so I tried to stop it—naturally. As I told you—I want you to marry me. "

"And you could still want to marry me—thinking what you thought? "

"Certainly I could"—promptly. "Don't you remember, I've told you more than once that the past doesn't count—that nothing a woman might have done would matter to me if I wanted her? I thought you would understand. "

"Understand? " Ann laughed mirthlessly. "How should I understand? Tony and I were trapped up there—at the Dents de Loup. It was a pure accident. Hasn't Lady Susan told you? Oh! "—with a quick, tortured movement. "What have I ever done that you could think of me like that? "

"I know—" Once again a fleeting look of shame clouded the blue eyes. "It seems mad—now. Now that it's all explained. But any man might have thought the same. And do me this justice—I loved you well enough to forgive you that, or anything else. "

"*You loved me!* " The contempt in her voice was like a lash across the face. "You to speak of love! Why, you don't know the first meaning of it! No man who loved me would have deliberately set out to destroy my happiness. Did you imagine for one moment that I would marry you after what you've done? Never! Even if I absolutely *hated* Eliot I wouldn't marry you. Oh! "—smiting her hands together—"I couldn't have believed that any man—even you! "—with blazing scorn—"could have been so wicked—so utterly devoid of anything decent or honest or straight. Have you no feeling, Brett—no mercy, or charity, that you could do such a thing? "

"I've the kind of charity that begins at home, " he returned, unabashed. "All's fair in love and war, you know. "

"Fair! Surely you're not trying to pretend that you've been fair? "

"I think it was a perfectly legitimate thing to do—in the circumstances, " he answered coolly.

She gazed at him, appalled. Lady Susan had indeed been right when she declared that Brett had no principles, and against his unshakable sang-froid Ann felt as helpless to make any impression as a wave beating at the foot of some granite rock.

"When you want something very badly, " he explained with the utmost simplicity, "the only way to get it is to forge straight ahead. You can't afford to be squeamish over trifles. And I want you! "—his voice deepening to a sudden intensity.

The old, familiar fear and dread of him rushed over her afresh. She felt sick—sick and terrified.

"Oh, go—go away! " she exclaimed desperately.

"All right, I'll go. But you'll kiss me first. "

He took a step towards her. She could not retreat. The wall was immediately behind her. With a sudden sideways movement she twisted and tried to escape him. But it was useless. With incredible swiftness he caught her as she turned, and she felt his arms close round her in a grip of steel. He stooped his head.

"No—no! " she implored piteously. "Brett, let me go! Please—*please* let me go! " She struggled frantically against him. Then, finding herself helpless in his grasp, she covered her face with her hands, pressing them hard against her cheeks. But she might as well have tried to pit her puny strength against an avalanche. In a moment he had forced down her shielding hands, bending her slender body backwards so that her face lay just below his lips—shelterless and at his mercy. And then she felt his mouth crushed savagely on hers and the turbulence of his passion swept over her as the hot wind sweeps across the desert—scorching and resistless.

When at last he released her she swayed unsteadily.

"Oh, go—go! " she whispered, her hand against her bruised lips.

For a moment he stared at her without speaking.

"All right. I'll go, " he said sullenly, at last. "But I shall come back. You'll marry me, Ann—I swear it! "

Vaguely she heard him go—the closing of the door behind him, and, a minute later, the sound of the latch of the gate falling into its socket. Came the trampling of a restive horse on the road outside, followed by the rhythmic beat of cantering hoofs. Then silence.

How long she remained where Brett had left her she never knew. She was oblivious of the passage of time, conscious only of a vast grey sea of misery which seemed to have hemmed her in on every side and which had now risen suddenly and closed over her head. But at last, with a quivering, long-drawn breath, she moved stumblingly across towards the window. The room appeared to her stiflingly hot. Her face burned, and her temples throbbed as though a couple of relentless hammers were beating inside her head. With fumbling, nerveless fingers she unfastened the catch of the window and threw it open, letting in the cool autumnal breeze. She leaned out thankfully, drawing in deep breaths of the clean, salt-laden air. It seemed to lave her face, washing away the hated touch of Forrester's lips on hers, and pressing lightly, like a cool hand, against her aching temples.

For some time she stood there, her mind almost a blank, content just to know that she was alone—freed from the presence of the man whom at this moment she felt she loathed more than any one on earth—and to drink in great draughts of the chill, revivifying air. But presently her thoughts began to stir once more. She grew conscious of her surroundings—of her body, which felt suddenly cold. With a shiver, she closed the window and went over to the fire. She crouched down on the hearthrug, and gradually, as her mind became clearer, she began to piece together all that had happened.

It was a bitter realisation. Her whole happiness had been ruined—utterly and remorselessly, because she and Tony had missed the train at the Dents de Loup. It seemed incredible! Such a trivial, unimportant small happening to have brought the whole fabric of a man's and woman's happiness toppling headlong to the ground! A little hysterical sound—half laugh, half sob—escaped her. And Brett— She could hardly endure to think of him. It was past belief that any man who loved her—and within herself Ann acknowledged that in his own selfish, masterful way, Brett did love her—could have so ruthlessly flung everything aside—chivalry, honour, and a woman's happiness—in his fierce determination to obtain his ends. Past belief, indeed! Yet it had actually happened, and the consequences would roll on, like the wheels of some dreadful machine, crushing out hope and joy and faith.

Faith! Ann's thoughts checked at the word. That was the one and only thing which could have saved the whole terrible situation. If Eliot had only trusted her, had had faith in her, then neither the unlucky accident at the Dents de Loup nor the treacherous misuse which Brett had made of it could have availed to hurt their love or to destroy their happiness. For a moment a tide of bitterness against her lover for his lack of trust swelled up within her, then her inherent sense of justice drove it back. He had learned distrust—learned it from bitter experience. The entire burden of catastrophe lay actually on the shoulders of the woman who, years ago, had taken a boy's love and faith and broken them like toys between her hands.

Dully Ann wondered who the woman was—wondered whether she would be a little sorry if she could know that another woman was paying so heavily for the wrong which she had done. And then a dreary smile crossed her face. It wouldn't make any difference if that other woman did know. There was nothing she could do to repair the harm she had worked. It was all hopeless—wheel within wheel, link added to link.

Well, it was over—finished. Ann tried to face the fact without blenching. Love had come, for a brief moment transmuting her whole world, and now love had gone again, and it only remained to take up the burden of life once more. Perhaps it would be easier soon. Some day, she supposed, this pain at her heart would cease, just as everything good, bad, and indifferent, comes to an end in time. But no power on earth could alter things—put back the clock. Even if Eliot, driven by the desperate hunger of love, came back to her, nothing would ever be the same again. He had distrusted her, and that distrust would lie between them now and always.

*****

Night came, but Ann could not sleep. She tossed restlessly from side to side, her thoughts going round and round in an endless weary circle. Tony and Brett and Eliot, three men who had loved and desired her, each in his own way, and between them they had managed to crush out every atom of happiness that life could hold for her.

Towards morning, utterly worn out, she dropped into an uneasy slumber, from which—it seemed to her—Maria roused her almost at once, and with the return of consciousness the whole deadening weight of recollection fell on her once more. She raised herself wearily on her elbow.

"Is it really time to get up? " she asked languidly. "I feel as if I'd only just gone to sleep. "

Maria, bustling about the room pulling up the blinds and drawing back the curtains, paused and looked at the slender figure lying in the bed with eyes full of concern. They were like the faithful, yearning eyes of a dog who senses that you are in trouble but is powerless to help. He can do nothing—only love you. And Maria knew that her adored young mistress was in sore trouble, and that she could do nothing to help—only love her.

"There, drink your cup o' tea, miss, and you'll feel better, " she said hearteningly. "A body feels different with a cup o' tea inside. I suppose you've heard the news—since Mr. Forrester himself was here only yesterday? "

Ann set down her tea-cup sharply, her heart beating apprehensively. What was she going to hear now? Something else that would hurt her afresh? She glanced shrinkingly towards Maria.

"No. What news? " she faltered. She did not want to be hurt any more. She felt as though she wouldn't be able to bear it.

"Why, 'twas the milkman told me. Mr. Forrester's off from White Windows to-day. Going away quite sudden like in that there *Minx* of his. " She nodded in the direction of the bay.

The ghost of a smile flitted across Ann's tired face.

"In the *Sphinx*, you mean, " she suggested.

"Yes, miss, jes' what I said, wasn't it? " agreed Maria. "You can see 'em all on board this morning—busy as bees in a hive. "

Ann stepped out of bed and went to the window. It was quite true. Far below in the bay she could see the shining *Sphinx*, and there were signs of unmistakable activity on board. She drew a long breath. If

Brett were going, it was good news—not bad! She had always been secretly afraid of him. Now—now that she was aware of the part he had played in the destruction of her happiness, she knew that she would never again be able to see him without recalling all that she had lost. He seemed to her to embody the whole tragedy which had befallen her.

And the yacht—his yacht—waiting, waiting always in the bay, like a cat at a mousehole....

Two hours later Ann stood on the cliff and watched the *Sphinx* steam slowly out to sea, and with the last gleam of the yacht's white stern it seemed to her as though some inexplicable, still lingering menace were removed.

CHAPTER XXVII

THE TRUTH

"Café noir? Bien, m'sieu."

The alert French waiter shot away like a stone from a catapult, leaving Coventry to lapse back into the reverie from which he had roused himself to order his coffee. He had dined rather early with a view to escaping the chattering crowd which thronged the hotel, and now he was sitting alone in a windowed corner of the *salle*, his eyes resting absently on the curving line of coast and sea.

Set like a round silver shield in the midst of the starry sky hung a full moon, rippling a shining highway across the deep night-blue of the Mediterranean and turning the common-place walks of the hotel garden below into silvern paths of mystery. But Eliot remained unmoved by the exquisite beauty of the scene. It hardly seemed to penetrate his consciousness. He was musing with a grim, sardonic humour on the strange chance which had brought him, after nearly three months' solitary wandering through Europe, to the identical hotel at Mentone where Tony Brabazon and his uncle happened to be staying. It seemed as though fate had deliberately mocked him—perpetrating a bitter jest at his expense. Ever since he had quitted Silverquay he had been roving from place to place, seeking forgetfulness, and had at last turned his steps toward Monte Carlo, hoping that in the keen concentration and excitement of pitting his wits against the god of chance he might temporarily drown the memories that pursued him. And then, who should he encounter on the very first night of his arrival but Tony Brabazon!

The boy had been seated at the next table to the one allotted to Coventry himself, dining in company with a haughty, irascible old gentleman whom he had introduced as his uncle, Sir Philip Brabazon. One of the most ironical touches of the whole queer jumble of events, Eliot reflected, had been the jolly, friendly way in which, the instant Tony caught sight of him, he had jumped up from the table to greet him, joyfully inquiring for all the friends he had made at Silverquay and, in particular, for Ann.

Eliot had been conscious of a curious intermingling of feeling. The very sight of Tony, bringing with it, as it did, a quickened rush of torturing remembrance, filled him with a kind of insensate fury. He wanted to strike the friendly, good-humoured smile off the boy's face. And yet, underneath the burning anger and resentment which he felt, he was fain to acknowledge the rank injustice of it. Tony had done him no deliberate wrong, and, ignorant of the fact that indirectly his was the agency which had brought Eliot's happiness crashing to the ground, his open-hearted attitude of friendliness was the most natural thing in the world. Moreover, Eliot admitted to himself that had things been otherwise he would have felt quite disposed to reciprocate Tony's evident good-fellowship. The boy had a distinct charm of his own, and he had liked what little he had seen of him at Silverquay. But, circumstances being as they were, he opposed a quiet indifference to Tony's friendly overtures, although with characteristic obstinacy he declined to be driven out of Mentone by the fact of the other man's presence there.

Sometimes the Brabazons had visitors—Lady Doreen, Neville and her mother, and on these occasions Eliot derived a certain misanthropic amusement out of watching the incipient love affair which was obviously budding between the two young people—a development which, he could see, was clearly a source of satisfaction to at least one of their respective elderly relatives. Doreen's mother was all smiles. She had other daughters coming on.

That Tony and Doreen Neville were rapidly drifting towards the condition known as being in love was unmistakable, and Eliot envied the pliant facility of youth which can put the past behind and embark so soon upon a new adventure. Surely a man who had once believed himself in love with Ann—Ann, with her warm vitality and pluck and humour—could never be satisfied with the frail beauty and helpless, clinging sweetness which was all that Lady Doreen had to offer! Ann was not an easy person to forget, as Eliot knew to his own most bitter cost. Yet Brabazon seemed able to forget. God! If only the faculty of forgetting were purchasable!...

*****

The waiter sped swiftly forward and deposited Eliot's coffee on the table by his side, rousing him out of his bitter reflections with a jolt.

"You've been an unconscionable time! " he flung at the man irritably, and then smiled wryly at his own irritability. His nerve must be going! A French newspaper lay on the table at his elbow.

Drawing it towards him he deliberately immersed himself in its pages to the exclusion of the thoughts which were torturing him.

It was thus that Tony found him an hour later when he strolled into the *salle,* looking somewhat at a loose end and rather sorry for himself.

"Going to the tables to-night? " he asked, pausing irresolutely at Eliot's side.

Eliot glanced up.

"No. Are you? You do most nights, don't you? " He recollected having seen Tony's flushed, eager face opposite him at one or other of the tables on a good many occasions.

"No. Feel off it to-night. Besides"—with a frown—"I've dropped an awful lot of money at it lately. May I sit down? " he added, laying his hand on the back of a chair.

Coventry put down his newspaper. It was obvious the boy wanted to talk, to unburden himself of something. Better let him get it over and have done with it, he reflected. A word of encouragement and the whole story came out. Tony, it appeared, was feeling hipped. The Nevilles were leaving Mentone, a new doctor who had been consulted having advised a more bracing climate for Lady Doreen, and simultaneously Sir Philip had announced his decision to return to London—a combination of events which had succeeded in reducing Tony to unplumbed depths of despondency.

"It's rather a break-up, you see, " he explained, "after nearly three months here together. We made a topping foursome"—ingenuously. "And now it's all over, I feel rather like a kid going back to school after the holidays. "

Eliot found himself sympathising against his will. It was as difficult to maintain an inimical attitude towards Tony as to resist the spontaneous advances of a confiding puppy.

"Couldn't you persuade your uncle that a more bracing climate might suit him, too? " suggested Eliot, with a faint smile.

Tony flashed him a quick glance from under his long lashes—half laughing, half deprecating.

"That's just it, " he admitted frankly. "I can't budge him. Doreen and I are—well, half engaged, you know—"

"Half-engaged? " asked Eliot, lifting his brows.

Tony nodded, suddenly moody.

"Yes. Depending on her health and my good conduct"—rather bitterly. "So they're swishing her off to the Swiss mountains for the one and my uncle is removing me from the temptations of Monte Carlo for the other. "

"What part of Switzerland are the Nevilles going to? " inquired Eliot, more for the sake of saying something than because the subject held the remotest interest for him. "Davos? "

"No. Somewhere up above Montricheux. "

"Montricheux? " The word left Eliot's lips involuntarily.

"Yes. You know it, don't you? "

"I've been there"—briefly.

"I had the adventure of my life there, " volunteered Tony. "I've never forgotten it, by Jove! Up at a place called the Dents de Loup. "

Had he been looking he would have seen a sudden smouldering fire wake in the keen grey eyes of the man beside him. But he was occupied in lighting a cigarette at the moment, and, failing to observe the change in Eliot's expression, he pursued reminiscently:

"Yes. I was up there with a girl I'd known ever since I was a kid—we'd almost been brought up together. And the first thing I did was to go and skid down the side of a ravine. " He puffed futilely at his cigarette. "Blow! It's gone out. "

He paused to relight it, while Eliot sat rigidly still, waiting in tense silence for the rest of the story. It all came out quite naturally and with a blissful unconsciousness on Tony's part that the tale could have any particular significance for the man beside him.

"She was the pluckiest girl I know, " he wound up loyally. "Took it like a real sport and never blamed me in the least. Most women would have clamoured for my blood. "

"Yes. I think they would. " Eliot replied quite mechanically. He was hardly conscious that he had made any answer, and when, soon afterwards, Tony took himself off with a friendly: "Well, so long. See you in the morning, perhaps? " he responded once more like an automaton.

He was aware of only one thing. His whole consciousness concentrated on it. Ann was innocent—utterly and entirely innocent! There was no longer any question in his mind. Tony's transparent simplicity and candour in recounting his adventure at the Dents de Loup and its immediate consequences was too self-evident to doubt, and although he had refrained from mentioning the name of the girl who had been his companion—the "pluckiest girl he knew"—it was equally clear that he had been narrating the mountain episode in which Ann had been concerned and for which she had paid so dearly.

Grimly, with a ruthless resolution, Eliot faced the facts. He had completely and very terribly wronged the woman he loved. His suspicions had been absolutely unjustified. With his own hand he had pulled down his happiness—his own and Ann's, too—in ruins about them.

And there could be no going back—no undoing of what had been done. A man cannot doubt a woman, as he had doubted Ann, and then, when she is proved transcendently innocent, go back and tell her that he believes in her. If he did, she would be quite justified in flinging his tardy assurances of faith back in his face and thanking him for something of very trifling value. Even if out of the limitless tenderness of her woman's heart Ann forgave him—as, God knows, women are forgiving men every day that dawns! —still their love would be robbed of something infinitely precious—tarnished by an ugly and abiding memory. What was it Ann herself had said about love? *"It's faith... and trust, Eliot. "* He remembered her grave, steadfast eyes and groaned in spirit, realising that he himself had despoiled love of its very pith and marrow, its deepest inner significance. There was no way out—no atonement possible.

Motionless, sunk in the inferno of his own thoughts, Eliot remained where Tony had left him until one of the hotel employés, who had several times glanced uneasily in the direction of the silent Englishman occupying the seat by the window, finally plucked up courage to begin switching off the lights for the night.

"*Pardon, m'sieu*". he murmured deprecatingly as he passed by the still figure in the course of his tour of the room.

Eliot stared at the man with blank, incurious eyes. Then he rose slowly to his feet and walked out of the hotel—moving with a peculiar precision like one who walks in a trance. After that he lost count of time. He went down into the depths and the dark waters of a grief and agony that was nigh to madness submerged him.

When he came to himself it was to find that it was late afternoon and that he was back again in his room at the hotel. He could not have given the faintest account of how he had passed the hours which had intervened since he had walked out of the hotel into the moonlit night—whether he had eaten or drunken or where he had been. He had a vague recollection of wandering aimlessly about the streets, and then of diverging from the town into the country because he had twice encountered the same *gendarme* and on the second occasion the man had followed him for a few yards suspiciously. Beyond that he remembered nothing. He was only conscious of a physical fatigue so intense, so racking in every nerve and sinew and fibre of his body that for the time being it deadened even the mental torture he had been enduring. He flung himself down on his bed and slept till the noonday sun was high in the heavens, flooding his room with light.

When he resumed the normal usages of life once more and reappeared downstairs, he found that the Brabazons and Lady Doreen Neville and her mother had all gone their several ways. They were the only people with whom he had any acquaintance, and in an odd, indefinable way he missed their presence. He spent almost all his time at the Casino, working out and experimenting with different systems. He had come to no decision as to how he should order his future life, and until he had formulated some scheme he found that he could only stop the hideous treadmill of his thoughts by focussing his whole attention on the crazy gyrations of the spinning ball.

And then one day, about a month later, a letter was put into his hand, bearing the Silverquay postmark. The writing was unfamiliar, and its unfamiliarity woke in him a sudden horrible fear and dread of what the letter might contain. Had some one written to tell him—what Ann could no longer write and tell him herself? He slit the envelope and his eyes raced down the lines of the sheet it had enclosed.

> "*Dear Mr. Coventry,* " ran the letter, written in Lady Susan's characteristically big, generous hand. "*Probably you'll think me an interfering old woman. I daresay I am. But try and remember that I was young once and that just now I'm looking at life for you and Ann through young eyes—and thinking what a long, weary lot of it there is still to be lived through if you each remain at opposite ends of the pole. The time will go a deal quicker if you are together—it's like dividing by two, you know.*
>
> "*I hear you ran across Tony Brabazon in Mentone, and I think that by now you probably know as much about what happened up at the Dents de Loup as I or any one, and are probably cursing yourself. Don't. It's a waste of time and happiness. Come to my party instead.* "

Attached to this characteristic document was a card of invitation to a dance to be given at White Windows by Lady Susan Hallett on February the seventh.... And to-day was the sixth! But it could be done. By travelling all night, catching the morning boat and then the midday train to Silverquay, Eliot realised that he could reach White Windows in time.

A bell stood on a table near by—one of those shiny metal bells with a button on the top which you press down sharply to induce the thing to ring. Eliot thumped it, and continued thumping till a half-demented waiter came flying towards him in response.

"Bring me a time-table, " he roared. "And bring it quick. "

CHAPTER XXVIII

THE GREY SHADOW

The ball-room at White Windows was all in readiness for the forthcoming dance. The floor, waxed and polished till it was as smooth as a sheet of gleaming ice, caught and held the tremulous reflections of a hundred flickering lights, whilst from above, where the orchestra was snugly tucked away in the gallery behind a bank of flowers, came faint pizzicato sounds of fiddles tuning up, alternating with an occasional little flourish or tentative roulade of notes.

The dance was not timed to begin for half an hour or more, but the members of the house-party had congregated together at the upper end of the room and were chatting desultorily. Sir Philip Brabazon and Tony were included amongst them, in addition to a couple of pretty girls, nieces of Lady Susan, and three or four stray men who had been invited down to swell the ranks.

"And how's Ann? " demanded Sir Philip of his hostess.

"Ann? Oh, you'll find her a trifle thinner, I think, that's all, " responded Lady Susan discreetly. To her own eyes Ann seemed to have altered wofully in the course of the last few months, but she reasoned that Sir Philip was no more observant than the majority of men and that if she prepared him for the fact that Ann was somewhat thinner than of old he would accept the change quite naturally and not worry the girl herself with tiresome questions as to the cause of such a falling off.

It had been a very difficult winter, but Lady Susan had the satisfaction of knowing that she and the rector between them had triumphantly routed Ann's detractors, and although it was well-nigh impossible to utterly stamp out of a country district such as Silverquay the hydra-headed monster called scandal, they had certainly succeeded in drawing his fangs. But if Lady Susan had been successful in her campaign against the tittle-tattle of the neighbourhood, she had been powerless to restore that sheer joy and happiness in living which had been so peculiarly Ann's gift until the day when Eliot Coventry went out of her life, taking from her, as he went, everything except the courage to endure.

Lady Susan had never forgiven Brett for his share in the work of destroying Ann's happiness, and she chafed bitterly against her own inability to help matters. It was only through the merest accident that she had at last seen the possibility of being of service. She had been up in town a few days prior to the date fixed for the dance and had encountered Tony shopping in the Army and Navy Stores. He happened to mention that he had run across Coventry at Mentone, and a chance remark elicited the fact that he had regaled him with the history of the Dents de Loup adventure.

Perhaps Lady Susan's face had expressed more than she knew, for Tony, perceiving that she attached some special importance to the matter, looked suddenly anxious.

"I say, I've not been giving Ann away, have I? " he demanded in honest consternation. "I made sure she'd told you all about it by this time. I never thought—"

"Don't worry, " Lady Susan reassured him hastily. "You're not giving her away. She did tell me—all about it. "

When she returned home she had taken her courage in both hands and written to Eliot asking him to come back. And to-night, doubtful whether her letter had reached him in time to allow of his returning for the dance, totally ignorant of the reception it would receive, and uncertain even as to how Ann would welcome him if he actually did return, she was on tenterhooks of nervousness and anxiety.

"You do grow thinner in the winter, you know, " she continued airily to Sir Philip, unwisely elaborating her comment upon Ann's appearance.

"You don't, " contradicted the old man with his usual acerbity. "You grow fatter if you've any sense—to keep the cold out. " He glared at her, then demanded abruptly: "How do you think Tony's looking? "

Lady Susan's dark eyes rested thoughtfully a moment on Tony's face before she answered.

"Not too well, " she admitted. "He looks a little strained and keyed up. Have you been bullying him, Philip? "

"Not more than usual"—grimly. "I've told him I'll pay no more debts for him. And a good thing, too! I fancy he's been keeping within his allowance since I put my foot down. Anyhow, he hasn't come to me again, begging for money. " He paused and shot a swift glance of inquiry at her, obviously seeking her approval, but Lady Susan preserved a strictly non-committal silence. She thought Tony exhibited decided symptoms of nervous strain. His eyes were restless, and his mouth wore a dissatisfied, thwarted expression.

"It's love, " pursued Sir Philip, as she made no response. "That's what's the matter with the boy. He doesn't know; whether he's on his head or his heels. "

"Love? "

"Yes. He's in love with that slip of a Doreen Neville. And because I brought him back to Audley Square instead of careering all over Europe after her and her mother he's as sulky as a young bear. "

"Doreen Neville? " Lady Susan felt that her replies were hopelessly inadequate, but she was too genuinely taken aback by the news to think of anything to say.

"I said so, didn't I? "—crustily. "I suppose I shall have to let him marry her in the end. She's all right, of course, as regards family. But a bit of a swear-stick—melt in a storm, probably. Confound the boy! "—irritably. "Why couldn't he have remained in love with Ann? "

"I'm very glad he didn't, " returned Lady Susan quietly. "It was only calf-love. Besides, he would have *leant* on Ann—she's such a stalwart little soldier, you know"—with a smile.

Sir Philip nodded.

"Yes. She'd have kept him straight, " he said gloomily. "Whereas Doreen Neville's the hot-house plant type—just the opposite. No good to Tony at all. "

"I'm not so sure, Philip. Sometimes the need to care for and protect some one weaker than himself helps to steady a man down more than anything else. Ah! " Lady Susan broke off, her face brightening. "Here is Ann—with Robin. I told them to come early. "

Sir Philip put up his monocle and glared in the direction of the newcomers. Yes, Ann was certainly thinner—too thin, perhaps—though, as far as appearances were concerned, he thought the change had only served to accentuate the charming angles of her face and give an additional grace to the boyishly slender lines of her figure.

Any one less like a love-lorn maiden than Ann looked at that moment could hardly be imagined. She was wearing a charming frock the colour of a pool of deep green sea-water, with a handful of orange-golden poppies clustered at the waist, and as the lights flickered over her, from the swathed gold-brown of her hair to the tips of her small gold shoes, she was as detail-perfect as a woman who hadn't a single care in life. The simple, appealing black frock generally adopted by the heroine in fiction who has been crossed in love did not allure Ann in the very least. Whatever happened to her, she would always confront the world with a brave face. And even if her small, individual barque of life were hopelessly foundered she would at least go down with colours flying.

Nevertheless, to the discerning eye the alteration in her was very palpable. In repose her mouth fell into lines of quiet endurance, and her eyes held a look of deep sadness. But, fortunately for most of us, the discerning eye is a rarity, and in public Ann rarely allowed herself to lapse into one of those moments of abstracted thought when the unguarded expression of the face gives away the secrets of the heart.

She greeted Sir Philip with all her old gaiety, and, when he told her she was much too thin, laughed at him gently.

"Don't be a fuss-pot, dear godparent, " she adjured him. "I was never one of the fat kine, and really I'm very glad of it. You can dress ever so much more economically when you're thin, you know, and that's quite a consideration these days. "

"Are you—do you mean—look here, Ann, " he floundered awkwardly. "Are you hard up? "

She laughed outright.

"No, of course not. Robin gets a topping good screw, and I'm doing quite a millionaire business in the poultry line. "

"Humph! " Sir Philip grunted. "Got any clothes fit for London? "

She nodded.

"Lots. Put away where moth and rust shan't corrupt their morals. "

"Well, get'm out and come up to Audley Square for a bit. You look—I don't know the word I want—peeked. "

"It's no use shelving it on to me like that, " said Ann teasingly. "What you really mean is that you and Tony are getting awfully bored with each other alone! "

A smile glimmered in the depths of the fierce old eyes.

"Perhaps that's it. Will you come? "

"I'd love to. But you may just as well tell me what's worrying you. "

"You're an impudent girl! Who said I was worrying? "

"Well—perhaps not worrying. But unsettled in mind, " conceded Ann. "What's Tony teen doing? "—shrewdly.

"Getting engaged—or trying to. "

She laughed.

"Pooh! I guessed that—months ago. And I think Lady Doreen's a dear. So you'd better be getting out your consent and furbishing it up so as to give it prettily as soon as it's required. You know you're pleased—really. "

By this time the guests were arriving, and very soon Ann was swept away from Sir Philip on a tide of eager young men, anxious to inscribe their names on her programme. She was an excellent dancer, but although she was physically too young and healthy not to find a certain enjoyment in the sheer delight of rhythmic motion, she was conscious as the evening progressed of a certain quality of superficiality in the pleasure she experienced. There was a sameness about it all that palled. What was there in it, after all? One of your partners knew a priceless new glide or shuffle which he forthwith imparted to you, or else you initiated him into some step hitherto unfamiliar to him, and after that you both went on one-stepping or fox-trotting round the room in the wake of a number of other people doing likewise.

Ann, in the arms of a tall young officer from the Ferribridge barracks, caught herself up quickly at this stage of her unprofitable train of thought. This was not the first time lately that she had found herself impressed with the utter staleness of things—she who had been wont to find life so full of interest—and she knew that thoughts such as these were best dismissed as soon as possible. They linked up too closely with searing memories. She made a determined effort to steady herself, and pulled herself together so successfully that the young Guardsman from Ferribridge told quite a number of people that Miss Lovell was a "topping little sport all round—good dancer and jolly good fun to talk to. "

She danced several times with Tony, and left him completely nonplussed by her uncanny discernment when, after he had stumbled through the revelation of his engagement to Doreen Neville, during one of the intervals, she promptly told him she had anticipated it long ago and wished him luck.

"And—and you and I? " he had queried with a certain wistful embarrassment.

"Pals, Tony, " she answered frankly. "Same as always. You must let me meet Lady Doreen when she comes back from Switzerland, and"—smiling—"I'll hand over my charge to her. Have you been good lately, by the way? "

He flushed, and his eyes grew restless.

"I lost a bit at Monte, " he admitted. "I was winning pots of money at first, and then all at once my luck turned and I lost the lot. "

"And more, too, I suppose? " suggested Ann rather wearily.

He nodded.

"I shall get it all back at cards, though, " he assured her.

"Have you got any of it back yet? " she asked pointedly.

"No, But it stands to reason my run of bad luck must turn sooner or later. Come on back to the ball-room and let's dance this, Ann—don't lecture me any more, there's a dear. "

She yielded to those persuasive, long-lashed eyes of his, and they returned to the ball-room and finished the remainder of the dance. But her conversation with Tony had added to the oppression of her spirits. She felt sure, from the way he shirked the subject, that he was getting himself into financial difficulties again, and if the matter came to Sir Philip's ears she was afraid that this time it might end in an irreparable cleavage between uncle and nephew. The former had paid Tony's debts so often, and on the last occasion he had warned him very definitely that he would never do so again. And Ann was fain to acknowledge that one could hardly blame the old man if by this time he had really reached the limits of his patience—and his purse.

She was still brooding rather unhappily over Tony's affairs when Robin came to claim her for a dance. He, too, seemed rather preoccupied and distrait, and as they swung out into the room together Ann cast about in her mind for some explanation of his unwonted gloom. A minute later she caught an illuminating glimpse of Cara, sitting alone by the big fire which still smouldered redly at the far end of the room, and a queer little smile of understanding curved her lips.

"You've only danced with Cara once this evening, Robin, " she observed. "Have you been squabbling? "

He laughed.

"Not likely. But Lady Susan caught me and trotted me round for some duty dances, and by the time those were fixed Cara had booked up a lot and we couldn't make our programmes fit. "

On a quick, sympathetic impulse Ann pulled up near one of the doorways, drawing him aside out of the throng of dancers with a light touch on his arm.

"Then go and ask her for this, " she said hastily. "She's not dancing it. And I—I'm really rather tired. I'd love a few minutes' rest. " She gave him a little push, and before he could say yea or nay she had vanished through the doorway, leaving him free to secure at least one more dance with Mrs. Hilyard.

A good many couples were sitting about outside, partaking of ices and other forms of refreshment, and Ann made her way quickly through the hall and bent her steps in the direction of the library where, earlier in the evening, she had caught sight of a cosy fire. As she passed, she heard the ring of a bell, followed by the sound of some late-comer being admitted. She did not see who it was, and with a fleeting thought that whoever had chosen to arrive so late would have small chance of securing good partners, she slipped quietly into the library.

The fire had burnt down and she stirred it into a blaze before she settled herself in a low chair beside it. She was genuinely glad to be alone for a few minutes—glad of the peaceful quiet of the comfortable room with its silent, book-lined walls and padded easy chairs. She had lost the real spirit of enjoyment. Her old-time zest for dancing seemed to have deserted her entirely, and the daily necessity of playing up in public, of pretending to the world at large that all was well with her, was becoming an increasing strain.

In addition to this, she was conscious to-night of a vague sense of regret. In another few weeks the term of Robin's six months' notice would have expired and they would both be going away from Silverquay. He had heard of several suitable posts, but so far he had not definitely accepted any one of them. Probably within the next fortnight his decision would be made, and Ann realised that leaving Silverquay would be somewhat of a wrench. She had known both great happiness and great grief there, and a full measure of those unreckoned hours of everyday fun and laughter and enjoyment which we are all prone to accept so easily and without any very great gratitude, only realising for how much they counted When they are suddenly taken from us. But now, as the inevitable day of departure drew nearer, Ann found herself face to face with the fact that, although she might leave Silverquay itself behind, memories both sweet and bitter would forever hold out their hands to her from the little sea-girt village. Sometimes she would not be able to evade them. However fast she might hurry through life, they would reach out and touch her, and she would feel those straining hands against her heart.

And then, across her bitter-sweet musings, came the creak of the door as some one pushed it quietly open, and entered the room.

"Ann! "

At the sound of that voice she felt as though every drop of blood in her body had rushed to her heart and were throbbing there in one great hammering pulse. Her hands gripped the arm of her chair convulsively, and slowly and fearfully she turned her head in the direction whence came the voice. Coventry was standing on the threshold of the room. A strangled cry broke from her, and she sat staring at him with wild, incredulous eyes. For a moment the room seemed to fill with a grey, swirling mist, blurring the outlines of the furniture and the figure of the man who stood there silently in the doorway. Then the mist cleared away, and she could see his eyes bent on her with an expression of such stark bitterness and despair and longing that it hurt her to look at him. Was this her lover—who had left her in such fierce scorn and anger only a few short months ago? This man whose face was worn and ravaged with an intensity of suffering such as she had not dreamed possible! If she had grown thin in paying for that bitter parting, then he must have paid a hundredfold to be so terribly marred and altered.

"Eliot! " The word came stammeringly from her lips—hushed as one hushes the voice only in the presence of a great grief or of death itself. She bent her head, unwilling to look again on that soul's agony so nakedly revealed.

"Yes. I have come back, " he said tonelessly.

Closing the door behind him, he advanced into the room and came and stood beside her.

"Look up! " he exclaimed suddenly, almost violently. "Lift up your face, and let me see what these months have done to you. "

She lifted her face mechanically, and for a full minute he stood looking down at it, reading it feature by feature, line by line—the proud, weary droop of the mouth, the quiet acceptance of pain which had lain so long in the gold-brown eyes. Then, with a groan he dropped suddenly and knelt beside her, holding his arms close round her, and laid his head against her knees. His face was hidden, and hesitatingly, with a half-shy, half-maternal gesture Ann touched the dark head pressed against her. Moments passed and he neither stirred nor spoke. At last she stooped over him.

"Eliot," she said quietly, "tell me why you have come back?"

Even then he did not move at once, but at last he raised his head from her knees and met her eyes.

"I've come back," he said slowly, "because, though I've doubted you, I can't live without you. I've come back to ask your forgiveness—if it is still possible for you to forgive me." Then, as she would have spoken, he checked her: "No, don't decide—don't say anything yet. Hear what I have to tell you first."

She yielded to a curious strained insistence in his voice.

"Very well," she said gently, "you shall tell me just what you will."

He left his place by her side and went over and stood by the chimneypiece, looking down at her while he spoke, and as she listened it seemed as though all that he had fought against, believed and disbelieved, suffered and endured, was made clear to her in the terse, difficult sentences that fell one by one from his lips.

"You knew that I'd once been deceived by a woman," he said. "Her name doesn't matter. She deceived me, and my love for her died—as surely as a man dies if you stab him to the heart. She stabbed my love—and it died, and I swore then that I would give no other woman the power to hurt me as she had hurt me. When I met you I knew, almost at once, that you were a woman whom—if I allowed myself to—I might grow to love. I think it was your sincerity, your transparent honesty that won me. You were all I'd dreamed of in a woman—all that I hadn't found in that other woman. But I was afraid. So I left Montricheux—went away at once. I didn't want to care for you. I'd been too badly hit before. Cowardly, you'll say, perhaps—you were never a coward, were you, Ann? Well, it may have been. Anyhow, I did go away and I tried to forget all about you. It wasn't easy, God knows, and then, by a trick of fate, I found you again, at my cottage—living there, sister of the man with whom I'd just made a pact. After that it was a struggle between my joy at finding you there and my determination never to let myself care again for any woman." He paused, but Ann did not speak, and after a minute he went on again:

"Well, you know how it ended. I was beaten. I loved you and I had to tell you so. When I yielded, I yielded entirely—gave you my utter love and faith. I believed in you completely—far more than I knew or even suspected at the time. And then, close on the top of that, I was told the story of how you had stayed at the Dents de Loup with Tony Brabazon. Even then I could hardly credit it. I came and asked you. And you didn't deny it. It was true. What else could I think? I argued that you had thrown Brabazon over because I was a better 'catch' from, a worldly point of view—just as that other woman had thrown me over for a similar reason! —that you'd deliberately deceived me, that you'd been faithless both to Brabazon and to me, as you would be faithless to any other man who loved you.... Remember, it had been your seeming sincerity, your truth, your *straightness* which had first attracted me. And just as I had loved you for your truth, so then I hated you for your falseness—your unbelievable falseness.... Why didn't you deny it all, Ann? Explain—clear the mists away from my eyes? "

"I was too proud—and hurt, " she said quiveringly.

"If you'd only stooped to explain—" He broke off, with a savage gesture. "Forgive me! What right have I to reproach or blame you? The whole fault was mine. Well, I believed you as disloyal and disingenuous as I had known you to be loyal and candid. And I went away. I went down into hell. You've at least the satisfaction of knowing that I paid for my distrust—paid for it to the last fraction owing—"

"Ah, don't! " She raised her hand swiftly, imploringly. But he took no notice. He continued doggedly:

"Then, when I thought I had suffered all that a man could be called upon to suffer, I met Tony—Tony over head and ears in love with quite another woman, as unlike you—oh, your very antithesis! He used to talk to me sometimes. God knows I didn't give him any encouragement! I hated the very sight of him. But he never guessed it. And one day he came and prattled out to me the story of an adventure he had had—at the Dents de Loup—how he got caught up there with a girl. And I knew, then, that it was *your* adventure, too—though of course he never mentioned your name. But it was as clear as daylight to me. It was as though scales had fallen from my eyes.... I knew then what I'd done. I'd pulled down our house of happiness about our heads. For a time I think I went mad. I could think of nothing except the fact that I'd made it impossible for me ever to come to you again—even to ask your forgiveness. "

He was silent a moment, leaning his arm on the chimney-piece and shading his face with his hand. When he again resumed it was with a palpable effort and his voice roughened.

"Afterwards, when I came to my senses, I saw that I *must* come to you. I had destroyed my own life—all that was worth while in it. But I had no right to destroy yours. So I've come back—to ask your forgiveness, Ann—if you can give it. And by forgiveness"—he eyed her steadily—"I mean all that forgiveness can hold—not just a mere form of words. I want the love I threw away—the right you once gave me to call myself your lover. If you don't feel you can give it—I shan't complain. I've no right to complain. I shall just go quietly out of your life. But if you can—now you know all—" He broke off. "Ann... shall I go... or stay? "

He made an involuntary movement towards her, then, checked himself abruptly and stood looking down at her in silence. From the ball-room there floated out the strains of the latest fox-trot, sounding curiously cheap and tawdry as they cut across the deep, almost solemn intensity that prevailed in the quiet room where a man had just stripped his soul naked to the eyes of the woman he loved and now stood as one awaiting judgment.

Ann remained silent. Speech seemed for a few moments a physical impossibility. She had been touched to the quick. Step by step she had gone with Eliot down into that place of torment where he had been wandering, suffering an agony of pain of which the keenest pang had taken birth in the bitter knowledge that it was of his own making, and in every fibre of her being she ached to give him back all that he had lost—all that he asked for. Ached to give it back to him complete, whole, unharmed—that love which had been his and which he had so piteously thrown away.

And she could not. By no mere shibboleth of words, no waving of a wand, could she restore the past, reconstruct what had been out of what was. Love she could give him in full measure, the same enduring love which would be his for ever, believing or unbelieving, living or dead. And his love she would take again—only she herself knew how gladly! But always their mutual love must lack something—that fine thread of utter faith and trust which he himself had cut asunder. It could be knotted together again, it was true. But one would always feel the knot—know it was there. He believed in her now—because she had been proved innocent. But she would never know if his belief in her would withstand the stress of another such test as the one under which it had gone down. To the end of life there would be a doubt, an unanswered question in her heart, as to whether he really had faith in her or no.

She looked up at last to meet his eyes still fixed intently upon her as he waited for her answer. Her own were rather sad. But her surrender was complete. She held out her hands.

"Stay! " she said.

Yet even as he gathered her into his arms she was vitally, cruelly conscious of the absence of the one thing needful to make perfect their reunion. Not even the swift passion of his kisses could convince her of his faith in her. She was not sure—could never be sure, now.

It would be bound to come between them sometimes—that terrible uncertainty. The grey shadow of distrust which had divided them in the past still followed them from afar—a vague, intangible menace. Would it some day swing forward, like the dark, remorseless finger of an hour-dial, and lie once more impassably between them?

CHAPTER XXIX

A PATCH OF SUNLIGHT

The days which followed were very wonderful ones to Ann. She had come through darkness into light, out of infinite pain into infinite joy, and perhaps the very fact that in giving herself to Eliot she had forgiven much—forgiven what many women would have found it impossible to forgive—added something precious, some sacramental spikenard, to the gift which flowed back to the giver, deepening the profound sense of peace and happiness which encompassed her.

Eliot had known how to accept her gift—had taken it with simple thankfulness and a wondering reverence for the shining ways along which a woman's love can lead her, and the hour which they had passed together after Ann had bidden him stay had been, in a sense, sacred—a mutual revelation to each of them of the secret depths in the other's nature. But afterwards, once that wonderful hour was past, Eliot strode masterfully back into his man's kingdom. He was not of the type to remain a penitent, on his knees indefinitely. Nor would Ann have had it otherwise. She would have hated a subservient lover.

Eliot was very far from being subservient. Almost before the neighbourhood's congratulations had ceased to rain about them both he was demanding that Ann should fix the date of their wedding.

"You impatient man! " she teased him. "Why, we're only just this minute engaged! We shan't be married for ages and ages yet. "

"Oh, shan't we? " he retorted. "We'll be married in May, sweetheart. That's exactly as long as I'll consent to wait. And I'm only agreeing to that because a woman always seems to think it's part of the ceremony to buy a quantity of clothes when she's married—just as though she couldn't buy them afterwards quite as well as before! "

"In May? Oh, no, Eliot. " Ann shook her head with decision. "That's the unlucky month for marriages. "

"You don't mean to say you're superstitious? "

"I don't know. " She spoke uncertainly. "But—we've had so much ill-luck. I don't think I want to tempt Providence by getting married in May. "

He shouted with laughter.

"Very well, you absurd baby, it shan't be May, " he conceded, adding cheerfully: "We'll fix it for April then. "

"No, no. That's too soon, " she protested hastily. "Let's decide on—June. "

"April, " he repeated firmly.

"June"—with an effort to be equally firm.

"If you say that again, " he returned coolly, "I shall make it March. I'd ever so much rather, too, " he wound up boyishly.

"That would be quite impossible, " replied Ann triumphantly. "I've promised to go and stay with the Brabazons in March. "

He took her by the shoulders and pulled her towards him.

"Let it be April, then, " he said, adding quickly, as he read dissent in her eyes: "We've wasted such a lot of time, beloved. "

She yielded at that.

"Very well, then—April. But I'm afraid you're going to be a dreadfully self-willed husband, Eliot"—smiling as though the prospect were in no way distasteful.

"I think I am, " he acknowledged, with all a man's supreme egotism. He laughed down at her, and, lifting her right off the ground into his arms, kissed her with swift passion.

"You're much too thin, " he grumbled discontentedly, as he set her down again. "You weigh next to nothing. "

"And whose fault is that, pray? " she asked gaily.

She was horrified to see his face darken with sudden pain.

"Don't, " he said abruptly, in a stifled voice.

"Oh, my dear—" She was back in his arms in an instant, soothing, comforting, and scolding him all in a breath. "You needn't worry over my boniness, " she assured him cheerfully. "When we're married and settled down and I've no worries, I expect I shall get appallingly plump and have to take to one of those anti-fat cures. "

"You—fat! " He laughed. "There's about as much danger of that as of Mrs. Carberry becoming a philanthropist. "

Eliot had been furiously angry when he heard of the gossip which had gathered for a time around Ann's name and of the part Mrs. Carberry had played in helping to disseminate it, but neither he nor Ann herself had been able to refrain from laughing at the complete *volte-face* which that excellent lady performed when the announcement of their engagement was made public. She had been one of the first to offer her felicitations, and had paid a special call at the Cottage—this time accompanied by the modest Muriel—to offer them in person. "It will be so delightful to have a chatelaine at Heronsmere at last, " she had gushed. Presumably, recognising that her daughter's chance of acquiring the coveted position was now reduced, to nil, she had decided—with the promptness of a good general—to accept the fact and adapt her tactics to the altered situation. With mathematical foresight she argued that when Coventry was married Heronsmere would undoubtedly become the centre of a considerable amount of entertaining, and from every point of view it would therefore be wise to be on friendly terms there. After all, there were as good fish in the sea as ever came out of it, and the prospective hospitality which she anticipated would emanate from Heronsmere in the near future should provide excellent opportunities for fishing.

Apart from Mrs. Carberry, everybody seemed genuinely delighted at the engagement—even Miss Caroline. She confusedly mingled regrets "for any misunderstanding" with her congratulations, and Ann, too happy herself to wish any one else to be unhappy, forgave her whole-heartedly. Lady Susan was overflowingly pleased.

"Though, of course, " as she characteristically informed Sir Philip just before he and Tony returned to London, "Eliot's been blessed far beyond his deserts—like most men. Anyhow, Philip, you may as well make up your mind to accept Doreen as a *pis otter* for Tony—

and do it gracefully, my dear man! Mark my words, marriage will be the making of the boy. Every man ought to be married. "

"I wish you'd held that opinion thirty years ago, Susan, " retorted Sir Philip. "I suppose"—he hesitated, his eyes curiously soft—"it's too late in the day now? "

"Much too late, " replied Lady Susan promptly, though her eyes, too, were unwontedly soft. "Besides, I could never bear to be parted from the Tribes of Israel—and you know you can't stand a dog about the house. "

"Drat the man! " she muttered crossly to herself, as the train bearing the Brabazons Londonwards steamed out of the station. She brushed her hand across her eyes as she hopped briskly into the car which had brought them to the station, giving the chauffeur the order "Home! " in a sharper voice than she usually employed towards her servants. "Drat the man! It looks as though a single engagement has demoralised the lot of us. "

It was certainly destined to be followed by far-reaching consequences as regards two, at least, of the other people in the neighbourhood. Robin's notice to give up his post as Eliot's agent had, of course, been suitably buried, a brief understanding handshake between the two men its only tombstone, and Robin had gone straight from his interview with Eliot to the Priory. He found Cara, surrounded by a small army of vases, arranging flowers, of which a great sheaf, freshly sent in by the gardener from the hot-houses, lay on the table.

"Aren't they lovely? " she said, when she and Robin had exchanged greetings. "Do you want a buttonhole? "

He looked at the deep-red carnation which she held out to him and shook his head.

"No, thank you, " he said politely. "I want a wife. "

Cara gasped a little.

"Robin! " she exclaimed faintly.

A lovely colour flooded her face. It had been a much happier face latterly—since Ann's engagement. The look of settled sadness had gone out of her eyes. She felt now—now that everything was made straight betwixt Ann and Eliot—as though the heavy burden she had carried all these years had been suddenly loosed from her shoulders. Eliot had found happiness, at last, and that terrible sense of responsibility for his maimed and broken life was taken from her. Of the existence of the grey shadow she could not know, or guess.

So she turned to Robin with a sweet hesitancy that brought him swiftly to her side.

"Cara! " he said eagerly. "Cara, are you going to give me that 'second-best, ' after all? "

Still she hesitated.

"It doesn't seem fair, Robin, " she faltered. "I'm older than you are, for one thing. "

"One year—or two, is it? " he mocked joyfully.

"Half a century, I think! "—with a quick sigh.

"You'll grow younger, " he suggested optimistically. "And anyway, can you bear to think of me living all alone at the Cottage after Ann is married? I should probably commit suicide. "

Cara stood twisting a spray of maidenhair fern round and round her fingers till the tiny pale green leaves shrivelled up and dropped off and only the wiry stem remained.

"When is—Ann going to be married? " she asked slowly, at last.

"In April. It's all fixed. But the thing that matters is when are *we* going to be married? "

April! Eliot was to be married in April! Cara was conscious of a muffled stab of pain. But she felt no active rebellion. With a wistful sense of resignation she recognised that his life and hers were separate and apart. She herself had sundered them more than ten years ago. But now, at last, Eliot had won through to happiness! She thanked God for that. And there was still something she could give

Robin in return for his eager worship—good comradeship, and that second love which, though it bears but a faint semblance to the rushing ecstasy of young, passionate, first love, yet holds, perhaps, a deeper, more selfless tenderness and understanding.

She turned to the man waiting so eagerly for her answer.

"Are you quite sure you want me, Robin? " she asked.

"Quite sure, " he answered gravely.

"Then, if you're really sure, I'll marry you whenever you like—after Ann is married. "

He kissed her with a deep, grave passion, holding her closely in his arms.

"You shall forget the past, dearest—I promise you, you shall forget all the things that hurt you, " he said with tender reassurance. Presently, when the first few minutes were passed, he smiled down at her, a gleam of mirth in his eyes.

"I shall see to it that Ann and Eliot don't postpone their wedding—if it means postponing ours! You said 'after, ' you know. "

She nodded.

"Yes. I can't possibly commandeer Ann's natural protector"—smiling—"until she's safely bestowed in some one else's care. "

But though she jested about the stipulation she had made, it was the outcome of a curiously definite idea. Since it was through her that Eliot's happiness had once been wrecked, she felt as though, until this new-found happiness which had come to him were assured—secure beyond any shadow of doubt—she was not free to take her own. It was in a sense an expiation, a pathetic little human effort to propitiate fate and turn aside any blow; aimed at Eliot's happiness by those jealous gods who exact payment to the very last farthing.

*****

Ann was overjoyed when she heard of Robin's engagement. To know that her adored brother would not be left lonely by her marriage, and to see Cara, whose former experience of matrimony had proved such a ghastly failure, with a new, brooding gladness in her eyes, added the last drop to her cup of happiness.

"*Dear* Robin, I'm so pleased! " she told him. "If I'd been choosing a wife for you myself I couldn't have chosen any one nicer than Cara! "

"Glad you're pleased, " Robin returned gruffly—the gruffness being merely the cloak to conceal his own riotous felicity which every Englishman in similar circumstances thinks it necessary to assume. But Ann saw through it, and was not to be deterred from frank rejoicing.

"It will be perfectly lovely to have my best friend married to my best brother, " she continued. "Where shall you live? At the Priory or the Cottage? "

"We haven't got as far as making such world-shaking decisions as that, " he grinned. "Perhaps we might live at the Priory and week-end at the Cottage"—whimsically.

Ann found a further cause for rejoicing in the continued absence of Brett Forrester. She had never seen him again since the morning when, with an intense feeling of relief, she had watched the *Sphinx* steam out from Silverquay harbour. Lady Susan was much too incensed against him to invite him to White Windows, and Ann rested fairly secure in the hope that she would never see him again, or, at least, not until she was Eliot's wife. After that, she felt she would not be afraid to meet him. He could work her no more harm then.

So that it was with a light Heart that she finally started on her journey to London to stay with the Brabazons. Eliot saw her off at the station.

"If you stop a day longer than a fortnight I shall come and fetch you back, " he informed her despotically. "I'm not going to spare my girl to any one for more than two weeks. And I grudge even that. "

And Ann, leaning out of the carriage window and waving her hand to the tall, beloved figure on the platform, felt no premonition, was conscious of no ominous foreboding that the train which was bearing her so swiftly away from him was actually carrying her straight towards the very danger from which she felt so sure she had escaped.

In the patch of brilliant sunshine which lay all about her, the grey shadow had paled until it had become almost imperceptible. But it was still there—only waiting for the sun to move a little in the heavens to fling itself blackly across her path once more.

CHAPTER XXX

THE KEEPING OF A PROMISE

Her first two or three days at the tall grey house in Audley Square sufficed to indicate to Ann that all was not going well there, Sir Philip had welcomed her warmly enough, and when she descended to breakfast on the morning after her arrival she found an envelope on her plate containing his cheque for two hundred pounds, together with a brief intimation that it was intended to "help towards the trousseau. " But, apart from the bestowal of this signal mark of favour, Ann found her godfather's behaviour extremely difficult to understand.

It was usually his custom to treat her with a species of crusty amiability, but, on this occasion, after the first warmth of his welcome had evaporated, she found that the crustiness became much more in evidence and the amiability conspicuously lacking. The old man was extraordinarily irritable, both towards her and towards Tony. It was as though he were labouring under a secret strain—prey to some anxiety which he was stubbornly bent on keeping to himself. Tony also, Ann observed, seemed to be living at high pressure of some kind. He was moody and restless, and unless some theatre or other plan had been proposed by his uncle he usually disappeared soon after dinner, and she saw him no more until the following morning.

It was all very unlike any previous visit which she had paid to the house at Audley Square. Formerly, if Sir Philip had felt disinclined to go out in an evening, Tony had always been eager with suggestions for their visitor's amusement, and many had been the occasions on which he and Ann had dined gaily at some little restaurant and gone on afterwards to a dance or theatre alone together.

But now the change was noticeable. Tony seemed entirely preoccupied with his own thoughts, and to judge by his manner, they were anything but pleasant ones. Sometimes he would sit in moody silence for an hour at a time, making a pretence at reading a magazine. Or he would get up suddenly when they were all three sitting together, and, without a word to any one, put on his hat and go out of the house. He never volunteered any information as to where he spent his evenings, and although Sir Philip would peer after him with angry, suspicious eyes when he took his departure, it seemed as if pride—or was it fear of what the answer might be? —kept the old man from questioning him. When eleven o'clock came, bringing no Tony, he would get up abruptly, fold his newspaper, and remark curtly to Ann: "Time we went to bed. No need to wait up for Tony. He has his latch-key. " It was always the same formula, and the next day at breakfast uncle and nephew would exchange a brief greeting, and no further reference would be made to the previous evening. It was as though a kind of armed neutrality prevailed between them.

Decidedly something was radically awry, Ann reflected unhappily. Her visit, of course, was spoilt. But this troubled her very little in comparison with her increasing anxiety concerning Tony. He had never kept her out of his confidence before. She had always been able to stand by him—as she had promised his mother that she would. But now it seemed as if he had deliberately assumed an armour of reserve, not only in his relations with his uncle, but also in his attitude towards Ann herself, and her helplessness worried her intensely. She felt convinced that there must be something seriously amiss to account for Tony's extraordinary behaviour, and finally, the day before her visit was due to terminate, she decided to consult Mrs. Mellow, Sir Philip's faithful old housekeeper, whom Ann had known ever since those childhood days when she and Robin had been invited over to Lorne to have nursery tea with Tony.

Mrs. Mellow was one of the old-fashioned type of housekeeper—a comfortable black satin person, with pink cheeks and kind blue eyes and crinkly grey hair surmounted by a lace cap. Her name suited her admirably. When Ann put her head round the door of the housekeeper's room with the announcement, "Mellow, dear, I've come to have tea with you, if I may, " she welcomed her with respectful delight.

"Now, come straight in, Miss Ann. As if you even needed to ask! I was afraid you meant going away this time without coming to have a cup of tea with your old Mellow. "

Ann shook a reproving forefinger at her.

"Now, Mellow, you arch-hypocrite, you know I'd never dare! If I did, I expect the next time I wanted to come up and frivol in town you'd tell Sir Philip that you were spring-cleaning or something of the kind and that you couldn't put me up. "

"How you do go on, miss, to be sure! " declared Mrs. Mellow beamingly, as she bustled about spreading the cloth for tea. "As if you didn't know you were always as welcome as the flowers in May, spring cleaning or no spring cleaning I And I suppose, miss"—archly—"it'll be 'Mrs. ' the next time you visit us—if all I hear is true? "

Ann laughed. Throwing her arms round the old woman's neck, she kissed her warmly.

"Yes, it really will, Mellow. I believe"—teasingly—"you're just aching to hear all about it? "

"Well, miss, " admitted Mellow, holding the kettle, suspended a moment above the teapot, "I don't want to seem inquisitive or disrespectful, you may be sure, but I *would* like to hear a bit about the gentleman who's going to marry my young lady. I always think of you as my young lady, you know, Miss Ann. You were more like a daughter than anything else to Master Tony's mother, God rest her! Perhaps you have his photograph, miss, that you could show me? "

Ann nodded smilingly—she knew her Mellow, and had anticipated this request! —and forthwith proceeded to descant on Eliot's various virtues and the beauty of Heronsmere until Mrs. Mellow declared that she could, as she phrased it, "picture it all as plain as if she'd seen it herself. " Then, when the good woman's kindly interest was satisfied, Ann embarked on the quest which had been uppermost in her mind when she sought the housekeeper's room.

"Mellow, I'm worried about Tony, " she announced at last.

The smile died out of Mrs. Mellow's face like the flame of a suddenly snuffed candle.

"You've noticed it, then, miss? " she parried uneasily.

"Of course I've noticed it. He isn't in the least like himself, and he's almost always out. "

"Yes, miss. " Mrs. Mellow shook her head. "I call it rare bad manners to ask a young lady to the house and then to leave her to entertain herself, as you may say. And I've told Master Tony so more than once. "

"You told him so? What did he say? "

"Why, miss, he looked at me in a funny sort of way, and he said: 'Don't you worry yourself, Mellow. Miss Ann will understand all about it one day—and before very long, too. ' I couldn't think what he meant, miss. But I didn't like the way he looked. "

Ann's brows were knitted.

"How did he look? " she asked.

"Why, miss, sort of reckless. Like he did that time when we were down at Lorne last year and he and Sir Philip quarrelled something dreadful. He came down to me then, Master Tony did, in the housekeeper's room, at Lorne, and he said: 'Well, I'm off, Mellow, and whether you ever see me again or not depends on whether you can beat any sense into the head of that obstinate old man upstairs. ' He was mad with anger, was Master Tony, or of course he wouldn't have spoken like that of his uncle. And I'm blest if he didn't go out of the house the very next day! Sir Philip was in a rare taking, I remember. "

"He needn't have been, " said Ann, smiling. "Tony only came to Oldstone Cottage and stayed with Robin and me. "

"So I heard, miss, afterwards. But, really, at the time I was frightened lest he should do himself a mischief—he looked so wild. "

Ann's heart skipped a beat.

"Do himself a mischief? " she interposed quickly. "What do you mean? How could he? "

"I don't know *how,* miss. But I tell you, I'm frightened for Master Tony. I am, truly. "

Ann gazed thoughtfully into the fire.

"Where does he spend his time, Mellow? Have you any idea? "

"I have not, miss. But I do know this—that it's sometimes two and three o'clock in a morning before he comes home. My bedroom's on the ground floor, as you know, and I hear him come in and go upstairs almost always after midnight. Last night 'twas near one o'clock, and another night it may be later still. It bodes no good for a young gentleman to be coming home at all hours. Of that I *am* sure. "

"I think you're right, Mellow, " replied Ann gravely. "Does Sir Philip know about it, do you think? "

"Indeed, miss, I fancy he guesses. But mostly he's too proud to speak what he thinks. Though he did say to me, one evening about a week or ten days before you came here, 'Mellow, ' says he, 'the boy's going the same way as his father. ' And then he swore, miss—something awful it was to hear him—that he'd not lift a finger to keep Master Tony out of the gutter. 'He'll end up in jail, Mellow, ' he said, 'and bring shame on the old name. All I hope is that I'll be dead and buried before it happens. ' And with that he gets up and goes out and slams the door behind him. "

Ann was silent. It seemed to her that things were even more seriously amiss than she had imagined. Mrs. Mellow glanced at her wistfully.

"Do you think, miss, that you could say a word to Master Tony! " she said. "Talk to him for his own good? He always used to take a lot of notice of what you said to him, I remember. "

"I know he did, " returned Ann. "But he doesn't give me any opportunity of talking to him now"—ruefully. "All the same, " she added with determination, "I shall certainly talk to him before I go home. I'll get hold of him this evening. "

But Tony proved obdurately uncommunicative.

"It's too late to *'talk'*! " he told her, with a roughness that was quite foreign to him. "All the talking in the world wouldn't mend matters. It's"—he looked at her oddly—"it's neck or nothing now, Ann. "

His eyes were feverishly brilliant, and Ann could see that even during the last few days his boyish face had grown strangely haggard-looking.

"Tony, you're in trouble of some sort. I wish you'd tell me about it, " she entreated.

"There's nothing to tell. Don't fuss so, Ann"—irritably. "I said it was neck or nothing. Well, it's going to be *neck*! I swear it shall be. I'm going to win through all right. And before long, too! "

To Ann's relief he made no suggestion of going out that evening after dinner—presumably in deference to the fact that she was leaving on the morrow, and, as Sir Philip appeared tired and Ann had still a few oddments of packing to finish off, by common consent they all retired early to bed. Half an hour later, however, as Ann was folding a last remaining frock into the tray of her trunk, she heard some one very quietly descending the stairs, and a minute later the house door opened and closed again softly. A sudden conviction seized her, and she ran swiftly down to the landing below, where Tony's room was situated, and tapped on his door. No answer being forthcoming, she threw the door open and looked in. She had switched on the landing burner as she passed, and the light streamed into the room. Tony was not there, nor were there any indications that he had contemplated going to bed. His room was untouched, just as the housemaid had left it prepared for the night—a fire burning in the grate, the bed neatly turned down, with his pyjamas laid out on it, a can of hot water, covered with a towel, standing ready in the basin on the washstand.

Very quietly Ann closed the door and returned to her own room. She had little doubt what had happened. In consideration of the fact that it was her last evening Tony had stayed indoors until she and his uncle might be supposed to be safely in bed. Then he had stolen out of the house and departed once more on his own pursuits. Ann could make a pretty good guess that these included gambling in some form or other.

She felt rather sick. It was so unlike Tony to resort to any hole-and-corner business such as this—slipping out of the house, as he believed, unknown to any one. That he must be caught in a terrible tangle of some kind she felt sure, and his mother's last words, as she had lain on her deathbed, came back to her with redoubled significance. *"And if Tony gets into difficulties?* " Vividly she recalled Virginia's imploring face, the beseeching note in her tired voice. And her own answer: *"If he does, why, then I'll get him out of them if it's in any way possible.* " It looked as though the time had come for the fulfilment of that promise. And ignorant of what danger it could be which threatened Tony, unable to guess the particular kind of difficulties in which he found himself involved at the moment, she was powerless to help.

Slowly she undressed and got into bed. But not to sleep. She lay there with wide-open eyes, every sense alert, listening for the least sound which might herald Tony's return. She could hear the loud ticking of the tall old clock on the staircase—tick-tack, tick-tack, tick-tack. Sometimes the sound of it deceived her into thinking it was a footstep on the stairs, and she would sit up eagerly in bed, listening intently. But always the hoped-for sound resolved itself back into the eternal tick-tack of the clock.

Twelve, one, two o'clock struck, bringing no sign of Tony's return, and finally, wearied out, Ann fell into a brief slumber from which she awakened with sudden violence to the knowledge that, at length, there was the sound of an actual footfall in the house. She heard the stairs creak twice, unmistakably, then the muffled closing of a door—and silence.

For a moment she hesitated, uncertain how to proceed. Surely she could sleep in peace now? Tony was safely in the house once more, and to-morrow she would have a heart-to-heart talk with him and induce him to confide in her. But instantaneously her mind rejected the idea. Something bade her act, and act immediately. Urged by that imperative inner impulse, she rose and, throwing on a wrapper, ran swiftly down the stairs, her bare feet soundless on the carpet, and paused irresolutely outside Tony's bedroom door. Her hand was raised to knock softly on the panel, when all at once an odd little noise came to her from the inside of the room—a curious metallic sound, like the dull clink of metal dragged slowly across wood.

Seized by a sudden overwhelming fear, she flung open the door. Tony was standing beside an old mahogany bureau, one drawer of which had been pulled open. His arm was half-raised. In his hand he gripped a revolver. Ann could see the light from the rose-shaded burners run redly along its barrel like a thin stream of blood. In the fraction of a second she had fled across the room and grasped his wrist.

"Tony! What are you doing? " she cried hoarsely.

She felt his arm jerk against her hold, resisting it, but she clung determinedly to his wrist with her small strong fingers.

"Give it to me! Give it to me! " she whispered hurryingly, hardly conscious of what she was saying.

His instinctive resistance ceased. She felt his muscles relax, and he allowed her to take the pistol from him. He stared down at her curiously.

"Pity you didn't come two minutes later, " he observed laconically.

Without reply, she proceeded to unload the revolver. He watched her with a faint, apathetic amusement.

"Shouldn't have thought you knew how to do that, " he said.

"I learned how to handle a revolver during the war, " she returned grimly. She crossed the room and very softly closed the door. "Now, Tony, " she went on, turning back and forcing herself to speak composedly, "you're going to tell me all about it. Things must be pretty bad for you to have thought of—this. " She glanced down with shrinking repugnance at the weapon which she still held. All at once the apathy which seemed to have possessed him vanished. He turned on her with sudden violence.

"Why did you come? If you hadn't, I should be safely out of it all!... Out of it all!... Oh, my God!... "

He dropped into a chair, burying his face in his hands, and the utter despair in his voice tore at Ann's heart. What had happened—what could have happened that Tony should seek to take his own life? Mechanically she stooped to replace the revolver in the opened drawer from which he had evidently taken it. A few loose cartridges still lay there, together with some torn scraps of paper and a blank cheque. Almost unconsciously her glance took in the contents of the drawer. Then suddenly it checked—concentrated. She caught her breath sharply and looked at Tony, a horrified, incredulous question in her eyes. But he was still sitting with his head buried in his hands, silent and motionless.

Very slowly, as though she approached her hand to something nauseous and abhorrent, Ann reached out and withdrew one of the torn sheets of paper and stared at it. It was covered with repeated copyings of a single name—sometimes the whole name, sometimes only one or other of the initial letters to it. And the name which some one was taking such pains to learn to write was that of her godfather, Philip Brabazon... Philip Brabazon... the sheet was covered with it, and some of the signatures were a very fair imitation of the old man's handwriting.

Ann snatched up the blank cheque. It was one that had been torn from Sir Philip's cheque-book. She could see that at a glance—remembered so clearly noticing the same heading on the cheque which he had given her towards her trousseau—the Watchester and Loamshire Bank. She held out to Tony the two pieces of paper—the sheet of scribbled signatures and the blank cheque.

"Tony, " she said, her voice cracking a little. "What—what are these? "

The tense, vibrating horror in her tones roused him. He looked up wearily. Then, as he saw what she held, a dull red flush mounted slowly to his face. For a moment he did not speak. When he did, his voice sounded dead—flat and toneless.

"Those, " he said, "are attempts on my part to forge my uncle's signature. "

She stared at him speechlessly. Then, a sudden new fear shaking her, she went quickly to his side, thrusting the blank cheque under his eyes.

"Tony—you haven't done it before?... This—this isn't.... How many cheques of his have you had? "

"One, " he said. "That one"—nodding towards the narrow pink slip she held. Ann gave, a gasp of relief. "Yes, " he went on, "I found I couldn't do it. The old man's been decent to me, after all. He'd have hated the old name muddied by—by forgery. "

"And do you think he'd like it stained by suicide? " she demanded fiercely. "Oh, Tony, you coward! You coward! "

It was as if she had struck him across the face. He sprang up, his eyes blazing.

"How dare you say that? " he cried stormily.

"I say it because it's true, " she returned, her voice quivering. "Thank God you haven't committed forgery! And thank God I was in time to stop your taking this cowardly—utterly cowardly—way out of things. You've got into a mess, and you wanted to get out of it—the easiest way. Did you ever stop to think of us—afterwards? Of your uncle, and me, or of Doreen Neville—all of us who cared for you? Oh! I wouldn't have believed it of you, Tony! "

"You don't know how bad things are, " he said desperately. "You've *got* to be hurt—you, and uncle, and—and Doreen. " His voice broke, then steadied again. "I've got myself in such a mess that a bullet was the best way out—for everybody. "

"I don't believe it, " answered Ann, with stubborn courage. "There's some other way. There always is—only we've got to look for it—find it. " Suddenly her heart overflowed in pity for this white-faced, haggard boy who must have suffered so bitterly, must have gone down into the veriest depths of despair, before he had been driven to seek that short and terrible way out of life. She held out her hands to him. "Tony, let me help! Let's look for a way out together. I'm your pal. I've always been your pal. Why did you bear all this alone instead of letting me share? "

At the touch of her strong, kind little hands he broke down for a moment. Turning aside, he leaned his arms on the chimneypiece and hid his face. A hard, stifled sob tore its way through his throat and his shoulders shook. Ann remained silent, giving him time in which to recover his self-command. Her heart was full almost to breaking-point with that eager, mothering tenderness which a woman instinctively feels for a man in trouble. She is the eternal mother, then—he the eternal child.

When at last Tony lifted his head from his arms he was very pale, but his eyes held a look of resolution.

"I'll tell you, " he said jerkily.

Bit by bit the painful story came out—the same familiar story, only infinitely aggravated, of high play, losses, then still higher play in a desperate hope of recovery, and finally, the confession of heavy borrowings, of notes of hand given and accepted—and now falling due.

"That's the devil of it—the time's up and they're due for payment, " wound up Tony hoarsely. "Payment! And I haven't twenty pounds in the world. "

As Ann listened to the stumbling recital, her face paled and grew very grave. This was worse—far worse than she had anticipated.

"How much, do you owe—altogether, Tony? " she asked at last, when he had finished speaking.

"Twelve hundred. "

"Twelve hundred pounds! " The largeness of the amount left her momentarily aghast, and the vague idea she had been harbouring that Robin and she might scrape up a hundred or two between them and so put matters straight crumbled to atoms.

Twelve hundred pounds! In her wildest imaginings she had never dreamed of Tony's owing such a sum. She shivered a little, partly from nerves, partly from sheer physical cold. The fire had smouldered to black ash long ere this, and the chill air which precedes the dawn was creeping into the room. Even the necessity of conducting the entire conversation in lowered tones, in order not to disturb the sleeping household, added to the aguish, strained feeling of which she was conscious.

"There is only one thing to do, Tony, " she said at last. "You must tell Sir Philip. "

A sharp ejaculation escaped him, hastily stifled as she raised a warning finger enjoining silence.

"Sh! Don't make a noise! We mustn't wake any one, " she cautioned him. "You *must* tell Sir Philip, " she resumed. "There's simply nothing else to be done. "

"It would be utterly useless, " he replied with quiet conviction. "He wouldn't pay. He said he wouldn't, last time. And he meant it.... You'd better have let me blow out my brains while I was about it, Ann"—with, a mirthless laugh.

"Don't talk rot, " she returned succinctly.

"It's not rot. Don't you see I'm done for—gone in? A man who borrows, as I've done, and *can't pay*, is finished. Outside the pale. You don't suppose they'll let Doreen marry me after this, do you? "

Ann shook her head voicelessly. She could see—only too clearly—all the consequences which must inevitably follow if the matter became public. It signalled the end of things for Tony. It meant a ruined life—love, happiness, a clean name, all would go down in the general crash.

"The only thing I can do, " he resumed hopelessly, "is to emigrate. Bolt, and start fresh somewhere. "

Ann set her teeth.

"You're not going to bolt, " she said doggedly. She was silent for a moment, thinking feverishly. There must he some way out—some way, if she could only come upon it.

"Whom do you owe this money to? " she demanded at last. "Several different people, I suppose? "

"No. One man offered to be my banker till—till my luck came round again, " confessed Tony. "And I let him. But I didn't know I'd borrowed so much. It seemed to mount up all in a moment. "

"'In a moment! '" There was a tiny edge of contempt to Ann's voice. "How long have you been borrowing from this man? "

"Oh, for a goodish time—on and off. I've paid back some. I'd have paid it all back if I'd only had a stroke of luck. But I've been losing every night for the last month. "

Luck! The weak man's eternal excuse for failure Ann felt as though she loathed the very word.

"Who is the man you borrowed from? " she asked.

Tony preserved an embarrassed silence.

"Who is it? " she repeated. "I must know, Tony. We can't plan anything to help if you're not absolutely frank. "

"Well, if you must know—it's Brett Forrester, " he said wretchedly. "It's beastly, I know, his being a friend of yours. "

Brett Forrester! Ann remained very silent, with bent head, absorbing the full significance of this confession. It seemed suddenly to have thrown an immense burden of responsibility upon her. Brett! As Tony said, he was a friend of hers. And desired to be much more than a friend, if Tony but knew! Were it not for this, it would have been simple enough for her to go and use her influence with Brett—ask him out of sheer friendliness to her to give Tony a chance—to grant him time in which to pay. It would have to be a very long time, she reflected. But perhaps, when she was Eliot's wife... Eliot was generous... he would not think twice about paying twelve hundred pounds to give happiness to the woman he loved—to purchase peace of mind for her. And she would economise in her own personal expenses and so try to balance matters. Eliot had told her that one of his earliest presents to her was to be a new and very perfectly equipped car for her own special use. She would forego the car—ask him to pay Tony's debts instead. Her thoughts raced along.

But all this presupposed that Brett would be willing to wait a little for his money. If there had been only friendship between herself and Brett, Ann felt she could so easily have begged a chance for Tony. But to approach the man who had desired to marry her so much that he had been willing to go to almost any length to force her into marriage with him, this man whom she had defied and scorned at their last meeting—to ask a boon, a favour from him, seemed of all things the most impossible. To do so would be to strangle her pride, to walk deliberately through the valley of humiliation. Oh, she couldn't do it! She couldn't do it!

Virginia's sad, entreating voice seemed to plead in her ear: "*Ann, will you do what you can for him—for him and for me?* " It was almost as though she were there in the room, an invisible presence, beseeching, supplicating mercy for her son—claiming the fulfilment of the promise Ann had made so many years ago. "'If it's in any way possible, ' Ann, " the voice seemed to urge. "'*In any way*' you said. And it *is* possible. You could save Tony if you would. "

After what appeared to Tony an interminable time, Ann lifted her bent head. Her face was white to the lips, but her eyes were strangely bright—like golden stars, he thought. They looked almost unearthly.

"Don't worry, Tony, " she said. Familiar little comforting phrase! "Don't worry, old boy. Leave it all to me. I'm sure I can put things straight. I'll talk to Brett—I'm certain he'll do what I ask and give you time to pay. "

"Time? " Tony laughed harshly. "If I had all the time until eternity I couldn't produce twelve hundred pounds! "

"But I could, " asserted Ann confidently. "Won't you trust me, Tony? I'm sure—*sure* that I can get you out of this scrape. "

He looked at her in blank amazement. But something in her face convinced him that she was speaking the truth—that he could rely on her.

"If you do, " he said, and his voice rang true as steel, "I give you my word, Ann, that I'll never get into another. I'll chuck gambling from this day forth. "

"Will you, Tony? Will you really? " she cried eagerly.

He took her hands in his.

"I promise, " he said simply.

The two strained young faces gleamed palely in the chill dawnlight—on each of them the impress of a stern resolution. Suddenly, moved by an irresistible impulse of compassion, Ann lifted her arms and laying her hands on either side Tony's face, drew it down level with her own. Then she bent forward and kissed his forehead—tenderly, as his mother might have kissed him.

"Good night, Tony boy, " she said. And a minute later her slender figure flitted, ghost-like, up the stairs to her own room.

CHAPTER XXXI

A BARGAIN

The day after Ann's return to the Cottage found her occupied in the composition of a letter to Brett Forrester, the number of torn, half-written sheets of paper which surrounded her testifying to the difficulty she was experiencing in the matter. The whole idea of appealing to Brett, of asking any service from him, was intensely repugnant to her and rendered the performance of her task doubly difficult, but at last, after several abortive attempts, it was accomplished. When completed, the letter read as simply and shortly as possible, merely saying that she was anxious to see him about a rather important matter and asking where it would be possible for them to meet. She had no idea where he was at the moment, but she had gathered from Tony that he had been in London as recently as a week ago, so she addressed her letter to his flat in town, posted it, and tried to possess her soul in patience until she should receive an answer. It might have eased matters somewhat if she could have shared her burden with Robin, but, as luck would have it, he had been obliged to leave home on the day following that of her own return. Eliot had unexpectedly commissioned him to inspect on his behalf a famous herd of cattle in which he happened to be interested, a matter which would take Robin up to Scotland and entail his absence from home for several days, and in the hurry of packing and departure there had been no chance of a cosy, confidential chat between brother and sister.

Two or three days passed, bringing no answer to her letter, and Ann began to be nervously agitated in mind as to whether it had reached its destination safely or not. She sought for reassurance by telling herself that, if Brett happened to be out of town, the letter was probably following him round and might not yet have caught up with him, but the knowledge that time was an important factor in the solving of Tony's difficulties, and the fear lest, in the interval, anything should occur to drive the boy once more to despair, kept her nerves on the stretch.

It was late in the afternoon of the fourth day that the response came to her letter—and in a form in which she least expected it. She had been out in the garden, gathering snowdrops, and was returning to the house, her hands filled with the white blossom of spring, when she lifted her eyes to find Brett Forrester standing directly in her path. Her heart gave a great terrified leap. She had pictured him as far enough away, and his appearance was utterly unexpected. Moreover, the very sight of him brought back a swift rush of painful memories, and involuntarily she recoiled a little. He regarded her quizzically.

"You don't seem exactly pleased to see me, " he observed.

"I'm—I'm surprised, that's all, " she said hastily. "I didn't—I wasn't expecting you. " Transferring her harvest of snowdrops to one hand, she extended the other towards him.

"Not expecting me? " he returned, when they had shaken hands. "After the letter you wrote me? "

"I thought you would write first, suggesting where we could meet. "

"I should have thought you would have known me better by this time, " he commented dryly, as he turned and walked beside her up the path to the house. "I never waste time in preliminaries. You said you wanted to see me—so here I am. "

Ann made no response—for the simple reason that she couldn't think of one to make. Brett always appeared t cut the ground from under one's feet, so to speak—certainly as regards the small change of social intercourse. Even behind his lightest remarks one seemed able to hear the threatening rumble of the volcano.

"What was it you wanted to see me about? " he continued.

"I'll tell you. Come in, will you? "

By this time they had reached the house and Ann led the way into the living-room. She was conscious of an acute feeling of trepidation and, by way of postponing the evil moment, paused to put her snowdrops in water in a bowl which she had left filled in readiness on the table.

"Are you staying at White Windows? " she asked, as she arranged the flowers with quick, nervous touches.

"I am not, " replied Brett. "I gathered, during the last conversation I held with my revered aunt, that my welcome had worn a trifle thin—as you are doubtless aware, " he concluded mockingly.

"Then—then where—how did you come here? "—in some astonishment.

"I came on the *Sphinx*. I am at present living on board, and at the moment she is anchored in Silverquay bay. Any other questions? "

Ann flushed hotly.

"I beg your pardon, " she said with downcast eyes. "I didn't mean to be inquisitive, only naturally I—I rather wondered where you had sprung from. You *did* arrive somewhat suddenly, you know. "

"I did, " he acquiesced. "I was on my way to the south, of France and your letter was forwarded on to me at Southampton, where I'd put in en route. So we steamed for Silverquay at once. Now, perhaps, you'll gratify my curiosity as to what is the important matter you want to see me about. I can only think of one matter of any real importance, " he added daringly, his blue eyes raking her face with the audacious, challenging glance which was so characteristic of the man.

Reluctantly Ann desisted from fidgeting with the bowl of snowdrops, and Brett nodded approval.

"Yes, I'm sure you've done your level best for them" he observed ironically.

She sat down, clasping her hands tightly together in her lap, while Brett remained standing on the hearthrug, looking down at her with quizzical amusement.

"I—I wanted to ask you—" she began, then halted abruptly and made a fresh start. "I wrote to you because—because—" Once again she came to a dead stop.

"Well? " he queried. "I'm afraid I haven't grasped it yet. "

Ann pulled herself together and made another effort.

"It's about Tony, " she said bluntly.

Brett's eyes narrowed, but he made no comment. He waited quietly for her to continue.

"He's told me—I've found out—that he owes you a large sum of money. "

He nodded.

"He owes me money, certainly. Whether you'd define it as a large or small sum would be a matter of relative proportion, I should imagine. "

"That's it! " exclaimed Ann eagerly. "That's just it. To him, twelve hundred is an enormous sum—a small fortune! To you—it isn't very much to you, Brett, is it? "

"I don't quite understand, " he replied cautiously.

"You hold some bills of his—notes of hand, don't you call them? " she pursued. "And they're due to be paid now, aren't they? "

"That is so. Well, what then? "

"Why, it wouldn't make much difference to you—would it, Brett? "—appealingly—"if he didn't pay just yet—if you waited a little longer? "

"I'm afraid I don't see with what object, " he returned coldly.

Ann caught her lip between her teeth. Oh, how difficult men were when it came to any question of money! How hard! Hardening all at once into cold and implacable strangers.

"Why—why—" she said entreatingly. "Tony hasn't got the money to pay you with just now, and if you'll only wait a little—give him a little time to pay—Oh, Brett, won't you do it? "

"Wait for my money, you mean? "

"Yes. "

"Do you think"—sardonically—"that I'm any more likely to get it at the end of six months than I am at present? If Tony hasn't got twelve hundred now—is he proposing to earn it in the next six months? "

The bitter, gibing note in his voice roused her anger.

"You'd no business to lend it him! " she exclaimed hotly. "He's only young, and you were simply helping him, *encouraging* him to gamble, when you know as well as I do that gambling is absolutely in his blood. You'd no *right* to lend it him! "

"I like that"—coolly. "Brabazon plays the fool—or knave, rather"—with a sudden harshness in his voice—"borrowing money which he knows he can't repay, apparently—and it's my fault! Not having enough sins of my own, I suppose you think you can saddle me with Tony's, too. Many thanks. " He bowed mockingly.

"You're the older man, " persisted Ann. "You ought not to have made it possible—easy for him to play beyond his means. Brett, please—will you give him time to pay? As"—with an effort she swallowed her pride—"as an act of personal friendship to me? "

"You still haven't answered my question. Supposing I agree, supposing I do give him another six months, how is he going to get the money by then—unless that old curmudgeon of an uncle of his shells out for him? " Ann shook her head.

"He won't, " she said. "I know that. "

"Then how is the young fool going to find the money in the time? Tell me that. "

"He *will* find it, " said Ann quietly. "I can't—tell you how. But if you'll wait six months, I'll give you my personal guarantee that the money shall be paid. "

Brett's eyes narrowed again in sudden concentration.

"*Your* personal guarantee? "

"Yes, mine. If you'll wait six months—or even *three*"—urgently. "Oh, Brett, you will wait? "

"'Even three, '" he repeated thoughtfully. Suddenly he threw up his head and laughed. "I see it—it's as clear as daylight! I believe"—smiling blandly—"you are proposing to marry Coventry next month. At least, I'm told that's the programme. And I suppose you count on paying off Tony's debt—with Coventry's money. Is that it? What a charming arrangement! "

Ann felt her colour rise till her whole face and neck seemed scorching with the hot rush of blood.

"Whatever the arrangement would be, you may be sure it would be a perfectly fair one, " she said steadily. "Nor does it concern you so long as you get the money owing to you. "

"On the contrary, it would concern me very much to be paid off with Coventry's money. I shouldn't like it a bit. He's got the woman I want—and he can keep his damn money! "

Sick as she felt under the insult of his manner, Ann forced herself into making yet another appeal.

"Brett, please be merciful! Put me outside the matter altogether. It isn't a question of you and me. It's Tony. And"—her voice breaking—"I want to save him. "

"I think it's very much a question of you and me, " he retorted. "You asked me just now to extend the time of payment 'as an act of personal friendship to you. '"

She was silent, Inwardly writhing under the lash of his tongue. She wondered if Tony would ever know or guess all that this interview had cost her.

"I know I did, " she acknowledged at last in a low voice.

Brett appeared to meditate a moment. Suddenly he looked across at her with eyes that sparkled dangerously.

"I won't take Coventry's money, " he said deliberately. "But I tell you what I will do—I'll let *you* liquidate the debt. "

"I? " She glanced at him swiftly. "I? How can I? "

"It's quite simple. Come and have supper with me—alone—to-morrow night on board the *Sphinx*, and in return I'll give you back those notes I hold of Brabazon's—every one of them. "

"Oh, I couldn't! " Ann drew away from him instinctively. "You know I couldn't do that, Brett. "

He shrugged his shoulders.

"Very well, then, Tony must pay up—or go under, " he answered nonchalantly.

"No, no! " She made a quick step forward. "Brett, it isn't fair—to ask me to do such a thing. "

"Isn't it? It's asking very little, I think. " His voice vibrated with a sudden note of passion. "You're going to marry Coventry. Very well. What am I asking? One little evening out of all your life—to call mine, to remember you by. "

Ann was silent. Her thoughts were in a whirl. Here was a way by which she could save Tony—put things right for him. But at what a price! She shrank from the risk involved. If Eliot were to hear of it, to learn that she had had supper with Brett on board his yacht—alone, what would he think—suspect? His faith in her had not stood testing once before, when a pure accident had forced her into a false position. Would it stand now, if she did this thing? If, being Eliot's promised wife, she deliberately spent the evening on board the *Sphinx* with Brett? She knew it would not. The faith of very few men would remain proof against circumstances such as those—least of all, Eliot's. The grey, relentless shadow had suddenly swung forward, completely enveloping her path.

"No, Brett, " she said at last. "I can't—do—that. "

"Then, as I said, Tony must go under" —coolly.

She clenched her hands in an agony of indecision. Tony, whom Virginia had bequeathed to her—whom she had promised to shield from harm "if it was in any way possible"! She had thought that already she had paid to the utmost in the fulfilment of her trust by stooping to beg mercy at Brett's hands. But it seemed that the keeping of her promise to the dead woman was to cost still more—

demanded the sacrifice of her own happiness, the faith and trust of the man who loved her. Piteously Ann reflected that could Virginia have known how matters stood she would never have exacted the fulfilment of any promise at such a fearful price. But Virginia could not know. And the promise held.

"Well? " queried Brett. He had been watching Ann's face closely while she fought her battle. "Well, will you come? "

She drew a long, shuddering breath.

"Yes. I'll come, " she said.

Her voice sounded curiously weak and strange to her own ears—like that of some one else speaking. She wondered if she had really spoken audibly, and, in a sudden terror lest he shouldn't have heard her, she repeated the words with jerky emphasis.

"Yes. I'll come. "

He made an abrupt movement towards her, but she shrank back out of his reach.

"You'll give me the notes if I come? " she asked rather Wildly. "You'll play fair, Brett? "

"Yes. I'll play fair. "

"Then—then—will you go now, please? " She felt as though her strength were deserting her—as though she could bear no more.

He paused, regarding her irresolutely. Then he turned to the door.

"Very well, I'll go now. The dinghy will be waiting for you at the jetty to-morrow night at nine o'clock. "

The door closed behind him and, left alone, Ann sank down on to the nearest chair, utterly overwhelmed by what had befallen her. An hour ago there had been not a cloud in her sky—the whole of life seemed stretching out before her filled with the promise of love and happiness. And now, with unbelievable suddenness, black and bitter storm-clouds had arisen and covered the entire heavens, till not even a flickering ray of light was visible. She remembered her strange, unconquerable fear of the yacht... like a sleek cat watching at a mousehole.... Well, the cat had sprung now—leaped suddenly, striking into her very heart with its pitiless claws.

No tears came to her relief. She felt stunned—stunned, and remained limply in her chair, staring with dazed, unseeing eyes into space....

*****

She was still sitting in the same position, gazing blankly in front of her, when Maria threw open the door to admit Mrs. Hilyard.

"I just looked in—" Cara, beginning to speak almost as she entered, broke off abruptly as she caught sight of Ann's stricken face. She hurried to her side. The girl's mute immobility frightened her.

"Ann! " she cried quickly. "What's happened? What is the matter with you? "

Slowly Ann turned her head towards her, regarding her with lack-lustre eyes.

"Nothing, " she said. "Or everything. I'm not quite sure which. "

She began to laugh a trifle hysterically, and Cara laid her hands firmly on her shoulders.

"Don't do that, " she said sharply, giving her a little shake. "Pull yourself together, Ann, and tell me what's gone wrong. "

With an effort Ann caught back the sobbing laugh that struggled in her throat for utterance. Getting up, she crossed the room to the window and stood there silently for a few moments, with her back towards Cara. When she turned round again it was obvious she had regained her self-control.

"I'm all right, now, " she declared, smiling more naturally.

"Then tell me what's wrong, and let's put our heads together to get it right, " replied Cara practically.

"Oh, yes, I'll tell you. But there's nothing in the world will put things right, all the same. "

Very briefly she recapitulated the facts of the case, while Cara listened with an expression of increasing gravity.

"You can't go, " she said with decision, when Ann ceased speaking. "Whatever else you do, you mustn't spend the evening on board his yacht alone with Brett. "

"And if I'm to save Tony, it's the only thing to be done, " replied Ann quietly.

"Then you must leave Tony to get out of his difficulties by himself. Sir Philip would pay, I expect, if the matter were put up to him. "

Ann shook her head.

"I'm quite sure he wouldn't, " she said, "There's no question of that. He's reached the limit of his patience. He'd simply turn Tony out of the house—turn him adrift. And that means shipwreck. Tony might—might even do—what he tried to do the other night. Kill himself. He's desperate. Don't you see, everything's doubly bad for him now—when he's in love with Doreen. Unless he's pulled out of this hole somehow, it means smashing up his whole life. "

"And if you pull him out of it the way you propose doing, it means smashing up yours, " returned Cara succinctly. "You know what Eliot's like—how jealous and suspicious. And you know Brett's reputation! "

"I can manage Brett, " insisted Ann.

Cara made a swift gesture.

"It isn't that! It's Eliot, and you know it. If he ever came to hear that you'd been to supper on the *Sphinx* with Brett, he'd never trust you again. "

"He might. I'm hoping—"

"He wouldn't"—with conviction. "It would wreck everything. Ann, don't be such a fool—such a *fool*! " Cara spoke with desperate intensity. "For God's sake, give up this crazy plan! "

"I can't. I must go. I've promised. "

Her brows drawn together, Cara reflected a few minutes in silence. She looked as though she were trying to work out a problem of some kind—balancing the pros and cons. At last:

"There's only one way out of it, " she said slowly. "Let me go instead of you. I think—I think I could make Brett see reason, and persuade him to give those notes of hand to me instead of to you. At any rate, let me try. "

"No good, " said Ann, shaking her head. "He wouldn't give them to you. He wants his pound of flesh"—bitterly.

"Why don't you ask Eliot to give you the money? " demanded Cara suddenly.

A deep flush stained Ann's cheeks.

"I've not fallen so low that I'll ask the man I'm engaged to for money with which to pay another man's debts. "

"You'd ask him if you were married"—defiantly.

"In certain circumstances—yes. But that's different. Oh, you must see it's different! Besides, Tony would accept money from *me*, even though my husband had given it to me. But he'd be too proud to take it from Eliot—or from any one else. "

"Too proud! It seems to me Tony's precious little to be proud about! "

"The more reason why he should keep any pride he has remaining. Don't be hard on him, Cara. Remember he's young, and that the instinct to gamble is in his very blood. This has been a lesson to him—a frightful lesson. I *know*—if he once gets clear of this—he'll run straight for the future. "

"Then you must let me go to the yacht, " insisted Cara with finality.

"No" The reply came with a definiteness there was no mistaking. "I've given my word to Brett that I'd come, "

"You know what Eliot will think if he hears of it? He'll probably—almost certainly—distrust you utterly, and it will ruin both your lives. "

"I must risk that, " said Ann quietly. "Tony's got to be saved somehow, and it's up to me to do it. He was 'left' to me, you know. Virginia trusted me. And I can't let her down. "

There was something curiously strong and steadfast in her face as she spoke—something against which Cara realised that it was futile to strive any further. Reluctantly she desisted, but it was with a heavy heart that she at last quitted the Cottage, leaving Ann firm in her resolve to save Tony, no matter at what cost.

Ann woke early next morning, feeling rather as though it were to be her last day on earth. She thought she could appreciate to some extent the sensations of a man condemned to be executed the following dawn. To-day she was tremendously alive, with happiness cupped betwixt her hands, while the future of rose and gold beckoned her onward. To-morrow, that whole future might be wrenched from her, leaving her like one dead, with nothing to live for, nothing to hope.

When Eliot paid his usual daily visit she went tremulously to meet him. This might be the last time he would ever look at her with the eyes of love—the last time they would ever talk together as lovers. For her, his kisses held all the poignant ecstasy and pain of kisses that may be the last on earth.

He had noticed the *Sphinx*, lying at anchor in the bay, on his way to the Cottage.

"I suppose that chap Forrester is going to favour Silverquay with another visit, " he remarked, as he and Ann strolled in the garden together. "I don't care for him, " he added. "When we are married, Ann, I'd rather you didn't see any more of him than you can help. From all I can hear he hasn't too savoury a reputation. "

Ann's heart sank. If Eliot thought that—felt like that about Brett, then there could be no hope of forgiveness if he ever found out that she had been to supper with him on the yacht. And now, appearances would be even stronger against her. It would look as though she had gone there deliberately in defiance of Eliot's expressed wishes.

She became unwontedly quiet—so much so that Eliot's solicitude was awakened.

"What's the matter with you to-day? " he asked, looking down keenly into her face as he held her in his arms. "Are you depressed or worried about anything, sweetheart? "

She roused herself to a smile.

"Worried? Why, what have I to be worried about—now we're together again? "

His face cleared.

"I suppose you're just feeling a bit lonely without that 'best brother' of yours. Is that it? "

"Yes. That's it, " she said, nodding emphatically. "I miss Robin. You—you won't have to send him away again, Eliot. "

"I don't think I shall, " he returned, smiling, "if it reduces you to such a wan-looking little person. You're quite pale, Ann mine. "

At parting, she clung to him as though she could never let him go.

"Why, what's this, child? " he asked, genuinely perturbed. "Are you really nervous at being left in the Cottage alone—even with the doughty Maria for company? If you are, I'll ride over to White Windows and ask Lady Susan to put you up there until Robin comes back. "

"Oh, no, no! " she exclaimed hastily. "I'm perfectly all right. I am, really, Eliot. I didn't sleep very well last night, that's all. "

"Well, then, take a rest after lunch. I shan't be able to come over this afternoon—I have to go to Ferribridge. So"—pinching her cheek—"your slumbers will be undisturbed. And go to bed early to-night, " he added authoritatively.

He went away, and later Ann made a pretence at eating lunch. The idea of "taking a rest" almost brought a smile to her pale lips. There was nothing further from her than sleep. Her brain felt on fire, and the time seemed to race along, each minute bringing nearer the dreaded ordeal of the evening.

At seven Maria brought in dinner, and once again Ann had to make a pretence at eating. Every mouthful felt as though it would choke her. Then, just as she was wondering how on earth she was to dispose of what still remained on her plate without incurring Maria's displeasure, there came a ring at the bell, and a minute later Maria herself reappeared, carrying a telegram on a salver.

"From Master Robin, maybe, sayin' when he'll be home again, " she suggested conversationally, while Ann tore open the envelope and withdrew the flimsy sheet.

"*Don't come to-night,* —FORRESTER. "

Ann looked up from the single line of writing and spoke mechanically.

"No, it's not from Robin, " she said. And tearing the telegram across she tossed the pieces into the fire, where a swift tongue of flame shot up and consumed them.

She was conscious of an immense surge of relief. She could not imagine what had happened. Possibly Cara had seen Brett and interceded with him. Or perhaps it was merely that some unexpected happening had made the projected supper an impossibility for that particular night.

But whatever it was, it meant a reprieve. A reprieve! She could hold her happiness unharmed a little longer....

CHAPTER XXXII

ON BOARD THE "SPHINX"

Brett glanced over the supper-table, laid for two, with an experienced eye. The lights, shining down upon dainty silver and crystal, added a more lustrous sheen to the crimson petals, like fringed velvet, of a bowl of exquisite deep-red carnations, and flickered gaily on the bright neck of a gold-foiled bottle which twinkled in the midst of the cool greyness of a pail of ice.

Satisfied with his inspection, Brett gave a little nod of approval. His manservant, Achille Dupont, who accompanied him wherever he went, had all a Frenchman's quick grasp of a situation, he reflected. Moreover, the man possessed the invaluable faculty of getting on well with the members of the yacht's company, so that his coming on board with his master and waiting on him exclusively failed to create any resentment. In addition to this, he was dowered with the golden gift of discretion. Achille never suffered from a misplaced curiosity concerning his master's doings. He accepted them blandly, and although Brett supposed there would be a certain amount of gossip on board the yacht concerning this night's doings, he felt serenely sure that Achille himself would preserve a strict reticence concerning anything that he might chance to observe or overhear in the performance of his duty of serving the supper.

The clock had struck nine some few minutes ago, and Brett pictured the dinghy slipping over the smooth water with Ann, hooded and cloaked, sitting in the stern. He could almost visualise her young, tense-lipped face with its courageous eyes gazing ahead into the darkness. She would have need of all her courage before the evening was over. That he admitted. But he comforted himself with the reflection, that, whatever happened, she had brought it on herself. She had refused to marry him, while he was fully determined that she should be his wife. In a way, he felt distinctly resentful that her obstinacy had driven him into employing such methods as he proposed to use to-night.

The door opened, and to the accompaniment of a respectful murmur of "*Mademoiselle est arrivée*" from Achille, a woman's figure, shrouded in furs and with a scarf twisted round her head, slipped past the Frenchman, and stood poised just inside the threshold as though uncertain whether to stay or go. Achille retired and closed the door noiselessly behind him, thus deciding the matter.

"Ann! " cried Brett triumphantly. "I wondered—I half doubted whether you would come, after all! Let me help you, " he added quickly, as the woman threw back the fur wrap she was wearing, and with a deft movement, untwisted the scarf from her hair.

"It's not Ann, " said a cool feminine voice, and with a swift turn of her wrist the visitor drew the swathing scarf aside and revealed the small dark head and pansy-purple eyes of the lady from the Priory.

Brett fell back a pace, his face wearing an expression of such blank amazement that for a moment Cara could hardly refrain from laughing out loud. But he recovered himself with surprising quickness, and looked her up and down with characteristic coolness.

"I don't think I remember inviting you for to-night, " he said slowly.

"No, " she replied. "I've come instead of Ann. Brett, you had no right to ask her here. "

His eyes flashed wickedly, but he preserved his coolness.

"That, I think, is my business, " he responded.

"It's not. " A note of deep feeling came into her voice. "It's the business of every one who cares for Ann to protect her from her own rash unselfishness. Just to please yourself, you asked her to come here, without a thought as to how it would affect her reputation—how people might talk. And you used those bills of Tony's as a lever. "

"Really, your perspicacity does you credit, " he returned ironically. "I saw no other way of getting her here, so, as you truthfully remark, I used those bits of paper as a lever. "

"Well"—quickly. "I've come for those bits of paper, as you call them. "

Brett shook his head regretfully.

"I never made any bargain to give them to—you, even though you have condescended to honour the *Sphinx* with your presence to-night, " he said.

Cara approached the table.

"No. I didn't expect them in return for that, " she replied. "I'm proposing to give you the usual return for notes of hand—payment of the amount owing. "

To make this proposal had been her intention when she had first suggested to Ann that she should take her place as Forrester's guest. She had not dared to offer the necessary money as an outright loan, realising that the girl would have refused it on Tony's behalf peremptorily, so she had inwardly resolved to redeem the bills Brett held without consulting her.

She opened a small, ivory-mounted wrist-bag she carried, and withdrew a bundle of crisp Bank of England notes.

"I think the sum owing is twelve hundred, " she said composedly. "There's the money. Will you count it, please, and let me have the bills Tony has given you. "

Brett stood quietly looking down at the small heap of notes, but he made no effort to pick them up.

"I'd forgotten you were a wealthy woman, " he remarked contemplatively.

Cara laughed rather bitterly.

"Heaven knows I've not found my wealth of much value to me before, " she said. "But I shall think more of it in the future if it can get a friend out of trouble. Come, take the money, Brett, and give me the bills, " she added, with a touch of impatience.

He picked up one of the notes and fingered it thoughtfully, then replaced it on the pile once more.

"I'm sorry, " he said mildly. "But it isn't you who owe me this money. It's Brabazon. So I can't accept repayment from you. "

Cara glanced at him swiftly. Her lips felt suddenly dry.

"What do you mean? " she asked nervously.

"Just what I say. Brabazon is my debtor—you haven't authority to act for him, by any chance, have you? "

"Authority? No. But I'm willing—I'm only too glad to be able to do this for him. "

Brett pushed the bundle of notes across the table towards her.

"I'm sorry, " he repeated pensively. "It's very good of you, of course. But I couldn't possibly take your money. I happen to be the holder of the bills, and I only give them back to Brabazon for the amount owing—or to Ann on the terms I suggested. Otherwise"—a sudden flame leapt up in his eyes—"I keep them. "

Cara stood as though turned to stone. The whole thing became perfectly clear to her on the instant. It had not been just a carelessly selfish proposal—that bargain he had made with Ann—but a deliberately thought-out scheme. Slowly she replaced the useless notes in the little silken bag which had held them.

"Ah! I see you understand, " he observed, watching her with some amusement.

She looked at him with a desperate demand in her eyes.

"Brett, what did you mean to do? What was your plan—if Ann had come? " she asked in a low, shaken voice.

He laughed.

"Can't you guess? Really, Cara, I think I complimented you on your perspicacity too soon! It seems to be—halting a little, shall we say? —now. "

"You didn't ask her here just for the pleasure it would give you—there was something else—"

"It was partly for that. I at least made sure of a few hours alone with her! " A note of passion roughened his voice for a moment. Then he forced it back and his blue eyes laughed at her again, audaciously. "But it was partly for the *dis*pleasure which I thought it might give to some one else."

"Eliot!"

"Even so. He's not got precisely what you'd call an equable temperament, has he?"

"And you knew"—slowly—"that if he discovered Ann had been here—"

"Exactly"—with a mocking bow. "You've guessed it. 'The marriage arranged'—would not take place."

Cara stared at him in frank horror.

"Then it was a trap!" she exclaimed, and beneath the utter scorn and contempt which rang in her voice any other man would have winced. But it affected Brett not one jot.

"Yes. And would have succeeded admirably, but for your interference. Tell me, how did you persuade Ann not to come? It isn't like her to back out of a bargain."

"No, it isn't," agreed Cara warmly. "Ann would always keep her word—even if the keeping of it half killed her."

"Then how?"

There was a suspicion of veiled triumph in her smile.

"It was quite simple," she said. "I sent her a wire, saying, 'Don't come to-night'—and signed it 'Forrester.'"

Brett burst out laughing.

"My felicitations! That was quite a stroke after my own heart! But still, you'll agree, it was rather a liberty to take with my name, wasn't it?"

"A liberty? Perhaps. But you were trying to *ruin* Ann's name—and her happiness. Won't you change your mind, Brett, and sell me those notes of hand? " she added, with a sudden entreaty.

"I hate refusing you, " he smiled back.

She realised the futility of pleading with him further, and drew her furs round her shoulders preparatory to leaving him.

"Then I'll go back. I'm sorry I've failed. But thank God I at least prevented Ann from coming here herself. "

She moved towards the door, but Brett was before her, and planted himself with his back against it.

"Let me pass, Brett, " she said quietly, though her heart beat a shade faster in her breast.

"Again I'm sorry to refuse you, " he returned mockingly.

"You can't—keep me here! "

"Can't I? If you interfere with other people's love affairs, you must be prepared to take the consequences. In this ease the consequence is supper with me. "

Cara hesitated. She could not struggle with him, and in his present mood she thought it quite possible he might oppose with actual physical force any attempt on her part to leave the yacht. If he did, of course, she would be perfectly helpless. Forcing herself to a composure she was far from feeling, she turned away from the door he was guarding with a slight shrug of her shoulders.

"I've no wish to have supper with you, " she said.

"No? Yet, after all, it's you who've despoiled me of my rightful guest, " he returned, with bland mockery in eyes and voice. "It's certainly up to you to provide a substitute. Perhaps"—banteringly—"we might even discuss the question of those notes of hand again—later on! A man's obstinacy sometimes melts as the evening advances, you know. "

A faint hope stirred in Cara's heart. Perhaps, if she yielded to his wishes now, without further argument, she might be able, later on, to induce him to reconsider his decision—to persuade him to be merciful. He seemed to read her thoughts with an uncanny insight.

"You'll stay? " he said.

She nodded, and he helped off the heavy fur wrap she was wearing. Then he pressed the bell-push and, when Achille appeared, gave a curt order for supper to be served. As the Frenchman departed his quick eyes flickered a moment over Cara's beautiful face and milk-white shoulders. Decidedly, he reflected, his master had good taste.

The supper, as might have been expected, was a very perfectly chosen repast, and as the meal progressed Cara was fain to acknowledge that Brett knew how to act the part of host most charmingly. On her side she played up pluckily, hoping that by falling in with his humour she might yet win the odd trick of the game.

It was not until they had reached the coffee and cigarette stage that he reverted to the avowed object of her visit to the yacht.

"It was really rather a sporting attempt on your part, " he remarked, "even though foredoomed to failure. Will you tell me"—curiously—"what induced you to do it? "

"I'm very fond of Ann, " returned Cara evasively.

He shook his head.

"I don't think that can have been all. You were running"—he regarded her through narrowed lids—"a pretty big risk, and you're woman of the world enough to know it. You are quite at my mercy, you see. A woman doesn't run that kind of risk—for another woman. " He leaned across the little table, his compelling blue eyes concentrated on her face. "Do tell me why you did it? "

For a moment she was silent. Then, lifting her eyes to meet his, she said simply:

"I did it because once—years ago—I robbed Eliot Coventry of his happiness. I wanted to give it back to him. "

"And you were prepared to risk your reputation over the job? "—swiftly.

"Yes, " she answered quietly. "I was prepared. "

"Then you must have felt quite convinced he was in danger of losing his happiness—to me? "—with lightning triumph.

"Not *to* you—through you, " she corrected quietly.

"Ann would have promised to marry me to-night. "

"I'm sure she would not. But it was almost inevitable that Eliot would misunderstand—distrust her, if he learned that she had been here with you—this evening. "

Brett nodded composedly.

"Yes. And I don't think the only explanation she could have offered would have helped her much—that it was done for the sake of Tony Brabazon! It was a big thing for any woman to do for a man—*unless she cared for him*! And"—he uttered a light laugh—"I fancy Coventry's jealousy of Brabazon would have wakened up again quite quickly in the circumstances. Oh! "—with an impatient gesture—"it was a lovely scheme—absolutely watertight, if only you hadn't meddled! "

He looked across at her with an expression that held a droll mixture of anger and mortification, not unlike the expression, of a child who, having banged a new toy too ecstatically upon the floor, sees it suddenly drop to pieces.

"Not altogether watertight, " observed Cara calmly. "There was a chance—quite a good chance, too—that Eliot might not have heard a single word about the matter—might never have known that Ann had been here. "

"Bah! "—arrogantly. "I don't leave things like that—to chance. I wasn't taking any chances. I arranged that Coventry should know all right. "

Cara started.

"What do you mean? " she demanded.

"What do I mean? " He smiled derisively. "Why, that old chap who lives at the lodge at Heronsmere, old chap with a face like a gargoyle—Brady, what's his name? "

"Bradley, " supplied Cara.

"Yes, that's it. Bradley. A cunning old rascal, if ever there was one—he'd sell his immortal soul for the price of a drink. I told him"—watching her keenly while he spoke—"that his master would probably like to know that a certain young lady in whom he was interested would be found on board the *Sphinx* this evening if he wanted to see her. "

"You told him *that*? " gasped Cara, stricken with dismay.

"Certainly I did"—triumphantly. "And I gave him a five-pound note to jog his memory. I don't think he'll omit to hand on the information as desired. I should say"—glancing at the clock—"that we might expect Coventry along at any moment now. "

Cara half rose from the table. Her face was very white, her eyes dilated with horror.

"Perhaps—perhaps he won't come—won't believe it, " she stammered faintly, with a desperate hope that she might be speaking the truth.

Brett smiled unpleasantly.

"I think he'll believe it all right. I gave Bradley very clear instructions. But, in any case, " he added easily, "I'd prepared for the possible contingency that the old fool might bungle matters. "

"How? " Her voice was almost inaudible.

"Why, then, I should simply have steamed away with my honoured guest on board. After a day or two's trip at sea, I think there'd be no question Ann would accept me as her husband. The position would be an even more awkward one than her predicament at the Dents de Loup. Her presence on the yacht could hardly be explained away as an—accident"—significantly. "But I preferred my first plan—it entailed less publicity"—with a short laugh.

Cara sprang up, her eyes blazing. In the torrent of scorn and anger which swept over her at his duplicity—at the nonchalant recital of it all—the embarrassment of her own situation was temporarily lost sight of.

"Brett, I think you must be absolutely devoid of any sense of right or wrong! I never heard of anything more utterly fiendish and heartless in the whole of my life. Have you *no* conscience, *no* decent feeling, that you could plot and plan to ruin a woman's happiness as you would have ruined Ann's? Oh! It's unbelievable! I think you must be a devil incarnate! "

He rose too, his eyes smouldering dangerously. The veneer of polished mockery had dropped from him suddenly.

"I'm not. I'm a man in love, " he said thickly. "I wanted her—God, how I wanted her! And, but for you, I'd have succeeded. You've robbed me—robbed me of my mate!... " His lips drew back over his teeth in a kind of snarl. "I think you deserve to be punished, " he went on slowly and significantly. "What's to prevent my putting out to sea—now—this minute—and taking you with me? "

"Brett—" She shrank back, suddenly terrified. His eyes were blazing with a reckless fury—mad eyes. She made a dart for the door, but before she could reach it he had caught her by the arm, his strong fingers crushing deep into her white flesh.

"Well, why not? " he jeered savagely. "You came here in Ann's place of your own free will! Supposing you *take* her place—altogether—"

A tap sounded on the door. Brett's hand fell away from her arm, and she stood quiveringly waiting for what might come. After a discreet pause Achille entered, advancing with soft, cat-like tread.

"For mademoiselle, " he said, tendering a note to Cara on a salver.

As she took the note she vaguely noticed that it bore no superscription. With trembling fingers she tore it open.

> *"I hear you are on the* Sphinx. *I'm quite sure you must have a good reason for being there, if you are there of your own free will. But in case you are not, and need help, I wanted you to know I've come on board and will take you home whenever you wish, —E. "*

Cara glanced across at Brett, who was watching her curiously. She slipped the note, intended for Ann, into the bosom of her gown and turned to Achille.

"Tell Mr. Coventry Miss Lovell is not on board the *Sphinx,* " she said quietly.

"Coventry! " broke violently from Brett. "Where is he, Achille? "

"He come in a boat from the shore, monsieur. Just now. He wait only an answer to zis lettaire. " The man bowed and retired, leaving Brett and Cara staring at each other.

"You would not have come between Eliot and Ann, after all, " she said proudly. "Your trick would have misfired. He trusts her—absolutely. "

She had hardly finished speaking when the sound of a scuffle came from the companion-way, accompanied by a stream of voluble French. Then: "Get out of my way! " came in good, robust English, and an instant later Eliot's big frame appeared in the doorway.

"I want an explanation, Forrester—" he began sternly. Then fell silent, while his senses quietly absorbed the whole scene before him—the man and woman in evening dress, the flower-decked table with its half-emptied coffee-cups and evidences of a recent gay little supper, the mingled scent of cigarette smoke and carnations. Last of all, his glance, cold and contemptuous, swept over Cara's white face.

He gave a short laugh.

"Bradley misled me, " he observed coolly. "There's no one here in whom I'm interested. " For a moment his eyes—accusing, utterly scornful—met and held Cara's. Then he looked across at Brett. "I understood you were alone, Forrester. I regret my intrusion. " With a curt bow he was gone.

As the door closed behind him Cara sank down mutely into her chair. She gazed wearily in front of her. There was no need to ask herself what Eliot thought. It had been written plainly in his eyes.

Presently she turned her head and looked across at Brett.

"Well? " she said tonelessly. "I hope you're satisfied. I don't think you need bother any more about—punishing me. "

The savage anger had died out of his face. He was regarding her with an odd look of surprise. There had been no mistaking the anguish of her expression as she had grasped Eliot's swift and cruel interpretation of the scene. She had looked like a woman on the rack.

"So... Coventry was the man... before you married that bounder, Dene. " Brett spoke very quietly, like a man communing with himself, fitting together the pieces of a puzzle.

She nodded.

"Yes, " was all she said.

He sat down on the opposite side of the table and leaned forward, still with that half-surprised curiosity on his face.

"Then why didn't you clear yourself just now? You could have done. Why on earth didn't you explain? "

A twisted little smile tilted her mouth.

"Because—because I wanted to keep Ann out of it. Don't you see—he thinks Bradley made a mistake. He need never know—now—that Ann even thought of coming. I've... made sure... of his happiness. I took it away once. Now I've given it back. "

Brett got up abruptly. That twisted little smile hiding a supreme agony touched him as no woman's grief had ever touched him yet.... The low, toneless confession with its quiet immolation of self.... He put his hand into his pocket, and, drawing out a packet of loose papers, banded together with elastic, flung them down on to the table.

"Oh, hang! " he said gruffly. "There are the bills Brabazon gave me. By God, you've earned them! "

Cara stretched her hand out slowly and touched the packet with hesitating fingers.

"Do you mean this, Brett? "

"Certainly I mean it. "

She stared at him almost incredulously.

"I believe you're—sorry, " she said slowly.

But in that she miscalculated. Brett would be an unrepentant sinner to the end of his days. He laughed and shook his head.

"Not in the way you mean. Frankly and honestly—Oh, yes"—catching the faint quizzical gleam in her eyes—"I can be both when I want to. The Devil quoting Scripture, you know! Frankly, then, I'm merely sorry that my plan miscarried. It was a splendid plan! Its only fault was that it didn't succeed.... But I know when I'm beaten. And you've beaten me. "

A few minutes later they stood together on the deck, waiting for the dinghy to come alongside.

"Good-night, Brett, " she said, holding out her hand.

He lifted it to his lips with audacious grace.

"It will be a bad night—thanks to you! " he returned with a last flash of mocking humour.

CHAPTER XXXIII

THE VISION FULFILLED

Ann opened her next morning's mail with nervously eager fingers. A couple of tradesmen's bills, an advertisement for somebody's infallible cure-all, and a letter from Robin saying that he would reach home the following day—that was all. Not a line from Brett. Nothing in explanation of his last evening's telegram.

There is a wise old saw which asserts that "no news is good news, " but Ann could extract no comfort from it. Such hackneyed sayings did not take into consideration people of Brett Forrester's temperament, she reflected bitterly. Something had occurred to prevent the carrying out of his plans for last night, but not for one moment did she imagine that he would allow anything to divert him permanently from his intention of compelling her to buy Tony's freedom on the terms he had already fixed. That fact must still be faced, and the absence of any word from Brett this morning increased illimitably the sense of strain under which she was labouring. Last evening she had keyed herself up to the required pitch for the ordeal which awaited her. And now the whole agony and terror would have to be gone through again!

She wandered restlessly from the house to the garden and then back again, her nerves ragged-edged with suspense. If she could only know what had occurred last night to prompt that wire, what Brett now proposed, what further troubles there were in store, she felt she could have borne it better. She was never afraid to face definite difficulties. It was this terrible inaction and uncertainty which she found so unendurable.

The minutes crawled by on leaden feet. When she returned from feeding her poultry she was absolutely aghast to hear the church clock only striking ten! It seemed to her that a whole eternity of time had elapsed since the moment when the delivery of the morning post, destitute of news from Brett, had plunged her into this dreadful agony of uncertainty.

Suddenly she heard the gate click. She had been unconsciously listening for that sound with an intensity of which she was unaware—expecting, hoping, almost praying for tidings of some kind. Surely, if he did not come himself, Brett would at least send her a message of some sort!

When at last the click and rattle of the wooden gate, as it swung to, smote on her ears, she felt powerless to go and meet whoever it might be whose coming the sound heralded. A curious numbness pervaded all her limbs, and she leaned against the table, almost holding her breath, while the measured tread of Maria's sturdy feet resounded along the passage leading from the kitchen to the front of the house.

Ann heard the opening of the cottage door, followed by the soft murmur of women's voices instead of by the high treble of the telegraph boy which she had expected. Then the swish of a skirt, the lifting of a latch, and Cara came quickly into the room.

The tension of Ann's nerves relaxed, giving place to a spiritless acceptance of the inevitable. There was no message from Brett, after all! It was only Cara—Cara who had come to ask the success or failure of her last night's interview with him. The irony of it!

Ann began to speak at once, anticipating the first question which she knew the other would be sure to put. It would be better to get it over at once.

"I didn't go to the yacht, " she said baldly. "Brett wired me not to come. "

Cara nodded.

"I know. But I went, " she answered quietly.

"You? " Ann stared at her. "You went—to the yacht! " she repeated in tones of stupefaction.

"Yes. And I got what I wanted. These are the bills which Tony gave to Brett—and there's a note for you, as well, " she added with a fugitive smile.

She slid the whole packet on to the table, and Ann picked up one of the stamped oblong slips of paper and examined it with a curious sense of detachment.

"'Bill or note.'" She read aloud the words which crowned and footed the Government stamp. Then she laid the bill back on the top of the others.

"But I don't understand, " she said. "How did—you—get these! "

"Sit down, and I'll tell you, " replied Cara.

Ann sat down obediently, feeling as though she were living and moving in a dream. Once she glanced almost apprehensively towards the small heap of bills on the table. Yes, they were still there. Those narrow strips of paper which spelt for Tony a fresh chance in life and for herself release from any future domination of Brett Forrester's. Not yet could she realise the full wonder and joy of it—all the splendour of life and love which their mere presence there gave back to her. For the moment she was only conscious of an extraordinary calm—like the quiescence which succeeds relief from physical agony, when the senses, dulled by suffering, are for a short space contented with the mere absence of actual pain.

At first she fixed her eyes almost unseeingly on Cara, as the latter began to recount the events of the previous evening, but swiftly a look of attention dawned in them. The realities of life were coming back to her, and by the time Cara had finished her story—beginning with the sending of the telegram in Brett's name and ending with the final surrender of the notes of hand—she had grasped the significance of what had happened.

"And you did this—risked so much—for me? " she said, trembling a little. "Oh, Cara! "

Cara was silent a moment. Then she leaned forward.

"Not only for you, Ann, " she said gently, "Do you remember my telling you that a woman once—jilted Eliot Coventry? "

Ann's startled eyes met the grave, sorrowful ones of the woman who bent towards her. But she averted them quickly. Something—some fine, instinctive understanding forbade that she should look at her just then.

"Yes" she answered, hardly above her breath.

Cara hesitated. Then she spoke, unevenly, and with a slight, difficult pause now and again between her words.

"I was that woman. I—robbed him of his belief in things—of his chance of happiness. I didn't realise all I was doing at the time. But afterwards—I knew.... Ever since then, I've wanted to give it back to him—all that I robbed him of. I made his life bitter—and I wanted to make it sweet again. To give him back his happiness.... Last night, I paid my debt. "

Ann had been listening with bent head. Now she lifted it, and her eyes held a terrible questioning. Behind the questioning lay terror—the terror of one who sees a heaven regained suddenly barred away.

"Then he... you.... " She could not even formulate the aching demand of her whole soul and body. But Cara understood. Love had taught her all there was to know of love.

"Eliot's love for me died ten years ago, " she said simply.

"And yours? " asked Ann painfully. "Not yours. Or you wouldn't—you couldn't—have done this—for him. "

For an instant Cara closed her eyes. Then she spoke, with white lips, but with a quiet, steadfast decision that carried absolute conviction.

"I know what you are thinking, " she said. "But you are wrong—quite wrong. There is nothing left between Eliot Coventry and me—nothing—except remembrance. And for the sake of that remembrance—for the sake of what was, though it has been, dead these many years—I have done what I have done. "

The question died out of Ann's eyes—answered once and for ever, and Cara stifled a sigh of relief as she watched the faint colour steal back into the girl's cheeks.

"I don't know how I could have thought you still cared, " said Ann presently. "It was silly of me—when you are going to marry Robin. "

"Yes. Robin and I are going to start a new life together. He knows—what happened—years ago. And he understands. I hope"—forcing herself to speak more lightly—"I hope he won't be too shocked at my flight to the yacht last night to marry me after all! "

Ann laughed.

"I don't think you need be afraid, " she answered affectionately. "But Eliot! " She paused in consternation, then went on quickly: "What did he think when he found you there, Cara? Do you know what he thought? "

Cara's expression hardened a little.

"Yes, I know, " she said shortly.

"And I can guess, " returned Ann. She sprang up from her chair with all her old characteristic impetuosity. "And he's not going to think—that—a moment longer. I suppose"—her voice seemed to glow and the eyes she bent on Cara were wonderfully tender—"I suppose you wouldn't explain because you wanted to keep me out of it? " Then, as Cara nodded assent: "I thought so! Well, I'm not going to be kept out of it. I'm going straight across to Heronsmere—now, at once—to tell Eliot the whole truth. "

She swept Cara's protest royally aside, and within a few minutes Cara herself was on her way home and Billy Brewster flinging the harness on the pony's back at unprecedented speed.

But Dick Turpin was spared the necessity of making the whirlwind rush to Heronsmere which loomed ahead of him, by the opportune appearance of Eliot himself at the Cottage gate.

Ann drew him quickly into the house.

"I was just coming over to see you, " she told him swiftly. "It's—it's about last night. "

His face darkened.

"About last night? " he repeated. "What about it? "

"You found—Cara—on board Brett's yacht. "

"I did—and drew my own conclusions. "

"Well, they were wrong ones, " said Ann. Then, seeing that he looked quite unconvinced, she went on quickly lest her courage should fail her. "If it had not been for Cara, you would have found me there—"

"You? Then it's true—true you actually intended going there? Bradley was right? "

"Yes, he told you just what he had been ordered to tell you. Brett believed I was coming—he was expecting me. I promised to go because he held some bills of Tony's—Tony had borrowed from him far more than he could pay. And Brett bargained with me that he would give them up if I would go to supper with him on the *Sphinx*. " The whole story came tumbling out in quick, vivid sentences. In a few moments Eliot was in possession of all the facts which lay behind his discovery of Cara on the yacht.

"So Cara had taken your place. " There was a strange new gentleness in his voice as he spoke of the woman who had first broken and then built up his life again.

"Yes. I was afraid—afraid that if you knew I had been there, you would believe—what you believed once before. "

A stifled ejaculation broke from him.

"You thought that? " he said, his voice suddenly roughened by pain. "Oh, my dear, do you think I haven't learned my lesson—yet? "

She looked at him doubtfully.

"How could I know? Oh, Eliot"—with tragic poignancy—"how could I *know*? "

For a moment the man and woman stood looking at each other in silence, separated once more by the grey shadow which had fallen again between them—the shadow of an old distrust. All at once Eliot's pain-wrung face relaxed.

"Didn't you get my note? " he asked eagerly. "Didn't Cara give it you? "

"Your—note? " For an instant Ann was puzzled. Then she remembered. Cara had said there was a note for her. At the time she had assumed it was a note from Brett, and in listening to the history of all that had taken place upon the yacht she had never given it another thought. She turned to the sheaf of bills still lying on the table. Yes, it was there, hidden beneath the bill which she had picked up to examine, afterwards replacing it on the top of the pile.

She unfolded the note and read it in silence, and, as she read, the grey shadow which had dimmed even the radiance of love itself unfurled its wings and fled away.

There could never be any more questioning or doubt. She knew now that Eliot's faith in her was perfected. He had written this—these words of utter trust—in circumstances which might have shaken the belief of almost any man. And his faith had remained steadfast. Love, which casteth out fear, had cast out this last fear of all.

"Eliot"—Ann's voice broke a little—"you've given me the one thing I still needed—the absolute certainty of your faith in me."

"I believe in you as I believe in God," he answered simply.

He drew her into his arms.

"And you, beloved—do you know what you have done for me? You have closed the gates of memory, shown me the way into the 'happy garden'—given me beauty for ashes."

A silence fell between them. But it was the silence of complete and perfect understanding. Together they would go forth into the future, unafraid.

Lightning Source UK Ltd.
Milton Keynes UK
UKHW011005231120
373921UK00001B/227